Murder at Swan Cove

Sharon Dobson

ISBN:1481156675
ISBN-13: 978-1481156677

DEDICATION

This book is dedicated to my daughter, Patricia Dobson, for talking me into writing a book during the National Novel Writing Month challenge and to the group of talented authors I wrote with in the Maryland NANOWRIMO.

Bill Dobson for dealing with me talking to myself about characters and the plot while burning dinner.

I would also like to give a special thank you to Bernie Moll for putting up with my many changes and edits to this book as he was trying to help in the edit process. His help and moral support got me to publication.

CONTENTS

ACKNOWLEDGMENTS

I would like to acknowledge the people of Chincoteague Island, Virginia and the Chincoteague Volunteer Fire Company. Growing up on this wonderful island surrounded by the best people in the world and my beloved Chincoteague Ponies gave me the inspiration to write this book. If you would like to donate to help support the Fire Departments efforts to maintain the wild herd their address is: Chincoteague Volunteer Fire Co., PO Box 691, Chincoteague Island, VA 23336.

DAY 1
CHINCOTEAGUE, VIRGINIA

I am called into the investigation on Wednesday, October 18th to assist the Chincoteague Police and the National Park Service. Before I make the three hour drive to Virginia, I look over the case report. On October 17, at 12:45 PM, a family walking the Wildlife Loop noticed a foul smell near an area called Swans Cove Pool. Park Service officers responded and just before night fall located the body of a young female. She was nude, curled into a fetal position surround by dried blood.

With no lights in the area, the coroner was called in and pictures were taken. The body moved to the nearest coroner's office in Pocomoke City, Maryland. Chincoteague Island Police have been called in to watch the crime scene over night to preserve the chain of custody.

When I arrive my first order of business is to see my crime scene and talk to Park Ranger Margie Meers, the first National Park Service Ranger on the scene. I make the turn onto the Wildlife loop stopping in front of two Park Service vehicles and a Chincoteague Police car.

A short slender female in a Park Ranger uniform steps towards my vehicle. Her silver badge glistens though the early morning sunlight breaking through the leaves. I assume she is Ranger Meers. She extends her hand grasping mine firmly, "Agent Clay?"

"Yes, ma'am. Special Agent John Clay from the Richmond FBI, I am here to assist you with the investigation of the body you found." The case file shines up to me from my tablet. The photos of the dried blood and pale skin are a start contrast to the lush greenery I see around me.

"Agent Clay---"

"Call me Adam, ma'am."

"Adam, we don't get a lot of stuff like this 'round here. Was a real shock, ya' know?"

"I understand. Mind filling me in on some of the details? Were you the first officer to investigate the crime scene?"

Ranger Meers begins to lead me through the low brush into the woods. We have to pick our path carefully around trees and areas of standing water in the marsh.

She seems at home picking higher ground to walk on as she talks. "Yes, sir. On October 11th, a family called about a wounded pony along beach road. They had stopped to show their children the wild ponies when they noticed one of them was covered in blood. They were afraid the injured animal would hurt their children, so they got back in their car and called to let us know. We called the Chincoteague Pony Association and one of their members responded to the scene with us. The pony seemed fine but her fur was indeed spotted with blood. We took photos of the pony in case there was a related report then she was released."

I stop to detach a few briers that have stuck to my pants leg, "Is that common practice ma'am?"

"Oh, Yes sir. People getting bitten and kicked by the animals in the park is a common occurrence. Yearly, over one hundred people ignore the 'please do not feed or pet the wildlife signs' and approach the animals. When that happens, occasionally people do get injured. Some call park service to file a complaint against the animal. Others knowing they were not following the signs don't make the call. In the past week, there were three reports of tourists being kicked by animals. None had reported any major blood loss, but hooves can be sharp."

"And did the blood on this pony match up to those common reports?"

"No, Sir. The blood transfer onto the pony seemed excessive for a kicking incident but we did follow up on it and checked with the local medical center to see if anyone had come in with an animal-related injury."

"Ranger Meers, can you tell me more about the state of the body when it was discovered?"

"The woman was lying on her side. Her arms were positioned in an attempt to cover her breasts and genitalia. When we saw her we backed away and called the coroner and the Chincoteague Police. It was just beyond anything we could handle."

"I understand, Ranger Meers. Your first body is a lot to take in. Can you tell me what happened once the coroner arrived?"

"He rolled over her for further investigation. It became really clear that she was murdered and by someone who was enraged. They did a number on her." Ranger Meers shudders stopping in her tracks for a moment, "Her body had been beaten and she had multiple stab wounds and her stomach had been sliced open. I have never seen anything like this in my life. It was gruesome."

She shakes her head and pushes past a few more branches. "The coroner is rushing her autopsy. What we know is that she was approximately sixteen to twenty year old girl. It looks like she had pretty rough sex before she died. The coroner did find a long white hair from a pony's tail in her right hand. The most significant information came from the stab wounds to the chest and abdomen. Someone had cut this girl open and removed her uterus. The coroner found human chorionic gonadotropin (hCG) in the girl. She was pregnant at the time of death."

My first challenge will be to determine the identity of the body. She was young and someone had to know she is missing. She was good heath and her body in good condition. This is someone's daughter and they are worried sick about her. My guess after we find out who she is our number one suspect will come to the surface. What I dread is telling her parents that after some pretty rough sex their daughter was cut up, her fetus removed and she was left to die alone in the marsh. Her only comfort was the mare that came close enough for her to try to pull herself to her feet and get help.

We reach a clearing near a small canal which winds through the marsh. In front of us, is an open plain of marsh grass with an island of trees in the center. The view ends at the rise of dunes which borders the Atlantic

Ocean.

"This is pretty far from the road. Do people normally hike out into the marsh or camp here?"

Ranger Meers shakes her head, "No, they don't hike out into the marsh, as you can probably feel they would be eaten alive by mosquitoes. The park closes at dusk and all non campers have to be off the island at closing. This late in October and during the week we had no record of campers on the Virginia portion of the Island and it is over ten miles to the nearest beach camp sites on the Maryland side of the island."

She pauses before stepping under the yellow caution tape, "This morning a pink string bikini top was found hanging off a bush right here. This is about one hundred yards from where the body was located. No other articles of clothing or shoes have been found. Also no tire tracks have been found off the roadway. The only footprints at the scene are of the wild ponies that roam the area and the officers investigating the crime scene."

Ahead I can see the bold nine inch letters identifying the FBI forensic team. As I suspected they are John Duncan's team from the Richmond office. This group is thorough. I have worked a few cases with them in the past.

The missing persons reports don't have a match for Jane Doe and she is not from around here so probably a tourist visiting the island from another state. A basic description of her is run through the National Crime Information Computer (NCIC) to see if we can get a match. Once again, while this case looks like it should be cut and dry, there are no recent reports of a missing sixteen to twenty year old girl with reddish blond hair that match her description.

I leave it to the forensic team to process and excuse myself to check in with the office. Ranger Meers walks over to the group of park rangers and Chincoteague Police who are watching the forensic team.

As usual, the normal assortment of crank phone calls has come in. We have gotten a couple calls from family members looking for runaways. Each one hoping that we haven't found their daughter, but also thinking if it was, they at least know what had happened to her. One particular call will go down in my annuals of weird. A homeless man called on the 800 number from Michigan saying he had seen her abducted by aliens in a flying saucer the weekend before. She had hovered over Lake Michigan and then flown toward Ann Arbor before being sucked up in the space ships light beam. I don't know whether to laugh or cry at this one. The girl did look a lot like the cow bodies found in fields eviscerated in the typical alien abduction thing. One thing you learn with a case like this is every once in a while you need a little humor. It keeps you from crying your eyes out or screaming like a loon in a public park. For all I know I may be looking for a couple little green men who dumped her body after they probed her.

The toxicology reports also come back with more questions than answers. I had hoped for drugs or alcohol. I had hoped for some reason this girl didn't fight back. Instead I find a perfectly healthy teenage girl. No drug, no alcohol, no malnourishment. Someone loved and cared for this girl. I just don't know why they hadn't stepped forward to say she is missing.

Her body was found about twenty feet away from a park service road that goes through the marsh. It is a beautiful spot on a normal day. I sit on a fallen tree on the warm October day and just looked around hoping the scene will talk to me. While I sit I watch a herd of sika deer graze on a marsh field. Off in the distance a large wild herd of ponies graze. My guess the pony that held the original evidence is happily grazing less than half a mile away. The rains that came in Wednesday and Thursday had destroyed any DNA evidence on the pony so there is no need to go find her again. I can leave her live in peace. After all she is just as much an innocent victim of this as the girl now laying in the morgue in Pocomoke.

I watch a white egret slowly walk through the shallow water, occasionally it stops and looks down, then quickly darts its head into the water and comes up with a minnow in its beak. I know FBI technicians will walk this marsh just like this crane hoping to look down and see something in the water or tall grass that holds a clue as to what happened here. More and more I believe the homeless man and his alien abduction.

Besides a name of the victim, we also lacked a primary crime scene. This girl lost a lot of blood, but this scene didn't have enough to show it. The area she was found is blanketed in pine needles. There was a pool of blood where she was found but not significant enough to have been where she was stabbed. There are no drag marks where someone pulled her dying body to the spot. There are no deep foot prints in the marshy soil showing someone carrying a one hundred and twenty three pound body. This is not where this girl was murdered; it was just where she died. I also need to figure out where the pony came in. Were these the girls hand prints? The tail hair gripped in her hand indicated the pony was there while she was dying. The ponies are grazing at a distance but they do not seem curious of me. I would assume a struggle and the noises that had to be made while this girl was being murdered would have scared the ponies away, not drawn one to her.

I excuse myself and head to my next meeting with a member of the Chincoteague Pony Association. These are the people who monitor the horses, provide medical care, maintain a census on the pony population. A few times a year, they ride their saddle horses the length of the island checking on the health and general welfare of the ponies. They also round the ponies up once a year for their annual firemen's carnival and the world famous wild pony swim. This event draws thousands of people every year to the island during July. Since Jane Doe is connected to the ponies, at least in death, I need to find out what I can about them.

Everet Chandler is one of those long lanky guys that you expect to see with a cigarette hanging out of his mouth, a cowboy hat cocked on his head and boots that have tromped through way too much manure to be worn in public. He is dressed in faded jeans and a flannel shirt with the sleeves rolled up. Under his collar, I can see the white t-shirt I expected. When he starts to speak, he doesn't let me down on his image. He has a slow southern draw and a voice thick with years of cigarettes and whisky. I put him at somewhere between 50 and 100 years old. He is just that type of person you can't tell. He either hasn't aged well, or he has and he is ancient.

The restaurant we meet is on Beach Road. The place is crowded with late lunch patrons. Plates of steamed oysters, fries and coleslaw flow from the kitchen. I order the house specialty fried oysters. Everet just taps the table and the waitress nods her head. In a moment, my ice tea arrives and for him a cup of black coffee. I find pretty quickly my authority on the ponies is a man of few works. He sips his coffee and either grunts or nods to most of my questions.

When our food comes I look at his plate of crab cakes, flounder fillet, hush puppies and baked beans. I decide he eats here a lot. I have wrongly assumed tapping the table indicated the same for him. I also find out I was wrong about him being the silent backwater type.

He begins to intently squeeze a puddle of mustard and another of ketchup onto his plate. Then takes a fork full of crab cake and dips it in the mustard before putting it in his mouth. He follows that with a fork full of baked beans. Then a bite of flounder and dips that into the ketchup. Watching him eat is almost as fascinating as trying to figure out how to get the man to open up and say more than yes and no to me. Each bite is meticulously measured and dipped before he puts it in his mouth and savors the flavors.

Finally, he finishes his meal and pushes his plate back before looking at me. I pause from eating and when he asks if I want to know what he thought happened to the girl I put my fork down and nod.

"Your girl wasn't from around here. I seen her body that night before they covered her up when I responded with the fire department to help the coroner with the body. She weren't no local girl. Not even one of the regular tourists. I'd recognize her. Besides that, if she was here all summer she'd have a tan. That girl's naked body didn't have a tan line on it. One of the things you learn around here is that the beauties in the bikini's all have nice tan lines. Some when they are generous will show you where they end. No this girl isn't one of the bunnies on the beach. She was too white, no color in her skin at all. Not just that dead purple color, she had no tan lines. I hear tell she was raped. So my guess she wore that skimpy little pink suit to take off for someone. Someone she wanted to do the nasty with out in the marsh. We get a lot of that you know, lots of wild open spaces. You got a girl, you just find a spot. We call that road lovers lane. It closes at dusk but before that you can drive up and find a spot. Few minutes later, when you are done, get back in your truck and go home. No one the wiser that you just had some fun. Someone brought that girl there for that and something went wrong, something bad from the look of her. I saw a pig once cut like her, cleaned its belly out before roasting. That's what someone did to her. As for the pony, she must have been grazing there. They come in close to the road at night because the black top is still warm. It gets pretty cold and damp out on the marsh when the sun goes down. The road's a good place to sleep for the night. That pony stumbled on her after dark I bet. She may have smelled the blood and went to see if another mare had given birth out of season, but she weren't around when the girl was cut. No she came by after whoever did that had left her."

Thinking back to the crime scene he was right. This is mid October and this girl has no tan lines. She didn't get out much. She didn't even have tanned legs. She doesn't fit the bikini clad teenager I am developing in my mind. Everet Jones has redirected my thoughts on my victim. Jane had a story to tell. What was a girl who never went out in the sun doing in a bikini at the beach in October? Bikini's in October are for the diehard tanners. These are the women who will put up with being cold to soak up the last rays of summer. I also know now why the pony might have been involved. She was just heading to the road to sleep on warm black top for the night. My current guess was Jane tried to grab on to the pony and make it back to the road but the pony spooked and ran leaving her where we found her body.

***

Back in my car, I see my phone has a message from the office. I figure I should check I it before driving off. If I am lucky, someone has called to say they are Jane's family and are coming to identify the body. Instead the message is another lead on a person who may have seen Jane Doe on Chincoteague Island the day she died. I see Everet walking to his truck and yell to him asking how to get to Captains Cove on East Side Drive.

"Take this road out of here and follow it to the light up there." He gestures wildly making a motion that looks almost like a fish swimming down a stream. "Turn down Chicken City Road and go on out there 'til you get to the fliggle at Ridge Road. Now there you want to make a left and that will put you on East Side Drive. Now go on down there about a click and you will see a little green cottage. You don't want to go there, that's Jonsie's rental cottage. He lives in the white house with the green shutters next to the boat dock. If you are going to see Jonsie at Captain's Cove I bet he's out by his minnow box about now. So go to the bait shop on the dock. Tell him I said 'Hi' you hear. Me and Jonsie go back to school together."

The only real indication I have of where I am going after that description comes from his flailing arms. As he gave me the directions his hands and body swayed and darted as if he is driving me there. I am a little curious about Mr. Jones at Captain's Cove. If he and Everet had gone to school together, maybe I can at least get an idea of the man's age. I really have a desire to understand something before the day is out --Even if it is to figure out the man I have just interviewed.

The trip to Captains Cove takes under two minutes. I figure out a fliggle is where the road makes an abrupt dogleg to drive around the front porch of a house on the corner. The longer I stay on this island the more I laugh at its strange ways. Of course I am not disappointed in James Earl Jones either. I might add no relation to the actor James Earl Jones. This man could be a twin to Everet Jones and I wonder if the last name indicates they are brothers, perhaps twins. When I ask James Earl Jones this, he slaps his sides and laughs.

"No we ain't related. Well, no that ain't the truth neither, and you being a law man I guess I have to tell the truth. Down here you got four main family names. Way back somewhere everyone here is related to everybody else. You live here all your life you start to figure out the difference between a brother, sister, first cousin and a cousin of a cousin three times removed. Now my daddy and Everet's daddy growed up in the same house. They both be Jones but my daddy was a Charles Jones and his daddy was a Richard Jones. Everet's daddy, Richard Jones was the bastard child of the next door neighbor and I think he was a Mason. You know it's hard to tell who might be related to who 'cause no one keeps the doors locked and at night. It use to be a game of cat and mouse. That don't happen no more 'cause people learned to behave a little more. Also, too many eyes watching out and women cluck like chickens if you get them talking about who might or might not be sleeping with who."

I think he lost me somewhere in the back yard of his grandfather's house and I worry if he and I speak the same language at times. The entire time he is talking, he is catching minnows in his hands and throwing them from one bait box to another. Then he lowers the wood and metal bait box back into the water, wipes his hands on the back of his jeans and holds out his hand to shake mine. We shake hands and he invites me inside his bait shack.

Those same hands that just fondled fish, grab two coffee cups and fill them, handing one to me. I look inside to see something the color and consistency of burned motor oil. He holds up a packet of artificial sweetener and asks if I want cream and in his words "you better not because I don't have none. Cream in your coffee is for women and pussys. Since I don't see you in no dress and I assume you ain't no pussy, well you can just drink it black."

One sip of the coffee leads me to believe I will be staying up all night. I'm not sure if I should chew it or drink it. My only fear now is whether my ulcer will survive a few polite sips. James Earl is not one to mince words. While I am still trying to decide if I am going to die from my first sip of coffee he starts into his information.

"I hear you are looking for information on a girl in a pink bikini. Well, Monday morning, I was out surf fishing just past the last parking lot. I drive my truck out there some mornings to fish. Well, I see this little hottie in a pink string bikini coming out from between the dunes. She was a cute little thing. Well stacked if you know what I mean. There was a guy with her. He was older and stayed back in the dunes. I saw him rolling up a sleeping bag. I didn't see his face or anything, just he had some gray in his hair and wasn't no teenager. Now you aren't suppose to sleep on the beach at night but sometimes people try to. The Park Rangers try to make sure all the cars are gone for the night but there are some who get a ride and sleep on the beach. It's cheaper than staying in a hotel and there are some who like to have some privacy on the beach at night for some nocturnal entertainment, if you know what I mean. Well I got the feeling these two spent the night on the beach. It was cold Monday morning and that girl wasn't wearing much. I wondered if the guy was her father. He looked old enough to be that. Then I thought, well no, what father sleeps on the beach with his daughter in one sleeping bag. So I guess she thought she'd gotten herself a sugar daddy but daddy was too cheap to spring for a hotel. Anyway, they headed off toward the main parking lot and I never saw them after that."

I ask him if there is anything more he can tell me about either the girl or the man she was with. Did they seem friendly together? This is possibly the first piece of the puzzle I have gotten. He shakes his head and I ask him if he could tell me exactly where he had seen them. He shakes his head again and says. "Dunes are dunes and beach is beach. I can get you to the general area but not sure if I can point out exactly where they slept. I got my pole planted just above the high tide line and I know what direction I was standing. I can get you somewhere around where they were but not exactly."

I thank him and put down the rest of my cup of coffee before walking out the door and back to my car. I guess my next move is to get the forensic team combing the dunes for signs a couple might have spent the night there nearly a week ago. I also wonder where they parked their car in order to be able to spend the night. It is a couple miles across the bridge and to the beach. If they had walked there from Chincoteague quite a few people would have seen them. I also figure before the five o'clock news it is time to update the description. Now, I know she may have last been seen in the company of an older man with gray hair. Hopefully, that will spark someone to remember more.

The search of the beach has to be put off until tomorrow morning. Storms have started to roll in off the ocean and the fear of a lightning strike is too great. Along the ocean, lightning can strike well in advance of the storm. Also, the team could be a distance from their vehicles and have to make a dash back up the beach to get to their cars if a storm hits. We hold a press conference away from both the beach and the crime scene. The location we choose is in front of the Assateague Light House. Word has gotten out that this is a pretty gruesome murder and the national press corps from DC has arrived. If nothing else, this gets the artists rendition of Jane Doe all over the evening news. We manage to get the press conference finished before the storms hit. The sky behind the red and white candy striped light house looks dark and threatening. I see the news crews casting glances at the sky hoping they don't get caught outside in the storm. Once again, all we can do for the night is sit back and see if anyone has seen anything.

***

I am sitting in my car at my hotel waiting for the rain to let up overlooking the swimming pool that is drained for the winter. On the other side of the pool, along the road is an anatomically correct statue of a stallion rearing on its hind legs. I keep thinking back to that pony. This girl had her entire stomach opened up. She had to be pretty strong to even rise up with that much blood loss to have put finger prints on the hind quarters. I was always taught to follow the evidence, but this piece of evidence just doesn't make sense. She was either standing and used the pony for support and then collapsed or these weren't her hand prints. Maybe that is my problem. Everyone assumes the blood on the pony is from our victim. What if there are more victims?

Once checked in, I go to my room and sit on my bed with the case file scattered across the comforter. There isn't much to it. I have initial toxicology reports and pictures of the crime scene. I keep picking up the pictures of the pony. I finally go to my lap top and pulled up the pictures there. I need to see them larger. My stomach is growling by the time I finally see what has been bothering me. I need to find this pony and measure the distance between markings on its hind quarters. I have the uneasy feeling these hand prints are too big to belong to the hands of my victim. The width of the fingers, the length of the palm and the fingers appear to be male, not female. Now I am wondering if I have a second victim. Maybe Jane Doe hasn't been reported missing because the man was her father and he ended up under the water in the marshes. If so, we may never find his body. That would explain no vehicle, no identification, and no clues. Someone may have killed them both and taken their car.

I flip on the TV in time for the news. It is a slow night and the story leads off the local broadcast. They do a pretty good job of creating hype. They flash pictures of the ponies grazing along the water and the drawing of the girl. Then they go to the news conference with us asking for leads. I hope we don't sound too desperate because we really have very little to go on. In this case we really do need the help of anyone with any information.

The hotel doesn't have room service and the nearest restaurant is about 50,000 mosquitoes from here so I run through the swarm of them and get into my car. I make a call to the head of the search team, John Duncan, and ask him to join me. I think he and I need to plan the areas to be searched in the morning and I think a call has to be made to the field office to send more help. This search scene is too big for a small team and the local force can't supply much. The park service as also a skeleton crew, pared down for the winter. Once the beach wanes for the season things quiet down to bird watchers and people who walk the beach for shells. The extra staff to clean the areas, guard the beach and patrol the parking lots are let go until spring.

I pick John up on Main Street and we leave the island by the five mile long causeway. As I drive, I keep thinking of the remoteness of this island. In order to get to the crime scene, someone had to leave the main highway and take the two lane road down through the marsh. The road crosses a series of bridges and roadways with water and marsh grass on both sides. Then they had to wind their way through Chincoteague to the north end of town to get to Beach Road. From there they had to drive a couple more miles to get to the Woodland Trail and the murder scene. This doesn't feel random. It feels planned. Someone had to know this town and had to know where to go to be alone and commit this crime. During the daylight hours, Assateague is alive with people. Even during the off season, people come to take pictures of the birds and ponies. The possibility of someone accidentally taking a picture of the murderer or the murder taking place was fairly high. The killer had to know he was safe from being seen and was alone to get away with this.

The clerk at the hotel recommended a seafood restaurant in Atlantic, Virginia. I was told to drive past the gates to Wallops Island base and then take the first left after that. There is a sign but I was warned it is easy to miss. It is about the size of a piece of paper hammered onto a fence post. The restaurant is out over the water. The view is nice and the food is home cooked. I manage to find it and when I open the door I am hit with the wonderful smells from the kitchen. One thing I have learned in the field-- if the locals tell you where to eat follow their advice.

John Duncan, the forensic team leader and I have worked together for a couple years. We have gotten to know each other well and work well together. I'm glad John has been assigned to this case. We both started working missing persons and homicide about the same time. I feel comfortable with him and trust his judgment. He and I have gotten to be friends both inside and outside work. It helps on a case like this. I have a gut feeling this is going to be long.

We are seated at a window table overlooking the channel. Before we even order, a big basket of cheese biscuits, corn bread and hush puppies are delivered to the table and a friendly woman asks us what we would like to drink to start with. For being an out of the way restaurant they have a full bar and a substantial food menu. We both order from the bar and each decides on the fried seafood platter.

One bite into the corn bread and I know how a restaurant with a sign smaller then the size of a stop sign about three miles off any main road and with no advertising can stay in business. The corn bread is sweet and buttery that melts in my mouth. I have been in the south many times, but I have never had corn bread this good. They serve it hot alongside honey butter. I fight my instincts to have another piece before our food arrives.

I let John unwind a little before we started to talk shop. He has spent most of his day walking around the marsh looking for anything that might help. Like me, he is coming up empty. When he works a case like this, he is tired and hungry by the end of the day. It is better to let him get some food in him before discussing plans for the next day.

Our tossed salads come with our second round of drinks from the bar. I don't realize how hungry I am until I start eating. Once again this place surprises me. Fresh leafy greens topped with lumps of crab meat. The house dressing is a spicy seafood dressing that brings out the flavor of the crab meat without over powering the greens. I notice John is equally as hungry as he scrapes the last drop of dressing from his salad bowl and asks me how I found this place.

Before we have a chance to start talking, the main course comes out. We each have a plate put in front of us piled about three inches high with seafood. I look at the fried oysters, clam fritters, crab cakes and filet of flounder on the plate. A companion plate is delivered to each of us containing mashed potatoes and fried apples. The waitress points out the mashed potatoes as a house specialty. They are Yukon Gold potatoes boiled and mashed then sea food seasoning and cheddar cheese are mixed in. After that lumps of crab meat are folded into the mixture before it is baked to a golden brown on top. My mouth is watering before she finishes telling us about them.

We started to eat and I realize we are going to have to wait to talk out our plans for the next day. The food in front of us is too good to waste between conversations. We mostly grunt and point at different things on the plate asking each if they have tried it yet. Pretty soon we have both cleaned our plates and are sitting back stuffed.

As we both pull out our tablets, the waitress comes around and asks if we want the table cleaned and if we want dessert yet. I haven't planned on dessert but then she tells us the pies are baked daily by granny who is the ninety-four year old mother of the owner. Not being one to insult a ninety-four year old woman I settle on the Snickers pie with a cup of coffee. John opts for the Smith Island Cake, a multi layered yellow cake with caramel and rum flavored layers in between.

Now too full to move and plates of dessert before us we finally get down to work. The forensic team has gotten nowhere searching the marsh in Swan Cove. John has spoken to James Earl Jones and they have agreed to meet at the parking lot at 7:00 AM. From there, they will walk the beach. James Earl is fairly sure he can point out the general area of the dune where he saw the girl walking and the place he thinks they may have slept for the night. Having searched beaches before John is worried about how much we will find. Beaches are collectors. People leave little bits behind all the time. The wind and the rain move things around and deposit more while moving things we need to stay put. Stuff can be buried in a day's time or blown away. That is the nature of beaches. His hope is that the dunes protected the area some from surf and wind. There is nothing we can do about the rain. We also discuss the pony. He agrees if the pictures are questionable we need to find her and take some measurements. If these are not Jane Doe's hands we need to find out who else had bloody hands on that pony.

We notice we are the only ones left in the restaurant and decide to pack it up for the night. We are both going to get a fresh start early in the morning so we pay our bill, thank them for the wonderful dinner and promise to come back before we leave the island. I drive back to our hotel in the dark. As we approach the island, I look at the lights of the town across the water. There is nothing from the main land to the island. Then there is a narrow stretch of land covered in lights from the houses and street lights of Chincoteague, beyond that the blackness of the Atlantic Ocean at night. The sky is still over cast and the night is pitch black. Slightly off to the north of the main clump of lights, I see the flash then break and then double flash of the light house. In my mind, I move a little bit to the north and see the absolute darkness over the area of the murder scene. Did Jane Doe die watching that same light pattern in the blackness of night?

DAY 2
CHINCOTEAGUE, VIRGINIA

I wake in the morning to the alarm on my phone. I hear water hitting the sidewalk and assume it is raining, which will hamper us finding any evidence today. I grab a quick shower and flip open my laptop to read my email. Nothing looks like it can't wait, so, I head out to the motel lobby to grab something from their complimentary continental breakfast. I pause as soon as I open my door and just hope what I see across the drained swimming pool isn't an omen of weird for the rest of my day. The water I had heard was a maid out along the road washing and waxing the stallion statue. At the exact moment I walk out the door, she is up on a ladder applying paste wax from a can onto the horse's penis and testicles. I've seen weird in my day but waxing a horse penis pretty much takes the cake. I snap a quick picture with my phone to file it away in my "look at this weird shit file" and continue on to find a couple boxes of donuts and a carafe of coffee. This isn't exactly my idea of breakfast but I grab two donuts and pour some coffee in a paper cup. As I walk back, the maid has climbed up two rungs on the ladder and is waxing his chest. I snap another picture because from almost every angle it looks like something from a fetish film. You just can't get weird like this on an average day. I smile as I walk back into my room.

The Richmond Field office has absolutely no new evidence or leads. Someone did suggest the mosquitoes did it. The itching welts on my legs confirm that possibility. I think the voraciousness of the mosquitoes in this place should be painted on big red warning signs as you approach on the causeway. The caller suggested the mosquitoes attacked her and drained all her blood. I assumed the person from Richmond had been here before and thought it only appropriate to put that as one of the top pieces of information. So far there have been eighty-five calls identifying Jane Doe as possibly someone's missing daughter. I know most, if not all, are a parents desperate stab at closure. Each of these leads will have to be investigated, well not the mosquito one, but all the missing persons will have to be ruled out. In this country, we have too many missing children. Whenever a body is found the calls pour in. It causes a lot of extra work for our team but, I understand. These people just want to know what happened. For many, finding her body would mean putting something in the cemetery besides a headstone.

A message from John is not promising. At the break of dawn, his team was on the south end of Assateague with James Earl Jones. At his last update, they have walked the beach a couple times with James Earl looking for the exact dune he last saw the girl. John is afraid they are going to have to search about a half mile of beach. James Earl knew where he had been standing but the girl is a little less defined in his mind.

Another team is once again combing Swan Cove. Meanwhile, the town sheriff and a couple members of the pony association are riding the marsh searching for the small herd of ponies that were along the road last Tuesday morning, once located they are going to be rounded up and penned in a holding area used by their vet team and for the wild pony round up in attempt to try and find the pony from the photo.

It is good to see there are multiple avenues of investigation going on. I hang up the phone with the coroner in Pocomoke after calling him to see if he has any more information or if the DNA evidence has come back. He has more to add but wants to go over some findings in person later in the day. For right now, he can tell me no pony bites. Yes, she has numerous mosquito bites. He can believe she spent the night on the beach from the number she had on her body. He also found beach sand in her hair. It is hard to tell what hit her head. It appeared to be an object not a fist. The rain had washed away any trace evidence before we found her. He is now waiting on a dentist to take x rays of her mouth and teeth to begin working through the eighty-five missing children cases. He warns me that identifying her isn't going to be easy. Some of these cases go back to when these kids were seven or eight years old. Kid's mouths change a lot from that point until late teens or early twenties. The dental records might not be much help because of the age when the children went missing compared to Jane

Doe's current age. This is a process of elimination until they have one or more they can't rule out. The DNA swab that had been sent to Quantico may help rule some. Less than half of the missing reports had DNA kits either created by their families before the kids went missing or from collection by police after. One disturbing bit of the conversation is that this sexual assault was not this kid's first rodeo. Scar tissue indicates old rectal and vaginal tearing consistent with some pretty rough treatment over a prolonged period of time. There is pitting to her pubic bone consistent with a vaginal delivery. He has also found some plastic surgery implants but those he wants to wait to talk about when he can show me why they are so unusual. He is still counting the number of stab wounds. He's marked them all on his chart but they bisect and overlap in some places.

First stop of the day is a return to the crime scene. The forensic team is in wading boots with rakes pulling them through the black murky water of the swamp. The smell coming up from the trapped gases in the silt is strong. It reminds me of searching the holding tanks of airplanes for flushed evidence. Who knew Mother Nature could produce noxious odors that would rival a septic tank. On the shore, I see a pile of goop covered articles recovered from the marsh so far. A couple mismatched broken flip flops, plastic bottles, an ancient beer can, some fishing sinkers and a plastic sand shovel. Each piece tagged with a number. Out in the water stakes with bright colored flags blow in the breeze, each with a number to correspond to the numbered articles on the shore. Chris Mulligan sits on a tree stump working on the grid map and labeling each item. Whenever someone calls with another item, she runs out and tags the GPS location. After that she places the marker on the grid map on her tablet.

I leave them with instructions to call if they find a magic bullet. I'd love something that says Jane Doe was here. A purse with a driver's license and her name would be great. As I drive on and approach the last parking lot, I see the satellite trucks from the news. Now every off air and cable network has picked up the story. This always adds to the problems. The news crews mean well. They are trying to do a job and they also help get information to the public. At the same time, it adds to our man power needs. Someone has to watch the news crews and let them get close enough to film but far enough away to not destroy something we can use. A few of the local news recognize me from the press conference and come running with microphone outstretched and camera person in tow.

I hate impromptu news interviews especially when I am as clueless about my victim as the network crews. I hold up my hands to the fifteen or so reporters yelling "Agent Clay, what can you tell us?" to give them something for the noon news. I tell them what I can. "By now every station has the artist rendition of our victim. We ask that you get it on the news. Someone lived next door to her. Someone's kid sat next to her in homeroom. So far no parent has conclusively come forward to say she was their daughter. We are following up on a bunch of missing persons cases but we are no closer now then we were yesterday to knowing her name. Our first step is finding out who she was. We know how she died, but until we can put a name to our Jane Doe finding out who murdered her is nearly impossible. Ask your viewers to look closely and if they know her call us. She needs justice and to be buried under her own name. Now if you can excuse me, I need to check in with the evidence search team. I promise as soon as we know anything I will call a news conference and let you know what we have discovered."

I walk up the path to the beach and nod at the FBI field technician acting as a buffer between the news crews and the beach. I have anticipated seeing evidence flags planted in the sand but maybe not so many. The dunes and beach to the water are covered in numbered flags. A camera person is going from person to person taking pictures. A lab technician is following close behind bagging and tagging the items then calling out a GPS coordinates to the technician plotting the crime scene. With this beach, we will probably collect a thousand pieces with hopefully one belonging to Jane Doe or her murderer.

I walk over to John and James Earl. They are near the water's edge. Sticking out of the sand is a piece of PVC pipe. I greet everyone and shake James Earl's hand and ask him if he would mind walking me through where he was and what he saw that morning.

"Well, see I was fishing here. This here is the pipe I stick my surf rod in. I just leave it. It don't matter if somebody else uses it as long as it stays put when they leave and if I show up they understand I dug a big ole hole to bury five feet of this here pole down in the sand. Now I think she came out from that dune there but it might have been that one or those over there. You know I was just minding my own business when I hear a noise and turn to look. What I saw was mighty fine. I don't mean to speak of the dead but she walked out from between the dunes and she was adjusting that ample set of knockers she had. It was a cold morning and that little pink bikini top was barely holding those nipples in. As she was adjusting them, I got a little peak. Then she walked over a bit and shimmied down her bikini bottom. Now that was a nice view. Then she squatted and peed in the sand. It wasn't until she had stood up and pulled her bikini bottom up that she noticed me. She seemed all embarrassed but waved. That's how I know she was your body. I got a good long look at her."

I asked him if he can tell me where she peed but to no avail. "Mister, I don't know about you but, when a girl is flashing some nice firm tits and then shimmies down a bikini bottom to a nice shaved V she could have been in front of a firing squad aiming at me and I wouldn't have noticed them. All I can tell you is that young thing got a rise outta me and it's a damn shame someone killed her. She was a beautiful little thing when she was alive."

I asked him where he saw the man and what he could remember. "Well after she waved she turned and ran back behind the dune. Now before you ask, no I'm not sure which one because she was wearing one of those thong bikinis so I was admiring the nice smooth mounds on her back side. I saw the man though. It was from the side or maybe a little toward the back, so I didn't see his face. He was folding and then rolling up a sleeping bag. I thought he might be her daddy or grand daddy with his gray hair but there was only one sleeping bag. She joined him and they walked down the path to the parking lot. Now my truck was the only one parked there so I don't know what their car looked like. I can only tell you what I saw."

I thank James Earl and go to look at the evidence collected and the possible camp site, nothing stands out that will break the case. One piece of evidence collected is going to be a handling problem. With a metal detector one of the lab techs found a copper Spanish coin dating back to the early 1700s. John has already done some research and a court case back in 1998 awarded all artifacts found back to Spain. There were two recorded Spanish ship wrecks off the coast of Assateague near the Maryland and Virginia boarder. The first was the La Galga in 1750 and the second was the Juno in 1802. Spain never declared either ship a loss so they retained sovereignty over the contents of the ships. The folk tales from these two ship wrecks were used as an explanation for how the wild ponies came to be. If this was the case, Spain never claimed the ponies but, they do claim anything from either ship that washes up on shore or is salvaged. This means we will have to document the coin, we can hold it until the case is over but eventually it must be returned to Spain for them to decide its disposition.

Already the sun is high in the sky. I have two crimes scenes being searched with little to nothing to show for the day except a nifty little piece of Spanish history. My next stop has to be to Everet Chandler who is out searching for the pony herd and the pony that was blood covered.

What I see when I arrive is something out of the Wild West. Heading toward me is a group of seven men on horseback surrounding a herd of wild ponies. The ponies seem to be accustomed to this procedure. They are sauntering between the riders as if it was something they do all the time. Everet and the town Sheriff ride up to me leaving the other five riders to steer the ponies toward the beach road.

They both point to a mare in the back of the pack. According to the pictures this is the mare we are looking for. A vet is waiting at the holding pen to look her and the other ponies over for any injuries or marks. Also some of my lab technicians are there to log and tag anything they can collect from them. The vet and technician will measure the pony and see if they can map out exactly where the hand prints were and therefore determine the size of the hands that made them. Hopefully by the end of the day, we will have more information on the pony and they will be able to be released back to their grazing land.

I pull my ringing phone out of my pocket to see it is from the coroner in Pocomoke. I excuse myself from Everet and take the call and hear Tim Clark on the other end. "I got a hit on the DNA and it's not something I want to talk about over the phone. When this hits the media, it's going to be a major shit storm and we both better have all our oars in the water before that. Can you meet me here today?" I look at Everet sitting on his horse and hope he hasn't over heard the message. The fewer people who know there is a pending storm the better. I tell Tim I will see him in an hour and hang up.

With that I say goodbye to Everet and the sheriff and hit the road for Pocomoke City, Maryland. The drive is about thirty-five minutes and the entire time I wonder just how big this might be. When I pull in, I only see one car in the parking lot. At least the man knows how to handle this. He'd sent his techs away.

Tim Clark motions for me to follow him into the lab. There is a small body lying on the steel exam table covered in a white sheet. I can tell from the size this is my victim. She looks childlike. Tim pulls back the sheet from her face. He has done a good job cleaning and restoring her dignity. I am not prepared however for his next statement. "Agent Clay, meet Kali Callahan, Kali, this is Agent Clay and he's going to help clean up this mess you have somehow gotten involved in."

Kali Callahan. That name is familiar. It takes a second for me to pull the name from my memory banks. It was eleven years ago and I was just about to graduate from the FBI Academy in Quantico, Virginia when Kali went missing. Because of the people involved and the location she went missing, all recruits were loaded onto buses and taken to help the search teams. I can still remember the image of the little pixie with big green eyes and strawberry blond hair in ringlet pig tails. It became a battle cry to find Kali, do whatever it takes. We never found her body but her mother, Samantha Callahan went to jail for twenty-five years for her murder. I am starting to see the growing clouds.

Back in 2001, Samantha Callahan was a topless dancer in a sleazy club in New Jersey. Somehow she had gotten hooked up with Jake Montgomery, a major Wall Street player and investment banker. Montgomery had a summer cabin in the Delaware Water Gap where he and his buddies went to hunt and fish. He'd leave his wife and kids at home and go to the woods to his little hide away. This case was an airing of dirty laundry of the rich kid club. Whenever Montgomery went to the woods with his buddies, they always hired a couple hookers to go with them and entertain. Samantha, being the mother of the year, took her six year old daughter Kali with her for the weekend. Friday and Saturday night, Samantha drank and partied with Montgomery and five other men while Kali stayed locked in a room. Now and then Samantha would check on her and take her food but for most of the time Kali was on her own. Saturday night was particularly wild and Samantha didn't remember seeing Kali after dinner. In the morning, Samantha woke up and the men had gone, when she looked so was Kali. She walked about five miles to a nearby town and called the police.

Police found a trash bag with a pair of Kali's jeans and her t-shirt. Both had blood on them. Samantha explained that on Saturday Kali had been running outside for a while and fallen. She'd cut her hand and scraped her knee. The clothes were torn and had blood on them so Samantha bagged them up and threw then away in the trash. With what she was making for the weekend she had planned to buy them both some new clothes and some new toys for Kali. No other evidence was found but, police didn't believe a hooker over the testimony of a bunch of Wall Street high rollers. According to an expert witness, the blood patterns on the pants and t-shirt were not consistent with Samantha's story. According to the men, Samantha hadn't mentioned the kid until they picked her up. She had been waiting on the corner for them with the girl and a suit case. They were ready to hit the road and told her with what they would be doing they wanted the kid to stay in a room locked away. Samantha agreed. When they got there, Kali wanted to explore but Samantha beat her and shoved her in the room. Then, she started to play some music and did a strip for them. None of the men saw Kali after that. They did some pretty heavy drinking Saturday night and when they were ready to leave Sunday Samantha told them she wasn't going. They left the house telling her to lock the door on her way out. That was the last they saw Samantha.

We searched the woods for a week. The Delaware Water Gap is a huge wooded area with marshland and a river running down the center. It is dotted with camps and large estates as well as small towns. It butts up against the Pocono's resorts. There were so many places this girl could have been abandoned or her body hidden. The area is also riddled with bears, bob cats and snakes, not to mention the ticks. If left alone in the woods, the child would not have made it long without being in big trouble. After a week the search was called off.

When it went to trial, Montgomery showed up with more attorneys any one man needed. Samantha had a public defender against the best lawyers New York money could buy. It was a media circus splattered with lewd pictures of Samantha with black boxes covering her nude body parts on the evening news. Samantha accused Montgomery and his friends of drugging her Saturday night and taking Kali. Montgomery's lawyer painted Samantha as a drugged out crack whore who took her daughter along on a weekend trick. In the end, the jury believed Montgomery and Samantha went to jail for her disappearance and murder.

All these years Samantha had maintained her innocence. She petitioned a group who had freed other falsely accused inmates to help her bring justice to Kali. Until this moment, there has been no evidence what Samantha Callahan had said was true but DNA doesn't lie and on the morgue table in front of me is the body of Kali Callahan. Tim Clark raises Kali's right hand and turns it over. There across her palm is a scar. All I can think is--Dear God we have held an innocent woman in jail. From what I am hearing someone not only kidnapped her, they have been having sex with her for at least part of that time.

The first blast of the shit storm is followed by the second as Tim Clark continues. "Now Kali, let's you and I talk to Agent Clay about the things that have been done to you during your young life. To start, she has had some work done to her face. While most women have cheek implants to make them look younger they usually wait until they are much older. Kali has very unusual work done." He pulls out a metal tray with small silicone pieces in it. "These are cheek implants but unlike normal implants these have no serial numbers or manufacturer identification. As a matter of fact, I think these may have been custom made for her and really expensive. They made her look more childlike. The weird doesn't stop there. She has had laser hair removal to her vaginal area, legs and underarms. You don't see this often. Especially with women who have her hair color. Laser hair removal works well with dark hair. During the procedure, the laser is directed at the hair shaft and the heat destroys the hair follicle at the root. It only takes two or three treatments at $3000 a pop with dark hair. With red and blond hair it can take five times or more. Someone spent at least $15,000 having all the hair follicles in her vaginal region, legs and her underarms removed permanently. Who does that to a girl this age? Perhaps if she was on the pageant circuit or was a model I could understand this. Of course none of this makes sense because both of those activities are in the public eye. You don't parade an abducted child in public. I don't know about you, but I have never seen pictures of her on a runway."

"From the sexual assault and the plastic surgery we are talking about someone who paid a lot of money to keep her looking like a child. We know it wasn't her mother; she's in jail for Kali's murder I might add. The other last person she was seen with, Jacob Montgomery, has recently been named President of one of the biggest banks in America. Just in time for him to rise to the top, the child he was connected to at the time of her kidnapping was just found dead in a marsh, not that different from the place she went missing eleven years ago."

I agree with Tim that we have to make sure we have everything confirmed completely and are one hundred percent sure the girl that was found at Swan Cove is Kali Callahan. He has already requested a second independent DNA test. For the moment, this is going to stay between very select people. If this is indeed Kali Callahan, I have to contact the New York DA's office before this becomes leaked. They are going to have to make a statement about Samantha Callahan. Since she is in jail for her daughter's murder, they are going to have to release her at some point. Even if she was involved, she will have to be released and retried at the very least. The scars on Kali's hand and on her knee confirm Samantha's story from the disappearance. This will also reopen the case against Jake Montgomery. He has never been charged with anything but that was because the blame had been put on Samantha. When she is removed from the equation, he and his friends become prime suspects. Since he has never been charged, there is no double jeopardy and one of the most influential banking heads in the world may go on trial for child abduction. Since I now have a name and a lead I have to regroup. I have to get the Kali Callahan case file sent to me and begin at square one, July 22, 2001, the last day of Kali Callahan's known whereabouts.

I get in my car and look at my watch. It's already 4:30. By the time I get back to Chincoteague the sun will be setting. I put in a call to John and ask him to meet me at the same place that we went last night. It is on my way back to the island and it is out of the way from the prying eyes of the media. He agrees to be there by 5:15 and I tell him to meet me at my car first. I think a conversation to bring him up to date in the parking lot is a better idea than in the center of a local restaurant. I did warn him to bring his rain coat and umbrella, after my meeting with Tim Clark I am thinking more shit typhoon then storm.

John and I arrive at the same time. He looks tired and lets out a groan as he sits down on the front seat and closes the door. He has spent a long day walking the beach and finding nothing significant. I don't know any other way to tell him then to just bring him up to date. He doesn't say a word as I fill him in on the identity of Jane Doe. In the end, he asks me if I have contacted the New York City District Attorney. To be sure I am waiting for the call from Tim Clark with the confirmation DNA sample. I really don't want to break this news until I am confident beyond a shadow of a doubt about who we have.

With nothing else to do at the moment we go inside to eat. I am torn between keeping my wits about me and drinking an ice tea or getting drunk and forgetting about my day. In the end, I settle on the ice tea. If I have to call the New York City District Attorney tonight, I don't want to risk sounding like a drunken loon. Our salads arrive and we both dig in. I don't think either of us stopped to eat today. I decide to try the baked stuffed flounder tonight. It arrives from the kitchen in a big brown baking dish. Once again I have a second plate for my side dish, this time a baked stuffed potato. The flounder is a work of art. The top is baked to a golden brown, it is crab imperial topped with white wine and cheese. The flounder fillet is cooked to perfection, light and flaky with just a hint of the wine flavoring. The baked potato is huge and filled with everything from chives to bacon, cheese, onions, mushrooms and sour cream. For dessert I go with pumpkin pie. It may be the best pie I have ever had in my life. As we leave the restaurant my phone rings and I see the number of the Pocomoke City Coroner's office.

The next wave of the storm washes over me. There is no question they body in the morgue is that of seventeen year old Kali Callahan, missing since 2001. John and I look at each other knowing this is going to be a long night.

We settle into my hotel room and I get the number for the District Attorney's office. It's after 7:00 PM so I'm sure no one will be there. I make the call anyway and District Attorney White answers the phone. After introducing myself I ask him if he is alone in the office. He is, some of the staff is still there because they are working on a high profile case but no one is within ear shot. So I begin…

"I am the chief investigator for a murder case on Assateague Island in Virginia." He tells me he has seen something on the news about an unidentified teenage girl found murdered here. "Are you familiar with the Kali Callahan disappearance eleven years ago?" He thinks for a moment and then asks if I think they are somehow connected. "I have two independent DNA samples confirming the body that I have in the morgue is that of seventeen year old Kali Callahan." Across the motel room John hears the expletive F bomb coming from the phone.

Then he asks "When are you going to the media? Can you give me a few hours?"

I tell him "We are going to make sure we have everything in order before we call a press conference. It's late for down here. The sidewalks roll up before dark. I think telling the media we are holding a press conference in the morning will be better." I also tell him at this point only the coroner, the head of the forensic search team and he knows the identity of the girl. He agrees and yells to a secretary to get him a flight to Salisbury, Maryland tonight. He promises to have a staff member email everything they have on the case file in the next few minutes. Then he would like to meet before the press conference so that we can all be up to speed before the questions start flying. We hang up both knowing tomorrow is going to be the biggest wave of the storm.

Within minutes the entire case file for the Kali Callahan disappearance appears in my email. I log onto the hotel print server and hit the button.

Then sprint out the door to the printer at the hotel office. I make it to the desk just as the first page spits out of the printer. The girl at the desk looks at me and asks if I know how many pages. I tell her it is ninety-eight pages. She stands there for a second before telling me this is going to cost a lot of money. Did I really want to print all those pages? I tell her yes, and go to grab two paper cups of coffee. John and I need to look at this case tonight. I watch it print and make sure the desk girl is not reading what is coming off. I don't want a leak and printing from a location like this screams leak. Luckily, the girl is more interested in the reality show on the TV then the printer. When it finally finishes I tell her it's done and she reaches behind her and hands it to me while telling me it will be on my bill at check out.

We divide up the case file against Samantha Callahan. I will get a copy of the court transcripts in the morning. For now, I want to know what the police on the scene at the Montgomery hunting cabin saw.

 The initial police report from Layton, New Jersey is first up on my pile. On Sunday, July 22, 2001 a young woman identifying herself as Samantha Callahan came in-claiming her daughter Kali had been kidnapped. She was visibly distraught and said she had walked from a cabin in the woods. She admitted she was a prostitute and had been working a private party at a home in the Water Gap. She had been picked up across the state and brought here for the job. Because this was so short notice she had been forced to bring her six year old daughter with her. The owner of the cabin, a man named Jake, told her he had no problem with bringing the child. He liked little girls. Ms Callahan said as the road trip continued she felt uneasy about the attention the men in the vehicle were giving her daughter and on arriving at the cabin she locked Kali in a bedroom and carried the key to the room on her person.

Friday night the men told her to dance and then took turns having sex with her in the great room of the house. This went on late into the night before they allowed her to get some sleep. She slept in the room with Kali. When she awoke the men were gone so she allowed Kali to go out and play for a while around the house. When she heard a car approaching, she quickly got Kali to go back inside. Kali tripped on the stone front porch and was crying when she took her back in and she tried to quiet her down before the men got back inside. She didn't want them thinking about Kali. She thought out of sight and out of mind was her best defense. Saturday night they made steaks on the grill. Then requested she strip and lay on the table while they used her as a human plate. At that point, she raised her shirt and showed the officer a burn mark on her abdomen she said was made by a hot steak. The officer also noted minor knife wounds that she claimed were from the men cutting pieces of steak off the main one. They poured steak sauce on her breasts to dip while they ate with their hands. They also dumped coleslaw and potato salad on her and licked that off. She described something akin to a Roman Orgy with her as the center piece. The entire time they were eating they took turns pouring tequila down her throat. The last thing she remembered was about 6:00 PM going to the bathroom and checking on Kali. She was drunk and felt very light headed. She woke in the morning, naked lying on the floor of the great room. The men were gone and the door to the room Kali had been staying was open. When she looked inside Kali was gone. She searched the house and found all the men's things were gone. She felt they weren't coming back. She threw clothes on and came here across the toll bridge. When an officer checked with the toll gate and the toll collector confirmed the woman was allowed to cross the bridge on foot. The toll collector gave her directions to the police station.

Ms. Callahan did not know the address of the house she was staying in. She only knew first names of the men who were at the house. During the interview she was not sure how to get back to the location. All she kept saying was that it was in the woods along the river. She rode with an officer back. It took nearly four hours for her to identify the house she said she had stayed at. The house was a summer cottage owned by Jacob Montgomery and appeared to be closed for the winter. Under Ms Callahan's insistence, a call was made to the Montgomery residence in New York. Mr. Montgomery claimed to have been home all weekend and had not been to his cabin for weeks. After a search warrant was obtained the lawyer for Mr. Montgomery did contact Layton police and admit Mr. Montgomery had taken a prostitute to his cabin with some friends for the weekend. He didn't want his wife to find out that he had been unfaithful but he felt being honest with the police was important. He then agreed to allow a full search of the property and volunteered the information that the prostitute had brought her child along. Mr. Montgomery said he had mandated that the child stay in a bedroom locked behind a closed door because he was a father himself and didn't think her actions were appropriate bringing a child to a trick. During the search, a trash bag was found in the outside trash cans that contained a child's pair of pants and t-shirt. Ms Callahan quickly added when Kali fell she cut her hand and a knee. She had gotten blood all over her clothing and Ms Callahan had thrown the clothing away, considering it torn and too spotted with blood to be salvageable. Since both the home owner and the mother stated the child had been in the house and appeared to be missing the police department initiated a search. The Delaware Water Gap is part of the National Park Service. Because the child was potentially missing in the 70,000 acres of the park the FBI took jurisdiction. They also provided eighty recruits to assist Park Service in the ground search of the park. At that point the Layton Police referred the case file to the FBI Missing Persons Investigation Division.

I next went to the FBI report of the interview of Samantha Callahan. The interviewing agent found her to be confused about the location of the house and the owner. She was vague about the timeline and was agitated thinking time was being wasted talking to her when someone should be out looking for her daughter. She insisted something was given to her in the tequila that caused her to black out and denied having a drug or alcohol problem. She also insisted she was a good mother despite taking her child to a house for the weekend where she had been employed as a prostitute. The interviewer spent significant time on the clothing in the trash bag and referenced the forensic report from the lab. Since the clothing was the smoking gun that eventually got Samantha Callahan convicted of her daughters murder, I look through the stack of paper to find the report.

The clothing was found rolled up in a ball in a trash bag and was the only thing in the bag. It consisted of a child's size small elastic band jeans and a size small pink t-shirt. The clothing appeared to be old; the labels were faded and almost unreadable. There was a ¾ inch tear in the center of the left leg of the jeans approximately where the knee would have been. This area was covered in blood. It was consistent with a blood flow from a wound. The stain measured three quarter inches in length and 2.8 inches in width. The back of the leg was also covered in blood with a matching stain. The technician had labeled this as a transfer stain. There were also blood drops near the waist band and on the right leg. In total there were eight droplets over one half inch in diameter. The t-shirt had a significant blood stain across the abdomen and center back with a one quarter inch tear in the front center of the shirt centered in the blood stain. This was determined to be blood pooling from a primary wound. There was also a blood smear across the left shoulder and down into the major stain on the center of the shirt. The recommendation of the forensic identification was that the t-shirt blood stain and tear were consistent in size and shape to a stab wound to the abdomen, possibly a through and through bleeding into both the front and back of the clothing.

Due to the amount of blood on the clothing and the characteristics of the transfer, Samantha Callahan was questioned a second time, this time just on the blood evidence. According to the interview, she stated her daughter had cut her left knee and right hand when she fell on the steps. The cut on her hand was deep and Ms Callahan was afraid her daughter needed stitches. The t-shirt had been used as a bandage to soak up the blood and help it clot, it was torn when she fell and like the jeans Samantha thought it was no longer any good.

The interviewer did not believe Samantha Callahan's story and she was charged with the disappearance of her daughter and held without bail. Meanwhile, the search had continued throughout the Delaware Water Gap. After no evidence was found to indicate the child was still in the area, the search was called off.

During the trial the District Attorney used the blood evidence and the lack of a body being produced against Samantha Callahan. Jacob Montgomery and his associates; Miles Wright, Prescott Hancock, William Derry, Phillip Duncan and Michael O'Harrah; testified against Samantha Callahan. They painted her as a drug addicted whore who took her daughter on tricks. Each testified on the beating she had given Kali when they arrived at the cabin. According to testimony, Kali had wanted to play outside and Samantha beat her and locked her in a room. Then proceeded to put on music and do a provocative strip tease for their benefit. Samantha Callahan was a professional hooker who worried more about her customer's satisfaction then about the child she had locked in a bedroom. The men each testified that Sunday morning the drunken Callahan was too out of it to wake up fully. She was told if she didn't get up she and her child would be left there. To which they said she screamed "then leave me!" Since there was nothing of value in the house, Montgomery told her to lock the door when she left and they drove back to the city. Montgomery planned to drive back in a few days and make sure the hooker and her child had left and not taken anything. They had even joked on the ride home that his wife wanted to remodel, if anything was missing or if the "dumb whore" burned the place down, he had insurance to cover it. They all also testified the child was alive and well the last time they saw her, but none of them had seen the child out of the room since they arrived Friday night.

I flipped through the charging documents. Samantha Callahan was charged with first degree murder, having reckless indifference to an unjustifiably high risk to the life of her six year old daughter, Kali Marie Callahan. The circumstantial evidence exhibited a severe loss of blood and while the body could not be located it was the opinion that the wounds sustained, as exhibited by the presence of a knife tear to the clothing, and significant blood loss was a mortem wound.

I put the case file down and looked out the window at the sky beginning to turn gray. Then picked up the phone and dialed the Richmond field office and ask them to notify the press. I am going to hold a press conference at 10 AM. While I grab a shower, John runs out to a local restaurant to grab breakfast. Since we haven't gotten any sleep we need something to fuel our bodies and a donut isn't going to do it. He comes back with eggs, bacon, French toast and coffee. While I start to eat, he grabs a shower and then eats. We are still eating as District Attorney Aaron White knocks on the door. He walks in coffee cup in hand looking like he hasn't gotten much more sleep then we have. I start to get him up to speed when Tim Clark knocks on the door. Now we are all together, we have a narrow window to prepare what we are going to tell the press and how we are going to present it.

DAY 3
CHINCOTEAGUE, VIRGINIA

We pack up and leave for the light house. Everet Jones is already at the site with a domesticated Chincoteague pony tied to a tree just in front. He thought it would add a nice touch to the scene and give a more positive plug for Chincoteague and Assateague. After all, the world is now watching and seeing Chincoteague as a murder capital, when this is one of the first murders to ever happen here. Seeing all the major networks and cable networks being joined by representatives of the foreign press is daunting. This story has gone worldwide and after today it might be an international sensation. Rarely does a person return from the dead to be the center of a murder investigation.

At 10:00 AM I take the podium. "My name is Agent Adam Clay of the Richmond, Virginia field office of the FBI. I am the lead investigator of the body that was found at Swan Cove on the Wildlife Loop on Assateague, Virginia two days ago. Before we begin I would like to introduce the people who are on the podium with me today. When we are finished we will open up the microphone to questions. You will be able to pick up bios of all who are here, as well as prepared documentation for this press conference. First to my right is Agent John Duncan. He is one of the leading field investigative agents for the FBI. He has been in charge of all evidence collection and leads the forensic team for this investigation. To my left is Coroner Tim Clark from the Worchester County Coroner's Office. Coroner Clark has been instrumental in evidence collection and identification of the body. Next to him is New York District Attorney Aaron White. I will start by saying that over night we had a positive identification of the body through DNA samples. Once we had a positive identification we followed that up with a confirmation sample at a separate lab to insure a correct reading. At that time we notified DA White because the victim was from his jurisdiction. We now know our victim is seventeen year old Kali Marie Callahan. Kali was a missing child from Layton, New Jersey on July 22, 2001. At the time, she was missing and presumed dead. Her mother, Samantha Callahan, was tried and convicted of Kali's murder. We now know that was an error. I will now turn the microphone over to District Attorney White."

White looks pale as he moves to the microphone. While District Attorneys are use to being in front of a crowd, they usually aren't there to admit there has been a mistake committed by his office. "As soon as I received the call from Agent Clay I notified the court. This morning at 9:00 AM an order was issued for the release of Samantha Callahan. As we meet, an attorney from my office is working on her final release and within a few hours Ms Callahan will be a free woman. Because of this grievous error, a financial arrangement will be made through the state to compensate her for the ten years she has been wrongly imprisoned. Once she is released, Ms Callahan and someone from my office will be in route to the area so that she may claim her daughter's body and arrange for a proper burial. Meanwhile, the case of the disappearance of Kali Callahan is being reopened. My office will be working with Agent Clay to find out where Kali has been for the last eleven years, who was responsible for her disappearance and for her murder. With that being said we will now open up for questions."

The crowd of reporters starts shouting trying to be heard above the others. I promise to take all their questions and answer everything. As we are talking DA White gets the call and announces Samantha Callahan is a free woman and is currently with the Assistant District Attorney for New York and will be arriving in the area in a few hours. Things are moving fast. We answer all the questions and break away from the crowd. I make a call to the restaurant and ask if I can reserve a private room for dinner. By tonight I will be sitting at the table with Samantha Callahan. I think all on the podium would like to hear after eleven years what this woman has to say.

As the press conference ends one of the lab techs walk up to John and pulls him aside. I can see the look on Johns face and the news isn't good. He walks toward his car. I follow and he pushes his passenger door open and looks at me. "Are you ready for the next bit of news? Those are definitely not our victims hand prints. We either have a second victim or the murderer touched the pony about ten times."

Every time we turn around we have more questions. It keeps going back to who was the man with her and where did he go. Right now we have two scenarios. One he murdered her and covered with blood walked away. Or two someone drove up on them, murdered them both and drove away without a trace. At this time, both areas of the crime scene have been checked and double checked and we released them to the media. They can finally get an up front and close look at the same nothing we have been looking at for a few days. At that, we both agree to go to our hotels and get some sleep. We want our wits about us when we meet Samantha Callahan tonight.

The alarm on my phone wakes me up and I grab another quick shower. The mosquito bites are itching and burning. I hope the water calms them down some. I throw on jeans and a sweater. Samantha Callahan has spent the last ten years in jail and I don't want to be another suit either questioning her or telling her what to do. I need this woman's help and trust. I'm not sure what her mood will be. I'm not sure how I would feel if I was wrongly accused and jailed for ten years, only to be justified by the death of my child. In the last twelve hours, this woman has been told she is free and her daughter's body has been found. That's a lot in a short time.

I drive to the restaurant and see four cars in the parking lot. One is a rental car. This means one of two things. A press car or the Assistant District Attorney and Samantha Callahan are already here. I walk in to see a man in a suit sitting with a stunning blond in jeans and a black sweater. I take the bar stool next to her. She looks like a slightly older version of her daughter. "Miss Callahan? My name's Agent Adam Clay."

She looks at me for a second and I see a tear welling up in her eye. "You are the one who had me set free. I have told people for almost eleven years that I didn't kill my daughter. It took someone finding her adult body to prove I didn't do it. I want to thank you for making the call so quickly and having them expedite my release. Thank you for giving me my daughter and my life back. This still feels like a dream and I'm so afraid I am going to wake up."

I reached over to her and put my arms around her. I have never met this woman in my life and I have never hugged a witness before but, at this time and this moment all I want is to comfort a grieving mother. I whisper to her "I'm so sorry for your loss and I am so sorry you have spent all these years in jail. I want to help you get justice for Kali and for yourself." She looks up at me with tear stained cheeks and mouths thank you. She then asks the Assistant District Attorney if it is ok if she goes to the ladies room. He nods and she walks away. He reaches over and shakes my hand. He's Assistant District Attorney George Hirschorn. I thank him for coming, at that I hear a group of people enter and see everyone who has been invited to this dinner meeting.

We wait for Samantha and then District Attorney White makes introductions from his team then I introduce her to our team. Everyone orders a drink from the bar while we wait for the private room to be ready. The waitress passes out menus while we are waiting. I see Samantha reach for her purse and pull out her wallet and put a hand on her arm. I keep trying to remind myself of where she has been and where she came from. I tell her dinner is on me. I know I am right when I see the look of relief spread across her face.

Samantha sits next to me when we get to the table. John sits on her other side and tells her he's my assistant. She nods and I can see she is trying hard to control both her emotions and fear. I know everything is a bit over whelming to her right now. If I want her to trust me and tell me everything I need to help her through the next couple days.

Once we order and the waitress leaves, I turn to Samantha and then look out at the rest of the table. "I'm not going interview you tonight. I think we should all get to know each other and our roles in this investigation. Samantha, we are your team now. Somewhere, something that you saw eleven years ago may be the clue we need to break this case open. I know this is hard on you. You have lost a lot over the past few years and now you have lost your daughter. Everyone here wants to bring justice finally to this case. We can't undo what happened. We can only go forward. While you are here, anything you need is being handled by my office. Because of the media coverage we would like to put you in protective custody. Not because you are still in prison, but because the press will have a field day if they corner you. This is to protect you. Of course, you are free and if you don't want protection we will back away and let you handle things with the press yourself. We just need to know your plans. You are in control now. We still control the investigation, but we need your help and to all be one team."

She nods and takes a drink of iced tea. "I don't know what to say or do. Look I was an exotic dancer and a whore eleven years ago. I made a mistake and trusted a man who had paid me a lot of money for a lap dance. Then, he offered to pay me more money than I have ever seen in my life to go with him for the weekend. I told him I couldn't. I had a six year old daughter. He told me no problem, just bring her along. When he pulled up and Kali and I got in he didn't say a word about the other car that had pulled in behind us. I should have gotten out of that car right then and I will regret that for the rest of my life. If I had gotten out of that car, my daughter would still be alive but, we needed the money. That money would have gotten us out of the hell we lived in. I could have gone to school and changed my life. Instead, I went to jail and the men who treated me like a piece of shit stole my daughter and I believe one of them killed her. I have gone over that weekend in my mind every day since I woke up and found her door open and Kali gone. I had a lot of time to think in jail. I also went to the jail library a lot and took advantage of the free education. I got my GED and then completed college. I have a degree in psychology now specializing in the mind of a pedophile. I always believed Kali was alive, at least for a while, and I knew how they treated me. No one ever wants a child to be treated that way she was. I have dreamed of one day being able to sit down with someone who would listen to my side of the story and believe me. I have dreamed of seeing Kali again. I have dreamed of seeing those bastards in jail for what they did. Now Kali has been taken from me one more time, but I will not rest until I see the men who kidnapped her in jail." She pauses when she saw three waitresses come in laden with trays of food. When they leave, the table is covered with hot steaming rolls, cornbread and hush puppies. Everyone has soup and salad along with a refresh on their drinks. Samantha sits there looking at the food and after the wait staff leaves and closes the door she says "Well they never served anything like this in jail. I don't even think someone on death row gets anything like this." I laugh and tell her this is just the start, dinner hasn't come yet and granny makes a mean selection of pies.

Everyone is hungry and the food is good. While we eat no one talks about the case. Samantha agrees to protection and is already checked into my hotel. Most of the rooms are booked by the forensic team with the over flow in John's hotel a half mile away. We shouldn't have any trouble keeping the press away from her. After dessert arrives, one of the waitresses comes back into the room and walks up to Samantha. She puts her hand on Samantha's shoulder and says "Honey, I know who you are and I am sorry about your daughter. Just know we on the island got your back and we want to find out who did this as much as you do. You need anything just yell. We islanders are loyal folks. Your baby is in heaven now but if whoever killed her tries to get to you, they will know what hell really is." Samantha smiles and thanks her. I find it funny eleven years ago the media hated Samantha Callahan and public opinion was to jail her for life. Now in an instant, she has turned into someone they love and want to protect. Having gotten to know some of the people on this island, I know the waitress's words are true. These people will stand up for what is right and they have Samantha Callahan's back.

Exhausted and full we all return to our hotels. In the morning, DA White is taking Samantha to the morgue to identify and claim Kali's body. Then he is going to assist her with funeral arrangements. I set up a meeting between her, DA White, ADA Hirschorn, John and myself for late in the afternoon. It has been a long day. The forensic team breaks into shifts. Two will patrol the exterior of the hotel outside Samantha's room. Another will sit outside her door. I unlock the connecting door from my side and tell her she is in charge of the lock on her side. She unlocks it and tells me if I hear her scream she assumes my gun will be drawn when I come in. She reminds me for the last ten years she has slept in a room with bars and men walking up and down the cell with guns. Being alone is a little scary. Knowing there are men with guns is reassuring, that she's grown accustom to.

DAY 4
CHINCOTEAGUE, VIRGINIA
TO NEW YORK CITY

After two straight days of Granny's pies, I wake up and put on a pair of sweat pants, sweat-shirt and sneakers to prepare for a run. I call John to let him know I will be out of cell phone range for about half an hour. As I hang up, I hear Samantha knocking on the connecting door. I ask her if everything is ok, I'm going for a run but she will still have guards at her door and outside the building. She asks if she can come along. During her exercise time for the last ten years, she has run around and around the yard. Being on a road running was something she dreamed about in jail. I wait for her to get changed and we set off down the beach road.

I'm surprised that she can keep up with me. I'm over a foot taller and one of my strides equals two of hers. I slow my pace down a little to make it easier on her and she tells me not to. Running was how she left the stress of being in jail behind her. Each lap around the yard was getting her closer to release. Being able to run on a road and taste freedom is wonderful and she doesn't want to slow down. We chat as we make our way to the Assateague Bridge and then turn around and run back. It's a nice flat run and we make good time. As the hotel comes into view, she yells "Race you to the horse" and we both take off at a sprint. She beats me by a stride and grabs hold of the outstretched tail to lean on it panting. Out of breath, I point to the hotel lobby and say "coffee".

By the time we have both made coffee and grabbed a couple donuts, we are able to speak normally again. She goes and sits at a table and I join her. It's nice to just sit with her and talk. I don't know what she was like ten years ago but the woman across from me is a person I could easily get to know. As I take a drink of my coffee, I try to remind myself I'm on a job and this isn't a club med vacation. In a little while, this woman needs to deal with the body of her daughter.

She takes a bite of donut and sits her coffee cup down. "I know not here and not now but you and I have to talk. If you mean what you said last night about me being part of the team to find Kali's murderer I am in and I know I have valuable information. No one wanted to listen to me when it happened. I have thought about what happened. I have run through things step by step. I also studied. I wanted to understand what happened. Not just from the act of them taking Kali but, the minds of the men who did this. I spent eight years studying the behavior of pedophiles and wrote my Doctorial thesis on it. Jacob Montgomery chose me because I was small and child like. He knew from the club and from visiting my home that I had a young daughter. I may have been targeted. He came to my house for sex and stalked my daughter. He may have known all along they were going to take Kali but, they had their fun with me first."

I stop her and suggest we take this to one of our rooms. If she is ready to talk, I want to hear what she has to say. We refill our cups, wrap up our donuts and head for my room. After I shut the door, I tell her I believe her and if she is ready, I am ready to listen. Setting my laptop to record the video, I tell her it is okay to begin.

"On the way to the house he kept looking in the back of the car at Kali, telling me I have a beautiful daughter. While we were driving he had his hands up my skirt. He was looking at my daughter and feeling me up. I figured he was paying me $25,000 for the next thirty-six hours so he had bought my merchandise. I spread my legs, closed my eyes and let him go. When we got there, he ordered Kali locked in a room and I did it. Then I did what he told me to do. I gave them all a lap dance. Jacob put me up on a table and laid me back. While two of them played with my nipples, he spread my legs and shaved me with an electric razor. He wanted me completely hairless and smooth like a little kid. He kept running his hand over me after that and saying this was just right. He took his turn first and they all stood there naked watching him. I felt their hands all over me while he thrust away. As soon as he was done another took his place. This happened over and over for a couple hours. When they were all done, I was so sore I could barely put my legs together to walk but I unlocked the bedroom and got in bed with Kali. The next morning I woke up and one of their cars was gone and Kali wanted to go outside. So we got dressed and I let her play. I heard the car coming back up the driveway through the woods and rushed her inside. That's when she fell. It was all I could do to keep her quiet and get her hand to stop bleeding before they knocked on the door. They had gotten bowls of breakfast food from somewhere and put them on the table. They told me to take breakfast to Kali and then come right back. Once again Jacob made me lay on the table and he shaved me again. Then they dumped the bowls of hot food on me. They licked it off of me while they took turns having sex with me. At one point, one took a link sausage and inserted it into my vagina masturbating me with it before putting it in my mouth and feeding it to me. The way they were treating me was horrible. I wanted to get dressed, grab Kali and run but, like I said I needed that money. When they were done with me, I went back to Kali's room and lay down. They were taking some kind of drug. My guess it was Viagra. I also know they were popping a lot of ginseng. They said it made them horny and helped keep them aroused. Jacob knocked on the door in the afternoon and told me to come with him. He told everyone he was going to go wash the dishes. They all laughed while he took me into the shower and bathed me. Then made me get on my knees and give him a blow job. When I came back out to the main room, I smelled meat cooking and he told me to lie back on the table for dinner. They poured a container of coleslaw on my stomach, on the other side potato salad. They dumped an entire bottle of steak sauce on my breasts and then they put a hot sizzling steak on my stomach. It burned and they took steak knives and cut pieces off the steak. I'd cry out when they accidentally cut deeper then the steak. They would just laugh. They licked food off of me and had sex once again, just standing around the table eating off of me. They called it fucking the plate. They kept pouring tequila in my mouth. I had to drink or drown. I started to feel out of it. Not a drunk out of it but a drug thing. Like when I had Kali and they put me under because she was partially breech and had to turn her some. I remember one of the other guys took me to the shower to wash the dishes. That's the last I remember until I woke up. I was still naked and I was lying on the floor. I didn't hear a sound in the house and got up and went to Kali's room. The door was open and she was gone. I checked the rest of the house. They were all gone. Both cars gone. Even my purse was gone. They left my skirt and tank top. I didn't even have shoes."

"In jail, I learned the shaving me and making sure I was completely hairless was one of the signs of a pedophile. I remembered at the club Jacob only liked the short small women, once again a sign. Finally, Kali was gone and they were the only other people in that house. They took my child and did something with her. Professionally, my guess is that she had severe sexual trauma to her genitals. I don't know whether one or all of them continued to have sex with her. She was their dirty little secret. In many ways over the years, I wished they had found Kali's body dead in the woods. It was better than the life she had. Children who are kidnapped by pedophiles are kept secluded from other children, usually in a room or small area. They are not allowed to go outside to play. The stimulation they get is sexual. They are trained to serve the man or men who own them. And yes, these children are owned. They are sex toys to these men. With the preference they showed to group sex she was brutalized by the entire group. Think of it as sex in a pack. She withstood hours of forced intercourse whenever the pack could get together. Because they fed her and bought her things she obeyed them. Because she was so young she didn't know what they were doing was wrong. They trained her to do what they wanted, and how they wanted it. And when she got too old or they got a younger girl, they either sold her to a pedophile who liked older girls or one of them brought her here and killed her. When Kali was found my guess is that she was pale. She was of perfect weight and size. She was probably shaved. She was kept as child like as possible. Her problem was that she got too old. She was pushing eighteen. That's the upper end for most pedophiles. She was no longer any use to them so they got rid of their dirty little secret."

If Samantha hadn't been in jail, I would have questioned her about her daughter's murder. She had described the body perfectly. I have thought of a pedophile.-The older man, one sleeping bag and the evidence of old brutal sexual encounters are evidence of a pedophile. I tell her I think she is correct, now we just have to find some proof. We talk a little while longer before DA White comes to pick her up.

I call John and we begin to make arrangements to go to the Delaware Water Gap and get a warrant to see the grounds of the Montgomery hunting and fishing cabin. DA White lets me know both he and Samantha will be coming along and his office is already working on that warrant as well as one for Jacob Montgomery's houses, office and personal accounts.

Montgomery's lawyer has been advised that he is once again a suspect of the Kali Callahan disappearance and now her murder. The other members of that sex party have also been informed they are under investigation.

We land in New York City at 7:05 PM. It's too late to drive to the Delaware Water Gap now and the nearest hotel is about thirty minutes from the cabin so we have arranged rooms just outside the city with me and John sharing a room and Samantha in the connecting room. Already Samantha's picture graces the cover of every daily paper and has made the cover of the tabloids. Once again in her life she has gained instant celebrity. Thanks to social media the press not only knows what flight we are on but our progress getting off the plane and coming through the gate. I see as we pass a TV monitor one of our fellow passengers is streaming us live and it has been picked up by the networks. I'm glad to see the black SUV waiting outside with a wall of police protection to the doors. Still, we are almost blinded by the flash of cameras and deafened by the drone of reporters yelling as we pass. I hate the feeling of the crowd pushing in on us, some reaching out to try to grab a piece of clothing or an arm to get our attention and hold us long enough for a statement. I hate the suffocating feeling of the press moving in for the kill. DA White handles a short press conference allowing us a few moments to get away. Even so we see paparazzi following us to the hotel.

We are hungry but the press camp outside our hotel makes it impossible to grab some food outside the room so we settle for room service. The TV is showing reruns of us getting off the plane and going to our hotel, it switches to a reporter outside in the parking lot. Samantha Callahan is now celebrity enough to have her movements breaking news during prime time.

We make an early night hoping to get away from the hotel without a lot of press coverage in the morning and go to bed. Throughout the night I see the bright lights of the video trucks in the parking lot and through the curtain I see an occasional reporter doing a live feed. The sun rises to the lot filled with satellite trucks and the morning shows all having reporters on the scene.

DAY 5
DELAWARE WATER GAP, LAYTON, NEW JERSEY

News from the Delaware Water Gap is not good. Word has leaked that police will be enacting a search warrant on the Montgomery hunting cottage. The local towns are now lined with satellite trucks. The local police call for help from the state police of both Pennsylvania and New Jersey to secure the woods around the property. Already the area is being called a media circus.

As our breakfast arrives, I turn on the TV to see a national network anchor in jeans, flannel shirt and a fleece jacket standing in the woods. "I am on the scene in the Delaware Water Gap. Across the river from me in that house sometime this morning the FBI, New York and New Jersey State Police will be enacting a search warrant on the weekend home of banking head Jacob Montgomery. According to sources, Montgomery has been informed that he is a suspect in the kidnapping and murder of Kali Callahan some eleven years ago. Recently the body of Kali Callahan was found in a National Park in Virginia. It is believed she was held hostage for the last eleven years until she was murdered early last week. In a statement released by the FBI, Jacob Montgomery is a person of interest and warrants have been issued on his homes and office. They asked that we not read anything into this other then Kali Callahan was last seen at his home in the Delaware Water Gap, according to our analyst, if found guilty Montgomery could face the death penalty for his role in the kidnapping, torture and murder of Kali Callahan. We will be on the scene all morning and will break in if there are further developments, back to you in the studio."

Behind me I hear Samantha walk into the room and stop dead in her tracks. Her eyes are focused on the house in the back ground behind the reporters shoulder. I expect to see tears but instead she has a look of confusion. She

49

walks closer to the screen and reaches out to touch the porch and then traces the roof line then turns around and looks at me and says. "I can't believe all he did to the house. I almost didn't recognize it. I can see it now, the original house, but it's barely there anymore. I wouldn't have recognized it at all if the person hadn't said that was the house." This made me curious and I turned off the TV and called DA White. After many missing persons cases where someone was detained, I know home construction makes it easy to build an extra holding cell for your victim. I want to see before and after pictures of this house and any building permits that were pulled on the property in the last eleven years.

We have to wait a few hours until traffic dies down anyway. One thing you don't want to do in New York is to drive during rush hour if you don't have to be on the road. So we settled in with breakfast and coffee looking over pictures of the Montgomery house, the building permits and the floor plans. Luckily the house had been extensively photographed by the New Jersey Police while it was an active crime scene. Samantha is correct. The once three step stone steps that lead to a small stone porch had become a stone deck that wraps completely around the house. It had been a rambling one story bungalow and was now a two story Tudor. The original foot print of the house has remained. The open court behind the house is now a stone swimming pool with waterfalls along the exterior wall. The aerial photographs we see compliments of the news helicopter show a glass enclosed area with steam covered walls and ceiling. Through the steam it is still possible to see the pool and hot tub as well as the waterfalls. Eleven years ago this was a simple brick courtyard with a barbeque grill and two wooden picnic tables. Now I want inside this house more than ever. If the outside has been upgraded this much I wonder what has happened to the scratched hard wood floors in the pictures and the simple rustic furniture. They just don't fit the new exterior. I'm sure with the second floor addition there were structural changes as well. This would make it easy to build a room to hold a hostage.

I don't want to tell Samantha about most of the hostage vaults I have seen. They are usually cement boxes with a bed and a toilet. The higher scale ones have a sink. They are built to be sound proof so that no one else knows there's a person inside there. They are accessed through hidden panels and the victim rarely sees light. Then it hit me, Samantha has studied pedophiles, I'm sure she has seen pictures of these places and she wants to get on the road as quickly as I do to get inside that house. Everyone standing in this room is expecting to find a hostage vault. I know my job is not to come to conclusions but to let the evidence guide me but, now and then you can't help having your emotions kick in. I want to find this man and his friends guilty of kidnapping Kali and murdering her. I want him to pay for the scarring Tim Clark found inside her. I want justice for both Kali and Samantha. They both were victims and served time for something they had no control over.

With traffic, the hour and forty minute drive from the city to Layton, New Jersey goes well. Traffic has died down enough to make travel smooth but the congestion keeps the pace slow. Once we reach Layton the roads are lined with satellite trucks and reporters milling around. As soon as the SUV approaches we can see the lights come on the cameras and the reporters excitedly speaking into the microphones. I'm sure somewhere someone in the country is cussing us out for the breaking news report that just interrupted their morning game show. It is 10:24 AM someone on TV was just about to give the answer to the winning prize and that answer will now be lost because we pulled into town.

We are met at the driveway to the Montgomery place by a host of lawyers blocking the way. There are days you are glad for blanket search warrants of property searches. We have no idea what is inside the house and the lawyers only want us to have access to what was there in July of 2001. The problem is, at least from the outside what existed in 2001 no longer exists. All we can do is move back away from the property line and wait for a New Jersey judge to make a decision. We withdraw to town among the satellite trucks and get a table at a fast food restaurant to see if we have driven here for nothing or if we can conduct the search. I feel a lot like an ant under glass. We are completely exposed to the media. We can't talk or we will be heard, we can't make a phone call or check a laptop because there are too many eyes and an unsecured network. All we can do is drink coffee and visit the rest rooms. An hour and twenty minutes later and two cups of coffee pass before we are green-lighted to return to the house. The good news is that a New Jersey magistrate will meet us there to help expedite any further attempts to block or restrict access. My general feeling in cases like this is that you have something to hide if you don't allow access. Putting up this size road block makes me look harder and deeper because once you piss me off I want to nail you with something for the trouble. I also know we have one shot. What the lawyers haven't gotten out of there by the time we got there today will disappear in the cover of darkness tonight. I have seen it happen many times before.

This time the driveway is open and we are waved in by the state police. The side of the house where the driveway ends is parked solid with various sedans and police cars. We find a place to park and walk around to the front of the house. There at the door are the lawyers standing in a row. At the bottom of the steps are various state police and a man I assume is the magistrate who is meeting us. He takes the warrant and looks at the lawyers telling them to "open the doors or I'm having these nice cops bust it down. Once we get inside if you are not a material witness or wear a badge you will be restricted to the foyer. You will not move beyond the foyer. Anyone who does will be charged with obstructing justice. Do I make myself clear?" I can see one of the lawyers is about to speak and the others stare him down. They move aside and accept the copy of the warrant from the judge.

The porch is a spectacular masonry job of an orange brown flag stone with a light grout. A bank of white painted Adirondack chairs sit on each side of the front door and continues down to the corners in both directions. Between every few chairs sits a small white wooden table looking like it is waiting for someone to sit a drink down on it during a summer evening. The door itself is a work of art made of heavy stained mahogany with etched glass depicting the woods filled with animals.

Inside the floor is now a checkerboard of black and white marble. The walls are paneled in a dark mahogany and reached from the floor to the ceiling two stories up in the foyer. I can see this room filled with a giant Christmas tree every year so that the lights show across the river to the occasional car that drives by. A grand stair case graces the back wall. It branches off six steps from the top to both wings of the house. The center of the ceiling is an intricate carved circle carrying the images of the animals from the door to the ceiling. From the center hangs a massive crystal and brass chandelier. To each side of the stairs are doors leading to the downstairs wings of the house and doors lead off on each side to rooms in the back of the house. I look over at Samantha. I don't want her speaking in front of the lawyers but

I badly want to hear from her. Two state police officers stay with the Montgomery lawyers and the judge while the rest of us go to the right and enter the door to the dining room and kitchen on the ground floor.

As soon as the door closes Samantha begins to speak. "That foyer wasn't there. There were two bedrooms on the kitchen side of the house. Kali was in one of those rooms. You could stand at the wall of the kitchen and see all the way to the family room on the other side. It was all open. Here is where they had sex with me on the table. There was a door somewhere about where the stairs are that led outside to the picnic area and the grill. Nothing is the same. I don't know how we can find anything. Nothing that was here when Kali and I were here is still here. It's all gone, even the walls have changed!" I can see her frustration and in her mind wondering how if this man kidnapped her daughter could he rebuild this house into something elegant. I assure her if there is something to be found we will find it.

The kitchen is filled with stainless steel appliances and counters. Like the dining room it looks nothing like it did in 2001. This could be a different house entirely. DA White mutters aloud this is a lot of money to spend on a summer house. The wife and his sons never come here because they hate being away from the city out in the woods. We leave the kitchen to the forensic team and head down the hallway. We are greeted by a glass wall that looks out onto the swimming pool and waterfalls. Out the open end, we can see the woods behind the house. A light snow fall has started. Every few feet there are French Doors that open up onto the pool area. The hall itself is designed as a theatre room. I slide open one of the French Doors and walk out into the pool room. I am hit with warm moist air and smell of chlorine. The pool and hot tub keep the area quite humid. Above, I can hear the sound of the news helicopters as they circle over head trying to get a view inside the house. Even with their noise, I hear the waterfall near the glass wall. Samantha has walked over to it and is watching the water cascading down off the rocks. She looks at me and says "who takes care of this place? There is not a speck of dust. This pool is immaculate. Look the rocks are clean in the waterfall. Someone checks this chlorine daily. Does someone live here and take care of it?" I have to admit I am thinking the same thing.

We continue across the pool area until we come to the back wall of the original house. There is a door that I hadn't seen from the foyer and suspect it is the original door to the picnic area. Instead it opens to a short tiled hallway. On each side is a door, one labeled Men the other Women. When we open the doors, we see a tiled shower and rest room area. Samantha walks around the women's room and opens a wicker basket and calls for a lab tech. There in the bottom next to a white towel is a red child's bikini. I see the look of horror cross her face. This isn't Kali's bathing suit but it belongs to another little girl. Montgomery has sons; this either belongs to a victim or to a guest's child. Regardless, it is collected and tagged. The men's room also has a towel in the wicker basket. It too is collected.

Next we open the French doors that go into the living room. It is decorated in what I would consider old world library. The walls are rich dark mahogany to carry over the feel from the foyer. Over-stuffed leather furniture arranged in a conversation area sits on a thick Persian rug. Mounted heads of deer and bear grace the walls. Around the room brass lamps with green glass shades provide a muted glow to the room. The way the house is situated and tucked into the woods, the lamps are needed during the day if anyone wants to read. On the back wall is a fireplace with a black marble mantel. I can still faintly smell the last fire that was burned in it.

Everything about this house screams elegance. It is nothing like the place in the pictures from eleven years ago. It also screams maintenance. The house sits in the woods and it is in the fall yet not a leaf lay on the glass roof. It appears to have been recently cleaned. The black marble of the mantel would collect dust in a few days, yet it is spotless. DA White makes a call to see if we can find out who cleans and takes care of this place. There has to be something in Montgomery's records to show a cleaning company or employee.

We make our way back to the foyer past the lawyers who are sitting in the chairs around the room. They stand when we enter but sit back down as we start up the stairs. We take the right side first. The master suite is decorated in a very manly fashion. Once again it is decorated with the hunter green tones and dark mahogany. There is no sign of Mrs. Montgomery in this room. The clothes in the closet are all men's clothing. Mostly jeans and dress slacks, a few blazers, long and short sleeve shirts. The drawers of the dresser reveal more men's clothing, socks, t-shirts and boxers.

The second bedroom on this side is also decorated in a male fashion. This one is in a solid blue motif, with dark furniture. It doesn't contain clothing and appears to possibly be a guest room. We cross the connecting bridge to the other wing. The first bedroom appears to be a second Master Suite. It is decorated as a twin to the first Master Suite. It also contains clothing. A lab tech goes back to the first Master Suite and notes the clothing in the second is two sizes larger. It appears this house was shared by two men.

I open the door to the second bedroom on this side. It stops me in my tracks and call for the lab team. This is a little girl's room. The walls are a light pink with a big white canopy bed. The quilt is covered with unicorns and rainbows. The walk in closet is filled with lacy party dresses and ball gowns for a small child. There are tiny high heels on a rack next to a shelf of dolls. A tech opens a drawer to find lacy bras and matching panties. With a gloved hand, he pulls out a see through black corset in a child's size. I hear Samantha run from the room. I find her in the hallway shaking. DA White is already making the call to put Montgomery in custody. Meanwhile, ADA Hirschhorn has walked down the stairs and tells the lawyer their client is being brought in for questioning and they might want to hit the road to meet him at the police station. He needs to explain some things.

Samantha is shaking too bad to walk down the stairs on her own and I put an arm around her to steady her. A lab tech from the kitchen calls to me to come take a look. I settle Samantha into a chair in the theater room and go back into the kitchen. There the tech opens the door to show a refrigerator stocked full of food. The partial carton of milk has an expiration date of next week. There is a leftover box from Chinese that still looks fresh. He directs my attention to a pink cardboard box. There is a partial round birthday cake that, says Happy Birthday Lexi. Another tech has found a partially burned candle with a 9 on it in a trash bag outside. I really hope this cake belongs to someone's grandkid.

We leave the house to the forensic team and head back to the SUV. As we pull to the end of the drive way everyone's cell phone goes off almost at the same time. As we stop to answer, Samantha sits there watching our faces until she announces "somebody better start talking or I'm getting out of this truck and marching over to the news media because they look like they already know what you are hearing!" I look at the window to see the throng of reporters once again talking excitedly into their microphones; a few have come up to the window and are tapping on the glass. DA White looks at Samantha and tells her to brace herself, we are going to have to get out of the truck and talk to these people. Montgomery has slipped away from the area on his private jet.

DA White puts his window down an inch and yells to the reporters "give us a few minutes to set up and we will give a news conference from the front of the Montgomery cabin." Then he yells to the state police blocking the driveway to let them come down to the house.

The Montgomery lawyers start to tell DA White he can't hold a press conference in front of the house and he yells back to them and the magistrate who is standing there in a state of confusion "then you shouldn't have stalled us letting your client get in his private jet. You and I both know he was instructed to not leave the state. Maybe you would like to stick around and talk to the press!"

In the past few days, I have gotten to know Aaron White and since we have met I have not seen him in this mood. We have all been frustrated by this case but now he is going for blood. He tells Samantha, John and I to stand in the back. It is better for us to be seen but not heard. He quickly brings the magistrate up to speed while the press set microphones up at the bottom of the steps of the house. When they signal him that they are ready, he steps up on the first step and begins to speak. "Earlier today we issued a search order on the three homes and two offices of Jacob Montgomery and Mr. Montgomery and his lawyers were instructed that he was a suspect in a disappearance, kidnapping and murder. He was instructed to not leave the state of New York. When officers arrived to serve the warrants and enact a search at each location they were blocked by lawyers for Mr. Montgomery. During the time police were guarding the residences and office and judges were making decisions on the warrants Mr. Jacob Montgomery boarded a private helicopter on a roof top less than a block from his home. He then went to the airport and boarded his private plane. As we speak, Mr. Jacob

Montgomery is in an unknown location. We have issued a fugitive arrest warrant. We ask anyone who knows the where about of Mr. Jacob Montgomery to please come forward. No detail is too small. At the end of this news conference I will provide the phone number for anyone with information to call. I will take questions now."

I had thought Samantha looked pale and shaky before. Now she looks as if she might pass out at any moment. I pull her off the porch and back into the house. We walk out into the pool area and sit down. A few minutes later, John and a state police officer come and get us. We are being escorted back to the city and away from this house.

On the ride back we are all quiet, lost in our own thoughts and trying to process all that has happened. I had hoped we might get a lead but I did not expect Montgomery to run. Running is the mark of a guilty man. As we approach the city, the sun is setting and I can feel the exhaustion setting in. It takes all the energy I have to get out of the car and go up the elevator to our rooms. John calls room service and orders dinner. Samantha is sitting on my bed with the TV remote in her hand flipping channels. Everything we see has our faces or Montgomery's on it. On the bottom of the screen the 800 number to report any information is scrolling. One of the richest men in America is currently a fugitive from the law and the country is sitting glued to their seats waiting for whatever might happen in the next act of this drama.

Room service arrives. I find myself eating without tasting. My phone rings and I see the familiar number of the field office on the display. The voice on the other end asks me to hold for the Special Agent in Charge Wade Bradford. I find myself sitting up in my chair and sitting at attention. Rarely do I get a call from the SAC, when I do it is usually not a good thing. This time he asks me if I am in a location to take a call. He has been talking to a young woman who has some information I want to hear. I inform him John and Samantha are in the room and he tells me to put the phone on speaker. Soon a woman's voice comes on the line and Wade Bradford introduces her as Caroline and gives her our names.

"Ms. Callahan, I am so sorry about the loss of your daughter. I never met her. She was kept in a different house but, I think I have information that will help you in the investigation. I go by the name of Caroline now. That was the name I was given by Jake. My name was Katie Nash. Jake took me from my mom when I was nine. She was sick. Her kidneys were failing and she was in and out of the hospital. He offered to help take care of me and my mom let him. It was a lot of help to her. I just want you to know what kind of life Kali lived. It wasn't that bad. Jake has a lot of money and he spends it on his toys. That's what he calls us. We are his precious toys. When you first start to live with Jake he buys you nice new clothes and he gives you things. We didn't have money for toys and clothes because of my mom's doctor bills. He let me pick out what I wanted for my room. I sat for hours with catalogues deciding and he bought every piece for me. He was like a dad to me. At night before bed, he would give me a bath and wash my hair and dress me in pretty night gowns. I was scared because my mom was so sick and he let me sleep in his bed with him. I was young and I had no idea that what he was doing was wrong. He said he loved me and wanted to take care and make me happy. Ms. Callahan, I was happy. I had everything I ever wanted. Slowly over a couple weeks Jake taught me how to make love to him. How to please him and I wanted to. I wanted to make this man happy and love me. I had never felt the way I did for him. The only time I was locked up in the house was when he wasn't home. Then he said it was for my protection. While he was gone he gave me homework and when he came home at night we went over what I had learned. He dressed me in ball gowns and gave me real diamonds and jewelry to wear. I never went hungry. I never felt like a prisoner. I loved Jake. When we were in bed, I did everything he asked me to do because he made it feel good. I'm not telling you this to get Jake in trouble. Most of my life I have lived with our secret but, whoever killed Kali broke the rules of the Co-Op." I hear Wade Bradford break in and tell Caroline to explain the Co-Op. "Oh yeah, the Co-Op. There's a group of people. They all have money and they all have different sexual preferences. It's like this, Jake likes young girls but once they start to develop he trades them in to the Co-Op and gets a new toy. When a girl becomes available, others look at her pictures and description and bid on the toy. The highest bidder wins and you are sent to them. There you learn what your new owner likes and how to please him. The members of the Co-Op get together now and then--for parties and events and you meet other kids who live in a similar situation. Besides pleasing our owners we are trained in performance art. It's usually girl on

girl stuff. You have sex with someone during the party for others to watch.
You learn to just blank out the other people watching and just enjoy the
other person. Now and then your owner might join in to make it a three
some. You get use to it; it's not a big deal. There's also a committee. They
oversee everything. Not just the bidding on toys but, the care and up keep.
Ms Callahan, Kali had the best of everything. She had a weekly manicure
and pedicure. She was waxed, tweezed and polished very week. She ate
gourmet food and slept on Egyptian cotton sheets. As she got older the
doors weren't locked and she would have been free to leave, but if you
leave you can never come back. You don't want to leave because you know
you are treated better than you would in the regular world. I have gone back
to the Co-Op two times. The first time I was eleven and my breasts had
started to develop. My next owner was just as kind and generous as Jake. I
stayed with him until I was seventeen and was traded in for another eleven
year old. The man who owns me now has provided me with an amazing
house and I have two children with him. I live a life of luxury. Look the
only reason I came forward is because whoever got Kali last broke the
rules. If you don't want your toy anymore you just send them back to the
Co-Op and get a new one. Oh My God, you don't have to kill them! And
who knows what will happen to the next toy he gets. My owner is in his
seventies and his health is bad. I have been visited by the Co-Op and told
he has included instructions with his lawyers to return me to the Co-Op
but, my house is mine and my kid's college is taken care of. Who knows, I
could end up with this guy if something happens to my owner this week.
The man who killed Kali needs a new toy. There is someone who is at risk
right now. I'm sure the Co-Op has approached him about his behavior, but
my fear is that he will be allowed to have another. For my children's safety,
I am telling you that this exists but, I will not give you names other then
Jakes because I need to protect my owner and my children. There is no law
against a man keeping a mistress, which now that I am of legal age, that's
what I will be seen as by the law. As for the one who killed Kali, if I hear a
name I will call you back. I think Jake ran because he knows who bought
Kali. I can't see him keeping her past eleven or twelve. She may have been
special, but that's not his age preference. He doesn't like breasts on his toys.
My guess because of her age the thrill of her being a minor was wearing off,
so it's someone who wanted a princess, one that he could dress up and take
to parties to watch her perform. That's who you are looking for, someone

who just bought a princess bride from the Co-Op." At that the line went dead. I hear the click and Wade Bradford came back on the line. "She hung up. She must have gotten scared. I wouldn't believe her except she was the forth call like this we have gotten. All are women claiming to be toys, dolls or princesses. All defending Jacob Montgomery and saying he didn't murder Kali Callahan. While we had Caroline on the phone we did some investigation. Katie Nash was turned over to a family friend at age nine. After the death of her mother, the family could not locate this friend. Her disappearance is a nineteen year old cold case. At the time of her mother's death, she would have been nine years old. If this woman wasn't Katie Nash she knew a lot of Katie's story and details that were not released to the press. I believe her. It looks like the death of Kali is just a scratch on the surface of what we have uncovered."

Wade Bradford promises to call if there are any other developments and hangs up. If this woman is correct Jacob Montgomery was responsible for kidnapping Kali, but he didn't murder her. We sit here mentally going over the conversation we just heard. Samantha is the first to speak. "I was in the sex trade. I understand her. Taking your clothes off and dancing or to have sex with a guy is a job. It meant nothing. Every girl dreams of having a man treat her well and put her on a pedestal.-Every hooker hopes that one trick will come along who falls in love with her and rescues her from that life. If I hadn't gotten arrested I would have probably died already, if not I would be a used and aging whore. Kali would have probably followed in my footsteps. We all want the best for our kids but face it, if you don't have an education and no prospects for a job lying on your back and spreading your legs pays the bills. I know this sounds crazy but I feel better about the last eleven years for Kali. I mean she was having sex too young but it gave her what I never could have. Maybe Jacob Montgomery did me a favor by taking her off my hands and giving her more than I ever could. Over the years there have seen some girls who were taken by pedophiles and held captive. They were trained by that person but they were also treated kindly and shown love. These pedophiles seek out kids who are in a bad situation and they take them away from that. They are taught that there's nothing wrong with sex. It is natural and as long as both people love each other it is ok. These young girls willingly go to their attackers because they feel loved and cherished. The sex is usually erotic and sensual. These are girls who learn the art of sex. After an arrest is made, the victims usually try to testify for their attacker. They feel genuine love and affection for this person. If they have children with the attacker, they beg to allow their children to visit their father. Assimilation back into the world is hard because they are caught somewhere in between. They love this person and they are told they were sexually abused by them. It is a hard concept for them to understand. Many become depressed because of the pressures of the real world and separation from the man that was their world. It will be hard to get inside this Co-Op because the women will protect the men they are attached to. There is genuine love and affection between them. This is not going to be easy but, gentlemen, somewhere, whether in a house we don't know about or on the plane with Montgomery is a nine year old girl who recently went missing." The red bikini and the birthday cake hit home. Montgomery has another child and he is hiding her.

I call the field office and ask them to send me a list of every girl who has been kidnapped over the past three years who would be nine years old now. Since Katie had been renamed, I assume her name is not Lexi, but I am hoping that candle is correct. The report arrives on my laptop in minutes. There are currently seven hundred and ninety-six missing female children in the United States at this time. Forty-six would be age nine right now and these are the ones reported. Caroline wasn't reported missing until two years after her abduction when family went looking for her.

I bring DA White up to speed. His only question is how many of these missing girls are possibly involved in this. I only wish I knew the answer. There are families who need closure. Not knowing where their child has gone and not knowing if they are dead or alive drains the life from them. Many relationships end in divorce with each side blaming the other or themselves for the child's disappearance. I think back to the calls we got from parents when Kail's body was found. Even though this was a dead body, they just wanted closure. Just getting to bury them gives them relief. Any time an unidentified body is found they hold their breath waiting for DNA results and the call that tells them what happened. What would happen now if some of these parents find their child is alive and living in luxury? Did Kali have an opportunity to call her mother and tell her she was alive? There were phones in the Montgomery house and in all the houses we searched. Was the life she led satisfactory to the point she didn't try to find her mother? Or worse knew her mother was in jail for her disappearance and suspected murder and chose to leave her there?

My sleep is interrupted by dreams of little girls in gowns and diamonds trying hard to look adult for the people who had abducted them. These children remind me of the little girls dressed up and marched through beauty pageants. These shows are always a pedophiles dream. They go to look at the little girl's parade around in various outfits and bathing suits. Their parents are oblivious. I have heard horror stories of children going through plastic surgery to give them a more adult figure in a child's sized body. I see very little difference in the level of abuse between a pageant child and these girls or Kali for that matter. They seem to have to live with being molding into someone's image, and not one of a child.

DAY 6
DELAWARE WATER GAP
TO LAYTON, NEW JERSEY

Morning comes and my mailbox is filled with missing person's case files. Room service delivers coffee, bacon, eggs, sausage and French toast while I am down at the front desk once again explaining to someone behind a desk that I understand printing this will cost me and will be added to my bill. I grab a cup of coffee in the lobby while I wait for the first few reports to print. When I have twelve printed, I grab them with a promise to have the others brought to my room as soon as they all print.

Back upstairs, I grab some breakfast and hand case files to both Samantha and John. I stop for a moment and look at Samantha sitting cross legged on my bed. It is hard for me to imagine she has just spent ten years in jail for something she didn't do and through a series of events she has ended up being a valuable part of this investigation. While she isn't a cop, her professionalism in her field has made her an expert in this case. She can only serve as a witness for Kali's abduction, but her insight into the world Kali might have lived has become important. It is hard to imagine a world that consists of not only pedophiles but an organized sex trade of children. I wonder what kind of will and determination it takes to sit in jail all that time and not be bitter, but to believe in your innocence so much that you push forward in your life and study to become something for when you are released. Even now with her child's body lying in cold storage as evidence in a murder and her concern is to not only find her child's killer but to bring other children home. To her that will vindicate Kali's life.

As we read files for clues, there's a knock on the door. I put the files I have done on the corner of the bed and open the door to get the rest of the reports from the desk clerk. John looks at Samantha and asks if she can describe Kali at the age she was abducted. If we know the profile of one of his victims we can narrow down his child preferences.

"I have been thinking about that. At the club he liked small blond women. I never once saw him look at a black or ethnic dancer. I put two girls from my pile aside already. Both were black. I remember a friend of mine who is black trying to get Montgomery to buy a lap dance and he got really nasty. He yelled at Joe, the club manager, to keep his black bitches away. He didn't want 'nigger pussy'. He also called another girl who was Hispanic a 'boarder beaner'. He was a racist. I can't see him taking a child who didn't look like she was out of a prep school. He wants a little girl he can dress up and fantasize about. That would be a blond girl with pale skin. Kali was quiet. She liked to sit and draw. I could get her a coloring book and crayons. That would keep her happy for hours. She was careful to stay in the lines. Even though she wore hand me down clothes she made sure they looked nice and would tuck her shirt in. She was always very careful not to spill anything on her clothes. She wanted to be clean. She was soft spoken. She was use to being out of sight and out of mind. That was my fault because to make extra money I would bring guys back to my place from the club. I was screwed up. Sex was a job for me and my apartment was my place of business. Kali would stay in her room when I had a man over. My guess being quiet and complaint made her an easier target. I have thought a lot about him and Kali and I don't think her abduction was random. I think he may have watched her for weeks. Everyone at the club knew I brought her with me when I came to work. She stayed in the back. For the record, I never brought her out front, but at night when I was leaving I saw Montgomery still in the parking lot. He would have seen Kali with me. I have always wondered if he picked me to go away for the weekend with them because all along he planned on kidnapping Kali."

We decide to use Kali as our model at the moment. She was at least the preference eleven years ago. Small, blond, quiet, obedient and agreeable is our current reference point. We have to read all the files but for now those are the girls that have the best possibility of being his target. After an hour, we come up with seven files we can't eliminate from a similar physical profile as Kali:

Morgan Tarp, age eight at abduction. Blue eyed blond from Missouri. Morgan was taken from a park while at an older brother's recreation football game.

Angie LaSalle, age seven at abduction. Green eyes, light brown to blond hair from Texas. She was last seen waiting for the school bus.

Jennifer Wright, age eight at date of abduction. Blue eyed blond. Jennifer was abducted from the play ground of a private school in Maryland.

Makayla Lewis, age six at abduction. Blond hair and brown eyes. She was abducted from a restaurant during a child's birthday party.

Sidney Harris, age eight at abduction. Blond hair and blue eyes. Sidney was abducted from a discount store in New York.

Rachael Simmons, age eight at abduction. Light brown hair and brown eyes. Rachael was abducted from West Virginia in her back yard while playing.

Elizabeth Cowl, age seven at abduction. Blond hair and green eyes. She was abducted from her bed at home one night.

We lay the pictures of the girls and their profiles on the bed. Samantha picks up Morgan and moves her file to the discard file. She has seen kids at recreation and park fields while their older siblings were playing. These kids had been at the field for a long time. They usually want to go do something else but the parent stays at the field to watch the one in the sport. The kids get tired and cranky. They are usually dirty from playing on the ground and to keep them quiet parents buy the kids junk food, which they spill on themselves. These kids won't be quiet. Someone might be able to get them to go to the playground but the description of the girls we know about didn't match. Makalya also went to the discard pile. Kids at birthday parties are hopped up on sugar and caffeine. They are loud and excited. They are not cooperative. They are already making noise before they are abducted. This isn't Montgomery's kind.

With five files, we begin to comb them for clues. Angie LaSalle kissed her mom and baby brother goodbye and walked up the driveway to the school bus stop. When the bus came, Angie was not there and it drove off. The school had a nine AM policy for parents. If your child was sick or for some reason not coming to school parents were suppose to notify school. Angie's parents did not notify the school so the school called home to check. By this time, Angie had been missing for two and a half hours. After weeks of searching, police found no evidence of foul play or clues to her disappearance and she is listed as without a trace.

Jennifer Wright was a bright eight year old only child of an up and coming oncologist in Towson, Maryland. She disappeared on a crossover day between custodial parents. Her mother took her to school and then left on a vacation with her boyfriend. The father was supposed to pick Jennifer up after school. When the children came inside from free play Jennifer could not be found. Her mother's cell phone was either turned off or she was out of range and the father was in surgery with a patient. Neither parent was aware of her abduction until the father came to pick her up and was met by police. The father had a solid alibi. He had been in the middle of a radical double mastectomy of a patient at the time. The mother was investigated for the potential custodial parent abduction. She claimed her innocence but other than the boyfriend had no alibi and did not return to Maryland even though she was informed her child was missing, instead continuing on to her vacation destination, returning two weeks later.

Sidney Harris was the child of a welfare mother. When she was abducted she was with her at a discount department store. People in the store remembered seeing the child playing and hiding while her mother shopped. A gentleman notified a store manager that the mother was shoplifting food. Store security watched her and indeed did see her hiding food inside her shirt and she was arrested. The mother was abusive and fought back against the store security and police were called. It was then that the mother mentioned her daughter. The child was not found in the store and in the ruckus caused by the mother's arrest no one saw the child leave with anyone. Store cameras show the mother but the child seemed to have just vanished.

Rachael Simmons was playing in her back yard with her two siblings when she left the fence to chase a ball. Her brothers saw her talking to a man in a green car and went to tell their mother. When they came back with their mother both the car and Rachael were gone.

Elizabeth Cowl was another high profile abduction case. She was the daughter of a Boston lawyer. She was at home sleeping in her Hyannis Port home. In the morning, her bedroom window was found open and the screen cut. Elizabeth also attended a private girl's school and was an avid reader. She had been sleeping with the book she was reading and it along with her favorite doll disappeared. Who ever took her appeared to know the families habits and the child's favorite things.

John has the pictures from the Montgomery cabin lying across the table and he picks up the pictures from the child's room. It is pink and white with unicorns and rainbows. There are stuffed animals and dolls around the room. There is an art easel, paints, crayons and paper neatly arranged next to the easel. A silver flute and music lay nearby. There are no books. He looks over the books on the library shelves. None appear to be for children. Caroline had spoken of doing home work and Montgomery going over it with her in the evenings. Of course Montgomery may have had her favorite toys and books taken with her when she was removed from the house.

I'm not sure what direction to turn next. John makes a call and arranges to return to the house to look for more evidence about Lexi. I look over at Samantha still in the jeans and sweater she arrived in and realized she has the clothes on her back. I call for a rental car to be delivered and find a way to sneak Samantha out without being seen by the press who are still camped in the parking lot.

Once out and away from the hotel we can breathe a little easier. I look in the review mirror and don't see anyone following us. John on the other hand has an entourage behind him as he heads off toward the Delaware Water Gap. As we pass a discount department store Samantha asks if we can go back there. She's sure she can find the clothes she needs but it's also the same name discount store that Sidney Harris disappeared from. Samantha has been out of circulation for a long time and hasn't been to one of these stores since her arrest. She wants to get a feel for the environment Sidney was in before she went missing. I turn at the next light and loop back into the store parking lot.

I'm not familiar with the store because I avoid shopping as much as possible. I will rush into a mall just before Christmas to buy a couple gifts for family. My only other shopping is the occasional trip to the men's store for clothes and convenience stores. We walk in and look around. The store is huge and seems to sell everything from groceries to clothing and shoes. We head first to the grocery section. It is a full grocery store running from front to back with isles filled. I look up at the ceiling and throughout the store see the tell tale blue bubbles of surveillance cameras and wonder how someone could grab a child and not show up on the camera. Then I look closer and see most do not have a light on inside the dome. My guess is that most are for show. Anyone who understands security would be able to see the active cameras versus the empty lenses. As we walk back up the outside aisle along the dairy and meat cases, we both stop and look at a door that leads to a storage area. Samantha asks an employee where the door goes and if we can look around. The employee tells us to the cold storage vault and that customers are not allowed in that area. I flip my badge and he goes to get a store manager.

While we wait Samantha says "look I know this mom. I was her. If I didn't have enough money to buy groceries we would come to the store. It was easier when it started to get cold. I'd wear a tight t-shirt under a sweater and stick the meat under the t-shirt and then tuck it into my jeans. I could afford the small canned stuff but meat was expensive. I couldn't feed Kali baked beans and pasta every night. I had to feed her meat. I would steal it. I know you and John are leaning toward a kid like Jennifer or Elizabeth because it would be easy to dress them up and have either look like the country club debutant. Elizabeth seemed to have good parents--she didn't need the Co-Ops rescue. Jennifer fits the profile of Montgomery; trying to rescue a child from a bad place but, he couldn't give her a life she didn't already have. She already had everything she asked for. The same situation with Elizabeth, what could he give her she didn't already have? Sidney on the other hand had a mom like me and a mom that sounded like Caroline's mom. She was not able to take care of her and gave her away. I know you have told me to not jump to conclusions but, I think Sidney might be Lexi. She even lived in the area. Do we know the address of the exact store? I can buy my clothes there. I have a feeling about this that won't quit."

I hate to admit it but, I have that same feeling. I had agreed with John that Jennifer and Elizabeth already looked the part and probably were easy to mold into the image he wanted. Both girls were only a few hour's drive from New York, but there is something nagging me about Sidney and standing here looking at the cold storage door and hearing Samantha talk, I am starting to feel we need to follow the leads on Sidney.

As we hit the road again, my phone rings and I see its John. I'm surprised because he should have just arrived. I can't believe we missed something that obvious that he found it so fast. I hear what he has to say and swerve to pull off the road, than ask him to repeat himself. I pull the blue tooth out of my ear and Samantha leans over. "You need to stop what you are doing and get here. ADA Hirschhorn and I walked in on the house keeper cleaning the house. He has staff coming here and she's agreed to talk to us with a lawyer present." I hang up and punch the address into my GPS. We are an hour out and traffic seems to be dying down for the morning. We are lucky it is a straight shot.

The trip is uneventful and we make good time. John calls to tell us deli is being delivered for lunch by the DA's office. We pull in soon after the lawyer does. In front of the house is the SUV of ADA Hirschhorn. Next to that a BMW sits still popping and cracking as it cools in the late October temperatures from the drive. Next to that is a silver Porsche. Samantha and I look at each other as we pass the car. On the front passenger seat there is either a really good fake or a mink jacket.

Inside we are greeted by John and ADA Hirschhorn. The lawyer has requested a few minutes to speak with his client before we interview her. All John will say with a smirk on his face is "just wait for this. It is worth the drive." The deli arrives and the clerk from the DA's office knocks on the door where the lawyer and house keeper are meeting to ask if they would like lunch. When the door opens I get a glimpse of a woman with stylish gray hair sitting with her back to me. I can't see much more before the door closes. The lawyer grabs a few sandwiches and two drinks and heads back inside.

Finally the door opens and we are invited into the study and are introduced to the lawyer, William Coates, and to the house keeper, Ms. Tiffany Burnside. Tiff as she prefers to be called is nothing like any house keeper I have ever seen. She appears to be in her mid 60's with time and age having been very kind to her. She still has an attractive figure, stylish hair and is immaculately dressed. From her manicured nails to her diamond bracelet, Tiff appears to be old money. I see Samantha is also staring at her and I motion for her to sit in one of the leather chairs next to me. Tiff gives us both an angry look as we stop staring and sit down.

I look at her and say "forgive me Ms. Burnside but I thought someone said you were the house keeper. I didn't mean to stare. Who are you in relation to Mr. Montgomery?"

She sighs and looks at a perfect thumb nail for a moment. Then takes her hand and sweeps back her hair. "I am Jacob Montgomery's house keeper of sorts. I have talked to my lawyer and the last thing I want to do is jail time. He has said if I cooperate the court will be lenient on me. Is that correct?" ADA Hirschhorn nods and she continues. "I am his house keeper and Lexi's nanny. I have been told you already know about Lexi and Jacob's involvement in the Co-Op. First I want to say that Jacob Montgomery is a good man and he had nothing to do with Marissa's murder."

John interrupted her "Marissa?"

"Oh, I'm sorry you know her as Kali. I never met her. I was a Princess Bride back then raising my own children but I know Jacob and he would not have harmed a hair on one of his dolls heads. He finds girls who need a father and he becomes one. He is one of the best daddy's a girl can have. He makes them happy little princesses and he won't release a girl to the Co-Op unless he knows she's going to a good home. He even checked out Alexandra's new father because he didn't know him. He cried when he saw the artists drawing of Marissa and called me. He was devastated and told me to pack Lexi's things because he was taking her on a trip. He needed to get away. Before you ask, no he did not tell me where they were going, only away. I saw on the news you people had been here and I came here today to straighten up for when they return. I'm sorry I did. So what do you want to know and how much do I have to tell you to stay out of jail?"

I am stunned. In front of us sits a well polished woman who is defending a child molester and a child sex ring as if we were having lunch at a nice restaurant. ADA Hirschhorn tells her she should start at the beginning because we need to know everything she knows.

"The beginning? Well I'm sixty-four years old so that would mean going back fifty-eight years. I was six when I became a doll for a man in upstate New York. He's long dead now but I won't give you his name I don't want to sully their name. I lived in a very nice summer home along the Hudson River. Like Lexi, I had a nanny housekeeper. She taught me how to be a lady and how to carry myself. All dolls are taught a foreign language, how to play an instrument, history and science. We are taught how to carry on a conversation with adults and are kept abreast of current affairs. Our nanny housekeepers are retired princess brides. When our husbands die or we get too old and they want a younger bride you move on to teach the next generation. I'm really surprised you have not been called off this case and told to let it die. The Co-Op has been around since just after the Civil War and some very powerful men are part of it. We have had Presidents, Senators, Congressmen, State Governors, business moguls, millionaires, billionaires…the Co-Op is the rich and famous. We are those dirty little secrets that are kept hidden from public view. If some schmuck who can barely rub two dimes together wants to be with a young girl or boy they end up going to jail as a sex offender. If you have enough money you keep your toys in lavish houses, they will hide your secret so that they don't have to leave. Most of us do not start out well in life. The Co-Op looks for children who need help. Most are poor and barely surviving. Some are badly abused. All are grateful for the new life we are given. For me, my father died in the war. My mother and I ended up living in a commune. I was begging on a street corner when a man pulled up and asked me when was the last time I had a hot meal? For me hot meals were boiled rice with some vegetables thrown in. This man was talking about something heavenly to me, a hamburger and french fries with a soft drink. My mouth was watering when I got in that car. He took me out to lunch and I ate until I could eat no more. Then he asked me if I would like a hot bath and a warm place to sleep. If not, he could take me back to the street corner. I went with him and left my old life behind. He drove me to the house on the Hudson. I had never seen anything like this. It looked like a castle. There he left me take a long bubble bath, than brought me some clothes to try on. They were all beautiful long gowns. He let me be the Princess of the castle. That night Anna was brought in and introduced to me. She was my nanny housekeeper. She cooked anything I wanted. Taught me what I needed to know and was a better mother then my own had ever been. On the nights that the man of the castle was there I slept in bed with him, and yes he taught me how he liked to have sex and what he wanted me to do. He took care of training me in the bedroom. I want you to understand that I have never met a toy, doll, princess, princess bride or nanny housekeeper who would trade the life we have for the life we had. You may think you are rescuing us if you destroy the Co-Op but you won't be. You will destroy the lives of every woman who is involved. I should mention there are boys and men also. There are those who prefer the same sex, but even they would not trade their lives for what they had. We are all very happy and live in complete luxury. I ask you what is the difference from a woman marrying a man and staying home to bear and take care of his children or a woman who is kept by a man for his pleasure?"

Tiff pauses then to reach out for a glass of wine sitting on the table and takes a sip. ADA Hirschhorn takes the opportunity to ask her if she understands sex with a minor is against the law. Tiff takes another drink before carefully putting her wine glass down. "Here is where your beliefs and mine differ. These laws are said to protect children, but the children gathered by the Co-Op are ones society has turned their back on. Not one toy or doll is held against their will. You willingly go to these men to please them. Your problem is that you do not understand the true age of consent. This is where actually learning history comes into the forefront rather than being told the history you need to know for standardized tests. From the inception of this country until 1885, the age of consent varied by state from nine to twelve years of age. The Women's Suffragette movement supported by the Protestant churches pushed for all states to adopt the age of consent at eighteen years of age. The church actually pushed for twenty-one. It wasn't until 1920 that the age of consent across the country was recognized as eighteen, but even today it is state based with some states maintaining sixteen. Part of the argument to raise the age of consent was not based off a child's ability to make decisions about their person, but about the average age a person lived. Prior to 1800, the average life span was thirty to forty years of age. By 1900, the average life expectancy had risen to fifty years of age. This allowed men and women to have more time to marry, have children and raise them. It was no longer necessary to have children at age twelve to eighteen in order to have them able to survive on their own after your death. This being a Paternal oriented society and one run entirely too much off of the will of the Church men decided to preserve the feminine virginity as long as possible so it was rape to have sex with a child under eighteen years of age. Of course this same society also imposed beliefs on women that they should not enjoy sex because it was not appropriate. Women should lay there and take it. It is a woman's job to spread her legs and bear her husband's children. If she enjoys sex she was a wonton whore. Even today a woman enjoying sex is taboo. In this male dominated world, a woman who enjoys sex is naughty, a tramp, a whore or worse. Our children are taught to enjoy sex. We are taught to explore it and to embrace the lust that all have in their souls but are restricted from acting on it. Sex is play and fun. It is an explosion of feeling and intensely enjoyable. We believe in teaching our children to explore themselves and their likes, then to be able to vocalize their wants and needs. Sex is not dirty or bad. It is a natural act between people. The sexuality of women has been suppressed to the point many women cringe at the act because they are dirty and violated. We have taken a different route. This is why we start children young. We want to educate them before the societal beliefs that sex is bad have become ingrained in the child. Imagine a world where both people are lovers first.

Seeing this world through the eyes of one who lives in it gives me a clearer picture of what we are against. The reports from the other calls we got were similar. These women indeed do not feel they are victims. They all stress their desire to not have this lifestyle end. All of my life, I have thought about the scum who sexually molest children as not worthy of having another breath. I imagined the fear and pain these children had when grown men violated them. I have seen the women who years later still suffer trauma from their abuse. Even with counseling, it is difficult for them to live a normal life. I think I must be going crazy wondering as I listen to her if we in society are not creating the pain and suffering these women endure. I remind myself I am a cop and I uphold the law. The Co-Op is breaking it and destroying young girl's lives in the process. At the same time, the woman in front of me does not appear to be your typical a victim of abuse.

ADA Hirschhorn asks her if she will tell us her role in Lexi coming here and what she can tell us about her. Tiff looks at William Coates and he tells her to go ahead. "I do not know where Lexi came from or her original name. I believe she may have been housed in the city for a while. I have a home not far from here, in the Pocono Mountains, and I was approached by the Co-Op to be her nanny last summer. She is a wonderful child. Her previous nanny taught her to play flute and I have been working with her on piano. She speaks fluent French and is now learning Italian. When we go out, the people around here believe she is my granddaughter and in many ways she is. I spoil her. Jacob comes to visit twice a week. Many times he spends the entire weekend. Then I leave them alone. When he is not here, we either stay here or at my home. She loves to shop the boutiques in the Pocono's. Last winter I also taught her to ski and she's quite good. As you can see with this house, she also has access to a lovely swimming pool and she is a good swimmer and loves the water. What more do you need to know? Her favorite color is pink. She has a cat who has either hidden somewhere or Jacob took Sakura with them. She is an excellent horseback rider and has been taking riding lessons at a local stable. She is currently studying the ancient Roman dynasty and their influence on civilizations, both then and now. Her favorite food is pizza but when Jacob is here she puts that love aside and goes with her next favorites which are blackened salmon or apricot crusted chicken. Really there is not much more I can tell you except we believe in leaving the past life behind us I have never spoken to her about her mother or where she lived before, we talk about the present and the future. The children who come into the Co-Op gladly leave their lives behind. They may miss parents or siblings for a while, but they are told they always have the choice of returning to that life. And Ms. Callahan, Marissa was happy here. I know from the news that she was your daughter. He built this house for her. He told me that on the phone after her body was found. He loved her and gave her everything her heart desired. He lost touch with her a few years back. Right now you have to trust the Co-Op to take care of whoever killed her. There are many who are angry right now. This murder disturbed our way of life and may be the end of it for us all. They will be punished. That I can guarantee. I wish I could tell you more but there is little else to tell."

John, Samantha and I excuse ourselves while the DA's office discusses an agreement with Tiff's lawyer on her release into his custody. None of us speak as we walk to the cars. The sun is already beginning to set as we pull back onto the main road and head toward New York. The trip back is quiet. John follows us. The address of the store Sidney was abducted from is about thirty miles outside the city. More and more the description of Lexi sounds like Sidney.

***

Samantha has been in jail for ten years and in that time big box stores have expanded. What was a store of housewares and clothing has now become everything from auto repair to groceries and household needs, and everything in between. She pauses as we walk in and looks around. Along the front of the store are the beauty shop, pharmacy, walk in clinic, optometry, photo studio, fast food restaurant, and customer service center. To the right is the grocery store. The center houses clothing, shoes and, to the far left of the store lawn and garden. Signs in the back locate electronics and auto repair. One stop takes care of all your needs and in the case of the Sidney Harris it also became the place to kidnap a child. I point to clothing first. While we want to see the location where Sidney disappeared from, Samantha needs to get some things to wear. John and I leave her to look around the clothing section while we go to find someone from store security. I figure she will feel more comfortable shopping for underwear without two strange men following her around. As we return, I see she took advantage of the opportunity and indeed did get her bra and underwear shopping out of the way and is working on jeans and sweaters. She also has a winter coat lying in the bottom of the cart. I hadn't even thought about the fact that she doesn't have a coat to wear and wonder if she has been cold but afraid to mention it.

Store security meets us as she is finishing putting a stack of jeans in the cart. We begin to walk with the security person toward grocery. As we pass an end cap, Samantha gets us to hold up a moment as she grabs a rolling suitcase and puts it in the cart. The security person gives her a strange look as she does. He's not sure why someone investigating a child's abduction is taking time out to shop.

In typical Samantha style, she looks at him and says, "Look I've been in jail for ten years and what you see is what I've got. We have a few choices here. I can go for yet another day in this dirty bra and I can wash out one of my three pairs of panties or we can take a minute for me to get some clothing. I'm sure these guys will be glad to see in me in something other than this pair of jeans and sweater. So give me a break if I want a bag to put my things in. Up until now I haven't needed a suitcase!" I can't help smiling at the security guards reaction. I think he's afraid she's going to shop lift the store or something.

The security guard takes us to the freezer cases near the front of the store. This is where the arrest took place. It is close to the front doors and it could have been easy for someone to walk out with Sidney. The security guard assures us they checked the cameras. The child had been wearing a blue t-shirt and shorts. Nowhere on store cameras did a child in a blue t-shirt even walk out of the store. We walk the store for a few minutes and ask about the door on the wall between the meat and dairy area. This leads to the back cold storage. While it is possible someone could sneak back there, they would have to travel the inside of the warehouse to get to the back loading dock to leave the store. Throughout the warehouse are cameras. These were also checked and there were no children seen on camera in the warehouse. The security person informs us the local police have a copy of all the cameras for a two hour period before and after the abduction. I make the call to have the images sent to my laptop to go over tonight. All we can do is thank the security person and go with Samantha to check-out. We notice some stares and people pointing. Samantha's few minutes of fame is still following her and we decide to get out of the store before it creates a situation. We are too late as we see a film crew entering the front of the store. Samantha Callahan buying clean underwear becomes part of the eleven o'clock news. Before she can finish checking out reporters are shouting and the store manager is asking us to leave. Samantha quickly pays for her purchases and we push our way to the door. We are all hungry but it looks like another night of dinner in the hotel away from prying eyes.

Back in the car my phone rings and John tells me he has pushed the food locator to order dinner. We swing in to pick it up on the way back to the hotel. As always the press camp heads toward the SUV as we park.

Samantha waves to them as she gets the suit case and bags out of the back. Someone yells to her and asks if she's been shopping. She responds back she thought they were getting tired of seeing her in the same clothes every day. They laugh and grab their film for the evening news.

Back in the room, Samantha unpacks the steaks, stuffed baked potatoes, salads, bread and blooming onion as I work on linking my laptop to the seventy-two inch TV screen in the room. It is becoming an evening ritual to work on case review while we eat dinner. We sit down trying to manage a steak with a plastic knife and fork as the videos finish loading and fifty-four camera images appear on the screen. Even with the size of the TV, the pictures are nearly impossible to see. We locate the bank of cameras in the grocery department and bring them up on the screen. After a few minutes, we see a woman pushing a cart enter with a child in a blue t-shirt and shorts. As the woman walks the aisles, the child wanders and explores the shelves. For identification, we pull a view of the child up and match it to Sidney's picture. Then we go back to the camera views. Her mother is concentrating on selecting canned goods and putting them in the cart, the entire time punching in numbers into a calculator. Sidney is on her own crawling into shelves and hiding to pop out as her mom goes by in an attempt to scare her and or get her attention. We watch as her mother takes a bag of candy and opens it then hands candy to Sidney. She must have told Sidney to put some in her pockets because the woman looks around standing guard as she hands her candy and it goes into the shorts pockets. Now and then they both open a miniature candy bar and pop it into their mouths. Samantha points out a man at the end of an aisle watching them. We pull him up on the screen. He's middle aged with gray hair. He's dressed like an average guy, jeans and t-shirt. There is nothing to make this guy stand out. We also note he does not have the same build as Jacob Montgomery. Sidney and her mother then head to the dairy case and her mother places a block of cheese in the front of her jeans. We see the man stopping a woman down the aisle and pointing it out that they are shop lifting. Now both the man and the woman are watching Sidney and her mother at a distance. She adds milk and butter to the cart then slips bacon under her shirt. Samantha seems to have been right about the tight tank top under the t-shirt. How she to shoplifted seems to be this woman's method as well. The man and woman point the shoplifting out to another woman. This one is young with a baby in the seat of the cart. They stand there watching and shaking their heads. Then the man walks off leaving the two women watching. Sidney skips around the meat department as her mother puts hamburger under her shirt and smashes it down to make it look smooth. Sidney wanders up an aisle and looks around while she opens a box of cereal and grabs a handful. She then crawls onto the bottom shelf in the soft drink and water section with the box. We see the man return with security and the mother begin to react to the shoplifting accusation. A crowd gathers around to watch as the woman resists the security guard. The man is still standing there watching. Samantha points to the screen at where Sidney had crawled into a shelf. A woman in skirt with high heels leans down to Sidney's hiding place and appears to be talking to her. We bring them up on the screen as Sidney crawls out and the woman points to her pockets making Sidney empty them of candy. The woman takes the candy and puts it on the shelf. She then reaches into her purse and pulls out a printed button down blouse and hands it to Sidney who puts it on. Then the woman holds out her hand. We watch as hand in hand the woman and Sidney walk toward the back of the store and make their way to automotive. They exit through the customer entrance.

Police and store security had been looking for a gray-haired man with a little girl in a blue t-shirt and shorts. Not a woman with a little girl in a printed top and shorts. They walked out unnoticed. The scuffle with Sidney's mother has ended and the crowd goes back to shopping. Their entertainment of the moment was over and their lives went back to normal. The man who reported the shoplifting walks out the front door of the store. The camera's roll for a few more minutes before store employees stop what they are doing and begin to look for Sidney. By now the woman and Sidney have been away from the store for over twenty minutes.

John starts to roll the playback on the front door and the automotive door to see if we can see when both the man who reported the shoplifting and the woman who kidnapped Sidney walked in. I want to see if they arrived together. The tapes show them arriving separately and at different times. Neither takes a cart. Both appear to check and send either a text message or read mail on their phones as they walk around. Just before the man starts to alert people of the shoplifting, we watch as they both pass Sidney and her mother. There is a brief eye exchange between them and it is hard to tell if the man nods or not. Soon afterward he goes to the first woman and points out the shoplifting. The exchange is subtle but it appears they are working together.

We next run the video of the parking lot after the abduction. We watch as the woman and Sidney leave automotive. We follow them as they walk out of view. A few minutes later, we see the man walk out the front and get into a black sedan and drive away. Finally after playing the video back a few times, we are able to get an image of the tags. I am not surprised when the motor vehicle database comes up blank. This car is running fake plates.

We sit here stunned. We have watched Sidney Harris being abducted on video and I'm not sure if we know anything more then we knew this morning. We saw two people, possibly working together walk out the door with a child in broad daylight. Throughout the store not one video camera caught a good image of either the man or the woman. They made sure they never looked up into the cameras and averted their gaze either down or to the side. We only saw their clothing and the tops of their heads.

I touch bases with the DA White's office. Tiffany Burnside is currently released to her lawyers. She has fully cooperated with the investigation and has agreed to be states' witness if needed. The conversation with her today has been eye opening. We arrange to meet with Sidney's mother in the morning and we all turned in for the night.

DAY 7
NEW YORK CITY, NEW YORK

It feels like I have only slept for an hour, but the sun is up when my cell phone rings. Karen Harris, Sidney's mother will meet us in an hour at the DA's office downtown. After her arrest, the judge decided the abduction of her child was punishment enough and she was given one hundred hours of community service at the missing and exploited children's center. There she worked through her need to find her daughter and help others who were in a similar situation. According to DA White, this experience has turned Karen Harris around.

This morning we walk right through the crowd of reporters as they scramble from the warm comforts of their vans to get into the SUV. As usual we have a few news chase cars pulling out behind us. A few even follow us through the drive up window for a fast food breakfast. This morning since we are driving to the DA's office none of us care if they follow. Once we reach the front door they will be stopped by security.

Karen Harris looks different then she did in the video. She is thinner, well dressed and stylish. As we enter, she stands to shake our hands. DA White and ADA Hirschhorn walk in and sit down. The meeting starts with an update on the investigation into the whereabouts of Jacob Montgomery. According to the flight plan filed before takeoff, the Montgomery plane was destined for Paris. After takeoff, the plane made a U-turn over the Atlantic and notified the tower they were changing destinations and would be notifying of a new flight plan. The plane was tracked on radar flying south over the Atlantic and was turned over to tower control at BWI. The pilot failed to contact BWI tower or radar and continued down the coast. It was lost in Georgia and suspected of having landed on one of many private or small airfields in the area. There were no reports of a plane crash or a plane in distress, nor is there any sign of wreckage. There is no reason to believe the plane crashed, but is being concealed somewhere in Georgia. After the briefing, DA White asks Karen Harris to tell us about the day Sidney disappeared.

"It's hard to know where to start. We got up, dressed and we had nothing to eat so we went to the store. We did that a lot. Sometimes we would just walk around eating things. You know grab a piece of fruit and pop it into your mouth, open a box and eat some. Some months we ran out of money for food before the next check came in. I know it was wrong but I didn't want my little girl to be hungry or taken away. When we would go to the store, I would let Sidney play. I never thought anything would happen to her. It was a typical day for us. Go eat some stuff and buy a few things to take home that we could afford. The District Attorney tells me you think she is connected to Jacob Montgomery. Is that true? Anyway we were shopping and the next thing I know there was a guy telling me he was store security. He grabbed me and lifted up my shirt. I tried to pull it back down. There's one thing to be caught shoplifting, it's another to have your clothes pulled up exposing you. In the middle of it all, that I forgot Sidney. These men were wrestling me to the ground and the next thing I knew I was being dragged into a security office kicking and screaming. Then they pushed me into a chair and told me to stay there. They locked the door and left me for about ten minutes. When they came back in, I was screaming 'where is my daughter?' I thought they had arrested her and put her in a different room and I just wanted her with me. I was afraid I was going to jail and I wanted to be able to say goodbye to her. I knew the drill, it had happened before and I wanted her to know I loved her and would be back. Instead, I ended up being sent to the Missing Children's Resource Center as part of my sentence. There I met other women, like me, who just needed answers to where their kids had gone. Most in New York City are runaway's who end up turning tricks on the street. I saw a lot of parents find their kid as a strung out junkie after just a few weeks. These kids turn up sick too. Some have deadly stuff after a few months on the street. Its hard Miss Callahan, I know I saw it in so many people's eyes. You get this hollow empty feeling. I am afraid every time my phone rings and I answer it because I'm afraid her body will be found in a shallow grave or dredged up out of the water. I will do anything you need to help find my baby and to make whoever is taking these kids pay."

I ask her if she would be willing to watch the video of her arrest and Sidney's abduction. I hope she might be able to give us more detail about the two people. They each passed her a couple times while she was in the store. Maybe she can give us a better description then we can get from the surveillance cameras. She agrees and I link my laptop to the smart board in the conference room. Soon the inside of the store comes into view. I select the camera views that have the best image of the events and start the videos running. Samantha hands Karen a tissue when the image of Sidney playing comes into view. The two women are comrades in pain. They understand each other too well. Karen wipes her eyes and watches intently as the man points her out to others and mutters "bastard" at his actions. She watches as store security grabs her and lets out an audible whimper. I change the camera views back to Sidney just before the woman approaches her. Karen reaches out toward the screen as she watches her and dabs her eyes. As the woman walks toward Sidney, Karen suddenly jumps up screaming and lunges at DA White "You bastards! You have had her all along! Why the hell didn't you tell me you had her? What the hell kind of game are you doing torturing me all this time? You better fucking answer me! Where the hell is my daughter?" She is inches towards DA White screaming in his face before either John or I can react. ADA Hirschhorn grabs a phone and calls security. It is Samantha who grabs Karen's arm just before she reaches for DA White's throat. Trying to get through to her Samantha is yelling "They don't have her, this woman is her kidnapper. Stop! Please stop before they have to arrest you! We want to help you! Please!"

Karen spins around and faces Samantha. "That woman works for THEM! That's Isabel Boyle! She's the social worker who wouldn't leave me alone. She was constantly coming to my house and taking her white gloves looking for dust. If she found just one speck, she told me my house was filthy and she could take Sidney away. She went to the school and pushed them around always threatening to take her, always looking for a reason. If Sidney was sick, the school called her and she came to my house demanding me to prove Sidney was too sick to go! They set me up! They had me arrested so that she could take Sidney and put her into foster care! Where the hell is my daughter? I want her NOW!"

We all stay there in silence for a second. Afraid Karen Harris will explode again, I go to her and ask her to please sit down so that we can work this out and get some answers. This prompts ADA Hirschhorn to make another call to ask for information on a social worker named Isabel Boyle. At that, security busts down the conference room door with guns drawn. Samantha releases Karen's arm and puts her hands in the air before freezing in place. Karen ducks down below the table while the rest of us turn and stare at the drawn guns. DA White tells them to stand down, things are under control. It is intense for a moment before the officers evaluate the situation and holster their weapons. Both Karen and Samantha are in no condition to carry on the and DA White calls out for some coffee so that we can all regroup. Meanwhile, clerks are frantically searching databases for information on the social worker named Isabel Boyle. I can feel my pulse coming down again. It has been a while since I was in a conference room with someone who has lunged at a cop. There is always that tense moment before the person is subdued that raises your heart rate to dangerous levels.

The coffee beats the clerk with the information by less than a minute. We are still fixing our cups when the clerk tells DA White there are no records of an Isabel Boyle in New York, New Jersey or Connecticut. Karen spins around and screams "No! I saw her credentials. She made sure she whipped them out and pushed them into my face every time. She is a Social Worker for the State of New York. She even drives your white state car. I have seen it outside my apartment building and outside Sidney's school. Even has the state of New York sticker on the door. She works for YOU!"

The clerk holds up a piece of paper and says, "Here look. I ran it as a maiden name and a married name. I even did past employees. I ran Isabel Boyle through the entire state and city systems and there is no one named Isabel Boyle working for New York City or New York State."

At that Samantha sits down hard and looks at me "Oh my God! The tags on the car at the abduction and her ID were fake. The car she drove was a fake state car. How many others handed their child over to a social worker who said they were there to take them? Does anyone else know what this means?" We all sat there as reality set in and we understood completely.

Our next stop is to PS319 in the Bronx to talk to the elementary school where Sidney went to see what information they can provide about Isabel Boyle. As always traffic in New York City is barely moving as we make our way through town. Eventually we make it and find a parking spot in a garage about four blocks from the school.

As we open the door, the smell of elementary school hits me and brings back memories. There is this smell that emits from every elementary school. It's a mixture of crayons, chalk and tempera paint with the disinfectant used to clean the floors and toilets. It seems there is a universal smell to them all. The sign on the door states all visitors must report to the school office. After that, we are left to guess where that might be. It appears our entrance must have been caught on video surveillance because about three steps in we are greeted by a uniformed officer. After a showing of badges and IDs, we are lead to the principal's office. The security officer keeps giving Samantha looks as if he is questioning why a woman her age has no identification or he recognizes her from the recent video coverage. It is hard to tell, but he is nervous allowing her in even though she is accompanied by the FBI and the DA's office. DA White had called ahead and the principal is waiting for us in a conference room.

Leona Haynes is a stereotypical buxom matronly woman looking as if she was cut from the elementary principal cookie cutter. She rises as we enter the door and shakes our hands before motioning for us to sit. She has planned ahead and has Sidney Harris' school records. I'm glad the woman is ready to get down to business. I begin by thanking her for coming in and unlocking the school. Luckily, under the circumstances she feels coming in today is the least she can do. When I ask, she pulls the information from the file on Isabel Boyle. Everything seems to be in order. There are copies of state records and a copy of Isabel Boyle's state ID as well as her business card. Before we begin, AD White calls his office with her badge number, the cell number and the address information. Leona Haynes is the only person surprised that the number comes back to a throw away phone which is now a dead number. The badge number belonged to a deceased Social Worker from five years ago and the case number belonged to another case file. An investigator at the DAs office is checking into whether any connection can be found to the actual case file, or if it is a random number that turned out to be active.

Leona Haynes is obviously embarrassed that she was duped by an impostor from Social Services as she begins to speak. "I can't believe it. I spoke with her myself. I personally check the people's identifications and make a copy. I called her many times to report Sidney had missed school or gone home early. She was very good at answering or returning my calls. She even called me after hours to talk about home conditions and asked if I had noticed behavioral issues. There were a lot of problems in that home and Isabel Boyle seemed to be really on top of things. I thought she was one of the best the state had actually. She was good for Sidney and I wished more of my children had her as a social worker. The mother could barely take care of herself, let alone a child. I was shown pictures of the home. It was a mess. Sidney slept on a bed filled with clothing and used that to cover up. The mattress was stained and dirty and didn't look fit for anyone to sleep on. The kitchen had dishes moldy and piled in the sink and trash overflowing on the floor and counters. The school was notified twice the child was treated for lice infestation. Then there were the repeated MRSA infections. The child had a reoccurring MRSA infection that was reported to the health department. We really didn't want her in school. From the reports the infection was usually either anal or vaginal. To me that signified some sort of sex offense. Sidney cried because when this happened we made her use the rest room in the nurse's office so that the toilet could be properly sanitized before another child used it. Sidney was on the school lunch program and so she had at least two good meals to eat each day. I was never sure why the child was allowed to live in the conditions she was forced into. And I heard when she disappeared her mother was in the process of being arrested for shoplifting food. Or am I wrong? Did this impostor mislead me on things? Now I'm not sure what to believe. Maybe this social worker was too good to be true."

We really didn't have many answers about the living conditions or the health of Sidney. We had Karen Harris's word that she kept her house immaculate but, it was never good enough for Isabel Boyle. As we look at the stack of doctor reports they all come from a free clinic in Queens. It is not surprising when the address comes back as the corner of a park. Nothing about the woman known as Isabel Boyle appears to be authentic; everything she provided seemed to have been part of a well manufactured ruse. More and more the evidence supports the story given by Karen Harris and makes me think of the words of Tiffany Burnside, maybe this is bigger than us. It's hard as a cop to think there are things we have never seen or dreamed criminals were capable of doing, but if what we are hearing is true then these people have created an alternative universe in order to abduct children for a pedophile ring.

We get copies of Sidney Harris's school files and thank Leona Haynes for her assistance. We are on the road for about fifteen minutes when DA White's cell phone rings. He pushes the button and tells Leona Haynes he has her on speaker phone in the SUV. Her voice comes over the radio speakers. "I'm sorry I didn't think of this while you were here. There was an incident involving Sidney about six weeks before she disappeared. Isabel Boyle brought a man with her. He identified himself as a judge with orphan's court. He gave me his name and asked if I voted for him. I don't live in this district so I didn't recognize his name. At the time, I didn't think his comment was odd but later in the day it dawned on me that it was weird. When I told him I didn't live in this district, so I was sorry I wasn't one of his voters, He laughed and said "that's right, you live in West Orange." I thought it was odd that he knew where I lived but I figured he was a judge in orphan's court so maybe he had looked at my city personnel file. Now I wonder if he was even a judge. I'm not sure if I would recognize a picture of him if I saw it. He was only in my office once for about fifteen minutes but finding out everything about Isabel Boyle being a lie made me think about the strange judge. I was told he was investigating Sidney's case file and was working on a court petition for Sidney's removal from the home. I gave them my support and copies of all her documentation. I wanted the best for her. Now I wonder if I gave personal information to frauds that used something in her file to abduct her. I really hope you find her safe. If I can help, even if you need me to look at photos of people please let me know. I feel horrible thinking I helped these people abduct a child." We thanked her for her information and told her if we got pictures of suspects we would give her a call and run a photo lineup. At this point every little bit helped put the puzzle together.

My phone rings and I see the Worchester County Coroner's office number. I answered and Tim Clark asks if Samantha Callahan is still with me. They have been notified by the crematorium that Kali's ashes are ready for pick up and he isn't sure where to send them. While we have all stayed focused on the crime, there is still the initial victim's body to handle. I pass the phone to Samantha after telling her who is on the line. I watch as she takes a deep breath and closes her eyes. She knows what this call is about and as with any parent this is not something she ever expected to have to decide, the disposition of her daughters remains. I hear her tell him she has no permanent address yet and can he just hold them until she knows what to do. I feel sorry for Samantha. During all this she has been a professional and helped us with the case. Meanwhile, she has not been able to start her life over. She needs closure for Kali. While finding who killed her will help with that, until her ashes are handled there will be an open door that can't be closed. I ask if she would like Kali's ashes sent to my office. There at least her ashes will be with people working on finding who killed her. Samantha agrees and hands to phone back to me to give Tim the address. After hanging up I call, my office and tell them to expect Kali in a few days.

One thing I know about my office is their respect for the dead and for our victims. I haven't been in for a week and yet I know what the operation board looks like. There will be the cherub face of Kali as a seven year old from her initial missing persons file smiling out across the room. Beneath that will be the cleaned face from the morgue shot used in identification with pictures from Swan Cove. The area is actually very beautiful and tranquil looking. It's hard to imagine the brutal murder that took place there. Somewhere will be the pictures of the pony that had blood on her. She was a pretty brown and white painted pony with a long mane and tail. She looks like very little girls dream. Below that will be a picture of Jacob Montgomery and his missing persons file information. Right now there are so many dead ends and loose threads in this case. All we can assume is that Kali left Jacob Montgomery sometime in her early teens and went to someone else. Who, we still don't know, nor do we know if that person is the killer. What we do know is that the story that is unfolding in front of us is not just Kali's. I think that is what is keeping Samantha Callahan going. We know there is another child out there. We suspect there might be many more. From people who have come forward we have an indication there is an entire network of people who are abducting children for their own deviant pleasure and raising them as part of this organization. When Kali's ashes arrive her urn will be put on a table in front of the situation board. I know my group. Someone will place flowers next to the urn. It has happened before. When the flowers start to wilt someone will grab more flowers at a store and put them in the vase. It's a way for us to stay connected to what is important, that face on the wall. Having Kali's ashes in the office will be one more reminder to everyone who we are working for. I tell Samantha Kali will be taken care of until she goes back to get her.

DA White decides to bring Leona Haynes in for a photo lineup. His office has gotten a few pictures of Jacob Montgomery that look different from the stock photo that have been plastered all over the news in anticipation that we may need to put his face in a line up. With the media exposure his picture has had, it is hard to get a positive ID that is not produced by familiarity with the overexposure he has gotten. We knew if we ever got a witness we didn't want the identification to be influenced by the news.

For the first time in a week, we are sitting at a spot where we have no new leads. We are able to return to the hotel early and sit down in the room to eat dinner. It's been a while since we have even been able to watch the evening news. I feel I have been so wrapped up in the case that the world may have ended with us the last to know. The local news is filled with a fire downtown, a shooting investigation and a politician being investigated for fraud. We all turn when a picture of a young girl comes on the screen. She was abducted walking home from school. We of course all wondered if this was yet another girl going into the Co-Op. The news switches to national with the protests at the G8 summit and live reaction to the world banking leaders meeting in Jekyll Island, Georgia. The screen flashes to a warm sunny beach with seagulls flying over head while a couple children fly kites on the beach. Jekyll Island was chosen for this G8 meeting because the island is off the Georgia coast accessible by a single road, which is currently blocked to everything but local traffic and those with reservations at the resort.

We all stare at the television. Jacob Montgomery's plane was last located flying over the Atlantic Ocean near Jekyll Island. What better location for a banker to hide then in plain sight among a bunch of other bankers. I am already dialing my cell phone before anyone else speaks.

An advance unit from the Atlanta Field Office is dispatched immediately. Our first priority is to locate Jacob Montgomery and the child. Our second priority is locating his plane. If we find that, we may hope to find DNA evidence that matches both Sidney Harris and if we are lucky Kali Callahan.

If we can establish a confirmed link to either girl then Montgomery's status jumps from fugitive wanted for questioning, to fugitive wanted for kidnapping, murder, child endangerment and a plethora of other offenses. Those will be up to the various DA's involved.

Once again the case is going into hyper drive. We have a good idea where Jacob Montgomery is located. Within an hour, we have confirmation that the plane did indeed land on the small airstrip on Jekyll Island. John immediately begins to send pictures and case notes to the Atlanta field office for them to be able to make a positive identification and the preliminary charging documents in the case. It will take Atlanta a few hours to alert agents and get to Jekyll Island. The hope is by morning we have a better handle on the case.

As we work to make flight arrangements, the Amber Alert interrupts prime time TV. Sidney Harris is back in the news this time as 'abduction by stranger'. A school picture of Sidney comes on with a split screen of a professional photograph of Jacob Montgomery. Someone in the New York police jumped the gun. Throughout the state of New York, smart phones begin receiving pictures of Sidney and Jacob Montgomery. This will be a double-edged sword for us. While all eyes are on the lookout for them someone will be picking up their phone and calling Montgomery. This man has already gone to ground; this alert will put him deeper underground.

There is not much more we can do for the night. Our plane leaves early in the morning. The Atlanta team is already preparing to go to Jekyll Island. If we are lucky, by the time we land Sidney will be on her way back to her mother and Jacob Montgomery will be in a holding cell. We say our goodnights and make an attempt at catching a few hours sleep. Tomorrow is already shaping up to be a fast paced day.

DAY 8
NEW YORK, NEW YORK TO
JEKYLL ISLAND, GEORGIA

My cell phone is ringing. I don't even open my eyes; instead I fumble around trying to feel it on the bed side table. As I answer, I try to get my wits about me and focus on what the person on the other end is telling me. "Montgomery's plane took off from the Jekyll Island Airport approximately ten minutes prior to the Amber Alert broadcast. A forensic team is currently onsite at the Jekyll Island Club Hotel in the Annex Suite previously occupied by Jacob Montgomery and his "daughter." The hotel staff has confirmed a positive identification of Sidney Harris. Montgomery's plane made a short hop to Miami. He's on the ground in Miami but, once again Montgomery and the girl have vanished. At this point there's no evidence that Sidney has been harmed. This in itself is a relief. I think in the back of everyone's mind is at what point does Montgomery kill the child to hide the evidence. No blood on the plane and reports of a man and a child getting into a car gives us hope. It appears they are still traveling together. Having Sidney with him will slow them down and hopefully, we can use that to our advantage.

I hear movement in the center suite and walk out to find Samantha bag and coat in hand. She looks at me and says "he's on the move isn't he?" I nod and look up to see John walking in dressed with bag-in-hand. The night is gone for all of us and I grab my bag and coat as we head out the door. As we walk outside the parking lot is lit by the camera lights of the news crews. Reporters look fresh and rested as they stand there microphone in hand giving the latest update to the public. Camera people and reporters run toward us yelling questions about Montgomery and Jekyll Island as soon as we exit the door. I wave them off, telling them they know as much as we do right now.

As we drive to the airport the over head signs list the Amber Alert and the news on the radio enters around Sidney Harris and Jacob Montgomery. "Late yesterday police confirmed banking mogul Jacob Montgomery is wanted for questioning about the disappearance of Sidney Harris, a child taken from a Suburban New York discount store last year. Federal authorities will not comment on the case at this time, but people close to the case have confirmed the investigation has now moved to Jekyll Island, Georgia. Earlier this week authorities were at the Montgomery summer cabin as part of the investigation into a body found October fifteenth on Assateague Island, Virginia. The body has since been identified of as that of seventeen year old Kali Callahan. Kali was last seen at age six while staying at the Montgomery summer cabin. Young Kali and her mother, Samantha Callahan, were hired by Montgomery and some business associates for weekend entertainment. Samantha Callahan, a known prostitute and exotic dancer, was charged with the murder and disappearance of her daughter and sentenced to twenty-five years in jail. Currently, Samantha Callahan has been released to the custody of FBI Agent Adam Clay. We have reporters on the scene in Georgia and will give you an update as soon as one becomes available."

At that Samantha reaches over and turns off the radio and says "I think we should just let the press investigate this since they seem to be all over it and telling Montgomery our every move! What I want to know is how they know what's going on before we do!" I don't have an answer for her, but we know since we hit New York there has been a leak in our investigation, one that appears to be informing Jacob Montgomery and the news before we even get the information.

A few minutes later, we are met and escorted by a transportation authority police car at Newark Airport. As we drive around the perimeter and enter the area reserved for private aircraft, I think back to the last time I was here. That was a murder investigation of a young woman found dead in the trunk of her car in long term parking. That case was a series of dead ends as we interviewed people through five states who had left threatening phone calls on her work voicemail. It turned out they were all innocent and got caught

Sharon Dobson

up in the investigation because they didn't know she had been reported missing. They had been waiting on her to call them back and complete paperwork to close their mortgages prior to settlement. That investigation took three weeks to determine we didn't have a good suspect. To my knowledge it is still in the unsolved murder files. Unlike hour long television drama's, the FBI does not always solve the case quickly or at all. I just hope this case is one we find the answers to. I now have two mothers with missing children and a public who want answers.

Our plane, a Lear 25, on loan from the New York field office is being towed out of the hanger as we pull in. Agent Cooper Woodle walks up and introduces himself. He has been assigned as our pilot for the flight to Jekyll Island. We follow him into the plane as he goes through his pre-flight check list. Before long we are in the air and heading south.

Jekyll Island is a barrier island off the coast of Georgia. In many ways, it is similar to Chincoteague and Assateague, Virginia. Both Jekyll Island and Assateague Island are part of the park system with Assateague being a national park and Jekyll being a Georgia state park. They are also both resort towns. As I look over the maps and information provided on the location, I am struck with just how similar both places are and the similarities to the Delaware Water Gap. All are accessed through one road. All have some sort of access control prior to entering the park. The Montgomery house can only be accessed by the Dingman's Ferry Bridge. That one-of-a-kind bridge is privately owned with a man standing collecting the one dollar toll from cars passing in each direction. Entering Assateague, you must stop at the National Park Service Booth and pay the toll. It seems odd that someone trying to hide their activities would do so with that kind of traffic control. There's no way to escape by road if the police are coming. Normally, an escape route is planned. I hadn't realized I was muttering to myself until Samantha pipes in "maybe they know the police won't come." I look at her and wonder how true this statement might be. Nothing in this case seems to follow patterns I am use to and the people involved seem to be notified before we can get near.

My thoughts are interrupted as over the cabin PA we hear "LJ25 N8459 this is Jacksonville control please adjust to south west runway three - six at heading three – five - four left you are cleared for approach at 09J Jekyll

Island please acknowledge." "Roger Jacksonville adjusting south west to runway three - six heading three – five - four left 09J Jekyll" Then Agent Woodle comes back on the cabin with "okay everyone buckle up we are going to need all three thousand seven hundred feet of runway to get to a stop."

For most of our flight we have flown over the Atlantic Ocean and now I watch as we swing inland somewhere over Georgia as we descend on final approach. The Lear 25 is equipped with eight tan leather seats in the passenger area with a full stocked bar in the back and luggage storage in the cabinet behind the two front pilot seats. Someone had put coffee and breakfast items on the bar but, none of us even touched it. Ahead through the space between the pilot seats, I can see the green lights of the runway quickly approaching us in the gray dawn of morning. Out the window to the west, I can see the sun just beginning to peak above the horizon.

We land and taxi back down the runway and take a left on an access road into the service area. Agent Woodle pulls the plane into a space and comes back and opens the door. Immediately a black SUV pulls up to pick us up. Even in late October, Georgia is warm and humid in the early morning. None of us are dressed for the humidity and immediately I feel myself beginning to sweat. Samantha wipes her forehead on her sleeve and then pushes it up over her elbow. It looks like it's going to be a hot day.

Agent Roy Banks from the Atlanta Field office introduces himself to us and motions to get into the waiting SUV. Lucky for us he has anticipated us arriving from New York where frost is on the ground in the morning and he has the air conditioning going full force as we put luggage in the back and find a seat. Agent Banks is local to the area and serves as our tour guide. As we make the left onto Riverview Drive, he begins his tour. I guess as much to catch us up on our surroundings as to tell us about an area he is obviously proud to call his local hangout. "Jekyll Island is seven miles long and a mile and a half wide. It has been inhabited since 1738. In the beginning it was a military outpost but soon people began to move here for the beaches. By 1888, Jekyll Island had become a private resort to one hundred of America's richest families. Everyone from Aldrich to Rockerfeller to J. P. Morgan bought a share for six hundred dollars in order to be able to come here. The Jekyll Island Club opened every January for the rich families to escape the cold winter in the north and enjoy life on the island. Where we are going now is the original Jekyll Island Clubhouse. As we make this turn look out to the left and you can start to see the beach houses built by some of the richer members of the club. Hopefully while you are here you will get to see a little of the island. It has quite an important history. In November of 1858, the second to last slave ship to ever land in the US, the Wanderer, came here and successfully unloaded four hundred and sixty-five slaves. By that time, it had been illegal for over fifty years to import slaves from Africa so they were unloaded on the island and delivered in secrecy to the mainland. Where we are going, the Jekyll Island Club holds a major part in US history. Around Thanksgiving 1910, the assistant secretary of the treasury, a senator and five of the leading financiers in the United States met here to discuss monetary policy and the banking system. The result of this meeting was the draft of legislation to create the United States Central Bank. This became the Federal Reserve Act of 1913." As he says this we are pulling up in front of a massive Victorian Era building. The sign out front says Jekyll Island Club Hotel circa 1888.

Walking inside is like stepping back in time. Heavy satin drapes decorated with braided cord grace the windows. The furniture appears to be hand tooled brown leather and mahogany chairs blending into the rich decorative wood paneled walls. Even the carpets appear to have lingered from the Civil War era. Small Persian area rugs are placed strategically on rich hued hard wood floors. Agent Banks passes the ornate front desk and walks through a parlor toward a carved grand staircase. He remarks that we have to pass through the river front rooms to get to the Annex. We are going to a deluxe king suite on the second floor, the room Jacob Montgomery stayed in.

It is at the end of a hallway on the river side. As we approach, I can see crime scene tape and the flash of a camera inside. The forensic team is still doing collection work as we arrive. In the hallway on an ornate chair sits a very nervous looking woman wearing a blazer and skirt. Her name badge identifies her as the hotel management. Each of us takes a look inside the room making sure to not break the threshold. There is a central seating area with a desk, flat screen TV and computer hook ups along one wall. The outside wall was floor to ceiling windows with a French door leading to a balcony.

Agent Banks walks over and talks to the hotel employee. She walks with him and he motions for us to follow. We enter a room down the hallway. This room is smaller and doesn't have a river view. There is a table with six chairs in the center of the room. On the bar there's a silver coffee pot with matching cream and sugar as well as cups and saucers. A silver tray is filled with pastry. Another has sliced bagels next to that a platter of cream cheese balls, lox, sliced tomato and sliced onion. The hotel manager, Shelly McKay, invites us to make something for ourselves. Since none of us had eaten the food and coffee are a welcome sight.

A cup of coffee and a bagel with lox and cream cheese hits the spot. As usual I didn't realize how hungry I was until I sit to eat. As we eat Shelly McKay tells us about Jacob Montgomery and his daughter Alexis. "Mr. Montgomery came in for the banking conference. He made his reservation months in advance. You have to in order to get one of the bigger suites. He has stayed here before and he has never brought anyone with him. He is usually all business when he's here. We were surprised when he showed up with his daughter and asked if we could send additional pillows and blankets for her. We offered to send up a roll away bed and he said she would be fine on the sofa bed. His daughter didn't seem at all distressed. She walked in holding his hand and was excited about some of our activities including horseback riding on the beach. Actually, Mr. Montgomery made a reservation for the two of them to go on one of the horseback excursions this morning. We didn't even know he had checked out of the hotel until your people showed up with a warrant to see his room. There was nothing secret about them being here. Most of their meals were taken either on their private balcony or in the Riverview Dining Area. I can't believe this is happening at our hotel. We pride ourselves for being an upscale resort for families. I hope the news understands that we don't condone this kind of activity."

I assure her we do not hold the hotel in any way accountable and will mention in the news conference to let everyone know they were cooperating fully and the hotel is in no way involved in this situation. I ask her if she knows approximately what time Montgomery left and if there was anyone with him except the girl. She sits there shaking her head before she speaks. "That's just it. We had no idea that Mr. Montgomery and the child were gone. They had dinner in the dining area. There was a band concert outside after the sun went down and most of our guests went outside to enjoy the nice evening and listen to the music. They were seen at that concert. Then around 8:30 last night, Mr. Montgomery and his daughter were seen dressed in running clothes and they headed out the path of the river walk. No one remembers seeing them come back. When we opened the door early this morning for the FBI team, it appeared no one had spent the night in the room. If they left the island, they had to be picked up by a car and driven off. There are eight miles of causeway between here and the nearest place on the main land. That would be the casino on Grisco Point. With the mosquitoes, at night no one in their right mind would try cross to the main land on foot." I interrupt her at this point and tell her Jacob Montgomery's plane took off from the airport last night. Her look is startled and then confused. "Jacob Montgomery and the girl weren't on that plane. Last night at the concert there was a charity auction. Mr. Montgomery surprised everyone by donating the use of his private plane and tickets for first class on a cruise to the Virgin Islands leaving this morning. It wasn't on the auction list. He walked up to the microphone and donated it right on the spot. It was one of our highest bids, ten thousand dollars for the item. As soon as it was auctioned off they were whisked away in a limousine and taken to the Jekyll Island airport for the flight to Miami so that they could board the cruise ship early this morning. By now, they are out to sea. If you would like I can call downstairs and confirm the name of the people who won the bid. They paid by credit card. It was a gentleman from Texas. He's a widower with two daughters, Mr. Calvin Montague and his daughters Anastasia and Maya." Now it is our turn to look confused and startled.

There is no doubt in my mind that we have a leak. Since we left Chincoteague, Montgomery has been one step ahead of us. Last night my initial call about Jekyll Island was made at about 6:10. It was right after the headline stories on the 6 o'clock news. The G8 conference led off the telecast and the call was made soon afterward. Within two and a half hours, he had thrown up a red herring and made their escape. I once again make a call to the Richmond field office, this time to confer with my boss on how to proceed. Once again Montgomery has blown away with the wind but my gut is telling me Anastasia and Maya Montague may be missing children and right now they are on a Bahamas registered cruise ship in international water.

The search of the room turned up the personal items and clothing of both Montgomery and Sidney. A rush DNA test confirms the child is Sidney Harris. Now there is no doubt on the fugitive kidnapping order. By taking Sidney from New York to Georgia, he had committed a federal level kidnapping, once caught he is going to a federal penitentiary. The problem seems to be catching up with him.

Samantha has been quietly sitting at my laptop for some time. Being around her these last few days I have started to learn her facial expressions. She is reading something which is making her both angry and confused. I watch as she flips back and forth between sites. Finally she looks at me and tells me to get changed we are going for a run. I remind her it is close to ninety degrees with eighty percent humidity out there, running in that heat is the last thing I want to do. She then tells me to get up, if I wasn't running we are going for a walk.

I am used to being in charge of an investigation and as a single guy I'm use to doing what I want when I want. Samantha telling me what to do is unsettling. At the same time, instinct tells me she's on to something. I think she wants to get me alone to talk. I look over and John is making eye contact with her as well and he asks if we mind him tagging along.

Together we leave the hotel and head down a path along the river. Once we are out of earshot, Samantha starts to talk. "Look I don't know who we can trust right now and who we can't. What I do know is that someone has been reporting to Jacob Montgomery since we left Chincoteague. Agent Woodle seems like a nice guy but I don't know who he's reporting to reporting to. My guess someone in the New York Field Office is connected to this somehow. Before you say a word about FBI agents being above that, police corruption happens and you have to admit somehow Montgomery has known our every move." I swat a mosquito and look around. We are on a paved trail along the river. It is lined by the manicured lawns of the Jekyll Island Club and trees with a few scattered houses having the view across the river to the mainland. Couples are walking the path and in a field a family plays with their dog. Around us people are enjoying the warm October day. To the right, stretching out into the river is a log pier with a restaurant out over the water and a connecting boat dock. Samantha points to the restaurant and asks if we want to get a beer. Normally at 11:45 in the morning, I am not ready for a beer, especially when I'm working a case but this morning is an exception. John gives me a look but shrugs his head and we head out the pier toward the raw bar.

Halfway out the pier, Samantha stops and looks around. Seeing no one, she leans out over the railing and says "First, Jacob Montgomery wasn't a runner. I read an article about him this morning where he out right said he hates most forms of exercise. He goes to the gym because he has to, not because he wants to and with his knees he even avoids the tread mill. So, why would a man with bad knees leave the hotel in running clothes and go for a run? Now what he did love was his yacht. Did you know he has a sixty-five foot yacht and that he has traveled around the world on? It's a three mast tall ship called The Lady Grey and last week it was in the parade of tall ships in Savannah, Georgia? And this weekend it is suppose to be in Daytona. I say suppose to be because just this morning it was announced the Lady Grey will not be visiting Daytona this year because of the ongoing police investigation into its owner. In their statement to the public, they felt the presence of the ship would be detrimental to the event and the publicity of the case would be the focus of the press instead of the money raised for the charity. So where in the ocean is the Lady Grey?"

I look out and see the small motor boats and Jet Ski's tied up on both sides of the long pier. Jekyll Island is about half way between Savannah and Daytona. It would be possible to take a boat around the south side of the island and head out into the Atlantic Ocean. From there board the yacht and disappear into the vast stretches of the ocean. If Samantha is correct, finding Jacob Montgomery might take a miracle. Ships at sea are hard to find. Even flying over the ocean you can look out for hours and not see a ship and when one is lost many times the remains are never found. After this revelation, I think I can use that beer. We go inside and find a table.

The waitress is a thin twenty something blond with a dark tan. From her accent, she is a local girl. She looks us over and asks if we are vacationing here. Samantha pipes in "yes, we are just staying a few days and then heading to Florida." Our waitress smiles and goes to get us our drinks. Then Samantha looks at me and says "I think we should look into getting rooms for the night. You don't want to make a liar out of me do you? I mean we have to sleep somewhere. Maybe we should rent a car and let

Agent Woodle fly back to New York, give ourselves a bit of mystery to whoever is tattling on us." At that, John starts laughing out loud. A few people in the restaurant look over at us and both Samantha and I break into laughter. This case is starting to get to all of us. Maybe she's right and we should make plans for where we will be staying tonight. If there is a mole, cutting ties with other field offices is a good place to start.

When the waitress returns Samantha starts to ask her questions about the island and whether the really rich people ever come here by yacht. The waitress tilts her head and thinks about it for a moment and then replies "We don't see any big boats on the river. I don't think its deep enough plus there's no place to tie up. Now and then a yacht anchors out in Saint Andrews Sound. If you follow Riverview Road over to Beach View Drive you can park in a parking lot on St. Andrews Road, there's a path out to the beach. From there you can see ships out in the sound now and then. Sometimes we locals go out there and picnic. It's a bit of a walk down the path to the beach and the tourists don't go there. The waves are also bigger and a few guys try to surf. You should really ask Jimmy, our bartender, he's the one who takes his board over there every chance he gets. I've gone to watch him a couple times. Jimmy works nights so you can catch him then or head out to the beach yourself. He and his group should be out there right now." Samantha thanks her and she leaves to check on other tables.

We really haven't gotten any closer to Montgomery but we now know it's possible that a small boat from the Lady Grey may have tied up here and they could have made their escape out to sea. As we are walking back toward the hotel, I hear a ping on my phone announcing an incoming email. I stop to look and see it's from my team with a report on Calvin, Anastasia and Maya Montague. Calvin Montague is a very successful corporate financier from Austin, Texas. Anastasia and Maya are his natural born daughters. They were born two years apart. Shortly after Maya's birth while breast feeding, Ellen, his wife, noticed tenderness and a rash around her nipple. One month later, she was diagnosed with a very aggressive form of breast cancer. She fought it for three years before losing her battle. This left Calvin as their sole parent. Rather than push the girls off on nannies or family, Calvin built an addition on his house and moved his office staff into his home. For the past five years, he has successfully built his business and grown his company. Earlier this year, he got zoning past to build an office building on his ranch so that he can increase his staff. I still want to talk to him but I now don't think he has any connection to the Co-Op. A field agent in the Virgin Island will speak with him as soon as the ship docks. I send the team a message to start looking into the Lady Grey. Since Montague seems to be a dead end, our next path has to be the location of Montgomery's boat.

The investigation has wrapped up in the hotel room and we have no clues to continue. I get permission to cut Agent Woodle and the plane loose and the Atlanta field office arranges for a car rental to be delivered to the island. Since this hotel is about three times the bureau's budget, we book three adjoining rooms in a hotel that is on the beach front. If nothing else, we can get a good night sleep before leaving the island. Once in the room I turn on the news. The lead story is about a tropical storm in the Atlantic. It's refreshing to see the news focusing on something other than our investigation.

We end up in an ocean view suite. This arrangement works best. This suite has a big dining room table, large wall mounted TV and a walk out balcony that overlooks the Atlantic Ocean. It's a nice night and Samantha opens the large glass door letting in the warm early evening air and the smell of the ocean. It seems our biggest decision of the evening is room service or eating out. We opt for carry out and a couple bottles of wine. We manage to find a place that sells barbecue chicken, corn bread, corn on the cob and baked beans. While we are waiting for the order to be packed up, Samantha walks down to the bakery and comes back with a chocolate cheese cake. She also found a liquor store and picks up a bottle of white and 2 bottles of red wine already chilled.

We eat dinner out on the lounge chairs on the balcony watching the sun sink down behind the ocean waves. In the distance, we can see the leading edge of the hurricane. The setting sun lights up the long thin tropical bands. There might be a decision soon to leave the island and head mainland to avoid being caught in the storm.

While I eat, I sit there contemplating Samantha Callahan. She's amazing. I have to remind myself this woman spent over ten years in jail for a murder she didn't commit. I have spent the last few days dragging her around the east coast. She has been able to adapt and go with the flow with everything I have thrown at her. On top of that, the ashes of her daughter are currently sitting on a table in the conference room adjacent to my office. She has taken everything in stride. It amazes me that she doesn't hold any anger or resentment. Instead, she made the best of things and improved herself. She has been an important part of this team and has been invaluable. I'm really getting use to having her around and turning to her to help sort this out. Even today when she took the lead, I was willing to follow her because I trust her judgment. When she said the money Montgomery was going to help her get a new life, I believe that was her intention. When it didn't happen, she grabbed the next best opportunity. It takes a strong person to be able to change their life as much as she hers. Now as the light fades, I watch as she picks chicken off a breast and dips it in extra sauce. Between each bite, she licks and sucks the sauce off her fingers. She's lounging back on the chair with her feet propped up and the plate on the arm of her chair. Once in a while, she takes a bite of corn bread or a fork full of beans. She looks over her plastic cup of wine at me and smiles, "classy glasses we have here, compliments of the ice bucket in the bathroom. Remind me next time to at least steal some coffee cups from the coffee in the lobby." Even her sense of humor works with the team and our ability to cope.

In all my years on the job, I have never had a witness or victims family member that I have gotten this close to. In the back of my mind, I wonder what will happen when this case is closed. At some point my boss is either going to tell us to put the case in storage or we will catch Montgomery and find Kali's killer. I'm not sure what will happen to Samantha after that. I wonder if being part of this is keeping her from starting her life over. She's still young and very attractive. At some point, she is going to have to deal with her daughter's remains and go back home. I don't even know if she knows a place to call home. She has no living family and no house to go back to. I wonder if I am hurting her or helping her by keeping her with me.

I also wonder why I have kept her with me. Ever since the morning we went for a run in Chincoteague, I have kept her by my side. At first I told myself it was to protect her from the media and let her fill in missing information from Kali's kidnapping. That should have ended in Layton. In the dark listening to the waves rolling in to shore I wonder why I'm not willing to let her go. I refill my plastic cup with wine and notice we have drained the last bottle. John looks at his watch and yawns. Then gets up, dumps his trash in the can and says good night as he heads off to bed. I ask Samantha if she wants to walk with me and see if the liquor store is still open.

Walking up the sidewalk, she links her arm in mine. Most of the stores have closed for the night. Music comes out the doors of a couple bars and restaurants as we pass. Out of a candy store the smell of caramel popcorn permeates the air; it imbedded itself in the bricks and mortar of the building. A couple approaches us on the sidewalk. They are walking hand in hand and I smile to myself, they look no different than Samantha and I. If this had been another time, another set of circumstances, maybe Samantha and I could be a couple on vacation taking an evening walk down the main street of a resort town. We get to the liquor store and go inside grabbing two bottles of Sangria.

We walk back in silence. There is something about the night that lends itself to thinking about your life. I look over at Samantha in the muted glow of the street lights. She is looking down at the cracks in the sidewalk as we walk. She isn't even looking up as we pass stores. There are times I wonder what she's thinking. She has learned to keep so much to herself and be so self contained. A couple times at night, I have woken to the sounds of her crying in the dark in her room. I can't blame her and I left her alone. I wonder if I should have gone to comforted her. I also wonder at what point I cross the line between agent investigating the murder of her daughter and a man who has grown to care and respect her. I have always kept myself from becoming involved with a victim or their families. An agent can lose his judgment if he does that and mistakes can happen. Getting too involved with a case has lost a job for more than one agent. Of course there's always that one case in someone's career that changes their life. If this case is as big as I think it might be, this is the case of my life. If the Co-Op is the size and scope we have been led to believe, Kali Callahan's body appearing in the marshes of Assateague Island is the window into a world that will, once broken, keep people up at night.

We reach the hotel and ride up the elevator standing on opposite sides of the car. After I swipe the room key, I hold the door open for her and once inside take a bottle from the bag. While I open the bottle, she goes out to the balcony and gets our glasses. I can feel some sort of unspoken distance between us now. The magic seems to have evaporated somewhere between the sidewalk and the door to our room. I take my drink and go back out onto the balcony.

Samantha joins me and sits back in the lounge chair closing her eyes after taking a drink she sighs, "Adam, I've been thinking a lot tonight. Maybe this is the first time since I was released from jail that I have time to think past the moment. We have been traveling and interviewing people, then moving on. Everything has been so fast paced. At some point, I'm going to need to stop and figure out my life from here."

"Right now-- all I have is today. I don't know what I will do tomorrow. I haven't thought that far ahead. At some point I am going to have to figure out where I'm going. I am so lost and I feel like I am drifting. In jail I had a room and board. Everything was structured and planned for me. Now, I have no idea what I am supposed to do. I need to find someplace for Kali. My daughter died and I can't cry for her anymore because she has been dead for eleven years in my mind."

"I have to find a place to live. To me one place is as good as another. I could take a map and stick a pin in it and call it home. I have to get a job. I know I have a couple hundred thousand dollars in the bank right now because the state of New York paid me off for sending me to jail. I don't feel like that money's really mine. Its blood money for ten lost years while my daughter's kidnapper walked free."

"That's why I want Montgomery. He stole eleven years of my life, not the state of New York. They were just duped into believing his lies. And, it hurts so bad to hear these women who have graduated from this little pedophile club tell me time after time my daughter was better off being in the hands of that bastard then struggling to get by with me. They remind me what a piece of shit I was. I don't think people realize that there's no pride in being poor. There's certainly no pride selling your body and your soul so that you can put food in your baby's mouth, but I did what I had to do. I can't regret finding a way to survive."

"Okay, I was a piece of shit whore who got herself knocked up. I sold myself, I stole what we couldn't buy and maybe they are right Kali led a life in rich luxury but it wasn't their right to make that choice for her. It certainly wasn't their right to pin the blame on me. Regardless, I remade myself and learned why these bastards do what they do. I got into his mind and the minds of the men around him that he calls his friends. I always dreamed when I got out that I would help women like myself who had a child disappear and I would help the kids who were victims of these scumbags. In knowing how they think and what motivates them, I see a brief glimpse into their world."

"Right now, I think we need to rethink what we are doing with Kali's death. We have two cases in front of us. Tiff thought recently she may have gone to someone else who wanted a wife or adult mistress on the side of his happy little life. She was pregnant at the time she was killed but her uterus and baby were cut out and she was left to die."

"If this was the killer's baby, he had something to hide from someone. I don't know whether just arresting Montgomery will bring justice to Kali. He at least kept her alive and if you isolate the sexual abuse from the rest of her life, she lived a life of luxury. We started out chasing Jacob Montgomery but, we haven't even begun to look for who killed her. That person is walking away from this without even a mention in the news. We still don't know who Kali was with on Assateague and who killed her. Adam, do you have any idea the scope of the Co-Op and who we might be up against? If what these women have been saying is true, we are talking a large group of people who have been outside the law since before we were born. This sounds like an organized group who has some sort of governing body that facilitates the exchange of human lives!"

I have to admit to Samantha that all this has crossed my mind. My hope is that once we find Montgomery he will talk and fill us in on the details. In my mind, there may be hundreds of victims, maybe thousands. When you look into all the child disappearances over the years, the figures are staggering. This case has the potential to be bigger than my team can handle and we may never know all of those involved. Right now my focus is on Kali. We have to take her disappearance one step at a time. We need to talk to Montgomery and find out who and where Kali went when she was traded back to the Co-Op. These are the only clues that we have until something new comes along.

I look at my watch and realize it is after 1:00 AM. I have no idea what tomorrow will bring and make the decision to turn in for the night. I realize in my semi drunken state my best move is to put some distance between Samantha and I before I do something that could side line my career. Whatever this is with Samantha has to be sorted out after this case is closed.

DAY 9
JEKYLL ISLAND, GEORGIA

Morning comes and still off in the distance we can see the outer bands of the storm far out over the ocean. We grab breakfast and flip through the news. The lead story is the pending storm. It currently covers over four hundred miles of open ocean and is building. Overnight it went from a category two to a category three storm with expectation that it will build to a category four sometime today. I check my email and call into the office. Nothing has changed. The Lady Grey is still unaccounted for somewhere in the ocean. The interview with Montague has concluded with no evidence linking him to Jacob Montgomery. Montague claims they had never met and the first time he heard of Jacob Montgomery was on the news while on board the cruise ship. Background investigations have found no link between the two men so Montague is released and allowed to continue on his trip with his daughters. We head out for the day to talk to the surfers on the local beach.

Our hotel has a bike rental stand and we rent three bicycles for the day. Samantha hasn't ridden in close to twenty years so we spend a few minutes letting her get use to it once again. Then we head south on Beach View Drive. The guy who rented the bikes told us if we want to check out the southern point of the island and look over St Andrews Sound, we should ride to the Glory Beach Boardwalk and follow the boards to the beach. Then walk south along the water to the point. Our bikes come with chains and key locks and we are advised to lock them up so that no one borrows them while we spend our day at the beach.

The island is flat and we make good time. It is three and a half miles from our hotel to the path for Glory Beach Boardwalk. The boardwalk is nothing more than a path from the road to a field and then a wooden walkway to the beach. We are told once we reach the end of the boardwalk turn right and walk about three quarters of a mile to the point. We will know we are there when we see the decaying ribs of a ship wreck on the beach. From there if we look out we will see St. Andrews Sound and the Hole. When we asked, we are told the Hole is just the deepest part of the water at the mouth of St. Andrews Sound. That's where the water runs the fastest as it enters the Sound and then into Jekyll Island Sound as it rounds the point of the island.

There is a strong breeze blowing when we reach the beach. As we walk, now and then, we have to turn our backs to the wind coming off the water as it picks up sand and blows it around. The storm out in the Atlantic has churned up the ocean and the waves pounding the shore are five to six feet high as they crest and roll onto the beach. The beach is unprotected and away from the hotels and with the storm brewing few have ventured out onto the sand. As we walk, Samantha occasionally bends down and picks up a shell and puts it in her pocket. We have all taken off our shoes and are walking in the hard packed sand. With each wave the water comes up and rushes over our feet. Sea gulls fly over us with interest looking to see if we have anything they might want to eat or if the surf is kicking up anything they might be interested in. It's been a long time since I just walked on the beach. It's relaxing and the sand feels good under my feet.

John occasionally picks up a shell and throws it watching it skip across the incoming waves. We watch as a sea gull swoops down to catch a thrown shell as it hits the water then spits it out disappointed it isn't food. After two weeks of investigating this case this is a great break. I point out ahead in the ocean there are a couple people on surf boards. My guess this is one of the people out in the water is Jimmy, the bartender from the Waterfront Café.

We pass a spot where it looks like the locals have an occasional beach bonfire. A pile of charred wood sits in the center of a ring of large pieces of drift wood set up like benches. A few feet away are the towels and beach blankets of the surfers. A few women lay out on blankets in bikini's tanning. Two ATVs are parked near the dunes with coolers strapped to the back.

As we approach, a blonde woman puts down her book and looks at us, then stands up and walks toward us and says hi. I realize it is our waitress from yesterday. "So you decided to check out the surf scene. Welcome to the Point. Well actually the point is down there where you see something sticking up out of the sand. That's an old ship wreck from years ago. It's pretty much rotted away now. It just looks like a dinosaur. This is where we surf. Well actually the guys surf and we lay out making sure they don't wipe out and drown. Let's just say I keep my phone handy to dial 911 if I need to." She turns and looks out over the ocean and holds her hand up over her eyes squinting from the sun's rays glistening off the water. She raises her hands and points out to a guy lying on his board out beyond the breakers. "There on the red board. That's Jimmie. He's pretty excited about the waves today. They normally aren't over about four feet but today he's gotten to ride a few he thinks are about seven. The storm is bringing in better waves then we normally see."

We watch as he starts to paddle and then stands up on his board as he catches one of the bigger rollers coming in. As he gets close to shore, our waitress starts to wave her arms and yell to him. Jimmie comes in from the water and pushes the tip of his board into the sand as he walks toward us. "Hey, Darla. What's up?"

She looks at him and smiles. I notice her posture has improved as he gets near and she makes sure she pulls her shoulders back and sucks in her stomach. I'd say Darla does more than just sun bath while Jimmie surfs. "Hey, these guys were in the restaurant yesterday and they were asking about big ships that might anchor here. I told them if anyone knew if a ship had been here you would. Hey, you want a beer or anything? I got some in my cooler. You've been out in the water for a while. You thirsty?"

He reaches down and grabs a towel and nods his head at her. She smiles again and turns to run up to the ATV. When she gets there she turns around and looks at us "Hey, you guys want a beer too? I got a case here iced down. There's plenty if you want some. You are welcome to sit down and have a cold one with us." We agree and she comes back with a six pack in her hand.

Everyone sits down on the sand and pops the top on a beer. It's a laid back afternoon and the local surfer crowd welcomes us as one of them. The other girls run up and grab some beers and the guys come in from the water and sink their boards in the sand. As everyone sits down, I let them know I'm an FBI agent investigating a case. At first they are afraid I'm going to bust them for drinking on a beach but I let them know its fine. This is not a public section of beach and I'm planning on sitting there with them having a beer.. What I need is information on whether a ship has been docked in the Sound in the last few days.

A surfer name Bogs answers "Yeah, there was this big ass ship here. It was sweet. I saw it two days ago. It was anchored just north of the hole. I was out here with a buddy surfing and saw it sail in. At first I thought it was an old fashioned pirate ship. I watched it out in the ocean under full sail. It was beautiful. I could see it a long way off and was surprised when it came in close to the island and dropped anchors. Now and then out in the distance, we can sometimes see the tall ships sailing but, I have never seen one sail this close to the island before, let alone drop anchor."

I ask him if he noticed the name of the ship. "No man sorry. I may have seen the name but I don't remember. I was too busy watching them stow the sails. I figured it was one of the ships that had been in Savannah and it was on its way to the thing in Florida. I thought they had to kill some time before sailing into Florida for the weekend so they anchored here. A while later, I saw them lower a smaller motor boat and head into the sound. So I guess they stopped for some food or something."

While not confirming this was the Lady Grey, they confirmed Samantha's suspicion that it was possible Montgomery and Sidney left the island on the tall ship. It could just be a coincidence but it is also very probable the ship anchored off the island was the Lady Grey and it stopped to pick up two passengers from the island.

We have to walk back up the beach and bike ride back to the hotel so we thank the group for the beers and head back. The bands of clouds block the sun more and more as the storm gets closer to shore. When it happens the clouds cast shadows on the beach and the air gets colder. I think it's time to get back to the hotel in case it rains.

The trip back is uneventful and by the time we return the bikes it is after five. We head upstairs in the hotel to get a shower and then out to dinner. Tonight we opt for dinner at our hotel. They are having a beach party with a jazz band out by the pool. We join what is becoming a dwindling group of guests at the hotel. With the threat of a hurricane, we are told many guests cancelled their reservations or left early to be away before the storm. I can't say I blame them. Overhead we still see stars most of the night but now and then they are blocked from view. It is impressive to watch this storm develop. It is still over four hundred miles from shore yet its bands are reaching out to us already. We spend the night eating and listening to the jazz band. At about ten, we are all feeling the effects of long days and short nights and head back to our suite for the night. I think I am asleep before my head hits the pillow.

DAY 10
JEKYLL ISLAND, GEORGIA

The morning is gray and a little cooler then yesterday. The cloud bands of the storm passing over head are thicker but morning news still puts the storm way off the coast. I check in with the office. With no current leads, we should head back for Richmond. Instead we are instructed to stay for another day. The Lady Grey is somewhere in the Atlantic Ocean. The Coast Guard has issued a maritime warning for ships at sea in the path of the storm. All vessels are advised to head to the southern Atlantic to ride it out.

Currently, the storm is covering over six hundred miles of ocean with a projected path making landfall in North Carolina, then follow the coast up into the Canadian Maritime. The storm coming across the country should join up with the hurricane sometime today forming a super cell. It will hit the steering winds from the Arctic Low currently sweeping along the Canadian providences late on the thirty-first or early on November first. Weather forecasters are calling this a perfect storm.

We eat breakfast at a beach side cafe watching the waves rolling in. They have gotten bigger since yesterday. I'm sure Jimmie and the other surfers are out on their boards trying to catch today's waves before the heavy wind and rain starts. Jekyll Island should only get brushed by the storm. There are news crews hanging around both for us and the storm so we have to be careful what we talk about sitting outside in public. We move the discussion from the beach to the suite. With nothing else to follow up on right now I decide it's time to take advantage of our expert and take a stab at defining a profile of those we are chasing and their associates. I make a pot of coffee and we set up around the table in the center room. Samantha opens the door to the patio letting the breeze blow in off the ocean. The storm has taken a lot of the humidity out of the air and it feels quite pleasant.

She then gets a cup of coffee and sits down. "I'm not sure where to start because this is a subject that has many layers. The obvious two are the perpetrator and their victim but there is a third and much bigger group, the people behind the veil of silence. You see we encounter people every day as we go about our lives and they make judgments about us. Normally you would think a judgment is something critical but people usually want to think the best about people."

"Let's take the profile of our perpetrators. These are men and women of money and power. For many of them because they have money, people automatically hand over power to them. For example, if you walk into a doctor's office you hand power to the doctor to tell you what is wrong with you and after allowing them to examine you, they tell you something like you have high blood pressure. Normally a person does not question a doctor unless they don't agree with the diagnosis. Then they will get a second opinion. We believe the person with the power because we are taught to do that. The same thing happens with the veil of silence. Someone who is a doctor, lawyer, business executive, banker or whatever the case may be, we recognize them as being someone in control and we believe them. They can't be wrong, they are successful people."

"In the instance of the doctor, what we might not know is that a pharmaceutical representative has visited them recently and told them if they can switch so many existing patients and prescribe to so many new patients for a new medication they will get a three night stay in a Las Vegas hotel. Your blood pressure may only be on the high side of normal or you may have eaten licorice in the waiting room, which raises blood pressure, but the doctor only sees that your blood pressure is high normal and he can get double points toward getting a weekend in Vegas. So he writes the prescription. As long as you fill the prescription he gets the points. If in a few days you almost pass out or you feel really out of it and the doctor tells you to take half a pill or don't take it until after you come back for a follow up. Maybe you can try to control your blood pressure right now with diet and exercise because your body reacts drastically to the medicine. In reality, you didn't need the medicine yet and the mild change in diet and lowering weight a few pounds would have solved the problem without medication. Yet, no one would ever believe their doctor didn't have their best interests at heart. Instead it is that their body is very sensitive to medication and the doctor had to take them off and try something else. We don't want to believe a person in power could do something wrong."

"It is hard to envision anyone deliberately hurting a child, especially someone who has a successful career. We want to think of the bad guys as some dirty man hiding behind a dumpster waiting to grab a passing child. We don't think of them as a family friend or favorite relative. Yet most child abusers first get contact with a child through the parent. Then they befriend the child and get the child to like and trust them. Little by little they begin to touch the child until what began as an innocent tickle becomes a sexual encounter. The Co-op is slightly different. Now and then it appears a child may be handed over to a Co-op member by the parent to help the child. From what I have heard abduction and coercion are more useful tools to them. They give the children what they are lacking in their regular world. The abuser becomes the person who gives them security, hot food, a warm place to sleep, toys and clothing they didn't have in their prior life."

"Of course the abusers are not going to talk. The victims don't see themselves as victims so they are silent. I think we need to focus on the third group. The people who interact with the abusers every day more than likely see the abuser with their victim on a regular basis, but they convince themselves that there is nothing bad about the relationship. We just encountered the justification at the hotel. Jacob Montgomery showed up with a child. Without asking it was assumed she was his daughter. He didn't want a roll up bed and he said the sofa would be fine for her and no one questioned it. My guess the pillow and blanket were never moved once they were put in the room. Yet the cleaning staff didn't question a young girl sleeping with a grown man. They mentally made excuses for the behavior. Everyone who sat around Jacob Montgomery and Sidney Harris at the concert and charity auction assumed she was his daughter. They created a veil around them and mentally created a picture that made his actions okay."

"People are afraid to ask questions. They are afraid to go to the authorities if they have any suspicion because they are afraid of what will happen if they are wrong and the situation is completely innocent. Instead, we tell ourselves it isn't our business or we are imagining things. Even if someone steps forward and asks for help, people are afraid to get involved. I'm sure you have seen this in your interviews and I know you have seen it on the news when they interview the neighbors. The first thing out of most people's mouths is that they can't believe this happened, or that the person next door was capable of something like that. They are such nice people."

"I sat in a seminar once taught by an FBI agent. He was addressing the veil of silence. In his case, he was talking about the 9/11 terrorists. For almost a year, people lived next door to these men. They saw them outside the apartment building. They were behind them at the grocery store. People interacted with them every day. Yet, no one questioned why a group of men lived together, didn't have jobs and said they went to college but never attended a class. Only a few people even questioned why someone would be interested in learning how to fly a plane, yet not care about landing. Normally the first thing someone wants to do is learn how to land. They want to be able to make it back down on the ground without crashing. Only after they crashed the planes did people who were in class with them ask that question. The instructor who did report it commented that it fell on deaf ears because it was never investigated. No one thought someone would learn to fly a plane so that they could hijack it and fly it into the side of a building to commit suicide. Yet, that is exactly what they did."

"At some point in this case, we are going to have to come forward telling people Jacob Montgomery kidnapped Kali, then he may have had another girl, and now has been involved in kidnapping Sidney Harris. We will have to shock them and tell them that he sexually molested them. He raped them. He made them perform sexual acts on him. He took their innocence and crafted them into child sex slaves. People need to get the picture in their mind that he can do bad things in order for them to come forward and tell us what they saw. These people have convinced themselves that what they saw with their own eyes wasn't bad. It will take shock and awe to break them from the delusion they have created and we are going to have to make them mad at him. This will break the veil and people will come forward. My guess, after we catch him, the walls of the Co-op will start to fall. People will start to question things they have seen in the past. I think these people have lived in a house of cards and as long as they can keep people believing in their power and position in life they can do no wrong."

"As for the victims we have a very long road ahead of us. Since the pattern indicated the children all come from homes where they struggled to survive, they have mentally accepted any pain or feelings of being uncomfortable as a payoff for the life they now lead. Not being hungry every night or cold when they sleep far outweighs the pain of intercourse in the mind of an eight year old. Intercourse only lasts a few minutes, hungry lasts until your next meal and when there is an uncertainty when that might be it is not hard to justify the two or three minutes of sexual trauma."

"I have talked to prostitutes and know from my own experiences one of the things women do while having sex for money is to count the number of strokes it takes for a man to orgasm. You begin to average how long it takes and lay there and count. The closer you get to the average the closer you are to knowing he will be getting off of you soon and this will be over. Then you take your money and move on. I assume these children having similar coping mechanisms. They might practice their counting in a foreign language. Then they get their sexual obligation and their homework out of the way at the same time. The victim becomes very disconnected from their bodies. It helps create numbness and allows you to hide behind the veil of silence as well. If you can drift off and think of something else it will pass the time until it is over and you can move on."

"I wonder about Jacob Montgomery. Eleven years ago he was already having trouble with erectile dysfunction and was taking medication. Eleven years on a man his age will not make the situation better. My guess is he had to train the girls to be more and more creative in order for him to maintain his erection and fulfill his needs. In the end, we will find some in the medical profession who are either part of the Co-op, paid for their silence or prefer to remain silent. These children have to occasionally have medical care. They would have frequent urinary tract issues, possibly tearing and scaring that have to be addressed. Any doctor outside the fold would take one look at these girls and be able to detect something is wrong with the situation. They would be required to report their findings. Why in the last eleven years did no one notice the scaring Kali had? I can't see that she never had an ear ache, sore throat or cold. Why did her doctor never ask about the obvious sexual trauma to her body?"

When she is finished talking I realize we missed lunch and it is dinner time. We head out of the suite and head back to the restaurant district. During the day some of the beach front places have boarded their doors and windows in case the storm track changes. I also notice the sidewalks are less crowded and it appears many tourists have left the island to avoid any danger. We find a bar that is open. The noise coming from the open door is lively and we walk inside. The discussion during the day has been intense and the live band playing on the stage with a group of drunken dancers is what we need.

We find a table in the corner and signal to a waitress. She arrives with menus and yells above the noise this is their hurricane party. The drink of the night is a pitcher of hurricanes for twelve dollars. She goes on to tell us their hurricanes are made of a mixture of rum and vanilla liquor mixed with three different tropical juices - passion fruit, orange juice and guava juice.

The alcohol flows and we are finished our first pitcher by the time our appetizers arrive. The theme of the night is wild abandon before the storm. Around us people dance and sing. The crowd is loud and lively. Life on a barrier island survives under the knowledge that any storm could remove all signs of civilization. While Jekyll Island has been inhabited for over one hundred years, what approaches is being called the storm of the century. Everyone knows this might be the one to have a direct hit and permanently put this island or another similar one permanently under water. History does repeat itself. Even today bits and pieces of buildings from Hog Island, New York wash up on Long Island and Rockaway Beach. Hog Island was an island used by Native American to raise livestock and became an amusement park and recreation park until 1893 when the eye of a hurricane made a direct hit and erased it. In a few days, what happened there could erase life here.

The owner is working behind the bar and routinely through the night he announces for everyone to eat and drink up. "If the storm turns, in two days this bar might be gone. Tonight we party and tomorrow the doors and windows get boarded up and put fate in the hands of God." Like those who live in Tornado Alley life for people who live along the coast or those on a barrier island can change at the whim of wind and water. Few people fully appreciate the power of nature until they have lived through it. I have looked out the window of my house and watched the power of water pull a two hundred year old tree from the ground by its roots and sweep it away in a heartbeat. I have also stood among toothpick sized pieces of wood that was once a family home. The surface of the planet is just a place we cling to and hope the forces of nature don't uproot us.

The second pitcher is gone by the time dinner arrives and it is followed by a third and forth. By the time the last pitcher is empty it is a challenge for the three of us to stand and walk back to our hotel. We each drank more than we should have. I blame some of our drinking on the need to chase the demons today's conversation manifested.

We stumble off the elevator and I am grateful for the invention of the swipe key to open hotel rooms. I don't think I could have managed a key with Samantha leaning on me for support. She has reached the drunk enough to need to go to bed stage. After ten years in jail, she's not use to drinking and her attempt to keep up with John and I, both seasoned professionals in alcohol tolerance, has failed. Her usual composure has slipped away and her hair which is normally immaculate has a sexy messiness about it. I head for my bed reminding myself she's drunk and beyond consent and I'm probably drunk beyond ability. Regardless, I make a mental note to check on her in a bit. She didn't drink enough for alcohol poisoning but, she will probably not feel well in the morning.

DAY 11
JEKYLL ISLAND, GEORGIA
TO COLLEGE STATION, TEXAS

I hear my phone ringing and try to pull myself from my sleep. It sounds distant and I can't remember where I left it. I open my eyes to Samantha walking into my bedroom with my phone in hand begging me to answer because her head is splitting. As I answer it, I hear her rummaging through her suitcase cussing about finding some aspirin. The voice on the other end is commanding my attention. I try to focus on the words and recognize Chip, an agent from my team. Meanwhile, I am wondering if I had just seen Samantha standing next to my bed wearing only a t-shirt. The words "letter from the Co-Op" brings me out of my stupor. I tell Chip to hold on and yell for John and Samantha. They both come running and I put my phone on speaker. I ask him to repeat everything he just said as much for my benefit as for John and Samantha's.

"Police in College Station, Texas got a call last night from a farmer who saw buzzards flying around one of his pastures. He had gone out on his four wheeler to check for a dead cow and instead found the remains of a naked man's body. His hands, feet and head had been removed and are missing from the scene. We got the call from the Dallas Field office because attached to his penis with piano wire was a note addressed to the FBI. Inside the envelope was a handwritten message 'The FBI no longer needs to investigate the Kali Callahan case. We will take care of and police our own. This man broke our rules and will never cross us again. Signed The Co-Op.' Boss, this was definitely addressed to us. Brazos County Sheriff turned the investigation over to the Dallas Field Office. With no head and hands, it will be hard to identify and my guess they wanted to pass the buck as soon as possible. We are running missing persons right now. Medical Examiner on the scene is guessing he was somewhere between eighteen and twenty-five by his muscle tone and build. Not much else to go on right now. No tattoos, scars or anything to talk about. It looks like he may have had some work done to one knee. This guy took pretty good care of what's left of his body. We will know more when we get him to autopsy and I've asked the Medical Examiner to rush the results to us. Other then no head, hands or feet the guy seemed pretty average. The letter, once again, plain white number ten envelope, just like millions of others and what looks like stock copy paper. The lab might be able to give us a little more. I can't promise much though until we find some other body parts. A finger print or some dental records would be nice. We aren't even coming up with a missing person yet. The guy looks pretty fresh. Maybe someone hasn't noticed he didn't come home last night. One more thing about the body, no blood, this wasn't our primary scene."

I hang up still sitting in bed. John stands in the doorway in sweat pants scratching his stomach hair as he thinks. Samantha looks down and suddenly realizes she is standing there wearing nothing but a t-shirt and excuses herself to go put on some clothes. Normally, I would have sat there admiring the view, instead I try to pretend I didn't notice the half naked girl in the room. Nor that the room is cold enough to make her nipples press against the material. I look at the display on my cell phone. It is now 5:28 AM. I hear the shower come on and figure Samantha is trying to wash the cob webs and alcohol out. John goes across the suite to his room to get dressed. Sleep is done for the night so I go out to the kitchenette and start a pot of coffee.

A few minutes later, Samantha walks out in sweat pants and the same t-shirt. This time I see the outline of her bra through the thin material. She grabs a cup and hovers over the coffee pot watching the stream of fluid pouring out. She finally pulls the pot out and quickly replaces it with her cup, then switches the pot back in a perfectly completed cup to coffee maker nab. Normally she puts cream and sugar in her coffee. I watch as she makes a face and takes a drink while it's still black. She looks into the cup, takes another drink and finally sits it down on the counter to put cream and sugar in the cup and stirs it. She looks up as I walk over and shake the filter cup a few times before pouring myself a cup. Her eyes are red. I put my hand on her back and tell her "this guy might not be Kali's killer. We have to find out who he was and how if any way he fits into the case." She sits her cup down and puts her head on my chest and starts to cry.

A million thoughts go through my head. The cop in me says help her go sit down and bring her the cup of coffee. The man in me tells me to put my cup down and wrap my arms around her. I listen to the man and hold her while she cries herself out. I rest my face down on her damp hair and close my eyes. Her small body shakes as she sobs. A hang over, exhaustion and reality finally break her and she gives in to a flood of tears. Then as quickly as she started, she stops and pulls away wiping her eyes and apologizing. This tough woman is embarrassed that she gave in to being human and letting emotion take over, even if only for a brief moment.

She takes her coffee and goes to a chair in the corner. "So, what now?" she asks. "Do we stay here and wait or jump on a plane to Texas? It's a lead right? We have to follow whatever leads we get. So what do we do with a headless, handless, footless man? And why the hell did someone cut off his feet? Has the FBI started foot printing people too?"

The foot removal does sound odd. Frequently hands or fingers are removed from bodies to make identification difficult but foot removal is a little different. Right now I don't have any answers. So, I pick up the phone and order room service for breakfast. Since we are probably the only guests awake at this time of morning in the resort town the food arrives before I finish getting dressed. When I walk into the center of the suite, Samantha is sitting at the table having a staring contest with a piece of French toast and some scrambled eggs. From the way she pushes the eggs around the plate, I think they have already won. Not that I expected her to eat much, I hoped she would though. Right now I don't know if we are about to make a drive to Jacksonville and fly to Texas or spend another day spinning our wheels on Jekyll Island. John has flipped open his laptop and is going back and forth between emails and files on his computer. I decide the email route is a good idea and put mine on the table next to my plate. Seeing us both about to hide in our computer screens Samantha picks up the remote and hits the button to turn on the TV.

As luck would have it, the network news is already on the scene in College Station. They switch from storm coverage to breaking news about our John

Doe. "Late yesterday afternoon, John Traynor, a College Station beef farmer, noticed buzzards circling his field. Mr. Traynor could you please tell me what you saw when you rode out to check on your herd?" John Traynor was tall lanky man with sun leathered skin. His gray hair dated him somewhere in his mid 50s, maybe older. He was dressed in work jeans and a blue t-shirt. Both looked like he'd already put in a long dirty days work on his farm. I wonder if these were the clothes he was wearing last night when he found the body. His life had been turned upside down when an army of police and reporters arrived at his farm. "I rode out on my four wheeler because it was about a mile away from my barns. There were a lot of birds so I knew it was something big. When I rode up on it I was surprised to see it wasn't a dead steer. At first I didn't think it was a man either. I had to get off and walk up to it to tell it was human. Whoever killed this guy kept his hands, feet and his head. It was pretty bad, the smell was what attracted the birds. I had my grandson with me on the back and I told him to stay on the ATV. This is the stuff that gives people nightmares."

"Was there anything else you can tell me?"

"Yeah, when I got up close I saw someone had tied a note to his…ummm…willie."

"There was a note tied to his penis?"

"Umm, yeah. It was addressed to the FBI. I knew there wasn't anything I could do for this guy and I definitely didn't want my grandson to see that so I left him there and went back and called the police. The police and FBI have been there ever since I took them out to the body. Now they won't let anyone near the field. It's bad though, real bad. Someone really cut this guy up good and left him for the buzzards." Out in the distance from the live shot the cameraman tries to focus in on the flashing lights of local police trucks, a couple SUVs and a crime scene van parked out in the middle of nowhere surrounded in total darkness. The screen switches to the reporter "an unnamed source in the police department has told us the note inside the envelope was addressed to Agent Adam Clay of the Richmond, Virginia FBI office. Agent Clay is the lead investigator in the Kali Callahan murder and the investigation into the kidnapping charges against banking mogul Jacob Montgomery. We will be following this story and bring you information as we get it. Now back to the studio." The anchor begins to rehash the case to this point and Samantha raises the remote and clicks it off. She stands up and walks to the patio and begins to open it, then suddenly shuts it and pulls the curtain closed. "Well, the press either knows where we are staying or the hurricane is heading for Jekyll Island because they are set up on the beach."

My cell phone now says its 6:15 AM. I was really hoping to not call the office back before 8:00 but with the press outside our hotel setting up on the sand means they have to know the room we are in. More than likely one of the rooms on either side of us has already been rented and microphones are set up to try to listen in on our conversation. To my surprise, the ASAC answers on the second ring. This is about three hours before he usually makes an appearance. I start to tell him the situation but he stops me. The medical examiner has rushed the report. Arrangements are already being made to get us to Jacksonville where we are catching a noon flight to College Station. The ASAC wants us out of here as soon as possible because the hurricane is closing in on the east coast. The current path puts it hitting north of our location, but late season hurricanes are very unpredictable. The drive to Jacksonville is a little over an hour. Since the press has already arrived to cover both us and the storm, he will issue a press briefing in about an hour. That should give us enough time to pack and for a driver to get to us to take us to the airport. We will be landing in College Station around five and the Sheriff will be waiting to brief us before going to the crime scene. My laptop pings with the verbiage for the official statement and a list of approved questions I can answer from the press. I then turn the TV back on and the sound way up as I walk to the shower and turn the water on full force. Luckily, the coverage has turned back to the storm. The coast from Georgia to Maine are bracing for the impact. The current storm path has it glancing by the coast of North Carolina and causing high tides and damage to the Outer Banks before a storm from Canada comes down and steers it into land. Reporters are standing on beaches giving reports from their location as the wave's crash behind them. I come back to the table and very quietly fill John and Samantha in on what is happening in College Station, Texas.

It's been a few days since I addressed the press and the office has been flooded with requests for information. I grab a shower and get dressed to face my adoring fan of reporters. Samantha has put on a pair of jeans and a short sleeve black sweater. She fluffs her hair a bit and puts on some eye liner. Even with a hangover she still looks stunning. She won't be speaking but the cameras and reporters lover her. John has opted for a pair of kaki's and a blue FBI polo shirt. The press has gathered on the beach with the hotel in the back drop. We walk out the beach exit and stand on the pool deck. Someone at the hotel has set up a podium and the sound guys from the networks have all set up their microphones. It always amazes me how prepared and fast the press are when the office calls a press conference. I guess reporting the same news gets old and their jobs depend on them getting fresh information. Today we offered them not just new information but breaking news during their live morning shows. The timing on this could not have been better. The first play will be live followed by recaps every thirty minutes leading to the noon news. It will get played again for the nightly news and for the late night. Already we are being told the morning talk programs have changed topics and are planning to discuss the case and the issue of child molesters. "Good morning. As many of you know I am Agent Adam Clay of the Richmond, Virginia FBI field office and the lead investigator of the murder of Kali Callahan. To my right is Agent John Duncan, also from the Richmond, Virginia field office. Agent Duncan heads the forensic team in the investigation. To my left is Dr. Samantha Callahan, mother of Kali and has been assisting us in psychiatric profiling of both the victims and adults involved in our case. To bring you up to speed on the direction of the investigation, first and primary is the location of Jacob Montgomery. Mr. Montgomery is wanted for questioning in the disappearance of Kali Callahan in 2001. He is also wanted for questioning in the disappearance of eight year old Sidney Harris, who is believed to currently be in his company. My office has issued pictures of both Jacob Montgomery and Sidney Harris. Yesterday evening in College Station, Texas a local rancher, John Traynor, discovered the torso of an unidentified man with a note addressed to this investigation. The body was rushed to autopsy due to the pertinent nature of this case. At this time, we do not know the identity of the man found and are asking for your help. He is estimated to be eighteen to twenty-five years old and weighed approximately one hundred and seventy-five pounds. Based on body hair he is assumed to have had blond to reddish blond hair. He had no other distinguishing features on his body. The medical examiner estimates his time of death as approximately two days ago. A Ziploc bag was found in his rectum containing a pink bikini bottom with a dried blood stain. Because the bikini bottom was protected in a container DNA testing could be done and has come back as a match to Kali Callahan." This new piece of information causes a stir through the crowd. I glance at Samantha and she is standing firm and not showing any emotion. I had been worried before we walked outside but she wanted to be able to stand next to me and look into the cameras. "We are now asking the public for their help. Please look at the pictures of both Jacob Montgomery and Sidney Harris. As for the body of the man found yesterday in Texas, even though this body has been found in Texas there is no proof that he was from there. Once again, the young man was approximately eighteen to twenty-five years old and had blond or reddish blond hair. He died sometime toward the beginning of the week but may have been missing since early October. My office has given the phone number of the FBI hotline for this case to all the networks in the press package and have asked for it to run at the bottom of the screen. If you see Jacob Montgomery, Sidney Harris or if you may have information on the body that was found yesterday in College Station, Texas please call us and. The information that you give us can be confidential. We are interested in finding Kali's killer and now the killer of this unknown young man. I will now take limited questions from the press. We have to leave soon to get to the airport and head to Texas." Arms shoot up and reporters start to shout questions. I answer those questions I am released to answer and pretend not to hear the others.

We walk straight from the press conference through the hotel lobby to a waiting SUV. The driver, Agent Craig Duggan from Jacksonville welcomes us aboard and takes off just as the horde of reporters exit the building cameras rolling as we leave for the airport. The drive to Jacksonville is quiet. Everyone is lost in thought and if they are like me trying to figure out where our body in Texas fits into Kali's story. I flip open my laptop and look at the picture of the note and the pictures from the crime scene. The writing is very steady. It always amazed me that a killer could end a life and write a note with a steady hand. This guy had been cut up, cleaned off, gift tagged and dropped off in the middle of a field to be found and deliver a message. On the surface the message tells us to leave the investigation to the Co-Op. Of course the idea is ludicrous. Anyone with any intelligence whatsoever would know that we would not stop investigating a case and allow vigilante justice to take care of their own. Plus this group, if they are half of what we are beginning to discover, is far reaching. We can't just walk away. And now we have two unsolved murders about six hundred miles apart. The second body adds to the investigation while doubling the work first to figure out how and why our body got there, and of course finding out who he was and why he was gift tagged with a note for us.

The plane we are scheduled to take is delayed due to weather conditions. Already the outer bands of the hurricane are affecting air travel in North Carolina. While we have time to kill before our flight, Samantha announces she's going to walk to the computer store on the airport concourse and asks if either John or I know anything about buying computers. We're guys and love gadgets, we both laugh and grab our bags to help Samantha buy a laptop. In twenty minutes, we have helped pick out a laptop, talked to the computer expert and figured out what software she needs. They promise to have the computer loaded, charged and ready before our flight is called. Moments later we are checking out, Samantha has a box in her hand for an eBook and the slip from the install desk for her computer and software.

As we walk out of the store, she looks around, spies a coffee shop and makes a bee line to it. Before she walks in, she looks and sees a WiFi sticker on the outside. John and I look at each other, shrug and follow her inside where she orders coffee for all of us and while we she finds a seat and begins to unpack her eBook. I laugh when we get to the table. She's already plugged it in to charge and is surfing the online book store for something to read. She reaches for her coffee, looks at me and says "you do know prison has changed and we are allowed to use computers. All my text books were on an eBook. They were cheaper for the prison system, plus you can't hide something inside an eBook. They are approved for prison use. Not that I was considered a violent inmate. They pretty much gave me free reign in the library and I took advantage of the online library as well. I had a lot of time on my hands for ten years. I am use to reading a lot. Plus, in case you guys haven't noticed, you spend a lot of time staring into your computer screens. I need something to do and I'm not getting back on another plane with nothing to do but stare at the back of someone's head for three hours. It's been weeks since I checked my email. I happen to have a lot of men who send me love letters. Now that I'm out I have probably lost my appeal, after all I'm no longer a bad girl but still, I do have a life!" John and I try not to laugh but when Samantha cracks up we both lose it. Of course knowing Samantha has an email address also makes me curious. What if someone involved in Kali's kidnapping has tried to contact her; we may have had a clue there all along. I had never thought to ask her about having email. I make a mental note to spend some time talking to her about prison life sometime She's right, things really have changed and the use of computers has changed even prison life and more than likely made smarter criminals.

After picking up her laptop, we head to the terminal to wait for our plane to be called. Our flight finally arrives and passengers begin to depart. I make a quick check with the car rental office at Easterwood Airport to make sure our rental will be ready when we land. Minutes later our plane is called.

We are booked on a mid-size commuter plane. About half the seats are full, but we are able to stretch out. Our plane swings out over the Atlantic Ocean before turning and heading toward Texas. The storm is visible out our window. Even from the air the clouds stretch as far as I can see. This storm is a monster. I wonder where in the Ocean the Lady Grey is and who is currently on board. Even if someone is running to escape the law, the last thing they should be doing is sailing into.

Once in the air, we are cleared to take out our computers and most of the passengers seem to be business men who open up their laptops and get back to work. I check email, as across the aisle, John pushes his seat back and closes his eyes. Samantha is sitting next to me at the window and looks out for a few minutes before turning on her eBook and starts to read. I wake up to the flight attendant tapping me on the shoulder and telling me we are about to land and I need to stow our electronics. Samantha's head is on my shoulder and her eBook has slid between our seats. I carefully retrieve it and slip it into my computer case. She wakes up as we begin to ascend.

Easterwood Airport is owned by the university with a well stocked rental car fleet. I chose a SUV from their fleet because I'm not sure how much off road we might have to do to get to the crime scene. From the news camera view it looked like it could kill a town car. The vehicle comes equipped with GPS. Since my one and only experience with Texas has been a week spent on a case in Waco I know the GPS will come in handy. One thing I learned about Texas, there are main roads, side roads, dirt roads and places the locals called roads that looked more like a cattle path then some place to drive a vehicle.

John and I settle in the front seat and Samantha sits in the middle of the back so that she has a view out the windshield. The area is pretty, populated with large homes and well manicured lawns. I suspect many belong to professors and administrators at the college. The land is flat and it is not hard to see the town of Bryan, Texas approaching. Our first stop is the Brazos County Sheriff's office to meet with the head of Criminal Investigations.

The officer at the front desk directs us into a conference room where a few other officers are talking to a closed circuit television. As we walk in, all stand and Sheriff Dewey Tarr offers his hand to introduce himself and his team. On the screen is Travis County Medical Examiner Dr. Doug Witting. Dr. Witting is the medical examiner who has been handling our John Doe. After introductions, Dr. Witting begins by apologizing for not making the drive to Bryan to meet in person but his office is one hundred and five miles away in Austin. "I'm sorry I didn't have the time to make the drive out to meet with you in person but we had an all hands on deck traffic accident this morning. We had too many people coming in to lose a pair of hands for the entire day. I'm sure you are a little confused about why your body was found south of College Station and his body was taken to Austin. The Travis County Medical Examiner handles the entire Austin-Round Rock Metropolitan area. Our team has to handle every death inquiry for nine hundred and eighty-nine square miles of land and thirty-three square miles of water ways. So we are a busy place."

"Your body of course is downstairs in our morgue until we hopefully make an identification and notification. We thought it was better for you to be nearer the crime scene then to have to make the drive out to me. You are welcome to do so if you would like, but we can handle most of what we need to this way. "

"I have sent ahead some of the toxicology reports and the pictures from the autopsy. Your body had given us very few clues other then the gallon sized zip lock bag we recovered from the rectum. We sent both the zip lock bag and its contents to our second floor toxicology lab. It was there that we had a positive identification with your female crime scene victim in Virginia. That and the note that was attached to his body indicates our victim is closely attached to yours."

I ask Dr. Witting what he can tell us about the male victim. "I am guessing he was eighteen to twenty-five years old. He took care of his body. His muscle structure shows a lot of time at the gym and from prior injuries to his knees and an old rib break I would guess he was an athlete. He has had surgery at some point on his left knee. There were signs of a meniscus tear that was repaired and a reattached ligament. Healed stress fractures shows that he had done some running, not as much recently, but there were the typical signs of pounding some pavement for long periods of time. I wouldn't say a marathoner though. His muscles weren't that long, more bunched like what I see in weightlifters. He also had well defined chest and abdominal muscles. This guy was lean and in good shape. Body hair tells me he had strawberry blond to blond hair. He had a nice tan from being outside so his skin was accustomed to exposure. Other then the breaks and the laparoscopic scars from the knee surgery there were no other distinguishing marks. His body had some light bruising on his wrists and ankles. I'd say he was bound prior to death. His hands, feet and head were removed post mortem. Prior to their removal his body had some time to lie on his back. The pooling is indicative of lying in that position for a few hours. Toxicology found a high concentration of both alcohol and Oxycodone in his blood. That combined with his stomach contents gives us some idea of the last few hours of the victim's life. Roughly two hours prior to death he consumed a steak, salad, baked potato and lobster tail. With that he drank a significant quantity of beer. I can't tell you whether this was an accidental death with dismemberment or a murder with dismemberment. I can tell you that the alcohol and Oxycodone levels in his body were more than likely the cause of death. He was a big man and from his body style he probably had a lot of fight in him. Drugging him may have been a way to subdue him. After he became unconscious or after death, he would be a lot to handle and move. The crime scene showed no signs of blood or struggle. It appears to be a secondary crime scene. If the body was dumped by one person they were very strong. I would consider two or three people needed to move his body. If I get hold of one of his hands, feet or his head I may be able to tell you more. His DNA is not in the system but we do have one anomaly that we have turned over to the Brazos Sheriff. Dewey would you like to handle it from here?"

Sheriff Tarr nods his head and takes over, "The DNA came back with a usual circumstance. Originally there was a match to Senator Duke Braden." I see Samantha's head turn and her face took on a quizzical look. "As you know Senator Braden has been hospitalized for the past month with a stroke. I of course confirmed with both his office and the hospice where he is staying and he is currently on a feeding tube and non responsive. The primary care doctor in Bethesda, Maryland told me it is only a matter of days before he passes. He is obviously not our victim. We then contacted his wife, Helen, to see if there were any other close male relatives and for her to confirm their whereabouts. The Braden's have two sons. One is in medical school in Baltimore, Maryland and the other is out of the country doing missionary work in South America. He is working with AIDs victims in the tribal regions of the Amazon. While both sons fit the physical profile, neither was in Texas in the last month and both have contacted their mother in the last week to inquire on their father's condition. The youngest son, Tyler will be coming home in two days from the Amazon to see his father one last time. His mother is worried he won't make it in time but it took a while to contact him because of the region he is working. The hospice has confirmed his other son, Joshua, has been visiting his father regularly."

"Now if you would like I can escort you out to the Traynor farm so that you can take a look at the crime scene. If we are going to do this today we need to get a move on. The sun will be setting in about seventy minutes."

We all thank Dr. Witting and head out to our vehicles. We follow Sheriff Tarr out onto the highway and head toward College Station. The twenty-five minute drive takes us through quite of bit of the college farm complex. The college is world renowned for their agricultural program and the facilities look immaculate as we pass. Interspersed around the farm complex are large houses, some bordering on mansions. Once again the landscaping surrounding the houses are well maintained works of horticulture. As we leave the farm complex and head out along the Brazos River, we begin to see fenced in properties with stone gateways and locked gates. I assume the driveways go to houses along the river. The road begins to narrow and the trees start to close in on the road and the black top turns to stone and finally a dirt road. Through the trees I can see buildings off in clearings in the woods. Most look like barns or storage sheds. Cleared areas are planted or grazing cattle can be seen.

Traynor Ranch is out on a peninsula on the Brazos River. On the map it looks like a tonsil of land. The house is built just before the peninsula. It's a big house with a few out buildings hidden in the woods and a swimming pool and picnic area with a patio connected to the back of the house. From the look of John Traynor on the news, I never thought the man on the TV lived in a house this nice but looks are deceiving. We pull up to the stone gate adorned with the Lone Star emblem in the wrought iron of the fence. The ends of the gate hold tall flag poles flying the Texas flag. Sherriff Tarr pushes a buzzer and the gate starts to creak open. With that a pack of dogs appear from nowhere and stand back from the gate waiting for our entrance.

John Traynor saunters out of the house and tries to shoo the dogs away from our SUV and yells "you all don't mind the dogs and come on out. If they sense fear they get a little feisty. So just ignore them and they will leave you alone." I take a deep breath and open my door. I figure today might be the day I become dog food in Texas but, as I step out the dogs continued to run around the vehicles barking. It seems they don't like SUVs, the humans inside mean nothing to them.

Sandy Traynor walks out on the porch with a pitcher of sweet tea and some glasses and yells to us to "come on out of the heat and get a glass of tea. You've been driving and I bet you are thirsty. Now John Traynor make sure you drink something before you go out to the spit to show them where they want to go. I don't want you getting dizzy from dehydration again! Sherriff, you keep an eye on him! I had him in the hospital last night because of all the excitement that man forgot to keep drinking and he damn near passed out on me. I won't have that happen again! Do you hear me! Everyone drink!" With that she walks back inside.

Traynor walks up and pours a glass and looks around "You all drink up. She may have gone inside but I can assure you that she's watching from somewhere and if one of us doesn't drink she will be back out here giving us all hell. She raised four boys while I was driving a truck and running this farm. I know the boys are afraid of her. I'm afraid of her for that matter. Even the cows are afraid of her when she's mad. You should probably have a drink."

Samantha walks up and starts pouring glasses of tea and handing them to us as we walk up to take a drink. The tea is fresh brewed and iced down to perfection. The heat and humidity have made me thirsty. After downing a glass, I reach over and pour another. Within seconds of the pitcher getting down towards the bottom she reappears with a jug and refills the pitcher. She nods approval and walks back inside without saying anything.

After finishing his glass, Traynor puts it on the table next to the pitcher and asks if we are ready to take a ride out to the field. He walks across the yard and opens the passenger door of Sheriff Tarr's truck. We follow his lead and climb into ours. Outside the gate the road ahead dwindles down from a dirt road to worn tire tracks in the brush. Even though the road has gotten some traffic lately I can hear the weeds and small trees scraping under the truck as we drive. Over head the trees close in over us at times blocking the sun. Through the woods I can see scattered bunches of cows sleeping in the shade. We stop for a moment as Traynor gets out and opens a gate for us to pass through. Once our SUV is through, he closes and locks the gate behind us before walking up to the Sherriff's waiting truck. Ahead where the tunnel of trees ends I can see a sun dried field and in the distance a barn.

We break through the trees at the barn and out buildings. Along the barn is a rusting trailer from an eighteen wheeler. On the other side is an old red tractor that has seen better days. It has more rust then paint. Around it are rusted plows and an old wooden sided hay wagon. On closer inspection the barn has some missing boards on its side and the door hangs open showing daylight through the barn. It is easy to see this is where things come to die.

We drive around the barn and park the cars. As I step out and look around, I see the river snake around the peninsula. We are surrounded on three sides by the river. Off to the right not far from the water's edge is the area roped off with crime scene tape. As I look around, the easiest way to dump the body would be by bringing the body in the way we came, which means someone drove by the house. I can't imagine this road is busy at any time during the day and a car driving by at night should be pretty obvious. That leaves an approach by river.

The water rushes by. It isn't too fast and would be possible to approach with a flat bottom boat. The trick would be tying up the boat and unloading a body, then to carry it across the field about one hundred feet. I wondered why if someone approached by boat, did they carry the body that from the river? Normally it would be dropped at the water's edge. Neither Sheriff Tarr's team nor the FBI team found fresh tire marks from a vehicle driving out and dumping the body. Someone carried it here and placed it here for some reason.

Sheriff Tarr walks over to the crime scene tape and opens the folder with the crime scene pictures and motions with his arm as he explains, "Here is where we found him. He was lying with what would have been his head toward the barn and his legs were pointing toward the tip of the spit. We found some foot prints that the FBI casted right here. We didn't see any fresh tire prints and the river was high because of a storm. There's no way to tell if someone pulled a boat up on the sand. The grass isn't full but it worked against us covering up any tracks leading toward the road or the water. If this man had crushed bones I would have said he fell out of an air plane but he didn't fall from heaven either.

Traynor volunteered his family wasn't home all day Saturday. Like almost everyone else in town they were tailgating in the stadium lot for the football game. "We were out of here by nine in order to get a good spot on the lot. Then we fire up the grill and the Misses starts cooking. She starts every home game with bacon and eggs on the grill. As soon as that's done, she puts on the slab of meat for pit beef. Like I said we have four boys to feed and they all have families now. It's a way for us to spend time with the grand kids. The game wasn't until four but we sit around with the neighbors and shoot the breeze. We got home a little after nine. After the game, we usually pull the food back out of the coolers and have a little more to eat as the crowd dies down. If not you could be stuck in traffic for an hour. It's better to avoid that and sit back with a cold drink and a sandwich. I would guess if someone came into my fields it was Saturday. Sunday we were up and out of the house for church but we are back in a little over an hour. The reverend is pretty fast when he wants to be and he wants to be able to get lunch in before the race starts. I have talked to a couple other people who live on this road. All of us were over at the college Saturday, so we are all pretty sure that's the only time it could have happened. We are still pretty shocked that someone drove onto our property, went through the cattle gate and came out to the spit to drop that body. We are out in the sticks so to speak."

I agree the body was probably dumped on Saturday. Perhaps the person took a chance that no one was home. There's also the very real possibility the person who dumped this body knows the Traynors and is familiar with the farm. While the town is only a few minutes away, once you leave the main road you are driving into the unknown, especially if this was done at night. There aren't any lights around. I suspect the Traynor house wasn't well lit with no one home, nor were the other neighbor houses since they were all at the football game. It was a risk though. Once you commit to this road there's no turning around without being noticed until you make it out into this field. Of course maybe that's why the body was left here. This is where the road ends. One thing I do know, this crime scene isn't giving up any of its secrets. Like the rest of this case, it is another dead end.

We thank John Traynor for showing us around and head back down the road. The sun is starting to set and it has been a long day. What we need now is dinner and to check into our hotel. The lights of the city are coming up and this area is flat. It isn't hard to find our way back to the city without even turning on the GPS. We agree while in Texas we have to find a good steak house. We should have asked for recommendations while we were with Sheriff Tarr and John Traynor but I hadn't thought about it. Now my stomach is growling and I realize we missed lunch about three hours ago.

The Taste of Texas Steak House is one of those barn décor places with peanut shells on the floor from the complimentary barrel in the waiting area. We are just ahead of the dinner crowd and are seated right away. Over us is the taxidermy head of a long horn steer. Big wooden timbers are attached to the benches of our booth. It's appropriate ours is adorned with a silver star like a sheriff's badge. The booth across from us is adorned with spurs. It's a little over the top in an attempt to look like a cowboy restaurant but I am more interested in the food. The house special is an eight ounce steak, thick cut with a stuffed baked potato, steak house soup and a slice of pie. We order three specials with a pitcher of beer.

Immediately the waitress brings the beer and the soup. At least service is good. The soup is good. I'm sure it's made with left over steak with some vegetables thrown into the broth but it hits the spot and calms the rumbling in my stomach. It is served with a loaf of brown bread. It's still hot from the oven and the butter melts into it perfectly. We eat in silence, all of us hungry. The waitress is right on things and clears the soup bowls as soon as we are done. We barely get into conversation when we hear the sizzling sound of our steaks coming to the table. The steaks are still steaming hot from the grill on plates warmed to add to the affect. They are topped with steaming mushrooms, green peppers and onions with cracked pepper, salt and garlic. The aroma is mouth watering. They are followed by big baked potatoes split and stuffed with bacon, chives, cheddar cheese and topped with sour cream. Everything is delicious and we dig in.

This isn't the place to talk about the case. I look around and see a few people who may be part of the national press. Outside we saw a few vehicles, some rentals, so it is possible we are sitting in the middle of a bunch of ears willing to listen. Instead we engage in small talk about the new laptop and eBook. The look on John's face tells me he's as impressed as I am about Samantha's knowledge of electronics. During the hour wait in the Jacksonville coffee shop, she had downloaded the back copies of a psychology newsletter she subscribes to and subscribed to and downloaded the last month of local College Station newspaper and the college newspaper. She managed to skim through them all before falling asleep. Since then, she has hot synced her laptop to her eBook so that she has access to all the information from her cloud.

The waitress interrupts our conversation about cloud technology to ask what we want for dessert. Options ranged from a simple bowl of vanilla ice cream to a chocolate torte with a pecan caramel topping. We all look at the chocolate torte and opt for it hot. Even though we are all full the thin layers of chocolate cake oozing with nuts and caramel entice us. With that we each ordered a cup of coffee.

The long hours along with being very full convince us we should leave and check into our hotel. My body feels heavy and my eyes are watering with each yawn. The drive to the hotel is not long and when we get there we each grab our suitcases and laptop bags. Around us in the parking lot are the familiar satellite trucks from the major networks. Our suite is on the top floor of the hotel and is accessible by a special pass key. The desk clerk in passing tells us the major cable network is in the suite next to us. I thank her for the tip. I'm sure by now our room is fully monitored for sound.

I wonder if we are disappointing the news crews. After locking the door, each of us put our laptop cases on the conference table before heading to our rooms to sleep. Samantha's room connects through an adjoining door to my room. I notice she leaves the connecting door open between our rooms. I hear her dumping her suitcase on the floor and then see a faint glow of light followed by the toilet flushing. Then the light goes out and I hear her blankets being pulled back before she gets into bed. She never even took the time to turn on the light and look around the room. I turn on the TV to see yet another reporter standing in the wind talking about the storm. It now appears the storm will cross over the mouth of the Chesapeake Bay and head north. Briefly, my mind thinks of Chincoteague Island. Right now it is in the target zone of the storm. Somewhere out there the pony that started this all will be fighting for her life on a barrier island during a hurricane. The next thing I know the smell of coffee drifts into my room waking me up.

DAY 12
COLLEGE STATION, TEXAS

From the light coming through the window, the sun has been up for a few hours. The clock next to the bed reads 8:45 am. I usually can't sleep past 6:00 am so the time surprises me. As I walk into the suite I see Samantha standing with cup in hand watching the coffee drain into the pot. She smiles and picks up a second cup and holds it out to me.

We both look as John walks into the suite rubbing his face. He looks as foggy as I feel. Samantha holds a cup up for him as well. This case has made us road warriors. We have been on it for nearly two weeks now. As Samantha pours each of us coffee, I wonder how far we have really progressed since I got the call about a body on Assateague Island. We are not any closer to identifying Kali's killer then we were the day her body was identified. Our only clue is Kali's bikini bottom in a bag up a dead man's rectum. I put my finger to my lips and walk over to turn the television on in the suite. Samantha walks into her room and turns on her television to another channel and stops in my room to turn the television on to a third channel. John laughs and goes into his room to turn his television on. Then I call room service to order breakfast.

The storm turned a little north during the night. I glance and see the current projection puts the eye of the storm hitting the Virginia coast with some weathermen predicting the eye coming on shore somewhere between Chincoteague Island, Virginia and Ocean City, Maryland. The irony of drowning out our conversation about the latest shit storm while a real storm was preparing to hit where this all began makes me smile. Let them have wind, waves and rain to drown out our conversation for a while.

I think it's time to review this case and the evidence we have. I miss having the wall in my office where I can put up a timeline with pictures of victims, witnesses and evidence. We each open our laptops and turn them on. Then I begin to timeline the case. On October eleventh at 9:38 AM, the pony is found with blood on it, which was later identified as being bloody hand prints and we can verify that the prints are too big to have belonged to Kali. On October seventeenth at 12:45 PM, the Reiner family reported the smell which lead to the discovery of Kali's body in the marsh. Her body was recovered and sent to Pocomoke for identification. I was put in charge of the investigation on October eighteenth and John was assigned to lead the forensic team. The only evidence from the crime scene is the pink bikini top which now has it's matching half in the College Station victim's rectum. At this point, John adds that according to the autopsy Kali was pregnant at the time of her murder. Along with other cuts, her uterus was removed indicating someone not only knew she was pregnant but, more than likely removed the fetus so that we didn't have that as evidence. Which makes him wonder if the fetus held DNA which might identify the father and give us another lead into the case. The question is whether the father of the baby had his DNA in the national registry. Would it be too far out of the question to assume a member of the Co-Op was a registered sex offender?

On October nineteenth we had a positive identification of Kali and by nightfall the wheels were put into motion for Samantha's release. We came to New York for the trip to the Delaware Water Gap to retrace steps at the summer cabin of Jacob Montgomery. The next day the case expanded out at this point adding the flight of Jacob Montgomery and the possible abduction of a child only know as Lexi. We got our first introduction to the Co-Op by the caller, Caroline, to the 800 line. We began to narrow down the identification of the child with Montgomery as nine year old Sidney Harris and Tiff Burnside filled us in on Montgomery and Lexis life. Karen Harris and Leona Haynes helped us find out either the Co-Op or Montgomery has an assistant, Isabel Boyle, who impersonated a social worker and facilitated the abduction of Sidney. By October twenty-fifth, we were on Jekyll Island chasing a lead that Montgomery had flown into there for the G8 conference. Evidence at the hotel confirms Montgomery was there with Sidney. We just left Jekyll Island for College Station when we got the call about the John Doe in the field. The Coroner estimated Kali was killed on October tenth which means she has been dead for nineteen days and we still have no idea who killed her or why.

We have very little physical evidence. A few finger prints, the bikini, some DNA samples and plenty of calls to the 800 number telling us how wonderful the Co-Op was to the women who have been abducted by this group. I am amazed by the number of people who have called with praise for the Co-Op. Normally victims don't praise the pedophiles who molested them. For that matter, none of the women claim to have been molested. Most give the same history that Tiff Burnside gave us of the Co-Op practice being the true empowerment of women and it wasn't sexual molestation because the history of this country allowed marriages as early as twelve years old. It makes me wonder if the Co-Op has its own home school kit where everyone learns a set curriculum.

John takes over at this point "We have a lot of unanswered questions and some peripheral evidence that will hopefully make sense in the end. I can't stop going back to the bikini. The top was left hanging on a branch but the bottom was taken by someone and kept in a plastic bag. I keep asking what the message is being sent with these two pieces. The bikini hanging on the branch seems like a natural act of someone taking off their clothes. Then her killer took the bottom and kept it. It wasn't a trophy because it turns up with victim number two. Killers don't give up their trophies. This feels like a crime of passion. It wasn't a random murder. This was a message to us or to someone else. If nothing else with confirms the two murders are connected."

"Next we have a missing person that we have no clue to their identity. I have a thin older man with gray hair. He is estimated to be between five foot ten and six feet. Kali appeared to have spent her last night with him. We have not found a vehicle, a body or any clue to identity. Who was this guy and what happened to him? He isn't our John Doe. Nothing about him fits the profile of John Doe. When someone killed her did he go into hiding? Did John Doe kill her and leave the scene or did someone kill both Kali and John Doe?"

"I want to address the Braden's as well. There's more to that story than meets the eye. The bikini bottom leads us to the Braden's. If not Duke,

Tyler or Josh, then Duke Braden has another son. I think we need to go to the source ourselves. We can't talk to Duke Braden but maybe we can talk to Tyler, Josh and Mrs. Braden. The killer or someone connected to the killer pointed the finger at the men in the Braden family. That screams someone who knows something or someone who wants to direct the attention on the Braden's and away from someone else. We never did confirm where Montgomery was around the time Kali was killed. Could he have possibly been in Chincoteague at that time."

"The killer or someone connected to them also brought us to Texas. Why did we have to come here? Why dump a body six hundred miles from the other crime scene? I would think if one of the Braden men was the father of the baby we wouldn't be handed a body to link to the crime scene or to Kali unless that is part of the message we were sent."

"Next up is Traynor farm. I can't see the body being brought down the Brazos River. If you take a boat down a river you are out in the open. Someone would have seen a boat in the area on Saturday. I just can't see anyone taking that risk. This leads us to look at dumping the body by land. This is also a huge risk. Not many people live down that road and my bet if a car drives down it everyone takes notice. If it's a local car you glance and go on with your day.

"We have to put the football game into the mix. If the person knew the patterns of people who lived on that road, they would know no one was home because they all tailgate. The river is still at risk. This would mean houses on both sides of the river would have to be away from home in order to go down the river unseen. I'm leaning toward the body drop happening by land. This leads me to believe who ever dumped this body is local. They know the people around here and their activities. This person very well may be connected to John Traynor. What do we know about him?"

That is a very good question. All I know about him is that he is a cattle farmer in College Station, Texas who found a body in his field. I pick up my phone and call the office to put someone on John Traynor and his family. I want to know if he had any connection to the Braden family. Out of curiosity I ask him to also check any connection to Jacob Montgomery. I call Sheriff Tarr and ask him to look into a connection as well.

John sits at his computer with a puzzled look on his face. "What about Calvin Montague and his daughters Anastasia and Maya. They are from Austin, Texas. We have thought Montague's bid on the cruise was coincidental. We didn't find a connection to Montgomery. I think I'd also like to know his possible connection to Braden and Traynor. Too many things are pointing to Texas to be a coincidence."

"Finally, I think we need to know where Kali fits into all of this. Where has she been over the last eleven years? If we are to believe Tiff Burnside, she left Montgomery at about age eleven and he had the Co-Op facilitate her next pedophile owner. Who was this person and how are they connected to her murder? Did Kali getting pregnant ruin it for that man and rather then turning her over to the Co-Op he killed her? The note said John Doe broke the rules and they police their own. Perhaps the Co-Op has rules that an owner of a teenager cannot impregnate her Perhaps the women are required to take birth control. What if only women over eighteen can get pregnant and someone at the Co-Op found out? "

Samantha has been sitting quietly listening then she broke John off in his forensic hypothesis. "The mind of a pedophile is about control. Many like little girls because they can mold them into the perfect pleasure provider. They follow the rules and live to provide for the needs of the man who is abusing them. These women do not see themselves as abused. They see themselves as pampered."

"The Co-Op seems to go for a specific profiled child. From what I see, they search out young girls who fit their profile. These are not your common run of the mill sexual predators. Those men prey on the children of families, friends and neighbors. These men are different. They have perfected the hunt and enlisted women who have graduated from their perversion. I am not entirely convinced that Jacob Montgomery facilitated the kidnapping of Sidney Harris. She was his age, but I don't know how he had a connection to her prior to the abduction. I have a gut feeling there is a group of hunters. Their job is to fill an order of the pedophiles in the Co-Op. These people are very organized. Perhaps the scandal and press from Kali's disappearance was more than he bargained for and he enlisted hunters for his next child."

"Also, if he did only keep Kali until she was eleven he had to get another child. Say he gets girls at age seven or eight then keeps them until they are eleven or twelve. He has girls for three or four years. He got Kali eleven years ago. That being the case there was a child after Kali and then another child before he traded her in and got Sidney Harris. As for Kali, she left Montgomery and went to someone else. If that person only liked girls from age eleven or twelve until sometime in the teenage years, she may have gone to someone else as well during that time."

"I keep thinking back to the words of Tiff Burnside as well. She gave us an insight into this group. The children and adult women who were kidnapped feel they have a better life as a sex slave then they did living in their birth family. They stay and become protective of the people who are abusing them because a need within them has been fulfilled. Many children who are sexually abused do not feel they are getting love at home. When someone touches them and shows love these girls respond. The lifestyle we have seen adds to the need. They never go hungry again. They are never cold again. They have nice clothing and a clean place to sleep; everything in their new life from the sex to the lifestyle feels good -- better then their past. So, they protect the new lifestyle and their abductors."

"I would love to know how they transition the girls. The victims develop Stockholm Syndrome. They connect with their sexual abusers. These men become their parent and spouse, so how do you take this girl who no longer sexually arouses you because she has lost the body type you want and prepare her to be traded in for a younger model? The next guy will be one who likes to look at women who are just developing breasts and pubic hair. They like their girls young and firm. What they aren't going to want to deal with is a sulking moody girl who misses her old pedophile. Something has to be done to entice her to switch her love and allegiance from her first pedophile to her next. What do you do for a child who has everything to make her accept the transition?"

"The next transition probably happens again somewhere between sixteen and eighteen. This will be when the girl develops a full woman's body. The thrill of sexual molestation goes away. These women are ones anyone can legally have sex with if there is consent. The men who take the women who have graduated are looking for a young beautiful woman who has been well groomed in society and in bed. These are the fantasy women. They will go to either older men who want to relive their youth or to men who are married and want to have a cute little thing on the side. From Tiff Burnside I got the impression these women go on to have children and raise a family."

"Kali was at a transition age. She had either been with someone for a year or so, was in the process of transitioning or had just gone to a new man. Maybe there was some jealousy. It could be anything from her getting pregnant right after she left and the prior owner wanted her back or she got pregnant before she transitioned and the new owner was pissed."

John interrupts Samantha at this point, "Maybe this means something. I'm looking at the autopsy report from Tim Clark. Kali's pelvis showed pitting indicating she had previously given birth. It wasn't fresh and could have happened months or years ago. There's no way to date that accurately. Her being pregnant didn't seem to be the problem. She had been pregnant once before and more than likely the baby was given up for adoption or something. I can't see a pedophile wanting to deal with a baby. It has to be hard enough to hide a teenage girl you are raping let alone her having a baby. So why kill her and cut the fetus out if she had already given birth once. That was handled somehow, what made this pregnancy different than the one she had before unless this was a new owner?"

"Let's play what if... Say you were a man whose wife was going through chemo. She wants a baby but no one is going to put an adoption through with a woman who might be dying. She can't have one herself because of the cancer and the chemo. How hard would it be to get a young woman from the Co-Op as breeding stock? His wife is too sick and too tired to have sex with him, but he loves her and wants to make her happy. Maybe he wants to give her hope. So rather than going out to get a surrogate who will have the child for them and then get paid to do it, he goes out and gets a girl who fits their needs. The wife doesn't have to know her husband is cheating on her by having sex with a teenage girl. He wants the sex for himself and the baby for his wife. The wife is told the baby is from in vitro, she believes the baby came from the turkey baster method instead of playing hide the sausage with her husband. We have even had cases where women have fake pregnancies in order to pass surrogate children off as their own. After the baby is born he brings the teenage girl in as hired help to take care of the baby. The girl gets to keep her child, the wife has a baby she thinks is hers and has someone to help take care of it and the man has a young thing to screw whenever the wife is sleeping. Everyone wins except there is a teenage girl who is being sexually molested by an older guy with money that bought her."

I look over at Samantha as John is talking. I have never sat down and read the full autopsy report and I know she hasn't as well. That little tidbit of information about Kali had slipped by her and I hadn't mentioned it. She is formulating something but can't find the words to speak. "So if Montague is connected to this case, when he was interviewed on the cruise ship there is a possibility Kali's daughter was sitting in the next room with someone from the ships staff? We may have had my granddaughter within arm's reach and released them? I may have a granddaughter or grandson out there somewhere, if not with Montague then with someone else."

With that she jumps up and runs to the bathroom. I can hear her vomiting. I wait and don't hear any other sounds. After a few minutes, I get up and walk into the bathroom. Samantha is sitting on the floor. Her head is cradled in her arms resting on the toilet seat. Her entire body shakes with her sobs. She is too close to this case. I am letting my attraction and feelings for her get in the way. I kneel down and put my arms around her. Then I work my way into a seated position between the toilet and the bathtub. I try to pull her body toward me but she is stiff as she hugs the toilet, so I lean toward her and wrap as much of my body around her as I can. Eventually, she looks up at me and puts her arms around my waist and positions her body so that it is cradles in mine. John is standing in the doorway with a disapproving look on his face. He also knows I have crossed over the line with Samantha and this case has become personal for me.

The door to the suite closes as John leaves the room. I've know John for too long and he won't go to the SAC about this. I know I am going to have to deal with my feelings for Samantha and what is best for this case and my career. I also find myself not moving from the floor and wanting to take the pain away from the woman in my arms.

I think both of us have body parts that are beginning to fall asleep from our position in and around the toilet. She moves and starts to wiggle backward on the floor to stand up. "I'm sorry. I don't know what hit me. Whether it's that Kali had a baby or that I'm a grandmother. I just found out I didn't just lose a daughter. I lost a grandson or granddaughter as well. I missed getting to raise my child. I screwed up the first years of her life and lost out on the last eleven. If the baby was a girl, I'm sure they won't let her out of their canopy. That's one less child they have to kidnap or she's being raised as someone else's child. It will be nearly impossible to locate the baby and even harder to fight for custody. I'm not getting any younger either. The possibility of me getting married and raising a family is ticking away. My possibility of being a mother and grandmother died alone in a marsh in Virginia."

I get up and stand behind her while slipping my arms around her waist. "I'm sorry. You lost eleven years of your life. No one can bring them back to you, but you have a future. When this case is over and we find out who killed Kali, you and I need to go out for a cup of coffee and talk. John's going to come back at some point and I'm going to have to deal with him. I'm not sure what this is between us, but for right now it has to be put on a back burner. If you stay with me on the investigation, we have to find a way to stay objective. If not, I'm going to have to put you on a plane as soon as the storm clears Maryland and Virginia. My team will help you find a place and get your life established. I'm going to leave it up to you."

She turns and I see a tear running down her cheek. "Adam, I want to stay. I want to be a part of finding out what happened to Kali. I know there are some things I might not be able to be involved in because I don't want to destroy any case you can bring against anyone. I've also know for days that there was something building between you and me. I know if this was another place or another time you and I could explore a relationship. Hell Adam, it's been eleven years since I've had sex with a man. I figure a couple more days, weeks or months aren't really going to make a difference there. You and I are adults here. We have already had quite a few cups of coffee together. When the time comes, we can skip the coffee. Just say the word and take me to bed. Not some one night stand mind you. I have invested the last two weeks sleeping in the next room. When the time comes, I reserve the right to wake up next to you in the morning and then get that cup of coffee."

We are both smiling and I lean down and kiss her. I may not be able to do this again until after the case is closed but this gives me incentive to get to the bottom of this and get working on that cup of coffee. For the first time in a long time, I am thinking house, wife, kids and a dog. I'm a guy who has never been home long enough to keep a potted plant alive and have to hire someone to take care of things when I'm not home. Now all I want is to make a new life. First, I have to find out who caused this to bring us together. Fate has a weird way of twisting things. From a call about a murdered girl in a marsh, my life has turned upside down.

I kiss her once more. Her body is pressed tight against mine. I can feel my arousal and her body responding to me. When we break off the kiss, I hold on to her as her body goes limp in my arms. We break apart when we hear the electric lock beep outside in the hallway as John returns.

Samantha switches on the TV in her bedroom. I hear a reporter talking about the hurricane, the waves in the background drowning out the voice of the reporter. I turn on the shower and start to get undressed. I need to shake off the mental image of Samantha in my mind.

John is sitting at the table when I come out. He doesn't say a word to me. He's researching John Traynor and his family. I get another cup of coffee and start working on Senator Duke Braden. I want to see if I can find a connection between the two families. Samantha has stayed behind her closed bedroom door.

It's getting late and I pick up the phone and dial room service. Even though we have not left the suite all day I feel exhausted. When the food comes we sit and eat. Tasting the food wasn't really important, just eating something because that's what you do to survive. The events of the day have left us all quiet. This has become yet another day of questions and no answers. I go to bed hoping the morning brings some clues.

DAY 13
COLLEGE STATION, TEXAS

John spent some of the night investigating the Braden family after I went to bed. The Braden's have lived outside Austin, Texas for thirty-five years. Prior to that they attended college together, married and lived in a small apartment in Austin while Duke got his law office established. He ran for office and won the first time with the backing of his father, Roscoe Braden. Helen Braden was a girl from the wrong side of the tracks but, her brains got her into college on a scholarship. That's where they met. They have two children, Tyler and Joshua.

The children attended a private Christian school through eighth grade and then switched to public high school for high school. Both sons played varsity football. Joshua was the brains in the family and went into the Ivy League for college where he continued to play football. After that he was accepted into Med School in Baltimore. Tyler was more of the rebel. He graduated high school with honors but, has only attended one year of college. After that, he volunteered with a Christian missionary group to spend a year in the Amazon. It is possible that they crossed paths with the Traynors while living in Austin. Duke Braden is a Republican and so is the Traynor family, of course so are many in Texas.

I can find no connection what so ever to the Traynors and Jacob Montgomery. There are too many miles and no business in common. I did find a connection between Traynor and Montague. Montague brokers the sale of cattle to farmers and Traynor runs a breeding station. He supplies steers to farms for beef herds. While remote, there is a link between them and Montgomery.

The connection between Braden and Montague is stronger. Montague is a major supporter of Braden's campaign and has served on his campaign finance committee. It makes me wonder why a cattle broker was in Jekyll Island for the banking conference. He isn't a banker and I didn't know livestock brokers had a say in monetary conferences.

Samantha walks out of the bedroom, turns on the TV and tells us to take a look at this. The hurricane has made land fall at Virginia Beach. At this point, it is following the coast line. Hurricane force winds extend two hundred miles from the eye and tropical force winds and rain extend out nearly six hundred miles. Because the storm is over the ocean, it is picking up massive quantities of water and dumping it on the land. Parts of Virginia could expect fourteen to sixteen inches of rain. The wind and rain have caused wide spread power outages and flooding. People are being moved away from the coast up into Maine. The storm is expected to keep on its current path and slam into New York and New Jersey then continue into Connecticut, New Hampshire, Vermont, Rhode Island, Massachusetts and Maine. Wide spread damage is expected from the Outer Banks of North Carolina into the Canadian Maritime and extending west two hundred to three hundred miles inland. The camera goes back to the anchor. "The Coast Guard has received a distress signal from the Tall Ship Lady Grey, owned by banking head Jacob Montgomery, in the Chesapeake Bay. The crew had tried to outrun the storm and make it into the quieter waters of the Chesapeake Bay but, the storm surge pushed eighteen foot waves into the side of the ship. She is feared to have foundered somewhere in the lower bay. Weather conditions are not permitting Coast Guard Helicopters to fly into the storm and any rescue attempt can't be made until the storm passes. There is hope that the passengers and crew boarded the two covered life rafts onboard the ship. At this point there has not been any rescue beacons activated on the life rafts, so the fate of the passengers and crew are not known. We will keep you informed of any information as it becomes available. Meanwhile, the search for Jacob Montgomery by the FBI continues."

We all sit in silence. We have speculated for days that Montgomery and Sidney are on the Lady Grey. I wonder if knowing we are searching for them stopped them from heading to shore sooner. Now we may never know what happened to Jacob Montgomery or Sidney Harris.

Samantha makes a cup of coffee and then says "I think we need to talk to Helen Braden, the senator's wife. Chincoteague might not be on the map anymore and the only solid evidence we have is the bikini bottom in a body with Braden DNA. For all we know Helen Braden was a child from the Co-Op. She has a rags-to-riches story. I'm ready to talk to someone who can give us some answers."

I agree and call Sheriff Tarr. I ask him if he knows the phone number in northern Virginia where we can speak with Helen Braden. I don't know with the storm if the phone lines are up in the area. I'm afraid if we wait any longer the possibility exists the hurricane might cut us off from speaking with her for days. I am a little surprised when I'm told she's in Texas. She has been home for over a week. He gives me the address and tells me he will call ahead. He has personally spoken with her and she has been very willing to help in the investigation.

The Braden ranch is a few miles from our hotel and we are there quickly. The driveway into the ranch is a tree lined dirt and gravel road each side lined with a single row of trees. To the left through the trees there is a lake with a green and white row boat tied up to a dock. Willow trees drape their limbs onto the water near a white and green painted gazebo. On the right a post and rail fence stretches out to the river. In the distance a herd of horses graze near a stand of trees.

***

The house itself is a three story Victorian mansion painted white with green shutters. The circular driveway curves in front of the house to the alluvial stairway that leads to a wraparound porch. As we get out of our car, we can look up and see the groupings of wooden rocking chairs and tables inviting people to sit and relax. Red and white petunias line the side walk and porch between tall leafy elephant ear plants. This place looks like it is cut from the cover of a Southern home and garden magazine.

Sheriff Tarr has called ahead and Helen Braden is expecting us. As we walk up the steps the front door opens and a stately blond woman in crisp tailored pants and a white button down blouse walks out. The best way to describe her is casual elegant. While her driver's license may say fifty-four, her stylist and surgeon are aiming for thirty-one. She looks the part of what money can buy and it was money well spent. She walks towards us offering the only giveaway to her true age, the hands of a fifty something adorn with a large emerald and diamond ring. "I'm Helen Braden and I assume you are Agents Clay and Duncan and you must be Dr. Callahan, the sheriff called and told me you would like to speak to me. Please come inside out of the heat."

We are led through the formal living room to the back of the house. We follow a hallway to a heavy oak door. Once she opens it, we step down into a tropical jungle. The floor is a flag stone path that winds through flower beds of exotic blooming plants and giant tropical ferns. Above us palm trees tower near a glass roof three stories above us. Orchids hang down from the crevices of large ponytail palm trees and the flutter of wings can be heard from unknown birds hiding somewhere near us. There is the sound of running water off to the right. The air is warm and moist, but not uncomfortable. We follow her to a set of wicker chairs and a table along a koi pond equipped with a waterfall. As we sit, foot long fish peek out from under the rock ledge to get a look at us.

She pulls out a chair and waves her arm toward the other chairs "please have a seat. My assistant, Jonathon, will be around in a moment to bring some refreshments. He's bringing ice tea, but would anyone like coffee or something hot? I can ring him and let him know if you do." We all mumble something cold would be appreciated. She smiles and sits at the table with her hands folded waiting for us to speak.

"Mrs. Braden, I'm sure you know we are here to talk to you about a possible connection to a case we are working on in Virginia and to the body that was discovered in College Station. First, I would like to tell you how sorry we are about your husband. I was glad you are back in Texas so that we can talk, we won't keep you, I'm sure you are returning to Northern Virginia soon." She just nods her head. "I am sorry we have to do this now but we need to try to identify the man found in College Station. I understand you have been in contact with both your sons, and I am glad they are alive and well. Was Senator Braden married before or do you know any other children he might have had? Do you know any reason the DNA in College Station was a paternal match to your husband?"

149

Helen Braden takes a deep breath and sighs, and then in her Texas draw begins "Agent, I am a politician's wife. My husband is dying in Virginia and I am home working with the state to plan his inevitable funeral. No, I'm not saying this for pity, nor to make you feel you are intruding on what should be a traumatic time in my life. I am not the grieving widow. My husband has been in politics for thirty-four years. He has lived in the state house, had apartments and a house in Austin and has a condo in Washington, DC. What he hasn't done is live for more than five or six weeks at a time in this house. I had my sons and raised them here with the help of my staff. I am not going to kid you or myself that the potential for him to have another child is impossible. We all have seen the headlines before about this politician or that politician having an affair and illegitimate children. A few times over the years, women have stepped forward and claimed to be his lover during campaigns. Like the good politicians wife, I have stood firmly beside him that we have a good relationship, and we do."

"Duke was the captain of the football team. He took the team to a bowl game two years running. I was a cheerleader and on the homecoming court. He and I were destined to be husband and wife. I bore the man his sons, and did my obligation, but Duke Braden is a self-centered man who will do what he needs to get ahead in his career. Having a woman by his side slowed him down. When the children came, we slowed him down even more. So we made the appearances as the happy family for the public, but our relationship was more of a financial one. I gave him the appearance of the all American family and he gave me the money create my own fairytale world behind the gates of this driveway. I have my horses, my bridge games, and my lawn and garden club. What I don't have is the emotion to mourn for that man when he dies. I really can't help you with the body you found in College Station. I know where my sons are and they are fine. Normally, I would say you need to speak to Duke and ask him what little tramp might have squeezed out a love child, but you and I know he's not talking anymore. I might suggest you speak to his personal secretary. Her name is Sally Gold and she probably knows more about what the man has done over the last thirty-four years then I ever will."

She pauses as a man in black slacks and polo shirt walks in with a pitcher of ice tea and glasses. He sits everything on the table and leaves promising to bring the rest of the refreshments. I watch as Helen Braden exchanges a glance with him. He's checking on her to see if she is ok and that we are not unwelcome guests. I get the feeling if she decides our conversation is over, he will appear instantly to escort us to the door.

"Where was I before Jonathan walked in? Oh, yes, Sally Gold. I can give you her contact information or you can fly to Virginia and speak with her yourself. When I got the call from my sons that their father was in the hospital, I flew there immediately. My boys had gone home to get a shower and change clothes but, she was still there holding his hand. If I hadn't seen her regularly over the years, I would say to ask her where her son is, but to my knowledge she never had a child. Her devotion to my husband's career was her marriage. I'm sure if he has other children, she will be able to give you their addresses and birthdates."

She stops and pours tea for everyone and offers sugar or artificial sweetener. I take the opportunity to ask her about the background on her husband's illness. She sighs again and looks down at her glass. "My son, Tyler, wants to save the world. He took a year off from college to go to the Amazon and work with the AIDS epidemic. He has been gone all summer and came home for a month in September. He spent three weeks with me and then flew to Baltimore to spend time with his little brother, Joshua. He flew back to the Amazon October twelfth; he was a few days late going back because of his father. On what would have been his last weekend home, Tyler had arranged an ocean fishing trip for himself, Joshua and Duke. They rented this huge boat that they were planning on sleeping in during the night and fishing during the day from Saturday until Tuesday. They were just doing a boy thing together. Monday night, Duke mentioned not feeling well but they had been having some pretty heavy swells because of a tropical storm in the Atlantic somewhere. Tyler and Josh just thought their father was sea sick. Then they found him on the deck face down during the night. They panicked. There they were somewhere in the Atlantic Ocean with their father barely breathing and it was dark as coal out there. Tyler took control of the boat and Joshua tended to his father while they got back to shore. It was early morning when landed in Ocean City, Maryland and docked the boat. There was no one to be found and since Duke was still breathing on his own they carried him to Joshua's car and drove him to the hospital. The prognosis was not good. He had somehow taken an overdose of his medications combined with drinking alcohol. He was diagnosed a vegetable. They said he could live for years like this. I know this sounds cruel but I love flowers, not vegetables. Duke was a vibrant man, he would not want to lay there breathing, wasting away on a feeding tube. So, I emailed Tyler asking what he thought we should do and consulted with Joshua. You have to understand it's hard to get in touch with Tyler in the Amazon and email is the fastest method. Together we decided discontinuing the feeding and letting him die with some dignity. That is what Duke would have wanted. Joshua visits his father every day and Tyler is due back into Baltimore tomorrow. He is somewhere in the air as we speak."

"I have already made arrangements, when Duke dies, to have his body flown back to Texas. You asked if I was heading back to be by his side and I won't be. I will make the arrangements here and dress in my finest mourning clothes. I will be waiting at the airport in my black suit and pillbox hat looking every bit the part of a lady of grace and elegance that has lost her husband. I'm sure people in Texas will compare me to Jackie O or Nancy Reagan. My sons will ride in the private plane that will bring their fathers body home. They will walk off the plane and stand with me while the honor guard brings Duke's casket home. Then, his body will lie in state under the capitol dome for three days so the people of Texas can come and pay their respects. He will have the full honors at the funeral for the former Governor of the State. It will appear to the world that a great man has died. They will be wrong. A great man didn't die."

She stops talking as Jonathan walks back in with a tray loaded with a silver tiered plate of cookies, tarts and petit fours elaborately decorated. He places the tiered plate in the center of the table and then puts small dessert plates in front of each of us. Helen Braden nods her head at him and he turns and leaves. She watches as he shuts the door and then waits a moment before continuing.

"You will find this out eventually anyway, so I will tell you what I know now. I only ask that you please wait to go public until after Dukes funeral. Let Texas bury their hero and let him have his final moment of glory. Dr. Callahan, I am truly sorry for what happened to your daughter. There is a secret I have had in my heart for many years and seeing the colored artist rendition of her brought the pain I have dealt with home. I don't know who that man is who is dead in that field, but I do know your daughter. I know in my heart my family is connected to this case. Marissa looked older in the picture, but I recognized her." There are tears in the corners of her eyes and she pauses to raise her hand to her lips, than reaches for Samantha's hand. "I once made a surprise visit to Duke's house in Austin. No one answered the front door and I had gone around the back to see if anyone was home. Sometimes Duke had meetings back there and the front of the house was locked. I was coming around the house to leave when I saw Sally Gold and a young girl. She was no more than twelve or thirteen. Sally Gold didn't see me, but I saw and heard them. That child was asking that woman if Duke would still love her even though she was growing breasts. I didn't say a word to them and stayed out of sight until they were gone. I know I should have confronted them but I was afraid. I stayed in Austin that night and waited until I knew Duke was home. It was dark and I went around the back of the house and looked in to see my husband kissing and fondling that girl. My husband, the man who hadn't touched me since I had my children, had his hand inside that girl's blouse. It seems I had gotten too old for him, he didn't like mature women. Duke Braden only likes women with firm little breasts and young teenage bodies. I tried the door and it opened. The fool had forgotten to lock it. I walked in on them just as his lips were about to kiss her naked breast. That son-of-a-bitch threatened me! He threatened to take away my children's private schools and my home. He told me if I ever told he would send me back to the small town I was born to waste away as nobody instead of a Governor's wife. Dr. Callahan, your daughter was an innocent victim of my husband, yet she cried and screamed at me pleading me not to take her daddy away. For almost an hour, she screamed how much she loved him and how much he loved her. Duke was trying to protect her and force me to leave but I wanted answers. I wanted to know what was wrong with that man. I wanted to know why he would want a little girl and in the end he told me I was old and didn't turn him on anymore."

Both Samantha and Helen Braden are racked with tears. They reach out for each other and hold on to the other crying. Jonathan reappears and stands behind Mrs. Braden, his hands resting on her shoulders. I reach over to lay a hand on Samantha's back. John rises and walks outside to make a phone call to the team. We have just landed in our next shit storm of this case.

Finally sniffing through tears, she leans back and continues. "He loved your daughter and she loved him. A few days later, Sally Gold called me and informed me that if I went to the authorities I would be ruined. My boys were not always angels and there was an incident with one of my sons. He should have gone to jail, but because he was Duke's son, he was released and it was kept out of the press. He had gotten a girl drunk and raped her. Duke paid the family to keep quiet and had it all swept under the rug. She also brought up my father and his indiscretions. My father made his money off of the importation of people from Mexico. He would laugh at the dining room table, bragging about how many people he brought over the border that day. To him they were something to be bought and sold like cattle. They paid him money for fake documents to establish themselves in this country. Five days a week he would drive across the border for business and sell the papers on the streets there. Then come home with a pocket full of cash. Telling anyone would have destroyed my world as much as Duke's. So, I kept quiet. Now that the son-of-a-bitch is laying there unable to threaten me anymore, I think it's about time the world found out the truth. I only wish I could tell you who you found dead in that field or how to get that information out of Sally Gold. What his body means to me is that while I was still the dutiful wife, he was screwing someone and had a child."

Helen Braden looks spent. Finally letting the truth out exhausts her. The only promise I can make to her is that we will not let this information get to the news as long as we can and we will try to spare her and her family as much as possible. She and her sons are victims of this crime as well. As the case evolves, I can see how many people will have to live with the shame of the actions of their loved ones. While we only have two dead, the head count of victims keeps rising.

We leave Helen Braden in the care of Jonathan and head back to the SUV. Samantha gets in the back and closes her eyes. The drive to the hotel is quiet. It is evident that Duke Braden is a member of the Co-Op. If he had Kali after Montgomery turned her in, Braden probably has another child now. With him in hospice, this child is either still with a nanny in one of his homes or has been turned back into the Co-Op again. Since I do not know the rules of the Co-Op, I don't know if the child reverts to the Co-Op at death or if something like this happens the child is left to fend for themselves. I make a call to District Attorney White and see if he can arrange a phone call with Tiff Burnside. I need to know how transactions work. Hopefully, she has some insight that can help us.

My next call is to the Richmond Field office. Instead of an answer I get a fast busy signal. Phone lines into Richmond have gone down in the storm. I spin through my phone book to find the cell number of one of my team who will answer their phone. Chip is the first to answer. The west side of the hurricane spawned tornados in Virginia and Washington, DC. Both the Richmond and DC field offices are closed. The Baltimore field office is open, but running on emergency power because of a wide spread power failure. There's no way for me to get information on Sally Gold or Senator Braden's DC apartment until the storm passes and the infrastructure has been restored.

Back at the hotel, we turn on the TV news. The situation looks pretty bad. Up until now the storm has been in the back of my mind. I take the time to sit down and assess the situation. This late season storm came at one of the worst times for many reasons. Coastally there is significant flooding. The storm is pounding the entire eastern seaboard with high seas compounded by twelve plus inches of rain falling from North Carolina into Delaware. The location of the storm has pushed water up into the Chesapeake Bay causing flooding to inland areas. The moon is full causing higher than normal tides further adding to the flooding. Much of the land under the clouds of this storm is flooded. People on the coast have been urged to move inland to higher elevations.

The storm is a category three hurricane packing winds of one hundred and twenty miles per hour for fifty miles around the eye. This is a worst case scenario. It has met up with a winter storm coming down from Canada and parts of Tennessee, Kentucky, West Virginia, Maryland, Pennsylvania and New York are getting snow. Blizzard conditions exist in all of these states with wind gusts up to sixty miles per hour. By staying along the coast, the storm is taking advantage of the warmer waters of the coastal shelf and it's not weakening. It is also able to continue to pull water from the ocean adding to the rain totals. The current storm track predicts the storm slamming into New York City.

Our investigation is now stalled as our entire investigation area slides under the clouds of the hurricane. We are left in Texas with nowhere to go or no one to talk to. John is sitting on the sofa flipping channels. I think he hopes somewhere he can find this is a joke put on by someone at the hotel.

Samantha is buried in her laptop. Now and then, I see her wipe a tear from the corner of her eye. She finally looks up with tear filled eyes. "I was thinking about the pony on Assateague. I think she was trying to get help for Kali. She's a mom and maybe she sensed Kali was one too. I have been trying to find out what they are doing for the wild ponies. I found a message on the fire departments web page. Before the storm, they rode out onto the island on horseback and went to a location where there are gates that keep the ponies in Maryland and the ones from Virginia from mingling because the Virginia ones are owned by the fire department and the Maryland ones are owned by the park service. Anyway, they opened the gates to let the ponies all go to the higher ground in Maryland. This has worked in the past. The ponies know when a storm is coming."

"I feel really connected to that pony. I think she may have stayed with Kali when she died. Now, I hope she has found somewhere out of the wind and away from the waves. I am seeing reports of twelve foot waves hitting the coast from Wilmington, North Carolina to Atlantic City, New Jersey. I don't know how the ponies can find high enough land. I know I have only seen a brief glimpse of the southern tip of Assateague, but the entire area is so flat and at sea level. The people there seemed so wonderful and the ponies are so beautiful. I hope the last experience Kali had was to see these beautiful creatures living in the wild and to have experienced the kindness of the people on Chincoteague. After this is over and hopefully the island survives, I want to go back there. Not just to thank the people, but to really get to know the area. Now, I don't know if I will ever get the chance. This storm could wash its existence off the map."

"I remember as a kid reading a book about the wild ponies of Chincoteague. In 1962, there was an early season hurricane that hit the island hard. Back then they did the same thing; they opened the gates and let the ponies have a chance to survive. The hurricane was really bad and waves split Assateague Island in half. A barge that was anchored near Chincoteague broke loose and hit the bridge connecting Chincoteague and

Assateague doing damage to the bridge. It was a couple days after the storm before anyone got a helicopter up to fly over Assateague and see if any of the ponies survived. They lost about half of the herd. When the water went down, they found the ponies back where they normally graze like nothing had happened. Chincoteague had over six feet of water covering the island at the height of the storm. The storm went on to hit New York City. It's funny; this storm was too early in the season to have a name so it goes by a couple names and is just recorded by most as a nor'easter. The winds, rain and characteristics match a hurricane. Regardless, these two storms look a lot alike and the destruction was massive."

"After the storm Misty, one of the ponies that had been bought at the wild pony auction and had her story made into a book and movie, was put in a horse trailer and taken across the United States to visit children at schools and libraries. Kids donated pennies and nickels to help support the wild ponies. Misty raised money to provide medical attention and to have feed dropped on the island for them in the winter. Misty became one of the most famous ponies to ever live. She died on October 16, 1972. Ironic isn't it. A pony with similar colors and markings was the one to first tell someone of the crime and the anniversary of Misty's death was right before you came on the case. I owe my freedom to a pony that is now fighting for survival. For all I know, it was a wild ancestor of Misty who walked onto the road covered in blood. What if it was the fame of the wild ponies that brought Kali to Chincoteague? She had years to contact me and she never made an attempt. I doubt, if she lived, I would have found her, at least not from jail. If the ponies survive, I want to try to find a way to thank them. I mean both the people and the ponies in Chincoteague. And Adam, I can never thank you enough for putting everything in motion so quickly for my release and for all you have done for me. You too John, I want to thank you for putting up with me. I know you didn't have to and I know I'm a thorn in your side sometimes. I know I have no official part in this investigation, but I know the mind of the people we are dealing with."

The look of shock shoots across Samantha's face as she scans something on her laptop screen. "Oh my God! The ponies! Helen Braden has a connection to Chincoteague! The herd of horses we saw on her farm are Chincoteague ponies. I think she has her own herd. They have the right markings and the right builds. I read today that the Chincoteague Ponies are a registered breed and owners across the country are part of the pony association." Samantha starts to feverishly type and scan pages, then stops suddenly and her mouth flies open. "Helen Braden is listed as an official breeder of Chincoteague Ponies. She owns a stallion and fourteen mares. Why didn't she mention that? Out on her damn web page is a picture of her summer house in Chincoteague, Virginia! That bitch knows something!"

I pick up the phone and call the Braden ranch but don't get an answer, so I call Sheriff Tarr. He dispatches a car to the ranch to see if he can have a talk with Helen Braden. Right now, there's nothing she can be charged with, but there's a big possibility she knows more than she's said to us.

John paces while I flip channels on the TV. Samantha files her nails and checks her laptop every few minutes. Time seems to have stopped. After forty minutes, my phone finally rings. Sheriff Tarr informs me the Braden ranch is locked up and no one is home. Not even the maid or Jonathan. The sheriff warns me to not read too much into it. Helen Braden and her staff might be working on funeral arrangements and everyone may have driven to Austin. He sent word to Austin to be on the lookout for her at the Braden house there. I ask him to have officers check the Austin house and make sure there is not a young girl living there. If there is a child there, take her and anyone who is staying with her into custody. This may be an abducted child and someone who is part of her kidnapping.

Samantha looks at me and says "I now understand the term shit storm. I think we just got hit with hurricane force winds!"

Outside the sun has gone down and the full moon shines bright over Texas. We walk to the SUV and get inside. Today we managed to have breakfast but lunch was forgotten somewhere along the way. Now we are all very hungry. As we head toward the strip near the college that is lined with bars and restaurants we see the annual zombie walk. I have forgotten its October 30. From 9:00 pm until midnight, the college students and anyone who wants to participate with them can dress as zombies and roam the streets in the Zombies Night Out.

The sidewalks are lined with people in torn clothing, white painted faces with black, gray and red face paint highlighting their deadliest and bloodiest zombie look. As we park the car and get out, a group of zombies come up to us telling us they want brains. It's hard to walk up the sidewalk because of the thousands of zombies out tonight. We pass in front of a bar and have to step out into the street to get around the crowd at the door. It seems college zombies also must have alcohol.

We walk into a packed burger joint and are given one of the last available tables in a room of zombies. The specials of the night all have night of the living dead themes. I go with something safe, a cheese burger and fries. John opts for a zombie burger medium well and baked beans. Samantha sits there flipping through the menu and decides on Southwest Egg Rolls and orders a 20 piece Buffalo Wing as an appetizer for the table. With that, we opt for the house special of dead man's beer in a never ending mug. The never ending mug explains the noise level of the restaurant. All the zombies seem to be in a great mood.

The food is good and the beer is cold. The zombies give us a chance to clear our heads of the case and watch something more entertaining. Drunken college kids dressed as zombies make a great comedy act. We have also started to classify the zombies into those that go for authentic night of the living dead look, those who just wanted a costume to pass enough to go out drinking with friends, and what we have labeled the slutty zombies. A few female zombies are dressed in bikini tops and micro band miniskirts. Some took the time to paint their bodies to look like the undead. Others walk up to a group of college guys with tubes of body paint all too eager to paint the girls for the night. No one seems to take offense that the guys are copping a feel as they paint. The bartender occasionally has to tell the girls to put their tops back on before the cops come and close the place down. It seems being a zombie for the night includes breasts painted as well.

As soon as we finish eating, we decide the place is getting too out of control to stay. The last thing John or I need is to be in a bar raided by vice for public nudity. Out on the street, the situation isn't much better. It has been over an hour since we arrived and the zombies have become really drunk. Acts of stupidity abound as we walk back to the SUV including a zombie grabbing Samantha and starting to run away with her. We finally make it to the SUV and weave our way through marauding groups of zombies in the street back toward our hotel. After parking, I walk across the street to the liquor store.

I hear the shouting before I open the room door. In my absence, John has decided to inform Samantha how she is ruining my career. I think he expected her to cower and agree with him. She didn't. I walk in to her pointing a finger in his face and yelling "just back the hell off of me! How dare you call me a two bit whore! If I had slept my God-damned way to the top, none of this would have happened. Instead, my daughter was kidnapped and murdered! I paid for what I did and then some. Don't you get that? I went to jail for my daughters disappearance and murder. I was tried and convicted off the lies. I would never do anything to jeopardize the case. I am not trying to seduce Adam. I have a doctorate and don't need a man to support me, so, I don't know where you got that idea, but you can hang it the hell up!"

They both turn and look at me when I walk in the door. I take a breath and shut the door, then walk to the table and put the bottle of rum down carefully. While I would like to deck John, at this moment, I decide their silence is sufficient and I let them both calm down. "John, Samantha and I have talked. Both of us have agreed that the outcome of this case is more important than any feeling we may be having. We are both professional and both want to see people go to jail for this. Neither of us will do anything that might jeopardize this case. All along, Samantha has been able to give us an angle on this case that neither of us has been able to see. She is a key to understanding what happened and hopefully anticipate what will happen. She's a professional in the mind of the people we are chasing. I have talked to the SAC about her being on the case and her input is not regarded as having any bearing on the murder case. Her only connection is to the initial abduction and that evidence on her has been thrown out. The DA has already charged Montgomery with the abduction and the men who helped him are already in jail without bail waiting on a grand jury. Montgomery's flight made them all a flight risk as well and they will be held as accessories to child abduction. Samantha is here because we need her here."

John walks over and picks up his laptop off the table "Whatever Adam. This is your career, not mine. I'm going to bed. You do whatever you think you should." He walks across the room and slams the door on his bedroom before turning the dead bolt.

Samantha starts to tell me she's sorry, but I hold my hand up to her. I don't even want to get into it at the moment. I grab two glasses; put ice in them and the pour Coke in each glass until they are half full. Then, I open the bottle of rum and fill each glass to the rim. Glass in hand I walk out on the balcony to watch the drunken zombies chanting "brains, brains" as a group staggers down the street. I notice she has walked outside also and she sits in one of the recliners. Neither of us speaks. It's probably better that way. Right now, this conversation could go a couple different ways. I don't want to think about either. I finish my drink and tell her goodnight.

DAY 14
COLLEGE STATION, TEXAS
TO SAN ANTONIO, TEXAS

I wake up hearing the television in Samantha's room. I knock on the door and open it. She's sitting on her bed with her laptop open while she watches storm coverage. The situation is bad. Most of Northern Virginia, Washington, DC and Maryland are out of power. The coastline is flooded. Both the Chesapeake Bay and Potomac are over their banks. The water of the inner harbor in Baltimore has surrounded buildings and is making its way through the streets. The next image is of the Washington Monument standing as if it was on an island in the middle of the National Mall. The Federal Government is closed, as are most local jurisdictions. People who had not evacuated on the coast are urged to shelter in place. Emergency Services had been suspended until after the storm passes. It has been deemed too dangerous to dispatch police or fire to rescue people.

Next the screen flips to New York City were sandbags and boards are being piled against the openings to the subway tunnels. Emergency services are worried the Hudson and East Rivers will flood the lower half of the city. The next shot is of the hull of the Lady Grey smashed on the beach at Sandy Point, Maryland. All are presumed dead with no signal reported from either of the rescue beacons in the life rafts. In the background, the image of the twin bridges crossing the Chesapeake Bay sit empty. Due to high wind, they are closed to all traffic. The next report is from Elkins, West Virginia which has already received a record three feet of snow for October with at least another twenty-four hours before the storm passes. The images appear to be surreal and part of some post-apocalyptic movie.

I remember what Samantha said yesterday about the storm of March 1962. It cost somewhere in the neighborhood of two hundred million dollars in property damages. This storm is more than forty years later. People have built closer houses along the coast and there are many more. I can only imagine the death toll and the price tag on the damage and recovery. My mind drifts to the ponies I saw on Assateague. I wish them luck through this. They have lived through storms like this before so I hope they do again. The irony of it all is that if all the wild ponies are lost it will be breeders like Helen Braden who return ponies to the island to replenish the herd. This reminds me of the task at hand today,-- the location of Helen Braden.

I walk out into the suite and John has already ordered breakfast. The argument of the night before buried so that we can get down to work. I check my messages and find a message from Sheriff Tarr that Helen Braden received a call that Duke had taken a turn for the worst and she had headed to his side. That made sense. Even though she is not the grieving wife she seemed like one who cares more about appearances. Being with him and making the announcement outside the hospice was much more dramatic and gives her the image she is looking for in his funeral.

As breakfast arrives, I tell John and Samantha where Helen Braden has gone. This causes Samantha to drop her fork, "How did she fly out yesterday when BWI, National and Reagan were closed due to the storm? Plus where was she going to go? I pulled up a map of the hospice yesterday. That area was on the news this morning. A tornado went through there and ripped things up badly. If I am correct, the hospice was damaged and patients were moved to a local hospital that had emergency power. I can't imagine there was more than one hospice on that block and the hospice lost part of its roof. There was a big deal about moving dying patients out into the storm to waiting ambulances."

She starts to type frantically and then spins her computer around. There on the screen is the front of the hospice. The portico is damaged and part of the roof is gone. The front circle is lined with ambulances as rain soaked medical teams push patients out the damaged entrance to be taken some place safer. The blankets covering the patients look drenched in the pouring rain. The headline reads "Did they make the wrong call? Hospice doctors and nurses brave the storm to move patients to safety."

She makes a face and goes back to her computer for a moment. "Hey Adam, yesterday didn't she say Tyler was flying back from the Amazon today to be by his father's side? I didn't think about it then, but they were already cancelling flights into the Mid-Atlantic region by then. She's a mother who hasn't seen her son in a couple weeks. Wouldn't she go to pick up her son? Where's the nearest international airport? Coming from the Amazon he'd have to clear customs right? Maybe he changed his flight to here."

I begin to call my office and instead stop and call the Dallas Field office. I'm in their turf so I should report in and play nice. I decide to throw them a bone and if Tyler Braden is flying in to Texas, let them grab him and ask him about the body in the field. While they are at it, I think a couple questions about what he knows of dear old Dad might not be a bad idea. I get a promise to be called as soon as they find out flight information from the FAA.

Breakfast is getting cold, so, I sit down to eat. Today I have the TV on and I am watching storm damage. My guess is much of the country is either watching this or living through it. So far seventeen states have been affected in some way by this storm. Higher elevations have several feet of snow piling up, the coast is flooded and up to two hundred miles inland are getting winds in the neighborhood of one hundred miles per hour. Right now, I am glad we left Jekyll Island. While it is south of the storm, the entire Atlantic Ocean is angry with high waves pounding the shore.

After eating, we put the tray outside and settle in to look at updates on our laptops. The TV continues in the background moving from location to location showing waves hitting the shore. I watch as a pier in Ocean City, Maryland gives in to the waves. Not long after, I see images of waves crashing around an antique carousel and roller coaster in New Jersey. These are followed by waves crashing against Ellis Island and the base of the Statue of Liberty. Nothing seems to be sacred in the path of this storm.

My phone rings and I see it's the Dallas Field office. I am hoping for a lead and something to do other then watch waves and wind destroy the east coast. Instead, there is no record of Tyler Braden on any inbound flights from the Amazon or anywhere else for that matter. He did not book a flight, cancel a flight, or land anywhere in the country in the last forty eight hours. Like Helen Braden, Tyler Braden appears to have evaporated into thin air.

We don't have any leads. We can't go home. We can't follow up with people because of this storm. We are stuck in College Station, Texas with a day on our hands. I look at my cell phone and it's not even 8:00 am yet. I call Sheriff Tarr back and ask him if he has any leads he thinks we should follow. If not, I think after two straight weeks of work it might be a good day to take the day off. When working a case, I rarely get that opportunity. With the Richmond Field office closed as well as the DC and New York offices, all I have is the Dallas office involved in the investigation. They can reach me by phone. Sheriff Tarr promises to see if he can track down Helen and Tyler Braden.

I stand up and grab the keys and ask "who wants to take a day off and have a road trip in Texas?" They both stand up and head for the door.

"Has anyone ever been to the Alamo?" I look at both and they are shaking their heads. I know this sounds crazy and completely against my personality, but I don't want to spend my day in the hotel watching the east coast of the United States melt under the wind and water of a hurricane. "Umm, anyone know the address of the Alamo? The closest I can get is San Antonio, Texas."

John pulls the GPS off the holder and starts to type in The Alamo, San Antonio, Texas. At that, the GPS spouts "Turn northeast onto Farm to Market Road route 60 University Drive." The Alamo is just three hours and twenty-six minutes away. We should be there before lunch.

Once we leave the traffic of College Station and hit State Road 21, the land stretches out for miles with big ranches on either side of the road. The weather is nice and we put the windows down. As we approach Bastrop, the trees start to get thicker. The road drives through the middle of the National Park. I can feel the temperature dropping as we go deeper into the forest. Samantha takes it upon herself to count the number of Farm to Market Roads we pass. She finds humor in stating the obvious.

About half way in the trip, I stop at a gas station to top off the tank and stretch my legs. We walk in and get a cold drink for the rest of the drive. Before we pull out, I ask if either mind staying the night in San Antonio. I pulled out my personal credit card and put two rooms on it for the night. I figure we have our cell phones and laptops and with the storm we are limited with what we can do. Since the drive is over three hours, this will give us an entire day in San Antonio. If something comes up we can hit the road and go where we are needed. Until then, today is a day off.

Back on the road, we make good time getting to Interstate 35 which takes us into San Antonio. It's been a while since I've been in the town, but the GPS directs me to the parking garage of the hotel I booked. In the back of my mind, I am thinking this is the first time not working that I am taking Samantha somewhere. I want to impress her. Our hotel is right on the river walk and a short trip to the Alamo. We go into the hotel and check in. The hotel has followed my instructions perfectly, two connecting rooms both with two double beds. We leave our laptops in the room and head down the elevator to the street. There I lead them down the River Walk and over four blocks to the Alamo.

I feel completely carefree. The oppression of the case peels away from me and getting out and walking makes me feel alive. Samantha is all smiles as we walk. She is looking around and taking in everything as we pass. The River Walk is like a never-ending circus of lights and entertainment. The streets are lined with stores and restaurants. Two more blocks and we break out into the open, facing the plaza and The Alamo. Even John has lightened up in his mood, trying to decide which bar and restaurant he wants to go to tonight. I feel like I can shake some of the cob webs out of my head and relax for the day. This may be what we all need right now. We have been cooped up in planes, cars and hotels for the last two weeks. I'm glad I made the decision to have a break.

As we walked in, I see the information desk and visitors center. Compliments of Sheriff Tarr, I look around for his daughter, Allison. I text her and see a pretty blond look up a few seconds later. She walked over smiling "Hi, I bet you are Agents Clay, Duncan and Dr. Callahan. Welcome to the Alamo. My dad called me and asked that I show you around and give you some of the history. Normally they don't have guided tours, but being that you are from out of town and today is my day off I figured a guided tour is in order. Why don't you come this way?" She walks off at a steady pace to the plaza facing the Alamo. I looked over at Samantha and John. Both were all eyes looking around in awe. Once we are where she wants us Allison begins "I should say welcome to Misión San Antonio de Valero. Construction began on this site in 1724 and served as a home for the missionaries and their Indian converts for almost seventy years. In 1793, the Spanish consolidated the five missions and divided the land among the Indians. The Indians did what they had done all their lives and farmed the land creating what we know now as the City of San Antonio. In the early 1800s, the Spanish stationed a cavalry unit in the old mission building. They were the first to call this the Alamo." As she talks, Allison walks us through the plaza of the Alamo. Her hand gesturing in the direction she wants us to see as she points out buildings and locations. She stops in front of the doors of the main gate.

"On February 23, 1836, the arrival of General Antonio López de Santa Anna's army outside San Antonio nearly caught Ben Milam, his Texans and Tejano volunteers by surprise. The Texans and Tejanos prepared to defend the Alamo. They held their ground for thirteen straight days against Santa Anna's army. William Travis, the commander of the Alamo sent runners carrying requests for help to communities around San Antonio. On the eighth day of the siege, thirty-two volunteers from Gonzales arrived, bringing the number of men to nearly two hundred. Legend is that as the possibility of additional help faded, Colonel Travis drew a line on the ground and asked any man willing to stay and fight to step over — all except one did. As the men saw it, the Alamo was the key to the defense of Texas, and they were ready to give their lives rather than surrender their position to General Santa Anna. Among the men at the Alamo were Jim Bowie and David Crockett."

Allison walked inside the doors and, after getting a few feet in, turned and looked at us again. "The final assault came before daybreak on the morning of March 6, 1836, as columns of Mexican soldiers emerged just before dawn and headed for the Alamo's walls. The men inside the Alamo beat back several attacks. Then the Mexicans scaled the walls and rushed into the compound. Once inside, they turned a cannon on the Long Barracks and church. They blasted open the barricaded doors. The battle continued until the men inside were overwhelmed. By sunrise, the battle had ended and Santa Anna entered the Alamo compound to survey the scene of his victory."

She pauses here and lets us look around. "There were at least eighteen women and children that survived the Battle of the Alamo. They were found here in the church after the battle by Santa Anna's men. The women were each given a blanket and two pesos. Then they were then allowed to leave. These women were the ones who told the story that the Alamo had fallen and the brave battle the men put up to try to save the stronghold."

We walk around for another hour before Allison tells us she needs to run for a study session. She makes sure we know how to get back to our hotel and reminds us to check out the river walk for dinner. We are all in a relaxed mood. John is a history buff also so this is right down his alley. I think Samantha is completely overwhelmed. A few times as we walk around, she has said she has never been to a place like this.

It's almost 4:00 PM when we walk to the River Walk. I have forgotten today is Halloween, but the small groups of children in costume remind me. Many of the stores and restaurants are decorated and their employees are wearing costumes. There is a party atmosphere as we walk. The children are laughing and playing as the merchants get ready to celebrate Halloween with trick or treating for them.

We find a restaurant with bistro tables on the sidewalk so that we can have an early dinner and watch the fun. The table we are seated at sits along the river so we also get a view of the boats making their way slowly up the river loaded with tourists. As usual, we missed lunch, but a nice leisurely dinner seems to work for us. This restaurant is famous for their forty-six ounce margaritas. I'm always in favor of the house specialty, especially when it comes in a monster glass. Perhaps the three of us getting giant margaritas on empty stomachs is not the wisest move, but this is a day of fun.

We start dinner off with supreme nachos and sopa de tortilla a la Mexicana. Samantha orders carnitas. I think the margarita is already getting to her. She giggles when she orders it because she likes the name. John settles on fajitas while I decide on enchiladas. The nachos and soup come out quickly so we start to eat.

Our conversation is light. We point out great costumes on some of the kids. There's a costume contest somewhere down the River Walk and parents are herding their children to get to the event. The wait staff is dressed in costume. We laugh because ours is a zombie. We don't seem to be able to get away from the undead. We talk about the Alamo and how great the River Walk looks. No one mentions the case. It feels good to laugh and relax. I haven't realized how tense and uptight I have become. Now letting it all go feels good. I can tell it has lifted a burden off of John and Samantha as well. We finish the meal off with a round of sopapillas and café.

After dinner, we walk the River Walk. Kids are everywhere laughing and running from business to business getting candy. Music is playing from some of the bars and restaurants. I'm glad we got a hotel for the night. We stop in a bar to use the bathrooms and grab another drink. It's hard to believe it's after 11:00 PM already. We finish our drinks and walk back to the hotel. Today was what the doctor ordered.

Slightly drunk and tired, we head to bed without turning on the television or opening a laptop. Tomorrow we will be back on the case. Tonight we sleep off forty-six ounce margaritas and a great day of sightseeing. Before she goes to her room, Samantha gives both John and I a hug and thanks us for the best day she has ever had. I'm proud of myself for this one. It was great to see her happy.

DAY 15
SAN ANTONIO, TEXAS

I wake to the sounds of Samantha trying to find aspirin. I stick my head into her room and ask if she wants to go downstairs for coffee. She raises the bottle of aspirin and I tell her I will take two also. We ride the elevator downstairs and follow the smell of coffee. The hotel has a nice continental breakfast set out. It is completely lost on me at the moment. My stomach feels like I had surgery over night. Samantha toasts a bagel and grabs a pack of cream cheese. I decide it is probably a good idea and I toast one as well. After all, I should have something in my stomach before I take the aspirin.

We haven't heard from John; so, I text him that we are downstairs getting breakfast and sitting at a table. Most of the people in San Antonio on business have already gotten up and left the hotel. Those that are here on vacation have not gotten out of bed yet. We have a corner of the dining area to ourselves. As I am getting up to get a second cup of coffee, I see John getting off the elevator. I pour him a cup and hand it to him. He looks as rough as I feel.

After breakfast, we ride the elevator back up to the room and turn on the television. The east coast is still being torn apart by the hurricane. Most of the Mid-Atlantic is out of power. Image after image is shown of houses sitting in the middle of water as if they have become house boats. The death toll is given by state. So far twenty nine people have lost their lives. In North Carolina, as the storm pulls away, there are images of police and Coast Guard helicopters air lifting people off their roofs. Image after image is of destruction. I try to call the team and get no response. From the quick busy signal, I can tell phone service is out in the area.

The images from New York City are just as bad. The subway tunnels are flooding and the flood waters in Manhattan have made it north to Canal Street. Long Island and Staten Island are completely under water. The National Mall in Washington, DC is completely flooded, a camera shot shows water standing in the mall and roads around the museums. The fountain at the World War II monument has filled the bowl shaped area and cascades down toward the reflecting pool and the Lincoln memorial. The Capitol and the White House seem to be on some of the only area on ground high enough to be out of standing water. The DC FBI office is at a lower elevation off the National Mall. My guess it is in standing water. According to the National Weather Service, there is at least a day left before the storm passes.

I think about my house. It sits on a rise in Northern Virginia. In the winter when the trees are bare, I can see the James River as it makes a bend around Dutch Gap and the remains of Henricus. My house will be high enough to escape the flood waters, but the conservation area at Dutch Gap and the ruins of the second English settlement will be under water as the James floods its banks. I can't image what the river looks like spreading out over the flat lands. I wonder why I am sitting in Texas watching this, but I know there is nothing I could do if I was home. It's one of the things I never understood about people who don't evacuate during a storm. There's nothing you can do when the water rises except watch it rise. If it gets too high, it will come in your house whether you are there or not. To me it is never worth risking your life to roll up carpets if the water raises enough to come in the front door. I know we are better off being away from the area but I still feel for the people we left behind. Right now I have no idea where my team is or if they are ok. I assume they are all at home with their families or in shelters above the rising water.

Samantha sits and watches with me. So many people are dealing with a storm of epic proportions. I know somewhere in the back of her mind the thoughts of Kali's ashes sitting alone in my office has to worry her. I reassure her even if the building floods or is damaged her ashes are on an upper floor inside a room with no windows. At the current time, all we can do is continue what we have in Texas and wait for the east coast to regain power and the water to recede.

John checks with Sheriff Tarr on both Helen and Tyler Braden. So far neither has surfaced. Whether it is because of the storm or Helen Braden wasn't telling us the truth about Tyler. He had not purchased a ticket under his name and has not flown into this country. There is no word on Duke Braden either. It is assumed he was evacuated from his hospice and is in a regional hospital.

We decide to take a walk around the river walk for a while. After we have lunch we can drive back to College Station. For now there is nothing we can do but wait. While waiting we might as well see some of San Antonio. The river walk is a path along the San Antonio River. Most of the path is stone lined landscaped with trees and flowering plants. Now and then, we see a pond with koi or goldfish swimming around in pools surrounded by lush floral beds. Ahead we heard a waterfall. We walk around a corner and see an ivy covered bridge crossing to the other side. Beyond that water cascades from a pool back down into the river. The air is already humid as the temperature tops eighty.

Samantha is bouncing back and forth between looking at the river walk and the many stores along the walkway. I hadn't realized that she has never been on vacation before and this is an entirely new experience for her. We offer to let her shop some more, but she has no idea what she would want to buy. Instead, we look at the sites and enjoy the warmth of the day.

At 4:30 PM, we stop and get lunch at another river view café. This time we opt for burgers and fries. We eat slowly and talk. Today has been a great day and this has been the perfect break from the investigation. The SUV is already packed and after eating we head back to the hotel parking lot and begin the drive back to College Station. The sun sets behind us as we drive through the miles of Texas landscape.

About forty miles out of College Station, I pull over along the road and get out. We get out and marvel at the canopy of light in the sky. I have never seen so many stars. It is breath taking. Even the Milky Way is a defined spot in the sky not just a hazy area. Samantha was from New Jersey near New York City and has never seen stars like this either. To her it is another world. John and I spend over an hour pointing out star formations in the galaxy. I think about this being another place and time and how I want to show Samantha the world. She has missed so much. It has become apparent to me in the last twenty-four hours that she has not even had a chance to live. In the back of my mind, I think about the future and how I can marvel and amaze her.

We finally get back in the SUV and head to our hotel. The news has changed very little since this morning. The reporters warn people to stay inside and away from standing water and down lines. There is no way to know if the power has been cut to an area or if the lines are deadly. The death toll has risen to fifty-eight. The news out of New York and New Jersey is grim. Millions are in the dark tonight. The water supply has been contaminated with storm runoff and water from the Hudson and East Rivers. In the higher elevations touched by the storm over three feet of snow has fallen. Power crews and relief efforts are in route to the affected areas.

Samantha has found a web page that is updating with pictures people are taking of Chincoteague. There is no news on if the ponies have survived. Two feet of water covered Chincoteague during each high tide during the storm. Houses and businesses are flooded and the causeway leading to the island has been closed to traffic. In the morning, the police hope to open the causeway and go to the island to survey the damage. People who stayed behind and ignored the evacuation order are posting pictures from their phones of trees down and high water. The area looks much different than it did two weeks ago.

The news is depressing. I get up and take the ice bucket out into the hallway. Then fill three glasses with ice. Everyone agrees it's a Rum and Coke kind of night. We sit and watch the news until after midnight. It gets to the point the news is repeating itself. I think of the reporters who are following our case. I'm sure many of them have family and friends in the disaster area as well. To all of us, news from the region is something we watch in horror and hope for the best.

DAY 16
COLLEGE STATION, TEXAS

In the morning, I wake to an email from my team. Chip has made it into the office. All is dry and intact, but there is no power to the area. He checked the computers and everything is fine but he shut the computers and the lab down because it was running on emergency power. The basement of the building is flooded and some of the cabling coming in may need to be repaired or replaced. No one realized the storm was going to be this bad. They had heard the National Weather Forecasters, but the depth of the storm was more than human imagination. When they left before the storm, they just turned off the desktops and left the mainframes churn along. Now the building sits dormant waiting for civilization to catch back up to the current day. Most of the team has generators at home but finding gasoline is getting hard.

Sheriff Tarr believes he has located Helen Braden. Her credit card is being used in Houston and twice it has been used in the same hotel. He has police checking with the front desk determining if she is a guest there. Flight manifests leaving the United States and flying or connecting to the Amazon have been checked back to October first and there is no record of Tyler Braden flying there--or anywhere for that matter. The only record of him in current manifests was from September eighth when he flew to Austin with an initial destination from Brigadeiro Eduardo Gomes – Manaus International Airport in Manaus, Brazil. It appears Tyler Braden either didn't mention he was not going back to the Amazon or his body is in the morgue in Austin. Sheriff Tarr is already trying to determine if anything about our torso matches Tyler Braden.

Meanwhile, the Coast Guard is listing all aboard the Lady Grey as lost at sea. Two days after the foundering, no remnants of the escape rafts have

174

been found nor has anyone come forward saying they are a survivor of the ship. The current Coast Guard manifest for the ship shows a crew of sixteen. If Montgomery and Sidney were on the ship, they were not listed on the official manifest, then again once they stepped out of the hotel on Jekyll Island their whereabouts are unknown. Once again, we are sitting around with no leads and nowhere to go. If this had been an average day, we would check out of the hotel and fly home. Right now the airports in the region are closed with emergency personnel checking the runways for damage and in some cases waiting for power to be restored.

With nothing else to do, I go online looking for something to do in College Station or Bryan. Other then the college and the Bush Library, there are shopping centers and bars. After failing to find anything that we can spend the day doing, while we wait on the east coast to come back to life, I start to sort through the book of attractions from the drawer in the hotel. I come up with hiking trails or horseback riding. Since none of us have ever gone horseback riding, we decide today is the day we will either learn or break something in the process.

I call ahead and make sure we can rent horses for the day and if there will be anyone to give us some pointers. I drive about forty minutes until I see the gates of a ranch. As usual for ranches we have seen here, the driveway is a hard packed clay road. We leave a dusty trail as we head toward the barns. No one is around when we get out so we walk toward noise in a barn. The man in the barn yells out that he is Luke and "come on in and let's get you mounted."

Luke is a cowboy. There's no other description that will apply. He's tall and thin with sloped shoulders and slightly bow legged. He's wearing dusty jeans and a black t-shirt with a beaten up black leather Stetson and boots that look like they are old enough to vote in the next election. Every few seconds, he spits tobacco juice on the ground. He surveys us as we enter and gets a big grin. "I was wondering if you were beginners and my guess is that we need to start at the very beginning. I'm right now aren't I?" We each nod and he grins just a little more. I get the feeling we may or may not live through today's events because this guy looks like he is going to enjoy any mishaps we might have. "Knowing you were coming, I grabbed a couple of the tamer horses we have around here. They are old and slow.

Young lady, I'm going to get you up on this one. Cloud knows what to do and all you have to do is stay seated on her." With that he pulls the horse up to a fence and motions for her to climb up and get on board.

Samantha looks at him and at the horse. Then she looks at the fence. She gingerly climbs up to the third rung and reaches out for the saddle, then with a deep intake of breath she swings her leg over the back of the horse and slides into the saddle. Luke then hands her the reigns and walks away. Samantha looks terrified as the horse stamps her feet and steps forward a few steps. "Umm… Luke. I don't know how to drive a horse. How do I make it stop?"

He turns and looks at her and says "Hold your horses. Cloud is just protesting having to work. She won't go anywhere yet and I will teach you all how to work the reigns in a minute. Let me get your friends on board." He repeated the same mounting procedure with John and I. Then he grabs the reigns of the fourth horse, puts one foot in the stirrups and swings up into the saddle. "Ya'll Giddy up now and come along." With that, our horses started to follow him out of the barn and into a round paddock. So far riding is pretty easy.

Once we reach the center of the ring, he pulls up beside us. "Okay, before we hit the trail we are going to learn how to start, stop, and turn the horses. See how my reigns are tight along the neck. This means stop. Now before you do anything remember there's a bit in their mouth. This is not a game of tug-a-war. Think about having a bar under your tongue and how you would like someone pulling at it. Be gentle. If you get rough and you tick off the horse, you have to deal with their attitude. Now let the reigns go a little slack and give them a little tap on the side with your foot. That means go. The more reigns you give them the faster they will go. Think this is your horse's gas pedal. If you want to fly across the field let the pedal out. If you just want to walk give it a nice gentle reign. Now say you want to turn left. Give it a little reign on the right and pull a little to the left. Horses don't make sharp turns. They have big bodies that only turn a little. You can't pull their heads around to touch their bodies. Just give them a little slack on one side and tighten up the side in the direction you are turning. You want to try that now?" We all nod.

Pretty soon we are walking around the ring and executing turns. We seem to be catching on enough for Luke to lean over and open the gate to let us ride out. He then rides his horse out and leans down and closes the gate. Ahead of us is a wide open plain that stretches toward the Brazos River. We are riding through tall grass and scrub pines. Our horses seem to pick the trail and where they want to walk. We are just along for the ride. As we reach the river Luke turns his horse toward the narrow strip of woods. We fall in behind him. The path gets narrower as we enter the woods and are forced to ride single file. I let John go first and then Samantha in case she has trouble. The smile on her face says she's having a blast.

Now and then, we have to duck and ride under low branches or try to stay in the saddle while holding a branch above our heads. The trail leads out to a narrow strip along the river. Ahead, the river goes through a series of exposed rock and the water rushes through sending white water down the river. We hear the falls before we see them. Across the river, Luke points out Hidalgo Falls. He explains the area across from us is a private owned camp for white water rafters. You have to be a member or have approval from one of the members to unlock the fence and go inside. I ask him if people frequently canoe on the river. He shakes his head. "Pretty much takes a damn fool to come down this. If they are letting water out of the dam, the water is high and a while later they can close the gates and the water drops down to a gentle stream. I have seen people fishing out there and they had plenty of water. Three hours later they have to get out and drag their boat across the river bottom to get the boat back to the banks. If you stay on the river too long you get to here. They say, depending on the river height, this is a class I to a Class IV. That's a big difference between a gentle ride and drown your hide, if you know what I mean."

This adventure answers a lot of questions about our torso in the field. Hidalgo Falls is about 20 miles south of the Traynor farm. If the water levels are unpredictable here, I am sure it is unpredictable there as well. I doubt anyone would risk putting the torso in a boat and going down the river. Beside the potential for being seen, there is the risk of being caught in shallow water with a body on board.

The ride lasts about two hours and I can feel the burn in my inner thighs as I dismount. Ducking and dodging the branches caused me to grip the horse with the legs. I didn't feel the stiffness before I got off the horse but walking back to the SUV I can feel the pull. I notice John and Samantha have a similar gait.

As I head back to College Station, I decide to pull into a mall to grab some lunch. I am also thinking about the hot tub downstairs in our hotel. I don't have my bathing suit but I am considering picking one up for this afternoon or evening and sitting back in the hot tub to relieve the pain. I'm not sure how much selection there will be in November but, I am willing to walk the mall for a few minutes to see if I can find anything. I mention my quest to the group and get a unanimous approval of the idea. Samantha is worried about the fact that we are going into a public place smelling like a horse but, I remind her we are in Texas. People will just think we are cowboys. That brings a smile to her face.

Luckily, the first department store we enter has a cruise department in both the men's and women's departments. We leave Samantha in the women's department promising to return and get her. For both of us, it is a matter of picking out a pair of trunks. When we get back, Samantha is at the register with a pile. I can see she's hit up the bras, panties, jeans and tops. I don't see a bathing suit but I assume it may already be in the bag.

From there, we go to the food court and grab some lunch. Samantha seems lost with so many choices. She ends up following me to an Italian place. Choice and freedom are still hard for her. I wonder if she will ever get use to being able to do what she wants whenever she feels like it. The years of jail and the life she led before have affected her. What I have always taken for granted is alien to her.

As we eat, we watch the people walking around the mall. Families are there with kids running around without adults present. In the back of my mind, I think about how easy it must be for a member of the Co-Op to find a kid and grab them. I see about twenty kids playing in a play area with only two adults paying any attention at all. A few other adults are standing around talking but, as I watch, a child falls and starts to cry with no one paying any attention or responding. Finally another child comes to the little ones aid and asks where a parent is sitting. The parent has no idea that their child has fallen or that a child has walked them out of the play area. It is only after they reach the table does the parent notice and react. I'm glad I don't have kids. This case has opened my eyes to the lack of education parents have in regards to their children's vulnerability from child sexual predators. I probably wouldn't let a child of mine out of my sight. These parents have no idea how lucky they are that it is me watching their children play instead of a pedophile shopping for a new playmate.

As we head toward the door of the mall, Samantha stops and looks at a pair of cowboy boots in the display of a Country Western Store. We walk inside to look around. Before we know it was are all trying on boots and hats. We laugh at the fact that we smell like cowboys, so we might as well look like one. If nothing happens in the case, we will be flying out of Texas and heading back to Richmond as soon as the airports open on the east coast. There's no reason for us to be here anymore other then not being able to get home. Authentic boots and hats from Texas make great souvenirs so we walk out with more bags. Samantha opts to wear her boots and hat out of the store. She's picked out a pair of black and gray boots with a black leather Stetson. She's tucked her jeans into the bottom of the boots and is wearing a black t-shirt. With that outfit and her blond hair she turns a couple heads in the mall on the way out. The look she gets from passing men makes her smile and puts a jaunt in her walk.

Back at the hotel we put our packages in the room before grabbing a towel and our new bathing suits. We decide to change downstairs rather then walk through the lobby dressed for the pool area. John and I walk out together and wait for Samantha.

I am looking at the instructions for the hot tub when I hear John exclaim, "Holy Shit!" I look to see Samantha walking out in a black string bikini. She looks absolutely stunning. What little material there is of the bikini barely covers her body showing off long lean lines and miles of flawless curves. John just looks at me and shakes his head. "Buddy, I take back what I said. If you don't ask her out, you are a fool.

I smile at her and say "looking good, Dr. Callahan. That is an excellent choice of swim attire." She giggles and spins to give us the full view. There is no bad view of her outfit. Every man, married or single in the pool area has turned to check her out.

I set the timer on the water jets on the hot tub and we get in. The hot water feels good and I adjust the jets on my back and shoulders. Samantha has laid back and closed her eyes. I try not to look at her, but the view is just too tempting. Her bikini leaves very little to the imagination and at thirty-four she could pass for her early twenties. I think about our conversation regarding when we get home and realize if nothing turns up in the case today, we will probably be on a plane back to Virginia either tomorrow or the following day. Then we will have to decide where Samantha will live. I would like to take her home with me. Spending the last few weeks with her we have grown inseparable. I'm sure she could live on her own, but I don't know if I am ready to let her go. I am comfortable having her near me. Maybe too comfortable because, at times like this, when I look at her all I can think about is making her that cup of coffee in the morning.

My thoughts are interrupted by the timer going off and the jets stopping in the hot tub. Samantha opens her eyes and looks around. "Okay, where in the hell is the button to turn those back on?" I point to the wall and she starts to make her way out of the tub. She wraps her arms around herself and runs to the wall to push the button again. Then wraps her arms around herself again and shuffles her feet back to the steps to get in. "Wow that was a shock! I didn't know it was cold out there! That was more than a wee bit nipple-y. It was full out chisel tits!"

John turns to her and cracks up. "What did you just say? A wee bit nipple-y and chisel tits? That's hysterical! I get the point, no pun intended, but where did you get that from?"

Samantha blushes and cracks up laughing. "You get out and push the button next time. At least, I just get chisel tits. You will get shrinkage so bad you will think you have an innie." Everyone in the pool area has turned to look and see what was so funny. It is a good thing this is just our personal joke.

When the jets stop again, John gets out and pushed the button getting back in quickly. "Okay, you win. I haven't been this small since I was in nursery school. Pardon while I defrost my nether regions." With that we start to laugh again.

Eventually we start to look like prunes. Our hands and feet are wrinkled and we know we have to get out. We have soaked in the tub for over an hour. The warning on the wall advises staying in no longer then twenty minutes. With our stiff muscles and how good the water felt, we decided to make an exception. Now, we race from the water to our towels and wrap up as we run to the changing rooms.

We meet up outside and head back for the elevator. The air still feels cold to us but, clothes make it a little more tolerable. When we get to the room Samantha goes into her bedroom and pulls her comforter off her bed. She brings it back to the center area and wraps up on the sofa.

John starts a pot of coffee and walks by her and laughs "Hey how are those nipples now?" Samantha rolls her eyes at him and responds "Fine, really fine!"

It's good to see them joking around. I flip on the television to see what storm coverage is being aired. One the screen is an amusement park with waves rushing over the rides. The top of a Tilt-a-whirl is barely visible and the roller coaster looks like a twisted sentinel in the open ocean. It switches to pictures of boats smashed together against a line of brick buildings. The destruction goes on and on. Then there is a helicopter view of some wild horses and Samantha yells "turn it up!"

"The winds have died enough for the National Park Service to get a helicopter up and they have been able to fly over the wild pony herds of Chincoteague and Assateague. According to the park service, it appears all of the ponies were able to find higher ground. They have not seen any causalities among the herds. The water is starting to recede and the ponies are beginning to return to their natural grazing area. Over the next few weeks, Park Service and the Chincoteague Volunteer Fire Company will check on the health of the ponies and if necessary drop food for them. Throughout the storm, there has been great concern for the wildlife on this island. Every year in July, the Chincoteague Volunteer Fire Company hold their wild pony round up. These ponies have been the central point of books and movies. America has a romance with these animals and I am glad to announce they ponies have made it through the storm. The people of Chincoteague Island are strong people. The island was covered in about two feet of water. As people begin to help their neighbors get trees off roofs and clean up the debris others felt the obligation to check on the pony herd. With all of the damage from this storm, we leave you tonight with a view of hope, as the wild ponies of Chincoteague return their lives to normal and pick up eating in the patch of grass they left off on four days ago."

I look over and see a tear run down Samantha's cheek. To her, these ponies mean a lot more. Somewhere, below that helicopter, is the pony that was by her daughter's side when she died. While that pony doesn't hold answers, in many ways her survival holds hope for Samantha that one day her daughter's killer will be found and she will get closure.

It's 6:00 PM and I'm starting to get hungry. I throw the room service menu to Samantha and tell her to surprise us. She grins and picks up the phone. Thirty minutes later, room service delivers chicken with asparagus and portabella mushrooms in a parmesan pesto sauce. With that she ordered, garlic parmesan Texas Toast and two bottles of white wine. I think to myself that she should order dinner more often. My mouth waters at the smell coming off the cart.

We joke and talk at dinner. The news mentioned that Baltimore Washington, Reagan National and Richmond International airports were expected to open tomorrow. After we finish eating, I make the call to get a flight booked home. Once done, I check one more time with Sheriff Tarr. They have not found Helen Braden. She was not a patron of the hotel and they are still looking for her. I thank him and tell him to keep in touch if he gets any leads. I don't see anything more that we can do in Texas.

I am happy and apprehensive about flying home. When we land, I have to make a decision about Samantha. I have extra room in my house. Even if she doesn't want to sleep in my bed, I have a place she can stay until she decides what she wants to do and where she wants to live. I decide to talk to her privately after John goes to bed.

As usual he turns in early and we stay up to finish off the wine. After I close my door, I walk to hers and ask if we can talk. I offer to let her stay at my place and I'm glad she accepts. I make it clear no obligations and no expectations. For now, it's an offer of a bed and a place to call home. What happens from that point, we will work out. I still need to stay objective about the case and can't let my feelings for her get in the way. When we get back to Virginia, she will get in the airport taxi with me and John can go his separate way. I live south of the city and he lives west so it will make sense. I know he will wonder what my plan is but, for now I really don't know.

I go to bed thinking about the flight home and taking Samantha to my house. It's been nearly three weeks and the storm of the century since I walked in the front door. Until now, I hadn't even thought about whether I still had a front door. I guess if one of the one hundred plus year old trees in my yard had fallen on my house someone would have called me by now. Of course, cell and phone service is still out in many areas and power is still an issue in much of the Mid-Atlantic. At least Richmond is far enough from the coast to not have the Atlantic pounding on it and the James River can get high but, it would take quite a bit for it to get to my house.

DAY 17
COLLEGE STATION, TEXAS
TO DUTCH GAP, VIRGINIA

Morning is a flurry of activity. We check email, eat breakfast and pack everything. We have all added a few things since we arrived in College Station. For once heading back to the office during a case, I feel refreshed. I feel a little guilty about having a mini vacation while everyone else was suffering through a storm , but I have a fresh mind and I'm ready to meet with my team and see if there's anything we can draw on to jump start the case. In the back of my mind is a fear that the flow of new information has dried up and we have nowhere to go. At that point, I will be assigned another case and hit the road chasing leads on it. For Samantha's sake, I am not ready to do that yet. Also, indications from this case lead me to believe what we have is not a small isolated incident. I think there are many other kids in bad situations that need our help.

The flight is bumpy and for the entire three hours the seatbelt sign stays on. The upper atmosphere is still unstable from the storm and another tropical depression is forming to follow its path. Samantha is not a good flier to start with and every time the plane drops she grabs the arms of her seat. I am glad when the pilot announces we are about to land and to stow all loose objects.

We grab our bags and head out to catch an airport taxi. John heads on his way home while Samantha and I head south to my house. As we pass neighborhoods, the sound of tree saws can still be heard. I see electric trucks from different states stringing lines. The full magnitude of the storm begins to hit me. My house sits on the back side of a golf course. We wind our way through the development and make the turn onto my street. Samantha looks out the window and remarks on how nice the neighborhood looks. We reach the end of the court and the driver pulls into my front circle. Samantha's eyes are wide as she looks around.

My house is a two story federal style. I thought it went well with the history of the area. I had it designed to look like one of the historic houses along the James. We grab our bags and I pay the driver. I'm trying to remember what condition I left the house when I left for Chincoteague. I try to keep things somewhat in order for when my pet sitter, Tara, comes in to feed Chaucer and Ebenezer, my rabbits.

I unlock the door and punch in the numbers on the alarm code and nothing happens. The panel isn't lit up so I check the light in the foyer. Nothing happens when I flip the switch on. I guess power is still off to the house. I make a mental inventory of what I may have left in the fridge and conclude there is really nothing in there so, there's not much to clean out.

I drop the bags next to the stairs and ask Samantha if she would like the grand tour. We walk through the living room and dining room into the kitchen. Then I take her over to the sliding door to the back. I'm particularly proud of this. The hill behind the house leads down to a sandy strip along the James River. It is on a portion where the river curves around a small island. The James looks high and I can see where it flowed up and around my boat house. My dock is a pontoon and I try to look and see if it floated back into the river or if I have to have it pulled off the bank. It's hard to tell from here and I make a mental note to walk down and check later.

Samantha screams as we start down the hallway to the game room. "What the hell was that? I saw something black run by! Please tell me you have a cat?" I laugh and look in the direction she was pointing. Under the book case I see Ebenezer hiding. I pick him up and show him to her. Her face lights up. "Is that a rabbit? You have a rabbit running around your house? It's adorable!"

I hand her Ebenezer and go in search of Chaucer. Once I find him, I carry him into the living room and pat the sofa for Samantha to come sit down. She is smiling and rubbing Ebenezer against her face. She sits and Ebenezer settles down in her lap letting her pet him. Chaucer hops down and takes off away from us. He's not as friendly as Ebenezer. "I guess I should explain these two. Two years ago, I was working a case and there was an elderly woman who was a hoarder. There was a call from the neighbors about the smell in the house. Everyone assumed it was from all the cat feces because she had twenty nine cats. Animal control went into the house and started to remove cats. As they were sweeping the house for animals, they found a body. It turned out a neighbor had come in to complain to her about the cats and she killed the guy. Instead of calling the police or getting rid of the body, she just shut the door. This house was a mess. Animal control removed both dead and alive animals. The stress of the raid and animal control pushed the woman over the edge and she committed suicide in the kitchen. While we were getting the body out of the house, they came across a dead mother rabbit. With her were these two. They were only a week or two old. Animal control was just going to take them and put them down because they were too young to be weaned and young rabbits don't thrive well without a mother. They were smaller then my hand. I couldn't stand two more lives lost in this house. I had spent over an hour stepping over dead cats. I asked if I could try to feed them. I was going to give them to my niece if they lived. After a few days, they had hooked me and I couldn't give them up. Before you ask, yes, they are potty trained. There are litter boxes in strategic locations. They pretty much take care of themselves. When I'm gone, I pay a neighbor girl fifty dollars a week to change their litter boxes and make sure they have food and water."

Samantha keeps petting Ebenezer and smiling as I talk. "I never thought of you as a guy to have cute and fuzzy bunnies. This is a new image for me, but I like it. I think it's pretty cool. I was always against killing animals from fur coats and things. It seemed such a crime to take such a beautiful creature and kill it just because it had beautiful fur. You have found a way to have the beautiful furry creature and it's alive and warm. You are pretty cool Adam Clay, pretty damn cool."

Finally, Ebenezer hops down and takes off down the hallway. I stand up and hold out my hand to her. Samantha stands up and I take her down the hall to the game room. Here, I have my wide screen television, a pool table and the game console. In any other house, it would be called the man cave. Since my entire house is my man cave, this is my play room. From there, I walk back to the stairs and grab the suitcases. When we get to the top I stop. This was the moment I was not looking forward to all afternoon. "Okay, the master bedroom is here." I lean over and open the door and let it swing open. "This is the hall bathroom. There's a door there that connects to the master bathroom. Then I have three other bedrooms up here. I told you no expectations and no obligation with staying here. You are welcome to either sleep in the master bedroom with me or move into one of the other bedrooms. I'm fine with you taking one of the spare rooms. What do you want to do?"

Samantha doesn't say anything. She bends down and picks up her suitcase and walks into my room. I breathe a sigh of relief. All I can do is smile and think I will have to get up and make coffee in the morning.

Samantha walks around the room and looks out the window. From here, you can see the curve of the James around Dutch Gap and over to Henricus Park. I put an arm around her waist and stand with her at the window and point out the different locations. "Do you see something in the distance over here to the left? That's Dutch Gap. In the summer, I will take you over there. It sounds strange but there's a tug boat grave yard. They are sitting there on their sides rusting away. It's sad to see them, but really beautiful as well. They look like they are dying wrecks but if you are really still and look in the water around the boats you see the little fish. They hide in and around the rusting hulls for protection. The bigger fish can't get in there, so the little fish are safe. Over here to the right is the second English settlement in Virginia. Sir Thomas Dale arrived here in 1611 and established a colony. It's now called Henricus Historical Park. The early settlers had problems with the local native tribes, the Powhatens. The Powhatens tried to take back lands that they thought belonged to the tribe and of course the English defended their right to take land granted to them by the King of England. The Powhatens burned down Henricus. It was rebuilt and they were more determined to establish English land here. Do you remember hearing about Pocahontas? After she was captured, she was first taken to Jamestown. They were so afraid of the Powhaten, they transferred her to Henricus. It was there that she learned Christianity and fell in love with the Colonist John Rolfe. When John Rolfe married Pocahontas, her father Chief Powhaten signed a treaty with the English. Their marriage paved the way for the expansion of the Virginia colonies and the eventual expansion into the territories that would become America."

I didn't realize Samantha was watching me as I was pointing out the view. She has a puzzled look on her face. "You love history don't you? That's why you knew so much about the Alamo. You bought this house so that you could get up every morning and look out over history. The more I am around you, the more you amaze me. I love your house and I love how you bring history alive for me. I've never met anyone like you. Thank you." She looks up at me biting her lip and all I can think of is how good it would feel to kiss her, and I did.

After the kiss, she leans her head against my chest. I close my eyes and rest my cheek on the top of her head. Everything seems right with the world and then my phone rings. I look and see the office phone number come up and sigh. I answer the phone and hear Chip on the other end. "Hey boss, where are you? I saw you were flying back from College Station. When we got back in here this morning, we found something I think you will need to see." I tell him we just got home.

"We-- as in you and Samantha Callahan? If that is the case, you should both probably come in here. First, we have Kali's ashes for her. I don't know what she wants to do with them. Also when we got back into the lab, there was a cooler sitting on the floor. No one recognized it. It looked old and dirty so we called the bomb squad. Boss, I don't know how this got in here, but we have a human head in a cooler dead center in the lab. It wasn't checked into any evidence log. It is just here. We were out of the building and it was locked up. I mean there weren't any alarms on the doors or anything. The power was out and the backup generators went under water. We got serious water in the mechanical room. We had to get it pumped out and mechanics are still working to get everything back up and running. We have power, but the computers are still a mess."

Samantha has been leaning against me listening in. She mouths "does the head belong to our torso?" I ask Chip his opinion of that. "It's a man's head. Until we get the lab back up and running, I can't do DNA to match it. The head has been around for a while. It's got pretty bad decomposition and it must have either been beaten badly or it was banged around in the cooler because it's a rotting smashed up mess." Great and he wants me to see this thing. I look at Samantha and mouth "do you want to drive in with me?" She nods, so I tell Chip we will be there in about forty minutes.

I had hoped to have a quiet night at home with Samantha and see where that kiss led us, but instead I find myself walking out the side of the house and pushing the mechanical override on the garage door. I have to reach up and pull down a chain to get the door open. Inside we get into my Jeep and I back out. Then, I have to go back into the garage to pull the chain back down and exit through the side door so that I can lock it. I finally get back into the Jeep and head into Richmond. The thirty two mile drive is uneventful. On a normal weeknight, I usually sit for more than an hour, sometimes longer in bumper to bumper traffic on I-95 going into Richmond. Today traffic is running smoothly. My guess this is because the area is still trying to recover from the storm and with the power out many businesses and most of the government offices are still closed.

We arrive at the office, and from the parking lot, there is only a skeleton crew working. I call my office and have someone meet me at the guard desk. Samantha only has an identification issued by the New York State prison system. This has gotten some strange looks and knowing glances as we have gone through airport screening. The assumption is that we are escorting a prisoner. While she has been on the payroll of our office since she joined the case, she does not have an ID to get into the building and normally the FBI frowns on a prison system IDs being used to enter.

We are met by Lyla from the team baring a green T badge. This will allow Samantha to move around the building without an escort. She will still need someone to open restricted areas, but it will do until we get a regular badge for her. At least for the duration of the case, she is working as a consultant for our team.

As the doors of the elevator open, we see the entire team in full panic mode. John has beaten us in and has taped off the area where the cooler sits. A finger print tech is on his hands and knees coating the box and the floor with powder. Another tech is crawling on the floor gently lifting foot prints. So far there are no finger prints. It appears the person was wearing gloves. The head has already been photographed in the cooler and has been removed to the lab table. I can see movement in the lab as the techs move around a table. There are flashes from a camera as it is being documented.

Lyla tells me to let John get me up to speed, she is going to get Samantha comfortable in the conference room and start working on her credentialing. As they pass my office, I see them pause and then enter. I know I should check and make sure Samantha is alright. The urn for Kali is in my conference room. Perhaps this time John is right and she has to face Kali's ashes on her own. Lyla is with her and will take care of her.

John has re-run the video cameras to see if we can identify who delivered the cooler to our office. It has taken the team over an hour to find how it even got inside. The facility was out of power from just after the storm hit until late yesterday. The cameras monitored the hallways for the beginning of the storm until the backup generators died. John runs the cameras on fast forward and I watch as the facility lights blink out and come back under emergency power. Six more hours pass under emergency power and then suddenly everything goes black. That was the point that the water entered the mechanical room and shorted out the generators. The next images are of a crew of three men repairing the electrical system. There was a twenty-eight hour time frame when the building was completely dark. As the cameras come back on, the image of the cooler is already sitting in our office. This means either someone entered the building during the storm and somehow got past the attention of the lone guard who remained through the storm or entered as the electrical system was being repaired. The agent who was here through the storm is driving to the building now. We are hoping he can shed some light on the cooler.

Samantha is in the conference room when I walk in. She is facing the time line board. I forgot there were crime scene pictures showing Kali before her body was bagged. I walk up to her expecting her to be crying. Instead she is looking at the pictures with a distant curiosity. Beside the board is the table with Kali's urn. A big stuffed teddy bear sits behind the urn and appears to be wrapping its arms and legs around it. A dozen red roses sit in a vase next to it. As usual there are notes on the table. It is therapeutic for the team to write notes to the victim. We try to connect with them so that we can enter their lives and possibly learn something that will be the break we need in the case. Samantha finally turns toward me and she has a look of confusion on her face.

"I don't understand something about these pictures. I was led to believe as Kali was dying she reached up to the pony. In these pictures, her body is posed." She sees the curiosity on my face now. She continues, "look at her arms. They are covering her breasts. She just had her baby cut from her womb. She was in pain. No woman would think of modesty then. She should have her hands on the cut to her stomach trying to hold herself back together. Instead she is rolled into a ball covering her gentiles. The natural reaction is to try to stop the bleeding not worry that your clothes were taken off of you. Plus, from all of the women we have talked to who were part of the Co-Op, being naked in front of a man was no big deal. Even for me it's not a big deal. I danced naked all the time and sold my body. I could walk down the street and not care. Clothes are just to keep you warm, modesty doesn't exist in my mind and I doubt it does in hers. It doesn't fit the profile. Only a person who is made to feel ashamed of their actions or their body worries about modesty. If she was taught sex was normal and healthy, as we have heard over and over, she would feel comfortable being naked. That's another thing. The bikini bottom wasn't cut off of her or ripped off. It was intact and the blood pattern looks like it ran down her stomach after it was cut. So someone took the bikini bottom off her after her uterus was cut out. Someone cut her and cut out the baby then watched her die. Then, I think they removed her bikini bottom and moved her to where she was found before posing her so that she wasn't exposed. We have discussed that her murder was a crime of passion, but I see two different stories. First there is violent angry passion. There is anger and spite in the stab wounds, then precision on the cuts to the abdomen. Look at how straight the incision is. It is almost surgical. There's no hesitation in the cesarean and it is a cesarean cut. And here, look at the bikini top. That was taken off and hung there before the murder. It looks like she or someone took it off of her and hung it up. Why not throw it on the ground? If you are going to kill her hanging it up makes no sense. And why take the bloody bikini bottom from the crime scene? The top was left. It was over looked, not thought of as significant or left so that the bikini bottom would be matched immediately to Kali. Finally, why if you strip her do you pose her after she died?"

She then walks over to the pictures of the pony. "These are the park rangers pictures aren't they? I see the bloody hand print, but look here. There are three finger prints leading to a big smear. There are others here and here. Have you ever wiped your hands off on your dog? I use to have a dog and when it was raining sometimes, when I was taking the leash off, my hands got wet. I use to laugh at myself for wiping my hands on the dog's back end like a towel. It looks like someone wiped their bloody hands off on the pony. This pony was a bloody rag to the killer."

I looked at the pictures as well and I could see her point. We have thought the blood pattern was odd, but I didn't think about someone wiping their hands. The original assumption was that Kali had tried to pull herself up as she was dying, but lacked the strength to grip the pony. The comparison after the pony was found and coat pattern measured it was determined the hand was bigger than Kali's. It was more consistent with the size of a man's hands. Perhaps one bloody hand rested on the pony while the other hand was being wiped off. Then the hand that rested on the pony was wiped off. She may very well be right and this pony was a hand towel for the murderer.

"So after murdering her and taking the uterus was there remorse by the killer? Or did someone else pose her so that she wasn't exposed? I also keep coming back to who was the man with Kali on the beach and what is the connection to the Braden family. We know the Braden's own a house on the north end of Chincoteague. We know that they were on a fishing boat somewhere off Ocean City, Maryland. Kali's body was found on the south end of Assateague Island while Ocean City is on the north end. The description of the man with Kali was not a Braden or at least the senator or his sons. To me, that gives us four people. Three are known – Duke, Josh and Tyler Braden, plus the unknown man. The bikini bottom turns up six hundred miles away in the fifth person and it holds the bikini bottom from Assateague."

I realize John has been standing in the door way listening when he joins in the conversation. "This is why I love the board. You can see all the puzzle pieces and begin to be able to sort them and put them together. I agree about the smears and will get the lab working on enhancing them. The uterine cut has been bothering me also; it is a textbook cesarean. Both Braden sons have medical school backgrounds. The cut does look too neat and planned to be random. The killer knew she was pregnant and my guess is that is why she died. I have thought that all along. What does anyone think the possibility is that Josh and Tyler knew Kali? Helen knew about her it is very possible their sons found out as well. Perhaps Duke even had Kali on the fishing boat with them."

"The boat story bothers me. No one on the team has been able to find the name of the boat or if there was even a rental. Duke was driven to the hospital in Salisbury, Maryland. It would have been just as feasible to have driven Duke from Chincoteague to Salisbury as Ocean City. It might even make more sense. There is a General Hospital in Berlin, Maryland which is closer to Ocean City then Salisbury. They would have had to pass that hospital to get to the other. If you are driving someone who was found unconscious and you suspect they had a heart attack or stroke why not go to the closest hospital? Josh is in med school and Tyler finished his first year of pre-med before taking his year off. These two both knew the importance of speedy treatment."

John's line of thought puts us in a new tangent. If the Braden's are somehow involved in the murder, possibly, the entire fishing trip is a lie. If Helen Braden is lying, she would be covering for her sons. If she's telling the truth, her sons lied to cover something up. Either they screwed up on their father's medical emergency or they are covering up where they were at the time. Unfortunately, the storm has shut down communications to both Ocean City and Chincoteague. We have to wait for answers to our questions.

Agent Marc Parker was the agent who volunteered to weather the storm in the facility after the power failed. He's a nice guy and a trustworthy seasoned veteran of the FBI. I have worked with him on cases many times in the past. As soon as we show him the picture of the cooler, he identifies it as one a workman carried with his tools to work on the mechanical room. He had looked in the cooler and there was ice, sodas and food when it was brought in. He didn't think there was room for the head. The guy did have a vacuum, some fans, a couple tool boxes and electrical wire. The three men pushed the equipment in on a cart. He looked at the log and identified the workman who claimed the cooler. The workers were all wearing the uniform of the company vetted to do electrical repairs in the facility. He couldn't pull up IDs because the computer was down from the power failure, but he did compare work IDs to driver's license. He checked the tool boxes as well. Everything checked out. As we talk to him, we figure out he did not check the contents of the vacuum cleaner. It was an honest mistake. The mechanical room was flooded and the workers brought in a shop vac. I doubt we check the vacuum cleaners used to clean the office or the buffer for the hallways when they are brought in. This just points out a flaw in our protocol that, when this is over, needs to be addressed. I can't blame the agent for this.

Now, I wonder how the person who brought in the head knew the company would get called to repair the mechanical room after the storm. Marc Parker came up with a possible answer. Two days before the storm, the company was in to service the generators and make sure they were working at full capacity in the event we lost power. While they couldn't anticipate flooding perhaps something else was booby trapped in ensure failure and a power outage?

Samantha chimed in "what if the owner of the mechanic company is a member of the Co-Op? Maybe they had an in to begin with." All of our heads whip and look at her after that comment. If she is right no contractor, no politician or banks-- no one was above suspicion. "Adam, someone in this building could be a member of the Co-Op. How do we know? It's not like they publish a directory of pedophiles that buy and sell in the child sex slave market."

I don't know how to respond to this. Never in my entire career have I wondered if someone I work with had been involved in a crime. My mind has put my fellow agents above that. I know how hard it is to apply and be accepted and then how hard it is to make it through Quantico. Is sex with a child a drive so strong that someone would be willing to throw all of that away?

Samantha sits down and tilts her head. "Okay, this is my area. I have studied these men for ten years. I can tell you about Montgomery and his friends. I can tell you the profile of a man who does this. I can guess about Duke Braden as well."

"Let me start with the mind of a pedophile. Most people think of a pedophile as someone in a trench coat masturbating in school yards or grabbing kids in the park. That's not the case. Your average pedophile is a friend, relative, neighbor, teacher-- they can be anyone. Many are in trusted positions. They want adults to feel safe leaving their child alone with them. They try to be helpful and trustworthy. Most people never suspect their child is being sexually abused."

"We have to broaden our description. The potential is there that women are also in the Co-Op. Pedophilia is not just about men. Women can be also. While the stereotypical Mrs. Robinson getting the teenage boy next door to mow her lawn and then come inside for something cold to drink and a roll in bed has been glamorized, these women are pedophiles. There is nothing hot about an adult woman taking a teenage boy to bed. Yet, how many boys look at an older woman and say she's a MILF? Most teenage boys would jump at the chance to just do it and if she's not too old or unattractive and if they get the offer, they will have sex with her. She feels young and desirable again. She has a hot stud that makes her feel alive. I watched an interview with a female pedophile once. She talked about the thrill of giving an erection to her own baby. Her sex life had changed with her husband after the baby was born. She didn't feel attractive and her husband looked at her as a mother, not the hot sexy woman he married. So from a young age, she masturbated her son. It didn't stop and progressed to intercourse by the time her son was in elementary school. He and mommy "played" together. This went on until his teen years when Mom got pregnant. She ended up in jail. Her son in therapy and her husband committed suicide. The baby was a gene pool of medical problems and died soon after birth. I think we may have to expand our thoughts that women could be members, not just victims."

"I want to address one of the leading causes pedophilia. Many pedophiles were violated as a child. They had no control then, so they get satisfaction controlling someone else in their adult life. They can manipulate a child and get them to do subservient or demeaning things that an adult might refuse. Many pedophiles are aroused by the control they exert over the child. I want to expand this to what I see with the Co-Op. They not only sexually control the children; they control every aspect of their lives. From the time the child is abducted, they are groomed for a fantasy lifestyle. What concerns me is that with each child they abduct, they create a potential new generation of pedophiles."

"The people we are looking at have money, lots of money. I don't know if this is a prerequisite of the Co-Op or whether the organization invites only a certain social status. They would not want the kid who has been abused by Uncle Charlie. Those children would not have the proper training. My guess is that children are traded like a commodity. Someone like Montgomery Jacob hunts and finds children. When he is done with the child he gets paid for the training and indoctrination he performs. These kids make money for them. If this is the case, the people who want the eighteen or older group pay the most money for a woman they intend on keeping for a lifetime. She will appear, like Tiff Burnside, to have the best societal training available. Once again, this is about control, but it is a different kind of control. In this case, they control their own environment and appearance. The woman is a mistress or a wife that he can pass for having a European education."

"Now for the children who are at risk, they are lacking something in their life. It is the only way I can explain the children not making an attempt to contact anyone. Kali lived in at least two houses where she had access to a telephone. She could have dialed 911 at any time. She never did because she felt the love and caring that I could not provide. Sidney Harris had the same situation. They appear to prey on struggling moms and give the child everything money can buy. A kid who has lived on the street will choose that almost every time."

"Finally, there is the potential for a homosexual element as well. We need to think about the closet man or woman who can't, for social reasons, allow their sexual preference known. Instead, they can buy a child and train them to serve their needs. A vast percentage of child sexual abuse is same sex. I can't believe this ring is strictly heterosexual. Any and every underprivileged child is at risk."

"The hardest part will be trying to rehabilitate any children we are able to locate. They have bonded with the indoctrination and feel they will be forced back to their old life. In reality, if they do not get significant psychological counseling, they will indeed end up back in a situation close to the lifestyle they led prior to abduction. They know the sex trade and even though they were trained for high society, they will be able to convert to street life. The potential is also high that they themselves will become abusers."

Most of this information is not new, but hearing it reminds me of what we are looking at. This is not just one child who has been abducted. For all we know there are hundreds, if not thousands, of potential victims. We have to catch a few to begin the process of infiltrating the entire organization. Right now, we are not sure if the head in the cooler is connected to our case. Since it was left in our office, we have assumed it is connected to our Texas John Doe. It could of course be a random head left for us as bait.

We will have to wait about three hours to get the answer to the question of whether our head matches the Texas body. It is pretty badly beaten and the flesh has decomposed significantly so a visual identification will be nearly impossible. The facial features barely look human. If it is the head from Texas, it is more than a week old.

Meanwhile, I have to do something about Kali. So far, Samantha has done a good job avoiding looking at the urn. It has become the elephant in the room. After John leaves, I sit down at the conference table. "We should take Kali's urn home with us this afternoon."

She turns and looks at me with this lost expression. "I don't know what to do with it. What do you do with someone's ashes? Is it ok to just sit them on a table or do you have to spread or bury them? I don't know the right thing to do. I don't know what people expect. I know Kali shouldn't be dead and she shouldn't be in that urn. I know that because of it I'm a free woman again and I wanted redemption, but I got it at the cost of her life. Do I celebrate a life that I know very little about? Adam, I don't know what to do!"

She says this without crying. I normally think of her as being so put together, but the woman in front of me is lost in the world. No matter how strong I think she is, when it comes to dealing with her personal life she struggles. "We can take her home and put her on the mantel over the fireplace for right now. When you decide what you want to do with the ashes, we can do it. There's no reason why you can't just keep the urn the way it is as long as you want. There are no rules and expectations about someone's ashes."

"Death is a personal thing but for the person who dies and those that are left behind. I deal a lot with both sides of the equation. Those who have died, they rely on me to find out what happened and if there was foul play to catch the person who did it. I owe that to Kali. For you, the situation is different. You have to learn to go on and live again. Not just that Kali died, but that you are no longer in jail. You have the rest of your life ahead of you. It's up to you to decide what you want to get out of that life. A wise old woman once told me that you have to choose to live or to exist. Those who exist lose out on living."

Samantha walks over and picks up the urn. Then carries it to the sofa in my office and sits down. She looks at it and turns it around. My team had a plate attached to the base. *Kali Marie Callahan, May her spirit live on and be with us to find truth and justice.*

She takes her finger and runs it over the inscription and smiles. I leave her there to have some time alone.

The New York DA's office sent video tapes of the interviews with the men who were with Jacob Montgomery at the time of Kali's abduction. The first time they were interviewed after the abduction, they accused Samantha of causing the disappearance. Their testimony had convinced the jury that Samantha was guilty. Now facing accessory kidnapping, child endangerment, human trafficking and possible murder charges, they are much more helpful. I download the videos to my laptop so that I can watch them at my leisure. I want Samantha to watch them with me and give me some background on the men as well as point out anything she knows is a lie. I doubt we will actually charge them with anything except perjury, but the potential is still there they are more deeply connected to the Co-Op. John has reviewed the tapes and doesn't think Samantha watching them will damage the case.

As I walk back into my office I pause. Samantha is curled on the sofa with her arms wrapped around the urn. She has fallen asleep with it in her arms.

I try to be quiet and get a few things done at my desk, but my shuffling wakes her up. It's about time for us to leave anyway. I have an evening of work cut out for me, so I decide to get a jump on the afternoon traffic and head back toward the house.

I call the power company to see when power is expected to be restored. I am reassured it should be back on within the hour. If not, I am going to check into a hotel. I'm sure Samantha is tired and I'm going to stop and grab dinner on the way home, but having hot water for a shower in the morning would be nice.

Once again, the drive is uneventful. I could get use to Richmond traffic being like this. I call ahead and order barbeque from a local rib joint and pick it up on the way. As I make the turn toward home I can see porch lights on. I know some are solar lights, but others aren't. My house is the last house at the end of a circle, but I am hopeful power is on. As I pull in, the house is dark and the outside lights aren't on. They are on a timer and I have no idea when the power went off to know what time of day my house thinks it might be. When I push the button for the garage the door raises.

Chaucer and Ebenezer scatter when I turn the lights on. It always makes me wonder what they were up to just before I walk in the door. Chaucer stands on his hind legs to look at us and then decides it's time to grab his long lop ears with his front paws and starts to clean them. Samantha is captured in his display of cute. This gets people every time. Nothing is more adorable then a lop-eared rabbit licking and cleaning its ears.

While Samantha is captivated by Chaucer, I put Kali's urn on the mantel over the fireplace. Once that is accomplished, I head off to put dinner on the dining room table and grab a bottle of red wine. We sit down to a tray of beef brisket with a spicy mustard barbeque sauce, baked beans, corn on the cob and corn bread. It's one of those meals you spend time licking your fingers and making sure you get every morsel. The wine is from Manheim, Pennsylvania. I had the opportunity to do some follow-up on a case there a few years ago and fell in love with their wines. Tonight I chose a full bodied red. We eat and talk while we manage to finish off the bottle. As I go to get more, the power goes back out.

Our choice now is to go to a hotel or try to sleep here. The power was on long enough for the temperature of the house to go up to bearable levels, but the outside temperature is forty three. Sitting on the hill over the James, there is usually a breeze. While the house has good insulation it will cool off during the night if the power doesn't come back on. I offer to get a hotel, but Samantha wants to spend the night here. I admit I have had enough of hotels for a while too.

Instead I go outside and bring in wood for the fireplace in the living room. I put a couple small pieces with fire starter blocks in the center to start the fire. The wood is damp. Even down in the woodpile, I find damp wood. I check the flue to make sure it's open. Wet wood sends up a lot of smoke until it dries and I don't need the house filled with smoke. After the wood starts to catch, I put a couple bigger pieces on. They smoke, pop and sizzle as the wood dries out. Before Ebenezer and Chaucer get too close to the fire investigating it, I put the fire screen up. Curiosity may have killed the cat, but after living with these two I can see the rabbit showed it to the cat and possibly pushed the cat to its death. Rabbits have a tremendous sense of humor.

We bring the food over to sit in front of the fire. I pull the coffee table over and we sit on the floor. The light from the fireplace and a candle I grabbed from the mantle give us enough light to see what we are eating. This is the first meal we have had alone. In the flickering light it is pretty romantic. I hadn't planned it this way but it is working out pretty well.

After we eat, I put the dishes in the sink and rinse them and take another bottle of wine out of the rack. This time I grab a red raspberry wine. It's one of my favorites. It's a sweet red that is great with dessert. Since we didn't pick up dessert and we are sitting in the dark next to a fire place it somehow seems right.

It's nice to sit and talk. Samantha made the mistake of asking me about my house. This doesn't look like a place where a single guy would live. Normally, I wouldn't get into Elizabeth. Her life and her death are too personal, but it's a cold dark night in front of the fireplace with a woman I am interested in. I have enough wine in me to be able to talk about it so I guess now is as good as any other time.

"I was married and had this house built. Elizabeth was a lawyer in Richmond. We had the big fancy house, lived the golf club life and everything was perfect. We had talked about kids and we were waiting until her career was established enough to be able to work from home other then when she was in court. I was on a bank robbery case in Kentucky for about a week. It was a hectic case and she was working towards a big trial herself. We were both really busy that week. I talked with her in the beginning of the week, but didn't hear from her for a day or two. I was so busy, I didn't even realize it. You know what it's like being on a case and falling into bed exhausted at night. When I came home, something felt wrong. I figured it was just that I had been gone for a week and I was just being paranoid. I opened the refrigerator and the milk was curdled. The food we had eaten before I left was still there molding. Here cell phone went straight to voicemail. I tried it a couple times and thought maybe the battery had died. I waited that night to see if she came home and she didn't. In the morning, I called her office and they told me she had text them she was joining me in Kentucky and taking a vacation. I convinced myself Elizabeth left me, but just in case I filed a missing persons report."

"I was in limbo for three weeks. Then her body washed up on the banks of the Shenandoah River in Harpers Ferry. She didn't have any identification and her body was in pretty bad shape. They thought she had been in the water for a while and had gone down the rapids before getting snagged on a tree. They didn't even let me see her to identify the body. They did the identification off of dental records. Her car was found in Brunswick, Maryland in the woods. Here I am a FBI agent and I can't even control the case on my wife's disappearance. It drove me nuts not being able to be part of this. I needed to find answers. Yes, I had my wife's body for closure but I needed to find out what happened. How she ended up in a river dead."

"In the end, it involved Maryland, West Virginia and Virginia State police as well as the FBI. She was prosecuting a case and a family member of the accused carjacked Elizabeth and made her drive to a deserted spot. There he raped her and beat her before driving her to the river and drowning her. I thought my life had ended. I had to bury the love of my life. I came home to an empty house. Work was a nightmare. I was doing a crappy job and my mind wasn't into it. I was told to take some time off and heal. How the hell do you heal when all you see is the house of your wife's dreams? I rented a roll off dumpster and threw every bit of furniture away. I gave away her clothes and everything she loved. I found myself sitting on the floor in an empty house. When I went back to work, I switched from bank fraud and robbery to criminal investigations. I understood the need for closure and could relate to the families of victims. I knew what they needed and the frustration they went through. I also know the anger that comes along. You end up blaming the victim and being mad at them for being killed."

Samantha takes a drink and puts her glass down slowly. "I understand the anger. Not at Kali getting kidnapped. I take full blame for that. She never called me. She never tried to contact me. I know that she liked being with them more than me. Anger I know well. At one point, I was thinking that she deserved to be killed. I was so ashamed I didn't mention it, but she never tried to get away from the men who were abusing her. She loved them and not me. I'm better now and I don't blame her anymore, but I still find myself getting angry that I was so horrible in her early life that she never tried to find me. I was easy to find. The trial was very public and the location of the prison was no secret. I understand Adam and I'm glad you turned your anger into action. I would still be in jail hoping some day to be free again."

I fill our glasses and empty the bottle. After two bottles of wine we are both getting a little drunk. The darkness in the rest of the house seems to close around me and the conversation has made me feel drained. I take the flashlight and go upstairs and grab pillows and two blankets. Those are dropped in the living room as I go outside to get more wood and my sleeping bag from the garage.

We push the coffee table back toward the sofa and spread the sleeping bag out along the fire. I make one more offer to get a hotel room, but Samantha stops me. "Adam, dinner was one of the most romantic meals I have ever eaten and the thought of sleeping on the floor in front of a fire sounds wonderful. I have never done anything like this. Please let's just lie down and talk. I want to get to know you. I have never had a boyfriend or a lover. I have had Johns. My love life hasn't existed so the first night I spend alone with a man that I like and having it in front of the fireplace is amazing. Please let's just lie down and talk."

With a plea like that it is impossible to resist. I lie down and wrap my arms around her as she snuggles her head against my chest. I hear the pitter patter of little feet as Ebenezer and Chaucer creep out to investigate. They have been hiding under the end table and since we moved they come out for a better look. I take my hand and stroke her hair. It's been a long time since I have held a woman in my arms. Samantha moves and starts to get up. I wonder if I have done anything wrong until she asks for the flashlight because she needs to go to the bathroom.

She comes back and snuggles back against me. "Adam I think you should know my past. I know why you do what you do and why you are so cautious with me. You should know Samantha Callahan also. I'm a little shocked that you have not backed away from ex hooker and topless dancer. I'm no angel but I'm not a devil either. You need to know what drove me to where I went before Kali disappeared."

"When I was young, my mom got a divorce. I never met my father and the break up was bad so my mother didn't talk about him much. She remarried when I was twelve. My mom worked in a coffee shop and one night she had to work overnight. She didn't think anything about leaving me with my stepfather. That night he came into my bed and raped me. I was afraid to say anything, but it started to happen more and more. I thought when I did tell her that I was doing the right thing. She accused me of trying to steal her husband and threw me out of the house. I was fifteen trying to find food and a place to sleep. A guy pulled up and asked me if I wanted to go with him. It was January and I could feel the heat coming out of his window. I got inside just to be warm. He drove around the corner and had sex with me. He gave me fifty bucks. I went with two more guys that night. I had enough money to get a hotel room plus money for food. About a month later, I was arrested the first time. It was a revolving door system. I was booked and released in an hour. I was back on the street working that night. I started to get some regular customers. I was young and didn't know about sexually transmitted diseases. I didn't use any protection and one night one of my regulars came back and beat the shit out of me. He blamed me for his gonorrhea and for him giving it to his wife. He left me unconscious covered in blood. When I woke up, I went to the hospital. That's when I found out I was pregnant with Kali. I was sixteen years old and I made my living catching a venereal disease and getting pregnant. I ended up in a church run halfway house for pregnant teens. They offered me a place to sleep and to get my act together. Instead, I ran into one of my old Johns and started seeing him. One of the girls staying there with me found my stash of money and told on me. Someone followed me one night and by the time I got back to the home they told me to take my things and leave. Kali was three months old and we ended up sleeping in a doorway. I was back to working the streets the next night. I didn't make as much. Most guys don't want to pick up a hooker with a baby and I didn't have anyone I could leave her with. That's when I started dancing in the club. Everyone thought Kali was cute and they let me bring her to work. She stayed in the back and other girls watched her when I was dancing. I split an apartment with two other girls and when one of us had a John the others took turns watching her. We all danced and made money on the side in bed. Jacob Montgomery became one of my regulars. Thinking back it wasn't me he was coming to see. He was plotting to get Kali. Adam, I am no angel and I have led a pretty horrible life. Jail was an improvement. I had a bed and three meals a day. I hadn't had that in seven years. I made a decision then that I could either continue to screw up and do my time or I could take the opportunity I was handed and make something out of myself. I knew I had a twenty year sentence and I would still be young when I got out. If anyone would hire me I would at least have a skill I could rely on. Those are the events that made me who I am. You are taking on a lot if you want me to stay. If not I will understand."

She feels good in my arms. Her past doesn't surprise me or scare me off. It just makes me want to protect her even more. I pull her tight against me and kiss the top of her head. "I think, in some way, everyone is broken. Sometimes those who are missing something in their lives find the piece of themselves that is missing. When it happens that makes you feel whole. For me when you are with me, I don't think of the world as being shades of gray. Since I met you, I have not woken up thinking about Elizabeth and how much I miss her. I think about making you smile. Let's just go to sleep and let tomorrow take care of itself. I am not going to promise you the world, but I will promise to accept you for who you are and to be open and honest with you. Right now we go from day to day."

She shifts and nestles her body closer against me. The fire cracks and sparks fly up as a log breaks. The wine and the warmth of being close together under the quilts draws me close to sleep.

DAY 18
DUTCH GAP, VIRGINIA
TO CHINCOTEAGUE, VIRGINIA

I wake up to the sound of the alarm beeping as it resets itself from power outage mode. Lights are on in the kitchen and dining room and I get up to turn them off. When I walk out of the bathroom, Samantha is sitting up on our make shift bed "do you want to get up and go upstairs?"

Her answer is to lie back down and pat the top of the sleeping bag next to her. Outside the gray of dawn is beginning to show. Morning will come soon, so I get back down on the floor and pull her back against me. I see Ebenezer and Chaucer sleeping against the stone hearth. I guess they were cold and decided to lie down close to the heat.

My phone rings from the coffee table and I crawl over to it to answer. The power company has informed the facility manager that the power is going to be off for most of the day. The lines have been temporarily repaired and the reason the lab did not have enough power was a failure in one of the three phases coming in on the main line. Yesterday, the engineers inside the facility had tested all the circuits assuming it was on our end after the mechanical room had filled with water. Instead, it appears the lines leading to our building had multiple trees fall. One of the repairs was failing on one third of the wiring and causing a short. The SAC decided to close the facility for the day rather than have everyone hang out waiting for the lights to come on.

Since there is no food in the house, we have to go out to get breakfast. We go to one of my favorite hole-in-the-wall restaurants about three miles from my house in the town of Enon. This place is owned by a local church group and serves southern-style "church lady" meals. They make everything from scratch and think meat and lard goes with everything. Fat is a food group. This is not the place for dieters. We choose a bacon, ham, egg, mushroom, onions, green pepper and cheese breakfast pizza. Their breakfast pizzas are piled high with toppings and as usual every table is taken with people waiting for a seat to open. We find a seat before our pizza is ready and sit down.

When we leave there, we determine a trip to the grocery store is in order. I'm sure the rabbits are almost out of food as well so I grab a bag for them. I decide to go light on anything that needs to go into the refrigerator or freezer since it has been unreliable since the storm. I pick up steaks for dinner. I figure I can fire up the grill. It's cold outside, but I have grilled in a snow storm so precedent has been set.

After putting the groceries away, I take Samantha for a walk down to the boat dock. I'm glad to see everything looks fine. The boat house doors swung open during the storm, but both my canoe and kayak are still on the racks. Luckily, I pulled my sixteen foot speed boat out and put it on the trailer for the winter a few weeks ago. It is still covered and chained to the tree along the boat ramp. We walk out on the dock and watch a bald eagle fish the river. These birds are beautiful and majestic, no matter how many times I see this I have to stop and watch. Across the water in Henricus Park, there are two nesting pairs. Over the summer, I watched as they taught their fledglings to hunt. There were times the young birds took a tumble into the river when they tried to catch a fish too big for them. I liked to get up early and take my kayak out and position it near the tug boat graveyard in Dutch Gap and wait for the eagles to come hunting. I shot over 100 pictures of the eagles last summer. I don't know what I will do with them. I have thought about getting a couple enlarged and framed. I just loved the time I spent on the water watching them.

My phone beeps for an incoming message and I take it out of my pocket to take a look. It's a picture of a beach and in front of a dune is a body half buried in the sand. The message attached was "guess what James Earl Jones found...Up for a road trip to Chincoteague?" I call him back and John's already on his way to pick us up.

We go back up the hill to the house and we both throw a change of clothing in a bag. Chincoteague is a four hour drive and it's already ten o'clock. By the time we get there, we will only have a few hours of daylight.

Plus, while I'm there I would like to check out the Braden house on the north end of Chincoteague.

From my house to Chincoteague, you have to take one of two routes. The first drives north to Annapolis, Maryland to cross the Chesapeake Bay Bridge and the other goes out the peninsula to Virginia Beach and across the Chesapeake Bay Bridge Tunnel. There are few bridges that cross the expanse of the Chesapeake Bay, but the trip through Norfolk to Virginia Beach is the fastest. We would take a commuter flight, but the nearest airport to Chincoteague is about forty five minutes away. So we drive knowing we will more than likely have to spend the night. En route I call the hotel and get two rooms.

The Chesapeake Bay Bridge Tunnels are a modern engineering marvel. There are two parallel bridge and tunnel complexes that are each just over seventeen and a half miles long. Counting the approach roads and toll facilities the length is actually twenty-three miles long. Each span has over twelve miles of bridges, two one mile long tunnels, almost two miles of causeway and four man made islands. This location has always fascinated me. It crosses the mouth of the Chesapeake Bay where it reaches the Atlantic Ocean. As it was being built, the engineers had to deal with the occasional ten to twelve foot wave. It has withstood tropical storms and hurricanes. It just recently reopened after the hurricane when the amount of rain coming down in the storm over powered the drains and flooded each of the tunnels with a couple feet of water.

One of the biggest thrills is to watch a battle group either leaving or returning to Hampton Roads and the Naval Weapons Station at Yorktown. As a kid, my parents use to take me to the point and we would watch the battle groups return. The planes on the carriers would always fly low over the water and tip their wings at the crowds. Sometimes we would watch the carriers cross over the tunnel portion and then head back to Hampton Roads to be there when the first ships started to dock. The band was always playing and there was a party atmosphere. The families waiting had usually not seen their loved ones for six months or more. It always seemed that there was a man or two on board who got to meet their newborn baby and do so for the first time as they get off the ship. Even as a kid, I found the return of the battle group to be an emotional experience. I mentally put that on my list of things to do with Samantha.

We are lucky to see a destroyer that had been doing sea maneuvers coming back in and crossing over the tunnel as we crossed the first bridge. Traffic is still light and we cross without any delays. We make a quick stop in Exmore to grab some lunch and have a bathroom break. We make good time and find ourselves turning onto 175 into Chincoteague at 2:30 PM.

As we pass the main campus of Wallops Island, we see the giant radar dishes and block buildings hidden behind trees and the traditional government fence. Back in the late 1950s and early 1960s, the secrets of the nation originated from here. The radar dishes tracked the space movements of the Russians and later until the end of the Cold War they tracked the Soviet Block via satellites. To our right, on the other side of a forest, are the Wallops Island launch pads. Back in the early days of space exploration, the first test flights took place there. At one time, it was in the running to be the main United States launch pad because rockets taking off from there didn't risk coming down on any human population. From launch to space, there is nothing but the wide expanse of ocean in the flight path. Today it is a privately owned Spaceport delivering both private and government payloads into orbit. I make another mental note to make a trip back to watch a rocket launch someday.

As we pass, I think how odd it is for this top secret location to be sitting here in the middle of nowhere. It isn't hidden. The road drives right by the satellite array. Yet, no one ever asked questions, they just drive by minding their own business. From reports I read, the Soviets on the other hand had a great interest in Chincoteague. During tests and launches, the ocean off Chincoteague was filled with fishing boats from around the world. Of course they fished for appearance only and while the US knew they were being watched there was nothing that could be said or done in international waters. Now the area is more open and the government has come clean about the history that took place here. The people still just drive by and mind their own business. After meeting the people I understand. This is just part of life and if it doesn't infringe on them, they don't care what is being done on the base. Now they just take pride in the history that is around them.

Our first stop is just over the draw bridge on the island to check in with the Chincoteague Island Police and let them know we are here. Karen Bowden is the only person there and she gets on the radio to let everyone else know we are on our way over to Assateague. As we are leaving she yells out "Hey, do you all know the storm tore the road up, right? You can make it down beach road to just before the circle. After that, you are either going to have to walk or if you got four wheel drive you are going to have to use it. The park service might get bent because you don't have a beach permit." She looks out the door at the SUV "okay so you do have four wheel. I will call them back and tell them to get the park service to meet you. They have been a little testy since the storm. A lot of people are playing tourist and getting hung up in the sand. I can't blame them none. Cars getting stuck have made the situation even worse down there. Good luck. I haven't seen it, but I heard it's a pretty rough ride over the bits of road that were washed out."

After we crossed the bridge we begin to see damage. There were a lot of trees that came down. For right now, they are either drug to the side or cut so that traffic can pass between the sections. As we hit the Tom's Cove, we have to drive down the center of the road. It appears waves from the bay eroded under the black top and broke huge chunks off. We see a park service vehicle parked at a set of saw horses at the end of the road. In both directions where road once existed there is now sand. I'm not sure if the road is still there and under a few feet of sand or whether it has been washed out completely. The place is still a mess. The ranger gets out and checks our identification. Then advises us to put the vehicle in four wheel drive and follow him slowly. There's still debris in the road. Our best bet is to stay in the tracks of the other vehicles. We are going to go down about a mile to the right. We follow him. Everything looks different then when we were first here. It looks as if the storm resurfaced the island and deposited a new one in its place.

He stops near a group of other four wheel drive vehicles and we get out. I can see the remains of the stairway we took to cross the dunes and get to the beach where Kali was last seen alive. The storm took half of it away. All that remains is one side of the railing with a few steps dangling from it. The dunes look beaten. The Park Ranger, Carl Truit, points down the beach. We can see where the waves split the island. He tells us during high tide the ocean crosses into the bay now. For the stability of the island they are getting ready to back fill and try to stabilize the dune again.

We can see the group of people and Tim Clark ahead. A Virginia State Trooper is taking pictures of the crime scene. I realize the body is still there and warn Samantha to stay back. She doesn't need to see what a couple weeks in the sand will do to a body. I also don't know what kind of damage the waves and windblown sand has done to it. Before I reach it I can smell it won't be a pretty picture. John is trying to flip through his crime scene pictures on his tablet as we walk. It's hard to tell if we are in the same place or not. From the stairs, I know we are in the general area where James Earl saw Kali.

I was right about the body. Most of the skull, the right arm and right side of the torso are stripped clean of flesh. Tim Clark has brushed back some of the wet sand still covering the body to reveal a torn flannel shirt and jeans. From what he has exposed, we can see his shirt is covered with blood and has slits on it suggesting the guy was stabbed multiple times.

From behind me I hear John "No way in bloody hell! A satellite doesn't lie! Take a look at this picture from the original crime scene. What we have on our hands is one sick little puppy." The targeting on the GPS is calibrated to within two inches and when we were here just under three weeks ago we had photographed the location of our current body. The storm had washed it away, but when we were here before there looked like a child's sand castle on this spot. Back then the sharp edges of the sand castle had crumbled in the wind and weather leaving it a little more rounded but the shape of a sand castle had been distinctly defined equipped with a moat. Someone had even collected sea shells and used them to decorate around the moat and as accents to the castle walls. We had photographed it as part of the crime scene but no one paid it much attention because it had just looked like a child's. Who ever built it had even used a sand mold to create the shapes of the walls and towers. This was just outside the search area we defined with James Earl and had never thought it might be a grave marker. If it hadn't been for the storm we may have never found this body. It would have been impossible to move and sift about one quarter mile of beach so we concentrated on the location where Kali was last seen.

John snaps a few more pictures and touches base with Tim to contact us when he gets something. The more the body is being uncovered the worse the smell gets. Even out in the open with a salt air blowing off the ocean the smell of dead body is permeating the air. I am glad to walk back toward our SUV. I think we are pretty safe assuming this body is somehow connected to Kali's. It is more than likely our missing old guy. Since we seem to have all the body parts on this one, it will hopefully be easier to identify.

It is already pushing four o'clock when we cross the bridge back onto Chincoteague. I want to drive out to take a look at the Braden house before the sun goes down. We drive north on Main Street until we come to a fork in the road. The storm appears to have knocked down the street sign and I get out righting the sign and determining which fork we need to take. Next to the sign is a broken tombstone cemented back together on top of a vault. I call John and Samantha to come take a look at it.

Here alone, on what use to be the north end of this island, is a single grave. It reads Capt. Joshua L. Chandler. Born October 1829, Died October 21, 1877 beneath that is an inscription:

> Farewell wife and children dear
> I am not dead but sleeping here
> As I am someday you will be ˙
> Prepare for death and follow me.

Samantha finishes reading and takes a step back "Well that is beautiful on the surface, but creepy. It almost seems like he wants his family to die and be with him. I don't see any other graves. I guess they didn't follow him here. Why would he be here all alone? This island is probably really crowded in the summer but this is where the road stops and the dirt road begins. It seems so desolate." She pulls her jacket around her as if the thought gives her a chill and gets back in the vehicle.

I have to agree with her and get back inside. John snaps a few pictures. From the map, we decide to take the crushed shell road to the right. Once again we are driving between fallen trees that had been pushed off the road to be cleaned later. Within a few minutes, we find the driveway and head out between the trees and marsh to the house.

The house looks out of place. The drive way is made of crushed oyster shells and ends at a crushed shell parking area. After that, the rustic homespun looks ends. My guess is the house is worth over one million dollars. Behind it we can see a long pier that extends out into the water for boats. The yard is landscaped in marsh grass and tall ornamental grasses. The pier has made it thru the storm intact, but the grasses are laid over and show signs the water covered them. From indications water may have made it up to or even entered the house.

We pull up to the front porch and park. John is the first the door to go look around. The smell hits us as soon as he opens the door. "Whoa! That's not the smell of a dead cat. Either a pony crawled in somewhere and died or we have a body around here somewhere and it's pretty ripe."

He gets back in and we back away from the house. I make the call to the Sheriff's office and within a few minutes his car pulls up. As he starts to get out he takes a few steps, gags and vomits in the ornamental grass. I try to tell him to breathe through his mouth to which he tells me "hell no! Now I can taste that shit!"

We wait for the state cop to come from Assateague before we go near again. He gets out of his car with "What the hell died." That is exactly what we all want to know. Samantha opts to stay in the SUV with the windows rolled up. Even then the smell has entered it and she is trying very hard to keep what is left of her lunch in her stomach.

The state officer opens the door and the smell magnifies. There in the living room sits a badly decomposed man in a suit. Flies have found a way in and they buzz and swarm around the body. There isn't much more we can do without Tim Clark. John snaps a few pictures and we go back outside. The air smells a little better out there, but not much.

When Tim Clark pulls up we have all retreated to our vehicles. We are using the excuse of preserving the crime scene, but in actuality we are hiding behind closed doors from the smell.

Tim gets out of his car and takes a few steps. "Aw man! What do you guys have against me? I have just had to double bag your last guy and now I get smelly guy in the house with the heat on? Do you have any idea what this is going to do to my morgue?" He walks inside and comes right back out. "Oh, hell no! You didn't tell me the guy was starting to turn to soup! I have to call my lab and get someone to bring a couple more body bags and a shop vac to get all of him."

He pulls out his phone and calls for back up and supplies. He then walks over to our vehicle. "If I were you, I'd back up a little down the driveway. I'm going to have to open the doors and windows to air the place out a bit. Someone did me a whole lot of favors by cranking the heat up to 80 degrees. You guys win on the two for one deal of the day, but you know it's not two for Tuesday, all right? By the way, any idea who Mr. Stinky Two might be?"

I shake my head. "Well, he's not the homeowner. He's in a hospice near Washington, DC. He looks too old to be either of his sons and he's dressed too well to be homeless. I was hoping once you scoop him out of that chair we might get a break and find a wallet."

I watch as Tim Clark makes a face. "Great so two more John Does with one smellier then the other. No offense but you guys are bad news. I usually get the occasional accident victim and have to determine if they died because of drugs, alcohol or medical issues. Those bodies are nice and fresh. You guys seem to find the ones who have been hanging out a while."

Right now there isn't much more we can do and even though I feel bad about leaving them with the smelly body my mind is focused on the hotel and getting a shower. I'm even contemplating burning my clothes. The smell of decomposition is a hard thing to get out of anything and right now I smell like a rotten body. John's car may never be the same.

As we put the windows up and drive away, Samantha makes a face and pushes the button on her window and puts it down. With just a few minutes exposure we stink. The trip back down Main Street to Maddox Boulevard doesn't take long and we pull up in front of the hotel. As we walk in, the desk clerk makes a face and tries to cover her nose. She gives us our keys and is grateful to get rid of us.

Samantha sits on the bed and pulls out her laptop while I am taking a shower. John is across the hall doing the same thing. I'm surprised he didn't say anything about Samantha and I sharing a room. I guess he has spoken his mind on it and has decided it's my career, my decisions.

As I walk out of the bathroom, Samantha looks deep in thought and is typing something. She stops when she sees me. "I was thinking. Let's say Duke, Josh and Tyler Braden have come to their home in Chincoteague because they were suppose to meet someone. When they get here, this guy is already dead. They panic and leave which causes Duke to have the heart attack and stroke. Tyler and Josh panic and drive their father to the hospital. He's in bad shape and they stay by his side. They figure their mother won't be coming to the house in Chincoteague until next summer which gives them time to dispose of the body and clean up. With him dying, they haven't had time to get back and we find the body. The killer is looking for a man with a young girl and he sees the guy on the beach with Kali and kills them. He then leaves the island and the bodies behind."

John has walked into the room and heard this. "What if the dead guy in the house was Kali's new owner and the dead guy on the beach was some sort of mediator. If Braden had Kali up until recently, the new owner might have complained about her being pregnant with Duke Braden's kid and wanted a refund. The mediator sides with the new owner and demands Duke pay up. Duke kills them both and Kali witnesses it so she dies also. He brought both his sons to help hide the bodies. What they didn't bargain for was Duke having the heart attack and stroke."

I have no idea. Right now I know we have a house full of players with no evidence. I'm hoping after the dead guy is gone and the house has time to fumigate we can get a crew in to comb the house for clues. My casts of characters right now are Duke, Josh and Tyler Braden, dead body in Texas, dead body on the beach, dead body in the house and Jacob Montgomery. For that matter an unknown number of people who are part of the Co-Op. I can't forget that someone living put the head in the lab and dropped the body in Texas. While the body in Texas is much fresher then the most recent finds, he also was found a week sooner.

I pick up the phone and call the office to let them know the situation here. What I really need are the identifications of the bodies and parts. I have too many unidentified pieces right now and I need to put names to them. Other than coincidence and location, I have no actual evidence to link them. The good news from the lab is that they are back up and running. They hope to have a DNA profile on the head in the next hour. As soon as they get the profile, they plan to run it against the database and see if we can find a match.

I need to clear my head. I think about going for a run, but it's cold and looks like rain clouds are approaching from the west. John decides he wants to get some sleep so Samantha and I decide to go for a drive around the island. This is our second time here and we have seen one section of the beach, Captain Chandler's grave and the inside of a hotel.

We head out Chicken City Road and when we get to the junction I laugh and tell Samantha this little turn is known locally as a fliggle. I decide to head down East Side Drive to show her Memorial Park. The last Wednesday in July, during low tide, the ponies are swum across from Assateague and driven up Main Street to the carnival grounds. There, on Thursday, they hold an auction of some of the foals before driving them back to Assateague on Friday. They do this to keep the herd at a manageable level. Memorial Park is the closest place on Chincoteague to Assateague. I hear the ponies are only in the water for a few minutes, yet; fifty to one hundred thousand people come each year to watch the event. The money raised goes back to the ponies for medical attention and feed during drought and the winter. My guess is that the television coverage from the storm on the condition of the ponies and how they rode out the storm will bring record numbers to the island for next year's Pony Penning.

Memorial Park is quiet and no one else is around. We get out and walk to the water's edge. From there we can look over at the west beach of Assateague Island. It's a narrow strip of land that leads to the water and marshy patches. Behind that is the wooded area that leads to the light house. The top three stripes peek out above the trees and one of the last rays of sunlight reflects off the prism in the light. A small herd of ponies graze along the beach near the water's edge. As we stand there, the cloud cover rolls in and makes the sky dark enough for the light house to come on for the night. It's nice to have a few minutes to ourselves watching the ponies slowly make their way down some marsh grass while just above the tree tops to light house blinks it's pattern of blink…blink blink…blink….blink blink… The water gently laps onto the shore and in the distance we hear a sea gull cry out. It's beautiful and one of those moments I want to savor.

Samantha is standing in front of me, leaning back against my chest as my arms wrap around her. "Adam, thank you. I didn't get to tell you this morning but last night was the first time I have ever slept with a guy and not had sex with him. It feels weird to do things like this with you. I'm not use to romance. I'm not complaining I love this. I've always felt like a tissue. Guys used me and threw me away. I accepted that as my life. You are so different and so wonderful. All my life I have wanted to be held and feel loved. I was always looking for someone who would make me theirs, not theirs for the moment. Maybe every girl dreams of a moment in time like this-- when all there is in the world are two people and a beautiful setting. I just always thought it was nothing more than a dream. Then I think of Kali and I wonder if she ever had a moment like this or whether she died waiting and hoping. On her last night on earth, did she lay there looking at the flashing beam from the lighthouse and see the beauty in it?"

I tightened my arms around her. I don't have any answers and all I can do is hold her in my arms. I want to take it slow because I want to be different than any other man in her life. I want her to want me. I can't tell her that I feel as broken as she does but I never thought I would find someone I loved again. I thought love had died with Elizabeth. Now I am not sure. I like being in this moment and knowing that Samantha is happy. I kiss the top of her head as we watch a flock of snow geese come for a landing across the water from us near the ponies.

The sky is darkening. Somewhere behind the clouds the sun is starting to set. We get back in the SUV and I head back to Ridge Road. I make the turn at Beebe road to go out to Main Street. The town is quiet as the porch lights come on for the night. When the tourist season ends, Chincoteague becomes a sleepy little fishing town. As we drive, I look around for a place to get dinner. I call John and tell him we will be there in about ten minutes. I'm thinking sea food from a place on Main Street just north of the draw bridge. When I was here before, a couple people recommended it and I didn't make it there. Tonight seems like that perfect time to try it out.

As soon as we sit down my phone rings. Caller ID shows it's the phone in the lab. I give my drink order and answer the call. "Hey boss, I have great news. We have a match. As we hoped your torso and head have come up being one and the same person. It's our mystery Braden. What I can't tell you is what Braden this happens to be or how the head and the body came to be 600 miles apart. It's as much of a mystery as how Kali's bikini bottom crawled up the torso's rectum. And hey, I thought you went to Assateague for a body. I have information coming in about two. How many bodies do you have there right now?" I explained we found an extra at the Braden house. "Ah ok. Did you get the report on the two bodies in Baltimore yet?"

I know cell service can be sketchy in parts of the island, especially on Assateague. The bodies in Baltimore are new information to me. "Ah ok, well Baltimore police think the two bodies they have are from the Lady Grey crew. They ended up in a place called Goose Pond just south of the Chesapeake Bay Bridge. That's not far from where the haul of the boat beached at Sandy Point State Park. While connected to our case, I'm just monitoring their identification. We still aren't sure if Montgomery and Sidney were onboard the ship or not."

I thank him and take a drink of my bourbon. As usual, I try to house specialty and start with clam chowder and make my way to clam fritters. I am a little surprised when they are delivered to the table. They look like little pancakes. I am use to individually breaded strips of clam. The waitress explains those are clam strips and are made out of the tough ocean clams. Restaurants have to cut them up because ocean clams are old and tough like chewing gum. A Chincoteague Island clam fritter is made with the little Cherry Stone clams chopped in only a few pieces and mixed with pancake batter. Then poured and fried. I take a bite and am surprised at the slightly sweet batter melding perfectly with the salty clam. Across the table from me, Samantha is having baked stuffed flounder and crab mashed potatoes. The flounder consists of a crab meat, mushroom, onion and bread stuffing sandwiched between two pieces of flounder fillet that has been baked in a white wine sauce and topped with a fine layer of Swiss cheese. She offers to let me try a fork full and it is excellent. After a sample, I think she may be right. This is one of the best baked stuffed flounder I have ever tasted. John opted for the crab fajitas. They look and smell wonderful with their fusion of Mexican and seafood. If nothing else this case has been a tour of good food.

Back at the hotel my eyes feel heavy. Between sleeping on the floor then a full day on-the-go then topped off with a big dinner and a drink, my body begs to lie down and sleep. We get into bed and I turn on the television just as the eleven o'clock news comes on. The last thing I remember is the report on tree removal and restoring power to the Delmarva Peninsula.

DAY 19
CHINCOTEAGUE, VIRGINIA
TO BALTIMORE, MARYLAND

I wake up to the gray of dawn and the flicker of the television. Samantha is snuggled against me and I untangle myself and go to the bathroom. Outside I hear a hard rain falling and I glance at the clock. It is six thirty in the morning. Samantha is still sleeping when I come out of the bathroom so I grab the card to the room and go down the hallway to the lobby and grab a cup of coffee for myself and one for Samantha. I also toast two bagels and grab a couple packs of cream cheese. As I suspected, she has woken up and is sitting on the side of the bed rubbing her face and then her hands through her hair. I hand her a cup of coffee and she grunts appreciation. I am learning to not talk to her when she first wakes up. She needs a few minutes to shake the cob webs from her head.

She takes a drink of coffee and puts the cup down on the bedside table. "Ok, I have to ask. Are we ever going to not be too tired, too drunk, too cold or interrupted and going to have sex? I'm not blaming you here. I think I fell asleep when I hit the bed last night."

I laugh and kiss her "I know so did I. The thought has crossed my mind. Quite a bit actually, but every time the opportunity arises something gets in the way. I promise you sometime very soon I am going to take advantage of the moment. How many couples can say they lived together for three weeks before they had sex? At least I have lived up to my promise that you are not a one night stand." We both laugh as John calls me from the lobby of the hotel.

Normally John is the kind to not get excited about anything, but after this case and the series of dead ends we have hit a break in the case is exciting. Something in his voice signals immediately something has happened. He tells me to come down to the lobby he's got a fax for me. I have no idea why I have to go down there and he can't come up here, but I play along.

He hands me a single piece of paper without a cover sheet or introduction to what I was looking at. I begin to scan it and look back at John. I don't know why he called me down to look at a paternity test from a laboratory in Richmond.

After testing the DNA of both Joshua Braden and Alina Braden it is a 99.99% probability that Joshua Braden is the father of Alina Braden. The print out continues with a copy of the DNA pattern for a Joshua Braden, a Marissa Braden and a child, Alina Braden.

John then prints something from his computer and pulls it off the hotel printer, scans it quickly and then hands two pages to me. The first is the DNA profile of Joshau Braden, the second is the DNA profile of our John Doe from College Station, Texas. "Meet John Doe, otherwise known as Joshua Braden and the mother of his child. He prints two more sheets and hands them to me. Now meet Kali Callahan, also known as, Marissa Braden. Adam, Kali has a daughter somewhere in the Richmond area and the address this DNA test was sent to was the Northern Virginia office of Senator Duke Braden. We got this fax a couple days ago and the lab handled it like all of the other leads we have been sent. No one expected to find anything, but we keep plodding away. Yesterday the judge gave us a search warrant and one of the techs contacted the lab and had them send an electronic copy of their DNA results from this test. Once it was loaded in the database, we first got a hit on John Doe and before anyone got over to the computer, it had the second match on Kali. This just came in with a third match to the head in our lab. We are going to have to notify the family and Samantha. Joshua Braden has been dead for some time and someone dropped his body in Texas and his head in our office. I would say it was delivered to us on a silver platter, but a cooler is close enough. Also, somewhere out there she has a daughter, which means Samantha has a granddaughter. I think you should be the one to tell her."

In my hands, I hold answers and more questions. John Doe has a name. We still don't know how, where or why he died, but having a name just opened up a world of information to pursue. Of course, the question when I get upstairs will be where is Alina Braden and how do I tell the woman that I am falling in love with that somewhere, possibly in the Richmond, Virginia area, she has a granddaughter?

I hold out the papers to Samantha when I walk in the room. She looks at them and has a puzzled look on her face then takes them. She sits for a few seconds reading and going back and forth between the sheets. I watch as realization sets in and she looks back at me in shock and asks "when are we leaving for Richmond?" I run my hand through my hair and let out my breath in a loud sigh "After we talk to Helen Braden, John Doe was her son."

John knocks on the door and I let him in. He has his laptop open and puts it on the desk next to Samantha. "I am working as fast as I can on this because I know you will want to know. I have a birth certificate for Alina Samantha Braden from the state of Virginia. Her birthday is August 6 and she just turned four years old this year. Marissa Braden is listed as her mother and the father is unknown. Hospital paperwork has Marissa listed as the adopted daughter of Duke Braden. Because of Marissa's age a social worker was assigned at the hospital as her advocate. Damn it! The social worker was concerned that she was only thirteen years old and giving birth. She refused to release the name of the father to doctors or social services. The doctor noted vaginal scarring prior to the delivery and felt she may have been sexually abused. Duke Braden was interviewed and said he had his daughter in a private boarding school until he found out she had gotten pregnant. He had pulled her out of the school and had hired a tutor to home school her. There were no charges filed and the case was dismissed for no merit by social services. They came close to catching the bastard!"

I need to think. Suddenly I have more pieces of the puzzle coming together, but in coming together, they have lead to more questions. I have a murder in Virginia whose evidence showed up in a body in Texas with his head showing back up in my office in a different location in Virginia. I have a mother who says she has talked to her son and denying that he is missing even though his body and head had been separated before that time. The mother is now missing, the other brother is missing and now I have a four year old who is missing. On top of that, I have a dead body in one of their houses. Now, I don't know if Duke Braden's stroke and heart attack were the result of natural causes or whether his is a failed attempted murder. To add into all of this, I have a dead guy on the beach that was possibly last seen with Kali, a missing millionaire and with him another kidnapped child. I also have two dead sailors and a smashed tall ship in the Chesapeake Bay.

On top of all of this, the woman that I would really like to get to know and possibly spend the rest of my life with is sitting in my hotel room in an almost catatonic state looking at a series of paternity tests spread out on the desk. I look at the clock on my cell phone as it changes to exactly eight. I announce I am going for a run.

Samantha looks at me with a blank look "Adam! It's raining! Are you going for a run in the rain? I can feel the cold coming off the window. You are going to freeze!"

I don't know any other way to work this out. I need the repetition on one foot in front of the other. Maybe I need it cold. I know I need to run fast and feel the burn in my lungs. I need to feel the road under my feet and put some distance from my confusion on the case right now. I put on my sneakers and head out the door.

I turn right leaving the hotel and head out Maddox Boulevard. I find myself still sprinting when I make the right on Main. I try to slow down and pace myself, but sooner then I expect I am at Captain Chandlers grave. I take the right and head out past the Braden house and follow the road to the end of the island. I have no choice but to turn back. I slow down at the driveway to the Braden house as I pass it a second time. The state police are there. I see three forensic vans in front of the house. I am torn between running up the driveway to see if they have any answers or to keep running. My decision is made when a state cop comes out to me and tells me to move on. I guess crazy man soaking wet running in a freezing rain doesn't look like he belongs here.

I reach into my back pocket and pull out my wallet and flash my badge. The cop looks even more confused and calls my name and credentials in to whoever is in charge of the crime scene at the house. I think he would have offered me a ride back up to the house if my jeans were not running with water. Instead he points up to the house. I run up and onto the porch.

Ryan Daisey looks me over and introduces himself as the head of the
Virginia State Police, Accomack County Forensic Lab. "Do you always jog
in your street clothes to a crime scene or was there another reason you are
thinking about contaminating my crime scene, Agent Clay?" I ask him if we
can talk because I want to fill him in on some things that have just come
down that might be relevant to our crime scene."

He makes a face when I stress the "our" in crime scene. Local cops, even
state ones, get very territorial over crime scenes and technically, I could pull
the trump card right now and bring in my own team. This crime scene can
be claimed as part of the federal case because I now have conclusive
evidence that links this house and the inhabitants to my initial crime scene
on National Park land.

He leads me into the kitchen of the house and pulls out a chair while
motioning for me to sit down. I in turn pull out my cell phone and press
the number for Tim Clark. Tim answers on the second ring. "Hey Tim, I
hope I'm not catching you with a hand in a body. I'm here with Ryan
Daisey of the State Police out of Accomack. I wanted to conference you in
on something." Tim tells me he's just gotten his morning coffee and was
looking over reports from yesterday. "Great. Have you gotten anywhere on
Smelly one and two from yesterday? I need some answers and I'm hoping
you can help."

He tells me he is looking at print outs now of the autopsies and is in the
process of putting things together for his full report. "Okay, then let me
start at the beginning. Kali Callahan. I read in your initial report that pitting
in her pelvic bone was consistent with a prior pregnancy. Is that correct?"
He answers yes, but it wasn't recent. It could have been a few years ago. "Is
there any way to tell if this was a caesarean or a vaginal birth?" He answers
vaginal. "Great. That is the confirmation I needed on this. I have DNA
reports showing a live birth four years ago to a baby girl. At least, as of the
beginning of October, this child was still alive. The DNA profile came back
as a match to Kali. The father of the baby is a match to the body in Texas
where we found her bikini bottom. And now to the head that was dropped
in my lab during the hurricane. Here's where it gets even stranger. The
father of this baby is the son of the owner of the house where stinky two

was found. Can you give me a guess as to how long stinky two was in that house?"

He doesn't hesitate "I was going to tell you this guy has been around for about three to four weeks. It was still warm enough when he died for flies to be in the house and I have a couple generations who have been feeding off of him. Whoever killed him did a butcher job after shooting him. It's hard to count the stab wounds there are so many. I originally thought he had turned to soup because of the heat of the house, but he had been cut up enough he started to fall apart. The heat didn't help much. I did look for a wallet or some identification on him and I have nothing. We have made dental impressions. I have to get DNA from his bone marrow because he was too rotten to get a tissue sample."

I think about this for the moment. "So whoever killed him sounds pretty angry. Would you say the stab wounds are like crime of passion wounds? Were they long incisions or rapid stabs and how deep do you think they are. I'm trying to determine the mind of the killer at this point. Kali we can definitely attribute to a crime of passion. Someone killed her and cut out the baby. Joshua Braden was also a crime of passion. The stab wounds were rapid succession stabs and varied in depth. Yet, the killer took the time to remove his hands, feet and head-- I assume to make identification hard. Then took the bagged bikini bottom and stuffed it up his rectum to link the crimes. Finally, he gift tagged the body to make sure we were notified as soon as the body was found. Both Kali and Joshua Braden were body dumps; we have no idea where the murders took place. Meanwhile, smelly number one was found buried a few feet away from where we think he was last seen and then it appears the killer built a sand castle on top of the body. I think possibly to mark where the body was buried. Smelly two was murdered and left at the crime scene. They are all connected in some way to Kali, but I have no idea how unless we go back to the Co-Op."

I hear computer keys clicking on Tim Clarks end. "Okay, well I have more. Smelly one is also a John Doe. I have no identification on him either, but he's right up there with Joshua Braden for creativity." He has my full attention. I urge him to go on. "You saw smelly one was pretty messed up. The wave and sand action from the storm ripped off a lot of flesh on his face, neck, shoulder and arm. I thought that was going to be the nasty part, but when I got his clothes cut off oh boy did this guy get worked over. He is another with multiple fast stab wounds but they look mostly post mortem. It's hard to tell with the degree of decomposition, but cause of death was spectacular. The first thing I noticed was that his penis and testicles were cut off. It looks like one swift slash while he was very much alive. That alone wouldn't kill him, but he would have lost a lot of blood. Are you ready for this? He died of suffocation. The sick-o that killed him stuffed his penis and testicles down his throat."

I needed to process this. I don't have a timeline yet, but right now if there's a single killer, I have four murders taking place in a short time. They seem rage based and there is a sexual sadist over tone to the murders of Kali, Joshua and Smelly Guy one. Smelly Guy two was just stabbed with no sexual over tones. Something made him different to the killer. I ask him about ages or anything else he can tell me about Smelly One and Two.

"Smelly one was older. There's a lot of arthritis in his joints and depleted bone density. I wouldn't put him under sixty. He was wearing high end clothing, the expensive western wear stuff and a watch I'd value at over a grand. Smelly Guy Two I'd put in his fifties. His size wasn't just bloating. He was a good 300 pounds in life. His suit was Italian as were his shoes. Besides reeking from decomposition the guy reeked of money. Did you find cars for either one of these guys? I'd like to buy one if it goes to a police auction." I haven't thought much about the vehicles these men might have driven. That was John's department and, so far, he hasn't turned up any vehicles missing owners. I try to direct him back to the stab wounds, I am curious about the knife used.

"The depth has varied. I don't think the killer took the time to punch it all the way in all the time. I would say he got off on the feeling of stabbing flesh and the depth was unimportant. For many killers like this, it is almost a sexual release each time the knife enters the skin. On the bodies I have seen from you, I would say the same weapon was used. It's a sharp sucker and I think your killer has had some practice with a knife. Maybe it's just the number of bodies he did in a short period, but there are no hesitation marks. The slashes are for removals of organs or body parts. No accidental marks and I think each looks like a planned jab. The knife itself is in the neighborhood of 10 3/4 inches. I would say full tang. It goes in really clean and deep when force is applied. Some of the stabs have been the full blade with hilt marks out the surface. Others went from four to six inches deep. The knife was pretty sharp and the blade solid. I'd say it was a tactical steel blade hunting knife. If you get me a knife, I can match the stabs from it."

"I have sent my findings to Austin and I'm waiting for their reports on your torso. We have also exchanged photos and reports with your lab. If I was a betting man, I would say right now these were done by the same person. Oh and your killer is right handed. Not that this will help much, about eighty percent of the population is right handed. It will only help to eliminate twenty percent, but any little bit, right?"

"Your killer also didn't care how much blood they got on themselves. Every victim I have seen from you has been part of a total blood bath. I also have heard they have not been found in a primary scene and they all look like they have been moved. If this is the case, somewhere on this island or just off of it, there's a whole lot of blood. Kali was still bleeding when she was dumped and I'd say posed. Which leads me to believe the original scene was nearby. He also had no problem transporting the body. So he doesn't care if someone sees him covered in blood or he has a way to change clothes and wash or conceal himself and the bodies while he transports them."

"I'm not sure what else I can tell you or what else you want to know. And hey, I'm not kidding about if you find one of the vehicles of smelly one or two. I'm driving a beat up old truck. I'd say these guys drive something pretty nice."

I hang up with Tim Clark and asked the Sheriff and the State Cop if there had been any vehicles found. This is something that has bothered me. Kali and Smelly one had to get to the beach somehow and no vehicle was found or abandoned on any of the beach parking lots or any hotels in walking distance. Smelly Two was found in a house that was supposed to be shut up for the winter. Once again there's no vehicle in the area. The island does not have any form of public transportation. People must rely on their feet, a bicycle or a vehicle to get around both Chincoteague and Assateague. Since one person can't drive two vehicles, it makes me wonder if there are two people involved. As for the primary crime scene, I have thought about that as well.

This is a small island and everyone who is local knows everyone else. Houses in town are close together. Ones like the Braden house sit off by themselves on the north end of the island. Money buys privacy that doesn't exist in the rest of town. Most people in the southern and central part of the island are long time natives. They know when strangers are among them. Even in tourist season, the natives to the island look out for each other. If the killer has a place that is local, they are hiding in plain sight, meaning people on the island are accustomed to seeing them.

The sheriff offers me a ride back to the hotel in his car. My jeans are wet and feeling uncomfortable and I readily accept the ride. The run helped me get my thoughts in order and the conference call began to assemble this puzzle in my mind.

I swipe the card on the door and open it. Samantha is lying in bed under the quilt. John is not in the room and I assume he has gone back to his to work. She looks up at me and she looks so tired. She then rolls over and pulls the comforter up around her tighter. I don't know what to say to her. I know she's probably mad at me for not dropping what we are doing at the moment and going on a wild goose chase looking for Alina. I assume part of John's retreat is to spend some time searching for where she might be living. By now, I hope he's working with a judge to get social security and internal revenue service records. She was born in a hospital and therefore there's a paper trail on her. She will have to have a social security number assigned to her and she will hopefully be listed as someone's dependent. Joshua Braden is a med student in Baltimore. I doubt he will have her living with him. It is possible she was living with Kali. In which case, I hope the child was left with someone and has not been on her own the last month. There is also the possibility that the child was given away at birth. All we can do right now is to begin to develop a paper trail to find her.

I am cold and my clothes are still wet. I go into the bathroom and turn on the shower. It gives me a few more minutes to think on what to say or do about Samantha. The water feels good. I stand and lean back against the wall allowing the water to hit my neck and shoulders. I reach up and adjust the shower head to a pulse. I could really use a hot tub with water jets right now. The cold rain and the stress have made my neck and shoulders stiff and sore. I close my eyes and concentrate on the water hitting my skin. Then I breathe in and out concentrating on each breath until I feel a little calm seep into my brain. I walk out of the bathroom in a towel and head to my suitcase to grab some clothes. I hear a sob coming from the blankets and instead sit on the bed and put my hand on the comforter at her shoulder. She looks up at me with red teary eyes.

I'm still damp from the shower and only wearing a towel but I pull the comforter aside and lay down in bed next to her. She slips her arms around me and rests her forehead against my shoulder. I pull her close to me and feel her body mold to mine. This is probably a bad move on my part with John across the hallway, but she has been through so much and I can't let her go through this alone.

She stops crying and looks up at me. "I know you can't go find her right now. I'm not upset about that. I don't want you to think I'm mad at you. All these years I have thought Kali didn't remember me or hated me. She did, Adam! She remembered me and somewhere in the back of her mind I must have been worth enough to give her daughter my name as her middle name. When I saw Alina Samantha Braden, I knew I was still in her heart." I tightened my arms around her and raised her chin so that I could kiss her.

As things go in my life, no sooner had I started to kiss her and let my hands start to explore her, John knocks on the door. I jump up and grabbed dry clothes and go into the bathroom while Samantha opens the door for him. I hate sneaking around like a high school kid, but until this case is over, we have to be really careful about our actions. John is already on edge about her and I being together.

I walk out a minute later dressed. John has set his laptop up on the desk and Samantha is standing behind him leaning on his shoulder. Alina was born in a Richmond area hospital fifteen miles from my house. Duke Braden went into an agreement with social services to provide for the baby. He applied for her social security number and for the last four years has claimed her on his income tax. She also appears on his health insurance. A judge is currently looking over his request for a subpoena for her medical records. John looks at me and clicks onto something else on the screen. "You want to be over here for this. Samantha, don't get excited, I can't guarantee this news article is correct but if it is--I have a picture of Alina."

I make it to them in two steps and have my arm around Samantha. I didn't even realize I have been holding my breath until I let it out slowly. John clicks and enlarges a newspaper picture full screen. Samantha lets out a small cry. "Oh my God! She looks just like Kali!"

In the picture, Duke Braden is standing on the capitol steps giving a speech. Next to him is a little girl holding onto his pants legs. She's dressed in a knee length party dress with little dress shoes. Her blond hair is down below her shoulders as she looks out at the crowd in front of them with big wide eyes. She is beautiful. The caption at the bottom of the picture reads "Senator Duke Braden giving a speech on the Capitol steps as he introduces his protection act for young teens with children. With him Alina Callahan, a young child he has sponsored through his unwed teen mother and children foundation. Every year Senator Braden donates over one million dollars to help unwed teen mothers afford education and training in order to make a better life for themselves and their children. Little Alina is a success story of his foundation. Born to a thirteen year old prostitute, little Alina and her mother have lived in a group home where her mother has been able to graduate high school and will attend college so that, eventually, they can be productive members of society."

I can feel Samantha shaking. The picture was taken in September. I guess the press corps had taken his word for the name of the little girl. If they had looked, they would have seen Alina's last name was Braden. Like me, Samantha is searching the crowd behind Duke Braden looking for Kali. She isn't there. From information I have seen from the Dallas Field office, I recognize Sally Gold standing a few feet away from Alina. Like everyone else connected to Duke Braden we have not been able to locate her.

I pick up my phone and tell my team to get a judge to give us access to the records from the Unwed Mothers and Children's Fund. I want everything Braden is associated with. I also initiate the alert for a missing child on Alina. I have asked for her to be labeled a missing and endangered child.

Within a few minutes, there is an alert tone on the television in the hotel followed by the picture of Alina.

"We ask you to be on alert for a missing four-year-old. She goes by the name Alina Samantha Braden or Alina Callahan. Alina is four years old with blond hair. She is believed to be a missing and endangered victim of a non-parental abduction. She is believed to be in Maryland; Virginia; Washington, DC; or Texas, but might be anywhere by this time."

After the alert ends, the television goes back to the noon news. There a reporter is reading a piece of paper. He looks confused at the paper and then looks into the camera. "I have received further information on this missing child from our news desk. Alina Samantha Braden has been linked to the Kali Callahan murder on Assateague Island. According to our source, Alina Samantha Braden is the daughter of Kali Callahan. We have also gotten word that the child is somehow connected to Senator Duke Braden who died three hours ago at a hospice in Northern Virginia. We will stay on top of this case and break into normal programming to give you updates as we get them."

In the chaos of the morning, we had somehow missed that Duke Braden died. We know this was coming, but now hopefully the missing Braden's will come out of the wood work. I know Helen Braden will not miss the opportunity to play the grieving wife for the elaborate state funeral she has planned for him. I think back to the promise that I made to her that I wouldn't break this to the news until after his funeral. She broke the rules when she went underground. Now I have to protect the welfare of Alina.

Samantha is pale looking and I take her hand and lead her to the bed. She has now gone from finding out she has a granddaughter to a missing persons alert going out in a short period of time. If nothing else things are moving quickly as we try to track Alina down and bring her home.

There is not much more that we can do here. I call Tim Clark to see if he has gotten anywhere with dental records and he's found nothing so far. The search of the house did not turn up any identification for the body there. My team has been running the description through the missing person's database and so far there is nothing that has hit a match. We are at a standstill so we get ready to check out and head back across the Bay Bridge Tunnel. I check in with my team before we hit the road and ask what has been seen or heard on the Braden front.

Other then Duke Braden's death, there has been nothing else surfacing about the Braden family. Helen Braden nor Tyler Braden have been heard from. Texas State Police are still looking for Helen Braden to make notification about the identification of Joshua Braden's body, because of that, we cannot release any other information about Alina.

We head down US 13 and are just outside Olney when my phone rings. I see it's from the Special Agent in Charge and I push the button to answer the phone. "Yes sir. We are driving south heading home. I have you on speaker phone."

"I think you should find a place to pull over. We need to make a decision about a phone call I just got from the Baltimore Field Office. I have two strange things. The original call is about a child that has been found walking around Fort McHenry. While the SAC from Baltimore had me on the phone, he let me know there was a human hand found in a back yard in Reisterstown, just west of the city." I have no idea why the SAC called me. There are children found all the time and while I am looking for two hands and two feet, they are not rare finds either.

The SAC continues "I wouldn't call you about the child, but when the US Park Service officer asked her what her name was and where her parents were, she told them her name was Alexis Montgomery and she had been with her father Jacob Montgomery. As soon as Park Service called the Baltimore City Police Department, they notified the FBI. Social Services are having the child checked out at the hospital right now." I'm glad I had pulled off in a parking lot because I probably would have driven off the road.

I thanked the SAC and set the GPS for Baltimore's Central District Police Station in downtown Baltimore City. We turn around and head back up US 13 toward Baltimore. The GPS displays four hours and thirteen minutes from our present location to downtown.

We begin to hit early rush hour traffic in Easton, Maryland. The traffic report indicates there's an accident just before the Kent Narrows Bridge. Currently there was a six mile back up leading to the accident. This has affected traffic crossing over the Chesapeake Bay Bridge as well. We decide to stop for an early dinner to let traffic die down some.

I call the Baltimore Field Office to let them know we are on the way. Alexis had to be sedated for examination and is being held overnight at the hospital. Due to the connection to our case, she was examined for sexual assault. Her body shows evidence of sexual abuse. The doctor will be available to talk to us when we are ready to interview him. A child psychiatrist has been trying to get information out of her as to the whereabouts of Jacob Montgomery, but has not been successful yet. The doctor is also welcoming Samantha in to speak with Alexis.

We finish eating and head out to deal with traffic. The accident has cleared and traffic is running slow. We approach the twin spans of the Chesapeake Bay Bridge as the sun is starting to set. This bridge is the northern crossing of the Chesapeake Bay. Stretching out across the wide expanse of water we can see three cargo ships heading into Baltimore Harbor to unload their stacks of metal cargo containers. As we descend to the eastern side of the bridge we can see the shattered hull of the Lady Grey still resting on the beach of Sandy Point. The Maryland State Police and the Baltimore Field Office have already processed the wreckage. The storm stripped the ship of most of its contents. Pieces of the sail caught in the rocks on one of the bridge pylons shows where the ship slammed against the cement buttress before being washed onto the beach.

Even though we need to get to Baltimore, I cross through the toll plaza and take the exit to the park. I pull up to the pay station at the park entrance. The Department of Natural Resources Ranger calls the main office and asks us to pull to the side so that we can be escorted down to the site. I'm glad to see it is still being protected as evidence. Within a few minutes, the black and green colored SUV of Maryland Natural Resources Police vehicle pulls up to us and puts down his window. "Hi. I'm Chris Chester. I have been told no one gets on the wreckage without authorization. I'm going to have to make some calls to see if it's ok to take you up to it. You can follow me down to the beach now though. The road is closed to visitors because we are still cleaning debris off of South Beach Road. We have cleared a lane all the way down to the beach, but watch where you drive. We had trees and flooding during the storm. Your SUV should be fine driving over the fine stuff and sand down on the parking lot but you might want to put it in four wheel drive once we hit the parking lot. We are going to have to plow the sand off the lot before we open it back up to day use."

We park and walk through the sand and debris out to a point of land right near the approach to the toll plaza of the bridge. The Lady Grey is on her side. The main mast is snapped as is the foremast. We walk around the wreckage. There is a hole punched at the water line. My guess either debris in the water or when it slammed against the pylons of the bridge. Farther back a long gash scars the exposed side. My guess this was the final blow to the crippled ship. It made less than one quarter mile after hitting the bridge before it came to rest on the beach. The bodies believed to be two of the crewmen were found just on the other side of the bridge between Moss Point and Goose Pond. The ship looks like a giant skeleton dead on the beach. I can imagine how majestic it must have looked just two weeks ago and now it is a shattered pile of wood, rope and brass fittings. The pictures online did not do its size justice. The length is easily four times the length of an eighteen wheeler and the deck lying sideways stretches up into the sky about two stories. Seeing it like this reminds me of the tugboat graveyard on the James. It's strange how something so majestic can take on such a haunting look when extracted from its natural element.

John walks around the ship getting pictures. The back of the ship still rests in a few feet of water but the bay is too cold to venture out and take a look. Samantha has stood back further up the beach and is surveying the wreckage from a distance. I think the horror of its final minutes is too much for her to take. Since Jekyll Island, she has speculated Jacob Montgomery was on board the ship. Now we are all wondering if his body is somewhere in the cold waters of the Chesapeake Bay.

We thank Chris Chester and head back to the SUV. We continue the trip to Baltimore. About an hour later, we pull in front of the Baltimore City Central Police District's building as the sun is going down. The desk sergeant is waiting for us and sends us straight back to an interview room.

There we are met by Officer Roger Price and Central District Commander Lenny Ross.

They shake our hands and offer us a seat. Roger Price opens his laptop and logs into the smart board mounted on the wall. After a few clicks, the picture of Sidney Harris appears on the screen. "This is Alexis Montgomery. We have confirmed the missing person dossier and we are fairly certain this is the same child. She is not giving us much information. She of course was scared and cold when she was found and turned over to us."

I ask him to give us the details to how and where she was found. All I know was that she was found this morning at Fort McHenry. "From what we can determine she entered the fort yesterday during the day. We had a couple school groups there and she more than likely slipped in with one of them. When the fort has buses pull up with kids, the groups have usually been prepaid. They get off the bus and come inside the visitor's center to watch the movie before taking them for a tour of the fort. They don't let it get out, but they don't really count the number of kids who get off the buses. They trust the school has given them a fairly accurate count. The kid seems pretty smart and we think she may have blended in with a school group. Once inside the fort, she may have taken the tour and when the school group broke out to do activities she must have gone off on her own. The park rangers are not sure how she did it, but she appears to have snuck off and hidden in the fort. She was locked inside during the night. After unlocking the gate this morning, the ranger opening up the various locked buildings of the fort found her sleeping on a display."

"It was forty three degrees last night and the fort isn't heated. She had a pretty cold night, but at least she was out of the wind. The ambulance crew thought it was a good idea to have her checked out. She fought with the ambulance crew and police. She did not want to go to the hospital or with an officer. Most kids after spending the night alone in a place like that usually welcome some place warm. Not this kid. When they got her into the emergency room they had to sedate her to get her to calm down. All we got from her was that her name was Alexis Montgomery and her father's name is Jacob."

"Something about her made the doctor in emergency do a rape kit. This kid was terrified to be touched. She is pretty messed up. The doctor's report says "profound scarring and bruising consistent with long term sexual abuse." On the side, he told me it looks like a grown man has been doing this kid for a couple years and she was young when it started. When we ran her description your case came up. This is all I can really tell you about her. The couple times she has started to come out of sedation, she clawed and scratched at people like a wild animal. She's scared and defensive."

We ask if it is possible to see her and try to speak with her. "The doctors, social services and all of us would like some information from her. I think if you can get her to talk it will help us all. We want to help her and this kid doesn't want to be helped. She's going to end up being placed in a foster home when she's released from the hospital if we can't get her to give us information. We have to prove who she is before we can hand her over to anyone claiming to be family."

We follow Commander Ross back downstairs and out to our car. He leads us through the winding streets of Baltimore. Even in the twilight, I can see the carvings and intricate architecture of Baltimore's historic buildings. Baltimore was an old sea port town and it still has a lot of its original buildings standing in the city. He pulls into a parking garage next to the hospital marked for the emergency department. We park on the reserved lower level and enter through a side entrance. There an armed security guard checks our identification and takes our vehicle information. We are issued identifications and sent up a service elevator to the fifth floor. As we are leaving, the guard is calling upstairs to let someone know we are on our way.

Outside the room there is a Baltimore City Officer playing a game on his cell phone. As we approach, he stands up and slides his phone into his pocket. He checks our identification and badges before warning us about going in to her room. Down the hall we see a doctor and a woman in a pants suit coming to greet us.

The doctor holds out her hand, "I'm Doctor Erica Ward the attending physician and this is Doctor Mary Ruhl our staff child psychiatrist. We would like a moment before you go in and try to talk to her. Because of her injuries, we have been asked to have Kim Palter escort you. Kim is a patient advocate and because Alexis is an unaccompanied minor, by law, an advocate must be there to keep the patients best interest at heart. You have to understand this child has been through some sort of trauma and she's very brittle right now."

Samantha introduces herself and gives her qualifications. "If this is ok with everyone, I would like to talk to her first. This is my specialty and the minds of the people who do this to kids. If there is a way, I would not mind allowing everyone else to listen in, but I think the fewer people the better in this situation."

Erica Ward agrees and she suggests we move to the adjacent room rather than the other half of the patient room. The child is very intelligent and will know we are there listening in if we just go to the other side of the curtain. With a plan worked out, we move out into the hallway and wait for Kim Palter. The door to Alexis room is open as is the adjacent room that we occupy.

We hear Samantha and Kim Palter make introductions before entering the room. "Hi Alexis. My name is Samantha. Do you like to be called Alexis or Sidney? You use to be called Sidney Harris weren't you?"

She pauses and we hear a tiny voice say "I prefer Alexis. I haven't been Sidney for a long time."

"I understand that Alexis. Is it ok if I talk to you for a few minutes?" Samantha pauses. I assume Alexis must have shaken her head because Samantha continues on. "I understand why you don't want to talk. It's ok. Let me tell you a little about myself. It has to be pretty scary being in the hospital with people around you that you don't know. I want to tell you why I am here. I want to know if your daddy is Jacob Montgomery? I came here to see you because I know your daddy."

We hear a timid, "You do? You know my daddy?" coming from Alexis.

Samantha continues. "Yes, I have known him for many years. Did you ever hear your daddy mention Marissa? She was my daughter before she came to live with your daddy."

We hear an even more timid Alexis say "Marissa died and that scared daddy. We had to leave home and he took me on vacation so that I would be safe."

We hear the bed creak slightly as Samantha sits down next to Alexis "I know. It had to be scary. I know Marissa died and I understand why your daddy was afraid for you. He didn't want to lose you. I'm sure he loves you a lot. Did he take you out on his sailing ship?"

The voice from the next room sounds a little stronger and more confident now. "Yes he did! It was cool. He let me help raise the sails. Before the storm, he let me lay out on the deck and look up at the wind in the sails. I even got to put a life preserver on and swing on a rope out over the ocean. Daddy was afraid I would fall in, but it was so much fun. The men on the ship made a swing for me and, as long as I wore my life preserver and someone was there to watch me, I was allowed to swing all I wanted."

"Wow, Alexis that sounds like fun." Samantha's voice was light and quiet. It was hard for us to hear from the open doorway. "You were on the boat when the storm started? I bet that was scary! When did you and your daddy get off the ship?"

Alexis sounds much stronger now "Oh that was scary! The captain thought we were too close to the coast and couldn't get out into the open ocean fast enough. Daddy and the captain argued. The captain insisted we try to head up to Baltimore for safe harbor. He thought the storm would pull back out and just brush Baltimore. The water was really rough and the sky was very cloudy. Daddy told me the rain that comes down for a few minutes and stops were tropical rain bands. He told me we were under the clouds of the hurricane. He was really worried. We struck all the sails and tied them tight. Daddy was furious and he said it made us sitting ducks. Finally, he told me to get my things. He lowered the run about off the side of the ship into the water. He went down first and I was so scared. He told me I could do it and he was at the bottom of the ladder. The ship was going up and down and the run about kept banging against the side of the ship and then drifting out. The wind was blowing a lot too. I cried, but daddy told me I could do it and he was there. It started to rain again and I had to climb this wet rope thing. After he pushed off the side of the ship and started the motor, we tried to make it to shore. We could see the lights of a town and we headed for it. I had to lie on the bottom of the boat because I was so scared. The waves were really high and sometimes it felt like there was no water under the boat and we fell back down to the water. It took forever but we finally made it to shore. Everything was closed and the power was out. Daddy's cell phone had gotten wet and we were stuck. A man in a car stopped and daddy told him we had gotten stranded. The man let daddy use his cell phone and call Miss Barbara. She came and got us. She had come across the Bay Bridge, but by the time we tried to go back the bridge had been closed due to high wind."

Alexis paused at this point. We heard the sound of a cup being set down before she continued. "Miss Barbara made a phone call and she found a place for us to stay for the night. We were there for two days. On the way back to Baltimore, daddy saw the wreck of the Lady Grey. We stayed with Miss Barbara for a couple days more, than daddy had to fly to Europe. That was two days ago. On the way back to her house, Miss Barbara stopped to get us breakfast. While I was eating, she went to the ladies room, but instead of coming back to the table she went to her car and drove away. I waited to see if she was going to come back but people started asking me if I was lost or anything and I left. She had argued with daddy that I was a risk because my picture was all over the news. I thought it was because of the Lady Grey had wrecked. I saw the sign for Fort McHenry and I have read about it in history so I decided to go. It was cool. I hid when they closed and spent the night there. I have read it's haunted but I didn't see any ghosts. I was hoping to see one. That would have been so cool. Instead I got caught and brought here."

Daddy told me people were hunting for him and they want to take me away from him. I don't want to be here! I want to go home! Please, now that I have talked to you, can I go home?"

I hear Samantha shifting on the bed. She has been able to do something the hospital staff hasn't been able to do. "Lexi, I don't think your father killed Marissa. I am one of the people looking for him, but I think he may be in danger. Other people who have been in Marissa's life have been killed. I want to find Jacob before that happens. Is there anything you can tell me to help me find him?"

"Daddy's in danger? No! He told me someone had hurt the senator. That's why we left on the Lady Grey. He wanted to get away from the man we saw in Jekyll Island. He told me not to talk to the man and to run if I saw him."

Now I heard genuine concern in Samantha's voice. "What man, Lexi? Can you tell me what he looks like? This may be the man we are looking for. We think he's killed a couple people including Marissa. Marissa was my daughter, Lexi. I loved her very much and I want to catch the man who killed her. I want to find Jacob before this man finds him too. I need your help."

The timid voice is back again in Alexis, "I don't know if I can trust you. I don't want anything to happen to daddy. I'm afraid. If I don't tell you and the man finds daddy, he might kill him. I don't know what to do!"

Samantha is staying so calm through this. She has the background both of the case and to get the confidence of a child predator victim. "I am working with an FBI agent to help find Marissa's killer. His name is Adam. He's one of the good guys and he can help us. Can he come in and talk with you too?" I wait holding my breath. I hear noise and then Samantha is standing in the doorway. "Lexi will talk to you, Adam. But Adam only, I gave her my word. Doctor, can we also get ice cream or something? I can see she's barely touched her dinner and she's had a couple pretty bad days. I think she can have a small treat-- if her health allows it."

The doctor agrees and leaves to have some ice cream brought up. I walk with Samantha and go back into the room. Samantha sits back down on the bed and reaches out to Alexis hand. She holds it in hers and the child seems to relax. "Lexi, this is Adam. I just thought of something else. Adam and I have met Ms. Burnside and she was worried about you." Alexis face lights up and she smiles. Samantha has completely broken through and disarmed this kid.

"You talked to Tiff? I miss her so much! She promised me we'd go horseback riding when I get home, but I think there will be snow on the ground by then." Her face suddenly goes dark, "Is Tiff ok? If you are worried about daddy might this man go after Tiff?"

I hadn't thought about that as a possibility, but to potentially help this situation, I pull out my phone and make a call to the New York DA's office. "This is Agent Clay, is DA White still in the office?" I hold while the phone is transferred. He comes on the line and we exchange pleasantries for a moment. "I am sitting here with Alexis Montgomery in Baltimore. She has become separated from Jacob Montgomery and Dr. Callahan and I have told her that we are worried about Jacob. Alexis has seen the man who might be trying to kill people and she's afraid for Tiff Burnside. In hindsight, Alexis might be right. Can your office contact her and see if we can get her some protection? As soon as I can, we will get a description sent to you so you know what the suspect looks like."

DA White pauses for a moment. "I take it you are with Sidney Harris. I will contact Tiff Burnside's lawyer and arrange protection. If you are sure it is Sidney Harris I will also notify Karen Harris. I take it since you are calling her Alexis she isn't ready for her mother yet?" I tell him no not yet but a protection detail is a really good idea and then I hang up the phone with him.

"Alexis if I get an artist in here do you think you can help that person draw a picture of the man you saw on Jekyll Island?"

She shakes her head. "I won't forget what Taylor looks like. He tried to grab me just before the auction. Daddy gave away the trip he had planned for us. It's ok though. It went to charity. Instead, we went out on the Lady Grey. That was just as good."

Samantha was sitting there watching the child and still holding her hand. "Lexi, do you ever wonder about your mom? Would you ever want to see her again?"

Alexis stops and looks at her. "My mommy died. They took her to jail and she died. That's how I came to live with daddy." I can see tears forming in her eyes.

Samantha reaches her arms out to Alexis and hugs her "Lexi your mommy is alive and has been looking for you. I talked to her a few days ago." She turns to me and says "Adam, do you still have Lexi's mom's phone number? I think Lexi would love to talk to her. Wouldn't you Lexi?" Tears are now streaming down Alexis cheeks and she shakes her head up and down. I push the phone number for Karen Harris and she answers on the first ring.

"Karen, this is Agent Clay." I smile because DA White has already contacted her. "Yes, she's in the hospital but she's going to be ok. She was cold and scared when she came in but the doctors are probably going to release her tomorrow. I'm sure I can make arrangements for you to see her tomorrow or as soon as you can get down to Baltimore. I think she would like to hear your voice. Is it ok if I pass the phone to Alexis?" I tried to stress the name she was insisting on using.

I hand the phone to Alexis "Mommy?" I can't hear what Karen Harris is telling her but she is nodding her head yes. Eventually she hands the phone back to me and I hear Karen Harris on the other end. "It's her isn't it? I never thought I would see her again. She said she wants to see me. I'm going to see if I can be there in the morning. I don't know how to thank you." I tell her that she will have to work with hospital staff but I'm glad we have taken the first steps in reuniting them.

The sketch artist from the Baltimore Field office arrives at the hospital and knocks on the door frame of Alexis' room. Samantha asks her if it is ok for him to come in and she nods. The artist shows her pictures of facial parts on his tablet and she helps him pick out the face of the man she met on Jekyll Island. In a few minutes she is done and he turns the picture around for us to see.

Behind me I hear someone gasp. Kim Palter is standing there with her mouth open. "I don't know his name but he's a med student here!" I jump up and tell the city cop outside to call for back up. I now wonder whether if word gets out that Alexis is here this person will try to silence her.

Samantha looks at me and tells me she would like to get some hot tea. I walk out with her and we both at the same time say "Tyler Braden!" We both wondered when Alexis said Taylor if she meant Tyler. The electronic sketch confirms our suspicion. We agree we don't want to alarm Alexis of how dangerous Tyler can be, so Samantha decides to not pursue any more questions about him. I send her back to be with Alexis and head to get her a cup of hot tea and to check with administration to see if Tyler Braden has identification for this hospital.

John joins me on the trip to the administration office. He has the sketch artist's rendition on his tablet. The office has closed for the evening, so we head back down to the security desk at the garage. There the security officer accesses the database of employees. He shakes his head. He does not have a Tyler Braden. He does have a Joshua Braden.

Joshua Braden has access to the hospital as part of the medical school and can accompany physicians on rounds, but has no medical privileges. According to the computer records, Joshua Braden has not scanned in to the hospital since October fourth. John gets a copy of the employee identification from the security guard and we head back upstairs.

I stop off at the lobby coffee shop and get a cup of tea for Samantha and we both get a cup of coffee before we head up the elevator. Alexis is sitting on the bed with Samantha eating her ice cream when we get back upstairs. She seems much more animated then before and she has relaxed with Samantha. I am impressed with her ability to disarm Alexis and get information from her. She's good at what she does.

Alexis is yawning as she finishes her ice cream. We still have to find a hotel for the night. We are told most of the hotels are full because of the football game this weekend. We drive out the Jones Falls Expressway and head up I-83 north to Timonium. We find a hotel and check in. Downstairs the bar is going strong and we opt to head out of the hotel to get dinner. I pull into a pasta restaurant. There are only three other vehicles in the front parking lot. It's a fairly upscale place and it seems the dinner crowd is winding down.

The restaurant is dark with tables scattered so that private conversations between couples can stay private. So far, there has not been a public sighting of Helen Braden, and not any flight information on Tyler Braden. The body of Duke Braden has been flown to Texas with no fan fair. It has already been announced that his body will lie in state under the Capitol Dome and the times the public will be allowed to view the body. The information of Joshua Braden's death is also being announced with a joint funeral for them both taking place next week in a state funeral. Both father and son are being buried next to each other.

As we wait for our meals to be delivered, we rehash the conversation and our notes on the interview with Helen Braden. She said she had talked to Joshua and had an email conversation with Tyler. At the time she said she had spoken with Joshua he was already dead. I am not convinced of the likelihood a mother would not know her own son's voice. If it had been Tyler, I could believe she didn't know he was dead. She only emailed with him. She also said that Tyler was back in the Amazon when we can find no proof that he either flew to the Amazon recently or flew back after his father's stroke. I believe Alexis saw Tyler Braden after Joshua's death on Jekyll Island. I don't see another way for her to have been able to give the description she gave the artist of him this evening.

The hospital has Joshua Braden not being back inside the hospital since just prior to Kali's murder. Yet, the nursing home identified the man who had been visiting the hospital as Joshua Braden. We now know that Joshua Braden had not been visiting his father. I wonder if the nursing home has been mistaken and it has been Tyler Braden visiting. If so, did Tyler know his brother was dead? This seems likely since he has been using his brother's name.

We also have to think about Alina Braden. With both Kali and Joshua dead, her life may be in danger as well. I don't want to bring this up because I don't want Samantha to think about it if she hasn't already come to this conclusion. Through all of this, Samantha has been quietly eating her baked ziti. "This entire case has gone back to the Braden's. Tonight when Samantha told Alexis she didn't think Jacob killed Kali, I agree. All along, I have had a nagging feeling that we have been chasing the wrong man. Not that I think he is innocent and from what I saw on the hospital report of the rape kit, the man deserves all the jail time he can get but I think Kali was killed by either Helen or Tyler Braden or both. This would explain a lot of things like what happened to the cars. Perhaps they found out about Alina and Helen got Tyler to help her. One or both did the murders and together they got rid of the cars."

John takes a bite of lasagna before responding, "I am worried about whether Helen Braden is still alive. You know those gut feelings? I think she and Jonathan are missing because they are dead. If she and Tyler were a mom and son killing team, she would still be in the public eye mourning her sons murder and now the death of her husband. She had it planned to be compared to the great women of this country at a time of national mourning. If they have gotten away with the murders to this point, I don't think she would go into hiding. Plus, it takes a lot for a mom to kill her son. That's a big step for most killers."

Samantha puts her wine glass down without taking a drink "You know you are right about that. She was all about appearance. I hadn't thought of that. If all of these murders are connected to one killer then we have a serial killer on our hands. His trigger seems to be the Co-Op. The messages he has sent us have been connected to the Co-Op. Joshua Braden was a billboard of finger pointing. First the note and then the bikini bottom telling us to follow that line of clues. The killer wanted us to know he was connected to Kali. Why would Tyler or Helen Braden want to also point a finger at themselves? That is unless Helen knew it was Joshua's body all along. I believed her, so she is either a really good actress, or she had no idea it was Joshua. I also can't drop the image of Jacob Montgomery being afraid of Tyler Braden. I had thought he left Jekyll Island because of having Alexis and us being on their trail. Did he just use Tyler Braden as a scapegoat for her or did Tyler Braden threaten him?"

I suggest we finish eating and get back to the hotel. I want to pull up our timeline again. More and more pieces are beginning to fall into the puzzle. We opt to skip dessert and drive back across the street to the hotel. The bar is still hopping and the music is loud as we get into the elevator. If we were going upstairs to sleep, it will be impossible. My guess is we have to wait until the bar closes to get any sleep. This is one of the things I hate about hotels with night clubs in them. While the party crowd loves the idea of drinking and dancing until they are ready to pass out, those of us who check into hotels to sleep would like to be able to do that. Normally, I won't check into a hotel with a bar in the lobby. It's a deal breaker for me, but tonight we got in late with no reservations and found a place where we could get two rooms. As it is, John is on another floor. He gets off on his floor to get his laptop and we continue up to our room.

I have rented a suite on the seventh floor. The window from our room looks out over the atrium in the center of the hotel. The way the hotel is designed all of the rooms look out over the atrium. With the noise level from the band and the yells of the crowd, there will be a lot of tired faces in the morning at the continental breakfast.

John knocks on the door and comments on the coeds vomiting in the elevator. Hotel hell doesn't get much worse than this. I'm glad I only booked us for one night. If we are staying in Baltimore for another night, I will find a quieter hotel. Our next hurdle is the slowness of the hotel Wi-Fi so we set up our own hotspot. I usually don't use that unless we are getting encrypted data. Tonight it is to keep the aggravation at a manageable level.

John starts the timeline. "First we have Duke, Joshua and Tyler Braden going to somewhere between Ocean City and Chincoteague. Duke has the stroke and ends up in the hospital in Salisbury about the same time as Kali is murdered. We also think the body on the beach and the body in the Braden house both die at about the same time. We get called on the case which leads to Kali's identification, Samantha's release and the search warrant for Jacob Montgomery. Montgomery flees with Sidney Harris, aka Alexis Montgomery and they go to Jekyll Island. Duke Braden is transferred to hospice and Tyler Braden supposedly returns to the Amazon. Instead he is seen by Alexis on Jekyll Island and they get onboard the Lady Grey. Meanwhile, Jacob Montgomery creates the diversion for us with the trip being given away at the auction. At some point, Joshua Braden is murdered and his torso is found in College Station. We interview Helen Braden and she seems convincing that both sons are still alive. She confirms that Duke had a sexual relationship with Kali. The Lady Grey must have gone north from Jekyll Island because they were caught along the coast with the hurricane approaching. Jacob Montgomery and the captain get into the argument and as the storm is hitting so he and Alexis leave the ship. Soon after, the Lady Grey snaps its masts and hits the Chesapeake Bay Bridge causing it to end broken up and beached with at least two crew members dead. Just after this, Joshua Braden's head is brought into the field office and left in the lab by employees of the vetted mechanical engineering company. The storm exposed the body of the victim on the beach and we find the body in the Braden house. At the same time, Alexis is abandoned by the woman she was left with because we were looking for her. Did I miss anything?"

I think for a moment. "Yes. The date of the paternity report was the middle of September. What if Duke took his sons fishing to have it out with Joshua about his sexual relation with Kali? According to Helen Braden, Duke took an overdose of his medications which caused the heart attack and stroke; perhaps, he was given the overdose? Both sons have medical backgrounds. Either could have drugged Duke and it went bad. That might explain why they delayed medical attention."

John taps a few things on his computer before adding "and Kali was pregnant again. We have no way of knowing the father of this baby, but the potential was there that it was a Braden baby."

This time it is Samantha who is looking through her laptop. "Wait. Who said maybe the dead guy in the Braden house or on the beach was some sort of mediator? If the dead guy on the beach was her new owner and he found out she was pregnant again perhaps he wanted his money back. Duke might have just wanted to get rid of her because he was pissed his son had been having sex with his sex slave. That had to piss him off and maybe it was enough to get rid of Kali. If the mediator determined because Kali was pregnant Duke had to give the money back and keep Kali until after the baby was born, it might be enough to murder her and cut out the baby. Whoever killed her knew she was pregnant and knew how to perform a caesarian. That got rid of the evidence of the pregnancy and if it was Joshua's baby it eliminated any way to track the DNA back to the Braden's. They have Alina hidden or have sent her away. If Duke had thought Alina was his and found out in September that she was having sex with Joshua, I can see this getting the whole thing started."

It passes back to John and his notes, "It was Joshua Braden that got a girl drunk and raped her. Duke threatened Helen Braden to take that public if she reported his sexual contact with Kali. Maybe Duke threatened her again and this time she had enough."

Samantha chimes in "but would she kill her son? I can see her having something to do with Kali's death, whatever happened to Duke and possibly the body on the beach and in the house, but she defended Joshua once. She was afraid to do anything out of fear of repercussions. I can't see her killing her son."

It takes a lot for a mother to kill her child. It happens now and then, but that usually happens with young children when a mother feels she is backed into a corner with nowhere to turn. Both of Helen Braden's sons have left the house to go to school and start careers. There have been occasions where a mother has protected a child that killed someone. It is possible Tyler killed and she protected him.

John takes a drink and has a puzzled look on his face. "What if giving the trip away wasn't to throw us off the trail but was to throw Tyler off the trail? What if he wasn't running from us at all? That would explain how he was always one step ahead of us. Sidney, Alexis, whatever her name is, told us Montgomery was afraid of Tyler and they went on vacation so that he could keep her safe. What if he was telling her the truth?"

I am tired and look at the time on my cell phone. It is after midnight and the music is still going strong downstairs. I can see where we are all exhausted and I call it quits for the night. We don't have any solid evidence to link everything together and we are just guessing at this point. While this might help point us in a direction, it can also derail us and bring us to a wrong conclusion. We have to let the evidence answer our outstanding questions. All I know for sure is that the Braden family is at the center of this series of murders.

John heads back to his room while Samantha and I settle in bed for the night. I lay down on my back and Samantha puts her head on my shoulder while draping her arm around me. Outside the window we hear the boom boom boom of the drum from the band. I didn't think we would be able to fall asleep, but I wake later with my arm asleep under her. I gently pull my arm out and get rid of the pins and needles. She shifts to her side and puts her arm around my waist and snuggles against my back. I go back to sleep wondering if one day we will be able to go to sleep in my bed.

DAY 20
BALTIMORE, MARYLAND

We wake up to the sound of the fire alarm sounding. Out in the hallway I can hear chaos. People are talking and wondering what they should do. We get up and grab a room card and our shoes. People are standing around the hallway wondering reluctant to leave the warmth of their rooms to go outside during the early morning in November. I have observed people for many years and I always find it curious that even though they drilled as children to get out in the event of a fire, as adults they question whether this is another drill or the real thing. I think because all they have ever done is drill, they have become trained that a fire alarm is always a test. I take control and tell people we need to go down the stairway, hotels don't hold fire drills in the middle of the night. The still drunk coeds want to argue with me. I finally decide to leave them to hotel security. Everyone else leaves the floor and they are making their way down the stairs.

As we reach the second floor, we can smell smoke. This prompts the doubters in the group to go down the steps faster. When we reach the lobby, we head out into the parking lot where I find hotel security and tell them about the two girls who went back into their room on our floor. Already fire engines are arriving in the lot. Two teams enter with hoses while two other teams start a room to room search.

Outside it is thirty eight degrees. Our SUV is parked out in the parking lot away from the building. We head there to get out of the cold. Luckily I have grabbed the keys on my way out and John is already standing by the passenger side door. I think of Sidney Harris spending the night out in Fort McHenry. I'm surprised the child made it through the night without succumbing to hypothermia. When the temperature gage starts to dip, I turn the heat on. None of us grabbed a coat on the way out. I see the hotel is trying to distribute blankets to the guests who are huddled together. Near our vehicle stands a man, woman and a small child huddled together trying to stay warm. I crank the window down a crack and ask if they want to come inside with us. They readily accept.

While we sit and watch the fire department enter and exit, there is little we can talk about except what we think is going on inside. With strangers in the vehicle, we can't talk about the case. At first the fire department is moving quickly. Then they slow down and seem to be discussing more than putting anything out.

It takes about forty minutes for the fire department to give an all clear so that we can re enter the hotel. Someone had put a cigarette in a trash can in the ladies room in the bar. The bar is a non-smoking location, as are all of Maryland's bars and restaurants, so the cigarette was one snuck in the bathroom. I'm sure right now the people standing in the cold listening to this announcement would like to wrap their icy hands around that person's neck. Running the heat in the SUV has kept us warm and the three people we piled into our vehicle, but many went outside without car keys or were parked too close to the building to sit inside.

It's 5:20 AM before we get back upstairs to our room. On the way back up the elevator, the two coeds are quiet. They have been ticketed by the Fire Marshall. Between the cold and the ticket, the girls have sobered up completely. Since they are worried it was one of their cigarettes that started the trash can fire, I have no sympathy for them. At the moment, I understand why someone would kill these two and leave their bodies behind a dumpster. Instead, I retain common sense and go back to our room. Hotel employees are running up and down the hallways with master keys letting people back into their rooms if they didn't take their keys.

We get back in bed and try to go to sleep. It doesn't seem like a long time before my alarm goes off. Karen Harris should be arriving at Baltimore Washington International Airport by 8:30 AM. The Baltimore City police will be picking her up and taking her straight to the hospital to see Sidney. I am hoping the police and medical staff on duty talks to her and remind her to call her daughter Alexis. For her psychological health, we have all been asked to call her Alexis. While it is easy for us, it will be hard for her mother. Hopefully Alexis will eventually want to go back to her birth name.

We go down the elevator to get breakfast. John looks as tired as I feel. Around us, I see others who have suffered the middle of the night interruption. The hotel staff is trying to be as friendly and helpful as possible as people shuffle through breakfast preparing for whatever brought them to Baltimore for the day.

The doctors and police have asked us to give Alexis some time before we ask her any more questions. Instead we go to the Fort Avenue area of the city. Alexis said she walked out of a restaurant and saw the sign for Fort McHenry. I want to try to retrace her path and see if there is some sort of clue to the mystery woman, Ms. Barbara. It doesn't take us long to find a fast food restaurant on East Fort Avenue. When we pull out of the parking lot, I see the brown and white sign for Fort McHenry at the corner of Lawrence Avenue. From there it is one mile to the gate of the fort.

Once again, I find myself on National Park Service land. Fort McHenry is a national historic park located at the mouth of Baltimore's inner harbor. During the Battle of Baltimore on the night between September thirteenth and fourteenth in 1814, Francis Scott Key was aboard the British ship HMS Tonnant negotiating the release of an American prisoner of war, William Beanes. It was from the window of the Tonnant that Francis Scott Key witnessed the bombardment of the fort and wrote the poem "Defence of Fort McHenry." He put it to the tune of a popular song by John Stafford Smith, *To Anacreon in Heaven*. This was the song that became known as the Star Spangle Banner.

I haven't been to Fort McHenry in over twenty years and there have been a lot of changes as the fort prepares for its two hundredth anniversary. The fort itself has remained untouched but there is a new visitor center and work done to the surrounding grounds. We park and enter the visitor center. Already I can see families and groups walking around the parapet of the star shaped fort. We show our identification to the ranger at the information deck and he tells us to have a seat.

A ranger approaches us and holds out his hand as we stand. "Hi, I'm John Armistead. I'm the person who found the little girl yesterday morning when

I unlocked the gates. Let me show you around." We follow him out through the side entrance and walk toward the fort. It is impressive. The park service has fully restored the fort and mounted the cannons on the battle works of the fort facing out toward the water.

A crowd has gathered around the flag post in the center of the fort. There a park ranger is standing on a platform with a flag at the tall white wooden pole. Next to the pole stand a drummer and a fifer at attention. They are dressed in 1812 military uniforms to fit the age of the fort. Another man walks out in a period uniform with a tall feathered hat of a commander. He calls the crowd and soldiers to attention for the raising of the flag. The drummer starts a slow beat as the ceremony begins. The fifer joins in with a period tune as the flag slowly rises into the air. Ranger Armistead apologizes for the delay in taking us to the area that Alexis was found. We all mumble that it is ok. Watching the Star Spangle Banner being raised over the fort is humbling. It is a ceremony every American should probably see in order to fully appreciate the meaning of the flag.

When the ceremony is completed, he continues, "We are standing in the Sally Port. I found her right here on the left. She was huddled in the back corner of the bombproof under the guardhouse. I heard a noise and thought it was an animal down there. We have problems this time of year with pigeons roosting to get out of the cold. We try to discourage them because cleaning their droppings off the rock is a constant problem. She had to be pretty uncomfortable. You can see its pretty cold and damp feeling in there. It kept her out of the wind, but did very little else. I called my superior and he called the police. The girl was defensive and scared. It was all we could do to restrain her until the police came. We also called an ambulance because she was so cold."

I try to get a feel for what it must have felt like to hide here for the night. The kid has to be pretty brave, not just from the cold, but she was excited about the place possibly being haunted. Very few adults would spend the night in a haunted location especially one connected to a battle field. It speaks a lot about her character and her adaptability to survive.

After showing us the location, he asks if there is anything else we would like to know. I have to ask him about his last name. He smiles "Yes, I am of that Armistead family. It was my great great great great grandfather who was the commander of the fort. My family has been the keeper of the keys to Fort McHenry since the battle of 1812. It is an honorary title, but I joined the park service and had a special request to be assigned to Fort McHenry. My son works here as well and when I retire he will take over being the keeper of the keys to the fort."

After he walks away, I see the confused look on Samantha's face. I laugh and ask her if she would like the tour of the fort from the history nerd. Both she and John agree, so I put on my imaginary tour guide hat and start the tour. "We are currently standing in the center of the fort. To our left we have the barracks for the commanding officers and their aids, beside that the powder magazine." We turn to face each building. "Continuing to the left was located the officer's quarters. Finally the last two buildings were enlisted men quarters. On September 13, 1812, there were about one thousand men living inside this fort. You can see it was pretty tight quarters. They knew from runners that the British fleet had attacked in North Point about five miles from here and were pushing this way. The British Navy had broken through the defenses and sailed north of Annapolis. General Armistead knew soon the British would attack the fort by both land and sea. Meanwhile, about ten thousand men of the Maryland militia were moving from Hampstead Hill, now known as Patterson Park, to confront the British land troops."

I take them both up onto the ramparts looking out over the water. "In advance of the British attack, General Armistead ordered merchant ships to be sunk across the mouth of the harbor in an attempt to block entrance. The attack began on the fort when the nineteen British ships arrived. For the next twenty five hours the fort was bombarded." I point out into the water "right over here would be the HMS Erebus. It was equipped to fire the Congreve rocket. This rocket had cutting edge cannon fire. It consisted of an iron cased twenty four pound cylinder warhead containing black powder for propulsion. There was a guide pole mounted on the side and the rockets were launched in pairs from the deck. These rockets were accurate up to two miles. In Baltimore, they were closer and more accurate. The warheads were loaded with incendiaries and shrapnel."

"Other ships alongside the Erebus were the bomb vessels Terror, Volcan,

Meteor, Devastation and Aetna. Originally they were positioned just off the fort, but during the afternoon, repositioned themselves just out of reach of the forts cannons. During the twenty five hour bombardment, they launched over one thousand five hundred bombs into the fort. Miraculously they only killed four Americans and wounded twenty four others."

"The defenders of Baltimore didn't give up and eventually the contingency including Francis Scott Key negotiated a cease fire thus ending the battle. This fort later served as a Civil War military prison and a World War I hospital. The fort was made into a National Park in 1925 and in August of 1939, it was designated as a National Monument and Historic Shrine. It is the only location in the country designated like this."

Samantha starts to laugh "Adam, how do you know all of this stuff? You can just pull it out of your head like some history book. Don't get me wrong, it is fascinating, but I have no idea how you know all of this."

I have to smile "this is my main love. I can't get enough history. My first time here was one Flag Day. I was part of a school group creating the largest human flag for the book of records. Another little known fact is that tradition has been set whenever there is a new flag designed for the United State it must be flown here on that flag pole before it can be flown anywhere else in the country. Both the flags welcoming Alaska and Hawaii were flown here first and are still on display here."

We spend a little more time looking around the fort. Everywhere we look there are children walking around looking in various display areas. It is easy to see during a school day how one child exploring alone might not be noticed by adults. The fort closes before dusk so she probably went to the bombproof as the school groups were leaving. We are dealing with a very smart kid. Most of the buildings were either just display or only the first floor is set up for display with the upper floors chained off to visitors. Of course it would not be hard for a child to wait until no one was in the room with her and sneak upstairs. Who knows where Sidney went or saw before hiding in the bomb proof or for that matter if she hid upstairs in a building until after dark and moved to where she was found.

I guess we were lucky that she followed the signs to Fort McHenry. If she had not gone to the fort, she may still be walking the streets of Baltimore or possibly picked up by someone else and disappear again. I feel we are lucky this time. Every day in this country, a child walks out the door and disappears without a trace. Many of these children turn up dead sometime later. I never thought I would think the lucky ones were taken by the Co-Op and sold into slavery.

We wait until we get a call from the Baltimore Police that the doctors have given the ok for us to talk to Alexis again. This time with Karen Harris present we can ask her questions about her time with Jacob Montgomery. First the child psychiatric team has asked to meet with Samantha and go over some areas that they do not want to push her into talking about. Of course the sexual assaults are completely off limits. That will come later. Right now she isn't ready to discuss the sexual trauma.

Samantha and I walk into the room and she immediately goes to Karen Harris and gives her a hug. Alexis watches the two women with curiosity. Then Samantha turns to Alexis. "Lexi did your mother tell you what she has been doing since she last saw you? She's doing something pretty cool. She's working now and is going to school. She's got a great job and is helping people find missing family members. Your mom has changed a lot since you last saw her. I went to visit her on her job and she's got this big office. She does a lot to make people happy too. You should be proud of your mom."

Alexis looks at her mother and smiles. Samantha sits down on her bed and continues. "I went to Fort McHenry. I've never been there before and you're right it's pretty cool. I watched them raise the flag in the morning. The buildings are old but nice. I can see why you stayed there but you were pretty brave. It had to be a pretty scary place in the dark." Alexis nods her head. "I bet Jacob would be scared if he knew you had slept there. I saw your house and your bedroom. It was very nice. Nothing like the cold night you spent in Fort McHenry. We need today to try to find Jacob. I told you I think there may be someone who might hurt him. I also bet he's found out that woman drove off and left you at the restaurant. He's going to be pretty angry with her. He won't be angry with you, though. I can tell from everything he bought for you at the house that he cares for you."

It was hard to tell what is going through Karen Harris mind. She looks puzzled at the soft line Samantha is taking. Samantha is trying to relay to her through eye gestures that she has to take it slow and not push the child. "Did Jacob say anything about where he was going or who he was seeing? Did you hear him make flight reservations or do you know what time you took him to the airport. Maybe even where he had Ms. Barbara drop him off at the airport? You may know something that will help us help him and let him know you are ok."

Alexis bites her lip and looks down. "He said he was flying to London. We took him to the international terminal. His flight number was 228 but I don't know what airline. He was told to be there a couple hours before his flight and we dropped him off at 8:15 in the morning. He was mad at Ms Barbara because he was going to have to wait all day at the airport. Does that help?"

John is already typing information into his tablet. He smiles and excuses himself to make a call. Samantha smiles back at Alexis "From the smile on John's face, I think you did. As soon as we find him, I promise to let you know."

The nurse walks in and Samantha pauses. She has papers for Karen to sign. They leave and Alexis is visibly nervous. "The doctor said I can leave the hospital. I am going to be staying in a juvenile facility for a few days. They tell me the house is nice but I'm scared. What if I get lost?"

For such a brave kid to have spent the night in what is proclaimed as one of the most haunted places in Baltimore, she suddenly sounds small and more like her age. Samantha reaches over and runs her hand down her hair smoothing it. "It will be fine. You won't get lost. Your mom is going to stay in Baltimore for a couple days. The doctors want you to get to know her again and when you feel better you can go home. It's going to be up to you when you feel you are up to it. The doctors and the people at the home you are going to know this and will work with you. No one will rush you. They know there have been a lot of changes in your life. I also promise you to let you know when we find Jacob. He will want to know you are ok. Everyone here is looking out for you and wants you to be able to feel happy and safe again."

Alexis lunges across the bed and bear hugs Samantha almost knocking her down. "Thank you! I didn't know if I would ever see my mommy again and I didn't know if I did find her if she would want me back." Samantha wraps her arms around her and kisses the top of her head. It's great to see the healing process beginning so quickly in the child.

John walks back in and motions for me to go back outside with him. I leave the room and follow John around the corner to the lounge. "First, we have a lead on Montgomery. He did fly to London; he had a car waiting for him and went to a hotel. According to the hotel records, he is still a guest there. London police are watching the hotel and will pick him up as soon as they see him. Next up when I called the office, I was told Duke Braden's body arrived in Austin. There it was met by a military band and the news crews. It was not met by Helen Braden or Tyler Braden. We do now know the location of Sally Gold. She flew to Austin with the body. She is being taken in for questioning. They didn't make a scene picking her up and she has been told they just want to talk to her. No charges are currently pending." Samantha comes out to join us. Alexis is about to be transferred. Karen Harris has checked into our hotel and will be riding back with us.

We see Alexis to her transportation and then follow the car to make sure she arrives safely. The house is going to be under twenty four hour surveillance. We have not determined if she is in any kind of danger yet. There is the possibility she is a lose end to the Co-Op and they might try to get to her. As we are leaving her at the home, Karen gives her one last hug and promises to be back tomorrow to see her. As Alexis kisses her goodbye, she looks at her mother and says "Mom! It's ok to call me Sidney. I just got use to the other name. It might take me a while to remember who I am." This kid is smart and seems to be bouncing back quickly. Samantha warns Karen on the way to the hotel that there will be set backs but having her back as Sidney is a big step.

Karen is given a room on the same floor as we are. It's already four in the afternoon. We agree to meet back up at six for dinner. Karen is alone in town and we are sitting in a holding pattern waiting to see where we have to go next.

I lay down on the bed and Samantha snuggles up next to me. The lack of sleep the night before is hitting us and I set the alarm on my phone in case we fall asleep. I wake to my phone ringing. It's five thirty four. I try to shake sleep from my head enough to answer the phone. "Boss. I don't know how to tell you this, but we have more bodies. This time it's Helen Braden and Jonathan Simon. It looks like a murder suicide. There's a note. The head of Austin police read the note to me. Seems she was having an affair with her man servant. The note said something about not being able to go on in life with her husband and son dead. She killed her lover and then herself. Both took bullets to the head. Sally Gold, the Senators assistant found them when she went to Duke Braden's house in Austin. They have been there for a couple days. You seem to draw the not so recently deceased. Morgues really are not going to like to see your name attached to a case soon."

We get out of bed and get dressed. I don't feel like eating even though it's been ten hours since our last meal. I feel that tired. John and Karen are already in the bar waiting for us. John looks like I feel. We order drinks while waiting on a table for dinner.

My phone rings again before we are seated. I take the call in private in case it has to do with Sidney or Alexis or whoever she is at this moment. Instead, it has to do with Helen Braden and Jonathan Simon. We are seated in a semi secluded table. I think the hostess thinks we are couples on a romantic weekend. "Karen, if you will excuse some shop talk for a moment, I promise not to get graphic. Jonathan Simons' next of kin came to identify his body. It was his male significant other. He is denying Jonathan and Helen Braden were in a sexual relationship."

Samantha interrupts "Are we talking he was bisexual and his partner didn't know about the relationship or are we talking gay and girls are off the menu?"

"I would say gay and girls are off the menu. This was his husband. I'm talking relationship to the point they left the state to get married and his husband brought a copy of the marriage certificate to the morgue to prove he was next of kin. The husband is demanding a murder investigation because he says the suicide note is a lie."

Samantha makes a face and twitches her nose. "So can we assume Helen Braden knew too much and she and her friend were murdered and made to look like a murder suicide? Did anyone besides Jonathan know she talked to us? Perhaps, with Duke dead, the murderer was afraid she had no fear of talking anymore. Do we know where Tyler Braden is? He is one of three things - a potential victim because he too knows too much, a murderer, or completely innocent and just in the wrong place at the wrong time early on in this."

Karen Harris is sitting there with her mouth open "so two people are dead in what appears to be a staged murder suicide and you think it's connected to the Co-Op."

I tell her we know they are connected. "From what we know, this is a very dangerous group who has, at this point, left a trail of bodies. This is one of the reasons Sidney is in protective services and you are in our hotel and John relocated his room to be next to you. I want to be honest with you about the people we are dealing with. This is our sixth or seventh body in this case. No one has determined if Duke Braden succumbed to natural causes or if someone slipped him a double dose of medication which brought on a heart attack and stroke. Tyler Braden is the last of his family standing at this moment; this is if he isn't also a victim. It seems to have started with Kali and the man she was with that day. There was a man in the Braden home that we assume was connected. Then Joshua Braden was found in Texas with his head delivered to the FBI field office in Richmond, now Helen Braden and Jonathan Simon. If Duke Braden death was murder that makes seven."

"Most of the victims have been cut up badly. Helen Braden and Jonathan Simon are the first shooting victims. I have to assume they are related to this case because most of this case is related to the Braden family."

Karen has a puzzled look on her face. "I thought Kali was with Jacob Montgomery. How does Braden fit in?"

I figure it won't hurt for her to hear the story. Maybe a new head in this will help and she works with abducted children and their families. Perhaps she has seen or heard something that can help link to the Co-Op. "The Co-Op appears to be a huge operation and from what we have been told goes back about two hundred years. A few people have told us this is older than the Civil War. They look for children who are from low income houses, usually a single parent, and living in poverty. They kidnap the children, possibly from a list. We think they stalk the children. We know both Kali and Sidney were stalked and then taken. It may be after the pedophile approves the child fits their needs. The child is then cleaned up, dressed up and given food that gets them back into good health. They are well educated with a slightly twisted view on history which makes child sexual encounters natural. The children are taught to meet the sexual needs of the men who order them from the abduction team. As you know, pedophiles have an age and appearance preference. When a child grows out of their age or development preference, it appears they go back on the Co-Op market where they are matched with a man who prefers their age and development."

"We aren't sure how the transactions take place; we have only been told the Co-Op facilitates the transfer of a girl to their next owner. Eventually, they become adults and they can once again return to the market. This time they are well-educated refined women who know all the graces of society and are experts at sexual arousal of their owners. They are offered up as mistresses or wives. Many go on to raise children with their owner. Eventually some go on to become nannies helping to take care of and train the next generation. These women have praised their abductors and try to protect them. This network seems to be well organized."

"The note left on Joshua Braden said that he had broken the rules of the Co-Op and they handle their own. There was no need for us to continue investigating it. We have since found out prior to the murders, someone found out Kali had a baby four years ago with Joshua Braden. We also know from her autopsy that she was pregnant again. We can only speculate this was the rule that was broken."

Karen just sat there for a moment "Eight hundred thousand children go missing every year in the United States. That's roughly ninety-one children an hour in this country. Most end up parental abductions, runaway, or just forgot to tell mom and dad they were staying late. Then, there are those who no one knows what happen to them. Sometimes parents never find out. Other times, years later, their bodies are found. I don't know if this will give parents of the missing without a trace hope or fear. Which is better? Not knowing or having the fear that your child is a sex slave to some pervert? I know my office has forty-three kids who appear to have stepped off the planet. Do you mean, if you get to the center of this and there are records, we could possibly bring many of the hopelessly lost home? Do you have any idea the magnitude of this?"

We all look at her and shake our heads. As this case has grown, the magnitude of what we have before us threatens to crack the very core of this country. The men involved in this are some of the wealthiest, most influential men in the United States. Already we have a Wall Street banking President and a US Senator kidnapping, selling and buying Kali Callahan over a ten year period of time. We have women, going back more than fifty years, who were kidnapped and raised by this group, who have come forward to talk to us. If indeed it does go back to before the Civil War and the threats that it has included Presidents and leaders of the country are true, it could potentially rewrite history. What if sexual philanderers such as George Washington or Thomas Jefferson were members of the Co-Op and part of their sexual history involves the purchase and sale of young girls in an organized pedophile ring. As a history buff, I wonder what that will do to the fabric of our history.

We finish our dinner trying to exchange small talk. I don't think anyone wants to talk about the case anymore. The potential scope of it all is bigger than we are. Instead, we get into a discussion about Fort McHenry and the Battle of Baltimore. Karen has no knowledge of the history of where her daughter spent the night and was found. The details astonish her. I am only too happy to paint the picture of that September night when Baltimore held the advancement of the British and helped make a turn in the war.

John comes back to our room for a wrap up of the night. It appears we are on our way back to Texas in the morning. A team from the Baltimore Field office is going to take over the detail with Karen Harris and Sidney. I make the flight arrangements so that we leave right after breakfast tomorrow and turn Karen over to the new team.

DAY 21
BALTIMORE, MARYLAND
TO AUTSIN, TEXAS

The night does not seem long enough and I could use more sleep, but we meet John and Karen downstairs for breakfast. We eat and wish her good luck. She has my contact information and I will be checking back in with her and the Baltimore Field office if more information becomes available on Jacob Montgomery. I check in one last time with the Baltimore County Police about the hand found in Reisterstown. DNA testing has come back to a body found on President Street in Baltimore City. It is determined this is not connected to our case. We drive to the airport, park the vehicle and get to the terminal just before our plane is called. Airport security gives us disapproving stares as we rush them through security. Even though we have FBI identification, we have to wait in line to pass through airport security. We end up running up the gangway just before the doors close.

Once again, we sleep through the three and a half hour flight, this time landing in Austin. After picking up our SUV, we head to the Austin police station to meet with the husband of Jonathan Simon. The nap on the plane has helped alleviate some of the exhaustion I am feeling.

We are met by Officer Brad Contress and taken to an interview room to meet Danny Plank, husband of Jonathan Simon. The Austin police don't find a reason to open this as a murder investigation. They feel Danny Plank just didn't know about Jonathan's sexual relationship with Helen Braden.

As we walk into the interview room, Danny is quite verbal that they need to listen to him, "what you fail to understand is that Jonathan couldn't have sex with a woman. His little man doesn't come to attention when he sees a woman. It just won't work. He tried in college and failed. He went back to men. Women just aren't his thing, so I know you are wrong about him doing that socialite. Look, she may have been one of the first ladies of Texas, but honey--I am the damn queen!"

I am amused by the scene in the room. Two Austin police officers stand with their backs plastered to the wall. Brad Contress may be the lead investigator, but he looks like he is terrified and would like to run from Danny Plank. In front of us is a man in tight hot pink jeans, a tight white shirt and pink stiletto thigh high women's boots. On the table sits a big hot pink colored sequin purse to go with the outfit. He is tall and thin with a dark tan, bleach blond messy hair looking like he had just gotten out of bed. The most remarkable thing about him though is his eyes. He has the dark smoky eye shadow that the starlets wear and dark kohl lines around his very long fake eyelashes. I have no idea why the police in this room are having a hard time believing Jonathan Simon is gay if this is his husband.

I ask if they would mind if I asked a few questions. Since they have no idea how to deal with him, they readily agree to let me take the lead. "Hi Danny, I'm Agent Adam Clay with the Richmond FBI office. With me are Agent John Duncan and Dr. Samantha Callahan. I believe you have information that can help in the case we are working on. Would you mind if we all sit down and have a conversation?."

Danny puts his hands on his hips and rolls his eyes. "Well, I guess. At least someone wants to listen to me." She sits down and says "ask away."

I take out my tablet and open a document. "I want to let you know that I believe you. I think your husband was murdered and this was made to look like a murder suicide. I need your help to prove both of our theories. Would you mind spelling your name for me and then tell me what you know about Jonathan's disappearance and death. First is that Danni with an "i" or Danny with a "y?"

I can see I have calmed her down already. "That's D...a...n...i. Simon. S...i...m...o...n. Honey, I was born Daniel Richard Simon and my driver's license still says that. I still have the equipment of a Daniel, but every day I tuck and tape into Dani." I think he wants to get a rise out of me but instead I thanked him for the proper spelling. He gives me a shocked but appreciative look. "Well then, let me start at the very beginning. Jonathan and I are married. I am talking leave the state to get a certificate that is not recognized by the state, but we had to do it because I wanted the ring." She holds out her hand to show a large diamond. "Ms. Socialite paid for that, let me tell you."

"Okay, so...I had gone with friends to Vegas to do a drag show. I knew Jonathan was busy with Ms. Socialite as she pre-arranged that troll of a husband's funeral." She puts her hand to her lips. "Oops, I'm sorry. I shouldn't speak ill of the dead but, honey, he was a troll and sometimes the truth just hurts. Well, while I was in Vegas, I tried to call Jonathan a couple times and he didn't answer his phone. He didn't call me back and I got worried so I called the police to report him as a missing person. And this man" He points across the table at Brad Contress "told me Jonathan wasn't a missing person until he'd been gone for forty eight hours. Well, I told him that he hadn't returned my calls in two days, but I was told maybe he was busy! Honey, my man knows to answer his phone or call me back. If he didn't call me back, then clearly, there was something wrong. When I got home, our house looked like no one had been there in days. I called his cell phone and this guy answered his phone. I asked him who the hell he was and he told me Tyler. I just screamed 'YOU BITCH!' and hung up."

I stop him there "are you sure this man said Tyler? Could it have been Tyler Braden?" Right now I'd like to leap across the table and hug her. Dani may have just given us the first real break in this case.

"Honey, I wouldn't know Tyler Braden's voice if I had his balls in my hand. All I know is that someone named Tyler answered his phone. Of course maybe Jonathan's phone was at his mother's house and he was there and answered it."

I turn to Brad Contress "Did Jonathan have his cell phone with him or was the phone recovered? He starts to flip through the file and pulls a picture of the crime scene. There on the table is a cell phone. "Dani, was this his phone?"

She looks at the phone and starts to cry and fan her face. "Yes, yes it is. Oh, I promised myself not to cry. I am going to mess up my makeup. I recognize the case. Ms. Socialite bought that for him in Italy. Its hand tooled Italian leather. Jonathan loved that phone case!" She then bursts out in full fledged sobbing.

John reaches over and puts his arm over Dani's shoulders. She looks at him and tries to smile, "you just have no idea what this feels like. I lost the man I loved. I know everyone is looking at me like some kind of freak fag but I have feelings too. I loved Jonathan. I lost my husband and just had to identify his body. I don't know what I'm going to do!"

John hands her a tissue "I do understand. I was in the Marines in Iraq. My partner and I were manning a check point together. We were a couple weeks from going home when a truck pulled up to the check point and screamed 'Allah Akbar!' The truck blew up right next to Chad. There I was a Marine during 'Don't ask, Don't tell', watching the man I loved, blown into pieces. He died on the scene in my arms. I wanted to run around the scene and put the pieces of him back together like that would make everything ok. Nothing makes it better. There was no one I could talk to and I had to try to keep it to myself. I had to just act like I lost my best friend. Chad was everything to me."

Dani looked around the room before settling his gaze back on John. "Thank you and I'm sorry for your loss. It helps to know I'm not alone."

Samantha gets up and walks to the other side of her. "Dani, I lost my daughter. After she was kidnapped I was accused of murdering her and went to jail for it. I was innocent but no one wanted to believe a hooker. Even Adam has lost someone he loved. His wife was murdered. You are among friends here because we have all lost someone in our life that meant the world to us. I know it's not a good club to be in, but we all understand what you are going through. We have all lived it." Dani hugs her and accepts another tissue to wipe her eyes.

Asking Dani any more questions right now would be a total waste of time. She has lost focus and redirecting her would be nearly impossible. Instead, I ask Brad Contress if he needs Dani for anything else and if we can drop her off anywhere on our way out of here. He shakes his head yes. I think he's glad to get rid of Dani and we leave.

Dani asked if we could drop her off there with her friends at a gay bar named Cocktails Bar and Grill. We park and walk in with her. She's a little shocked, but offers to introduce us around. It's lunchtime and we decide to grab something to eat. It is in part a gesture to Dani and in part to see into Jonathan's world. Dani walks in to a crowd of drag queens hovering over her and helping her to a seat. She gets to be the queen of the court as she begins to plan Jonathan's funeral. There's a Dolly, Liza and a Cher helping plan flowers and music. While Jonathan didn't go public in life, he was going to be made public in a full queen funeral.

Cocktails is a tapas bar and our waitress ChiChi recommends the calamares a la romana, chorizo and the gambas al ajillo with the ensalada tropical. With that she recommends the Cigales. After she leaves the table Samantha asks what we are eating. John and I laugh. "Calamares are squid, chorizo is ham, gambas al ajillo are shrimp with a tropical salad. Cigales is a wine from a specific region in Spain. It is known for its sweetness and smoothness. You need something like that to offset the spiciness of the tapas." She nods ok, but full understanding comes into play when she pops a spicy piece of calamares in her mouth. The salt and spice cause her to take a big drink of her cigales.

The queens at the bar keep us entertained with their banter while we eat lunch. One offers to go shopping with Samantha because she loves her style. We all eat and get a little drunk throughout the afternoon. By the time we are ready to leave, my head is spinning and John offers to drive. He switched to water sometime during the meal. I hand Dani my card and hand it to a couple other queens in the bar. If they can think of anything, I want them to call me. Jonathan is a victim outside of the pattern.

It is a fun afternoon and we head back to the hotel to sleep off the cigales. Instead I get a call from Doug Witting at the morgue. "Agent Clay, I heard you were in town again, this time because of Helen Braden and Jonathan Simon. I got your bodies if you would like to meet up and discuss my findings. I have something a little odd with their murders."

I ask him is it any odder then spending the afternoon getting drunk in a gay tapas bar because that's what we have just done. It might not be the best time for us to discuss the case. I suggest he gives us a couple hours and maybe we can meet at the morgue. Instead, he suggests dinner in two hours at an Italian place he knows.

I take another shower and walk out finding Samantha lying across the bed hugging a pillow sound asleep. I set my alarm and lay down beside her. I think we both need to sleep off lunch. It seems like only minutes before the alarm is going off. Samantha jumps up and runs to the bathroom before I can turn it off. I hear the water running as she jumps into the shower. She comes back out fully dressed and ready to go. We meet up with John and head to the restaurant.

This is our first time meeting Doug Witting in person. The last time we spoke was on video conferencing when Joshua Braden's torso was found in the field. Now, he has Joshua's mother and her personal assistant. We shake hands when we get there. Doug has brought two assistants, Kevin and Leah. They both worked on the bodies and he thought it was a good idea for us to speak with them as well. He has reserved a small private room so that we can eat and talk. These are usually used for parties. Tonight the atmosphere is not for a party.

The restaurant serves family style. Dinner begins with a big bowl of salad with a house dressing. They are generous with a big parmesan grater putting cheese on the salad. The wine flows freely as we begin to eat. A pair of servers brings in platters of chicken parmesan, spaghetti and meatballs, and lasagna. The servers leave us to serve ourselves. We begin to pass the platters around and Doug asks if we want to wait until we all eat before we talk about the autopsy. We all agree to discuss it while we are eating.

Doug opens his tablet "okay, let's start with the suicide note. It was written by Jonathan or at least it is his name signed at the bottom. Here's a picture of the note. The note reads:

I have nothing left to live for. I thought when Duke Braden died I would finally be able to live openly with the woman I love. Instead I find she will not have me. If I can't have her no one can. I'm sorry world, but I can't go on."

"If we hadn't done the autopsy I may have believed this letter. I have the autopsy and toxicology report here on both people and I can say without a doubt that Jonathan Simon did not kill Helen Braden."

"I will start with the stomach contents if that is ok?" We all nod. Even though we are eating, I didn't think it would affect us. "I asked you here because this is where I believe they had their last meal. In both their stomachs, we found the salad and a mixture of chicken alfredo, veal parmesan and shrimp scampi on linguini, also residue of wine and tiramisu. When the police checked the receipts, Helen Braden purchased that exact meal for three. Unfortunately, there are no cameras to be able to tell who the third person might have been and the servers don't remember Helen Braden being here."

"The toxicology report shows that both Helen and Jonathan were drugged. Neither one would have been able to put up a fight. I found five times the normal dose of triazolam in their systems. If you mix a normal dose of triazolam and alcohol it could put you into a coma. Five times that amount may create an irreversible one. If you had told me they had a last meal and took an overdose together, I would give them the Romeo and Juliet award. Instead, there's no way Helen Braden took a gun and shot him in the head and then put a gun in her mouth and shot herself. The drugs and alcohol would have made her near comatose if not completely comatose."

"In my personal opinion, who ever murdered them drugged them where they died. It would only take twenty or thirty minutes for that amount of drugs mixed with alcohol to render them unable to walk. They may have been talking still but slurring their words. People would think they were falling down drunk."

"I would say they died about an hour after eating dinner based on the condition of the food in their stomachs. They ate a lot of food, but it was not broken down. It was all identifiable. We have Helen Braden paying her bill at nine fifteen. It takes ten minutes to get to Duke Braden's Austin home. That gives the killer about forty five minutes to drug them before murdering them. Triazolam is a tablet. It can be crushed into a white powder that is soluble in alcohol. If Helen Braden and Jonathan Simon were already impaired, they might not have noticed the taste mixed in a sweet wine. I can't see someone getting them both to take an overdose so I would like to assume they had the drug slipped to them."

Austin police are trying to find the third person at dinner with them. At this point they are just a person of interest. It is possible that whoever ate dinner with them left and went home. These are questions that have to be answered.

We finished dinner with the house specialty tiramisu. It feels eerie having a meal similar to the victims. I have heard of investigators who relived their victims last hours in order to connect to them. It's not something I have ever done. I usually walk through crime scenes, but I don't recreate their last moments.

We get back into our vehicle and decide to drive by the Austin house. I put the address into the GPS and it does indeed only take us ten minutes to drive from the restaurant to the house. With Helen Braden and Jonathan, they would be dead within the hour from gunshot wounds.

We now have a timeline-- nine fifteen they leave the restaurant and drive home. We can assume they were home by nine thirty. They were dead between ten fifteen and eleven o'clock. I stop and make a call to the Austin police to see if they know the time that Dani called Jonathan's phone and it was answered by Tyler. Austin has not subpoenaed the phone records. I now believe Dani that they disregarded everything she has said. I ask for them to get the phone records for me.

My next call is to Dani. I need to know about what time she made the call to Jonathan. She checks and tells me she made the call at 9:57 pm. This fits into the time line. If Tyler Braden is the murderer, I don't know why he picked up and answered Jonathan's phone, but this was within the timeline of the murders. I don't tell this to Dani. I don't want to upset her anymore. She may have either talked to the murderer just before or just after they killed Jonathan. With this in mind, I make a call back to the Austin police and ask for her to be put under protection. For part of the time after the murder, she was in Las Vegas, now she is home and if she spoke to the murderer she may be at risk.

Back at the hotel, we settle in Samantha and my room going over the timeline. We know Helen Braden's credit card was used in an Austin hotel before we left to go back to Richmond. She had checked out before the police got to the hotel to investigate. We don't know where she went from there. We can assume Jonathan was with her. Since Dani was in Las Vegas, there's a possibility they went to Jonathan and Dani's house. It's possible at some point they returned to Austin, perhaps to work on the funeral arrangements. We also know Tyler was expected to return home, but we have no passenger manifests with him flying here. This suggests either a private plane or he never returned to the Amazon. Duke Braden's body flew back to Texas with Sally Gold accompanying him. Helen Braden's plan had been to have both her sons fly home with their father. Joshua of course had been killed. If it was Tyler Braden who answered Jonathan's phone, it is possible he drove to Texas.

There is a warrant out for Tyler Braden as a person of interest. Until he has been found, we just have a lot of unanswered questions. John decides to head back to his room and get some sleep.

I have noticed Samantha has been quiet today. After John leaves, she is still sitting on the bed with her arms crossed. "So why didn't you just tell me you are gay?" I spun around and looked at her. "All this time have you been leading me on? Why? Have you been using me to help solve the case? Am I just a piece of the puzzle?"

My mouth is open and I have no idea where she got this idea. Her words shock me. "I'm not gay? Why the hell do you think I'm gay? I think I'm falling in love with you! I don't believe this! I have tried to be a gentleman and be considerate of what you have been through. The first time I make love to you, I don't want you to feel like a one night stand or someone who paid you! You are amazing! You're smart and beautiful. I haven't felt like this about a woman since Elizabeth died. What the hell do you want me to say or do Samantha?"

She's still sitting there with her arms crossed, almost hugging herself. I can see she is close to tears. "You and John travel around the country together. You readily tell people you are partners." She stands up and takes a few steps toward me "I didn't know John was gay and that you were that kind of partner! Adam it's okay, you don't need to lie to me. Just don't pretend there is something between us! Tell me the damn truth!"

270

There's a knock on the door and I open it expecting to see hotel security. Instead it is John. "Okay, first everyone in the hotel can hear you. As a matter of fact, part of Austin might be able to hear you. Samantha, Adam is not gay. We are partners, as in we work together. Yes, we travel around together and he is one of my best friends, but I'm not sexually attracted to him. As for Adam, since Elizabeth died he's been as celibate as a monk. I am talking the man has a stronger grip with his right hand then his left from using it! The man hasn't even dated! Did you ever think maybe he hasn't touched you because he's on the job? That and he's still dealing with the loss of the love of his life. The man is broken. He needs to be fixed. I know the man and see how he looks at you. Hell Samantha, you come into his life with your brains, beauty and a body even a gay guy can admire and you are driving the poor man insane. He can't stop looking at you and drinking you in with his eyes, but fear of job and the memory of his wife scare the hell out of him." He stands there for a second holding up his hand and shaking his finger slightly. There's something more he wants to say, but I think he's trying to find the words. "You know what? I'm going to go back to my room now. I suggest you get undressed and get in bed. You two need to get first time sex over with. The longer you wait the worse this situation is going to be. Just turn off the light, go to bed and have sex. Its first time sex, it will be awkward and not really good, but it will get you over the first time. You can work on perfecting it and making it romantic or whatever after this. Now go have sex! I'm sure the other people in the hotel will be glad that you have stopped yelling so that they can go back to sleep. Maybe you will inspire them to have sex. That's okay too. Just go do it, now! Goodnight!" He turns and leaves mumbling as he walks. "I don't believe I had to just tell them to have sex!"

He shuts the door and we both laugh. Samantha looks at me still laughing "Did the guy who yelled at me to keep my distance from you just tell us to have sex and get it over with?" I nod my head and put my arms around her. "Then I guess I should get undressed and we should get in bed." I kiss her and feel her body melting into mine. When I stop, she is breathless.

She then reaches over and turns off the light and breaks free of my arms. In the dark, I can hear her taking off her clothes and them hitting the floor. I take a deep breath and get undressed. Not that John has put a lot of pressure on me or anything, he just put me out to stud with the ears of the hotel focused on our room. I hope he hasn't created too much stress and I can do this.

DAY 22
AUSTIN, TEXAS
TO RICHMOND, VIRGINIA

I wake up in the morning and get a shower. Samantha is awake when I walk out of the bathroom. I smile and walk over to her and kiss her. She kisses me back and then goes into the bathroom to take a quick shower. We both need coffee and breakfast.

John is sitting at a table nursing a cup of coffee when we get off the elevator. He looks at his watch and looks at us before grinning. "Well you two slept in today. Did everything go okay last night?"

I thought about punching him for his cockiness, instead Samantha looked at him and in her sweetest voice said, "Why yes it did. Last night I had to take the situation into my own hands and defrock a monk. It was a very satisfactory defrocking I might add. Of course, you gave him a challenge that lot of men would not have been able to rise to. There's a lot of stress involved in a performance like that, but I am glad to say Adam rose to the occasion and met the challenge head on. I am quite happy with the outcome." She giggles and walks away with a satisfactory switch to her hips.

I follow her admiring the view knowing I am a lucky man. If all goes well, this cute pert little fire ball is going to be my wife. I owe John for pushing the issue last night. He's right, the longer this would have gone on the harder it would have been when we finally got together. Until now, every time I have gotten close to getting my nerve up, something happened and the moment was lost.

People think it's easy for a guy to get a woman in bed. Maybe it is easy for some guys. For me it isn't. I analyze everything too much. It's part of my job to read the clues and look at all possibilities. It carries over to my life.

After Elizabeth's death, I built walls around myself. I have been afraid to love anyone or get close to them. Until Samantha, I have not allowed myself to get close to a woman. John was right about me being celibate. I have looked for excuses the last few years to not get into a relationship. Deep down, I think I blamed myself for Elizabeth's death. If I had been home, I would have know as soon as she went missing. I would have called the police and she may have been found before she was murdered. Maybe I would have noticed someone watching her. Instead, she died alone being terrorized, beaten and sexually assaulted prior to dying from her injuries and having her body dumped in the river like a piece of trash. There are still so many questions in my mind about what I may have done to contribute to her death and if I deserve to be with another woman. Last night, after he pushed me into the situation, I had no choice except to follow through. Luckily, Samantha was more than willing and quite helpful.

I try to put last night behind me and get back on track with the case. I think we are close to the end. In my gut, I am pretty sure Tyler Braden is our killer. I just don't know why. Of course we are sitting at a dead end again. We are waiting for Tyler Braden to be found. Unfortunately, he is off the radar. I call the Austin police and they have no trace of him even being in Texas. The only thing we can do now is return to Virginia and wait for the next break.

We pack and leave the hotel for the flight home. I hate this part of an investigation. All we can do is sit and wait. The evidence cannot tell us anything right now and we need something to link everything together. After we land, we drive back to Richmond.

We head straight into the office. My staff is working on other cases at the moment as we wait for movement. The timeline in the conference room has been updated and I go in there to look at it. Samantha joins me. We sit at the table looking at the board. I feel like we are so close, yet I don't know how to prove Tyler Braden is the murderer unless we get him into an interview room.

Samantha goes out to the outer office to get two cups of coffee. She sets one down in front of me, "Where is Alina? Duke Braden owned a house in College Station and in Austin. He has an office in Washington, DC and one in Northern Virginia. We know he has a DC apartment. Does he own anything in Northern Virginia or when he's not in Texas, he's in the apartment? If Tyler Braden didn't go back to the Amazon, he wasn't at Joshua's apartment in Baltimore and not in his mother's house in College Station. He wasn't at the house in Austin. No trace of him was found there. We also didn't find traces he was at the house in Chincoteague. Where is he? Duke's apartment in DC has been checked. So we have Alina and Tyler staying somewhere. Where is that? I'm not asking just because I want to meet my granddaughter. I think her life is in danger and we need to find her."

I agree with her. With the exception of Tyler, Alina is the only person with the Braden name who is alive. For Samantha's sake, I hope she is still alive. Since we have no clue to where she lives we can only look for clues. So far we have not found another house in Duke Braden's name.

The SAC decides to issue a plea to the media. He asks them to run another report on the case and ask for anyone with information on the location of Alina Braden to come forward. Someone in the Richmond or Washington, DC area knows where this child is located. Hopefully, this will bring someone with information to come forward.

With nothing left that we can do in the office we leave and stop at the grocery store on the way home. My goal is a nice dinner at home, some wine and going to bed like a normal couple.

As I open the door, I hear the sound of running feet. Ebenezer and Chaucer stand in the dining room on their hind legs peeping behind the table legs trying to see who came in the door. They come hopping out when they see it's me coming home. I bend down and give them each a scratch behind their ears. They follow me into the kitchen and I give them each a piece of banana to eat while I put the groceries away.

I am tempted to turn off my phone, but a sense of duty makes me keep it on. We both work in the kitchen. I make the meatballs while Samantha cooks the sauce and noodles for spaghetti. We also cut crusty bread and spread it with butter, minced garlic and grated cheese before putting it in the broiler. I light some candles and open a bottle of wine as we sit down to dinner.

After a few glasses of wine and dinner, I feel tired. We put the dishes in the dishwasher and head upstairs to the bedroom. While I check my email, Samantha gets a shower. Then I get a shower while she gets ready for bed. By the time I get out, she's sound asleep. I try not to wake her. We are both exhausted from being on the road for three weeks. I remind myself we hopefully have a lifetime ahead of us. One more night falling asleep won't dampen our relationship.

DAY 23
DUTCH GAP, VIRGINIA

Morning comes quickly. It seems I have just gone to sleep when I wake to the smell of bacon and eggs. Samantha is downstairs in the kitchen cooking. The toast is popped up in the toaster and the coffee is just finishing perking. It's good to see her making herself at home.

It's a slow morning and at the moment, I have nothing to go on in the case. Instead, I decide to take Samantha over to Henricus Historical Park. We hold hands as we walk through the recreation of the village in 1611. I feel like we are kids. It's a nice day and the re-enactors are demonstrating everything from blacksmithing to hanging and drying tobacco. We can almost feel Chief Powhattan and Pocohontas walking around the recreated village with the early colonists.

It is a perfect afternoon and I decide to extend this feeling into the evening. I head up I-295 to I-64 and toward New Port News. We stop in Colonial Williamsburg for an early dinner in one of the historic inns. Samantha is enchanted by the town and I make a note to myself to bring her back when it's a little warmer. As the sun sets, we walk up Duke of Gloucester Street toward the Market District looking at the holiday decorations. We watched as costumed interpreters stack wood in the wire baskets of the cressets then light them up and down the street. Toward to Palace Green a bonfire has been lit. The street is quiet except for the quiet conversations of people walking arm in arm. The air smells of the burning wood and you can hear the popping of the wood as we pass the fires. We stop and get a cup of hot apple cider and ginger cakes from a table along the street. We finally make it back past Bruton Parish and head into the small garden and through the fence to my Jeep.

I have one more surprise for Samantha tonight. I drive south on I-64 toward Newport News and get off at the park. After driving through the entrance, I pull into the parking lot and call my friend, Mike. We wait a few minutes for him to walk out from the park on the road. "The crew is just finishing. Give us about ten minutes and I will turn it on." Samantha looks at me with a puzzled look. My friend walks over and opens the gate to the park road. I smile at her and wait.

A few minutes later the lights begin to come on. We watch as throughout the woods the holiday display lights up. In a week, the holiday light celebration will be open to the public. Today and tomorrow the crews are finishing the lighting displays and checking them. I had brought Elizabeth here on the night I proposed. Mike told me they would be doing the final lighting tests and working on timing the moving light displays. That night we drove the two mile road looking at the lights. Then I took her to an over look of the James and proposed. Tonight I am not going to be as dramatic. The park has sustained some damage in the storm and they had to clean up the downed trees before doing the lighting. Parts of the road are still not completed so instead we get out and walk the display.

In the distance we can hear Christmas music, other than that the woods are silent. The quiet and the lights are magical. We pass a man who looks up and says hello as he works on timing the arch of penguins that cross over the road. When timed perfectly, it looks like the penguins are sliding down a sliding board over the cars. As we exit the woods we see displays out in the water with the colored lights reflecting off the calm lake.

As we turn the corner, we can see Santa's sleigh in lights and the source of the Christmas music. There Mike is stringing lights along the road. He stops to shake my hand and I introduce Samantha. He looks her over and smiles. "You must be pretty special. While this guy makes it here every year to drive through the lights, you are only the second person he's brought on a private tour. He's a good man. Give him a chance."

Samantha is gracious and smiles back at him "I know he is. Thank you for letting me visit here tonight with Adam. I have never seen anything like this. It's so beautiful. Adam has made tonight completely overwhelming and it's been wonderful. I will remember this for a lifetime."

I lean over and kiss her then give Mike a wave as we walk back to my Jeep. It's getting late and it's cold. We didn't feel the cold while we were in the woods, but now back in the vehicle I turn up the heat as we head home. The traffic is light on 64 and we make it home in under an hour and a half. Ebenezer and Chaucer are getting use to Samantha and don't even run and hide when we open the door.

After I set the alarm, I walk down the hall to my office and in the back of the center drawer I take out the spare keys to the house and remote to the garage. "Samantha, I want to make sure you have keys and know the alarm system. You live here and I want you to feel this is your home. There are a couple alarm panels in the house. There's the one at this door, one at the dining room sliding doors to the patio, and one to the kitchen door for the garage. I also had one put in the Master bedroom. Elizabeth had me put one in the bathroom in the hall. She had a fear of being in there and hearing someone in the house. All you do is push this button to arm it and, to unarm it push the pound key, then nine, six, three, one and the pound key. This red button is the panic button. The panic button is a silent alarm that notifies the police. It also sends a page to my phone. The yellow button turns on the motion sensors and the cameras. I set them at night. Don't worry there are no cameras in the house, they are all pointing outside. The remote that is by itself is to the garage. The other is the remote to the Jeep and you have a key."

She takes the keys and turns them over in her hands. "Adam I can't drive. I appreciate you trusting me with keys to your house. I'm honored. No one has ever given me keys to their house before. This means a lot to me. I don't know what to say besides thank you." She wraps her arms around me and kisses me.

I take her hand and lead her up the stairs. I don't want anything to break the spell of the night. For once in my life, everything has gone according to plan. I love to see her look of wonderment when I show her new things. It makes me love her more and more. Now, all I want to do is kiss her and get her clothes off so that I can end the night making love.

DAY 24
DUTCH GAP, VIRGINIA

I hear my phone ringing and as I wake up look out the window into the darkness. Samantha stirs in my arms as I pick it up off the headboard. I hear one of the team investigators, Doug on the phone "Boss I know it's early and I know it's Sunday, but we have a lead on Alina Braden." Samantha and I both sit up in bed. "We got a call about ten minutes ago from a woman identifying herself as Christina. She called from a cell phone and we didn't get a lock from the cell company, but it appears the cell phone is being used in the area she said she was located. I don't think this is a hoax. She said she has Alina and she's scared. They are hiding right now, but she thinks someone is going to hurt them. She has asked for help."

Samantha is gripping my arm so hard it hurts. I break my arm free from her hand and wrap it around her. Her shoulders feel cold and I pull her tighter to me. "Where are they and do we have anyone on the way to them?"

"Christina says she's in Alexandria. We have contacted the DC Field office and they are on the way. She has instructed us to call her when someone gets there. She will tell them where to go and how to find them. She has asked for protection. Do you want them transferred to us or held in DC?" I look at Samantha. I know she wants to meet Alina. I ask if we can arrange a transfer on I-95. This will put even more distance between her and whoever is chasing her.

Samantha is already up and getting dressed. Doug hangs up. We have to wait for a call that the DC team has Christina and Alina. Doug left as soon as he hung up with me to head to Fredericksburg. DC will pass them to us and transfer them to our protective custody. He has promised to call as soon as he has them in his vehicle.

Murder at Swan Cove

I get dressed and we head down the steps. Samantha is a nervous wreck. I stop her and put my arms around her and ask her to calm down. Alina won't know her and we will have to introduce her slowly. She's a toddler and we don't know what she's been through. Samantha knows we have to take it slow, but this is something personal and it's hard for her.

We get in the Jeep and make the drive into Richmond. We are the only car on the road and get their quickly. The office is brightly lit and everyone is in full mode manning phones and computers monitoring police reports, traffic and communications with DC. By the time we get to the office, the DC Field Office has Christina and Alina in their vehicle and are on I 95 coming south. Virginia State Police are not escorting them because they don't want to bring attention to the transport vehicle. Instead, they are set up every few miles monitoring the progress and standing by if they are needed.

A little after five a.m., the transfer is made to Doug's vehicle. He has two people riding with him fully armed. We have no idea the level of danger and are on full alert. I won't feel comfortable until the car is in our garage and they are in the building. Already a safe house and security detail are preparing. Christina, and possibly Alina, will be going to the safe house. If it is determined to break them up and Alina comes with us, a security detail is prepared to escort us to the house.

The sun is coming up as Doug pulls into the garage and they are quickly ushered inside the building and up to our office. At this point, the building is in full lockdown. No one without secure identification will be allowed inside until further notice. Samantha is standing next to me as they come up the elevator. She reaches for my hand and I can feel her shaking.

The elevator opens and two agents come out followed by a middle aged woman in jeans and a leather jacket. Doug is the last off with a small blond child in his arms. Alina fell asleep in the car. It is probably better for her and less traumatic. We just need to make sure she stays with Christina so that she's in familiar surroundings when she wakes up.

Everyone heads to the conference room next to my office so that we can talk. Two agents guard the elevator. No one gets onto our floor who is not one of our team. Doug lays Alina down on the sofa at the doorway.

Samantha sits next to her and cradles her head on her lap. After everyone is seated, I turn on the recording device on the center of the table.

"As we begin, I am turning on a video recording. As we go around the table introducing ourselves, please acknowledge this is being recorded and everything said in this room will be on record as part of the official interview. My name is Agent Adam Clay, lead investigator of the Kali Callahan murder and subsequent related murders. Now if everyone around the table can identify themselves for the recording."

One by one my team, John, Christina and Samantha identify themselves. We conclude with Samantha saying that Alina Braden, a minor child, is sleeping on the sofa next to her in the advent she wakes and her voice is heard on the recording. Because she is a minor and we do not have a child advocate in the room representing her, anything she says will be stricken from the written record.

"Christina I know you have spoken with the FBI Field Office in Washington, DC, but for our records would you please tell us the information you gave those agents. Would you also give us some background on yourself and how you came into guardianship of Alina Braden."

She nods her head and in a scared voice at a near whisper she began. "My name currently is Christina Montpatten and I am fifty-three years old. I say my current name because forty-seven years ago my name was Lilly Dupree from Baton Rouge, Louisiana. I was sleeping in the back of the bar my mother worked at when I was kidnapped and taken out of state to the home of then Governor Talmadge Cain. Tal has died and I feel no remorse naming him. He trained me in the finer points of sexual gratification before turning me over to the Co-Op to be sold to Franklin Martin, yes, the Franklin Martin of the steel industry. I was twelve at the time. Franklin kept me in an apartment in New York City and when he was in residence, he made me walk around nude and have sex on demand. Franklin Martin is still alive, but the scars you can see on my arms and legs are from him. When he had sex with me, he liked to smear blood on his penis and pretend he was taking my virginity for the first time. The sight of blood on his penis aroused him. I tried to run away from him and eventually he had enough of me and turned me back in to the Co-Op. By then I was fifteen years old. I was sold to William Bridge. With him I had nine children. He took them all from me and gave them up for adoption. Now I am owned by Duke Braden as a caretaker for his daughter."

A few people around the table gasp when she said daughter. She continues her voice not getting any steadier. "I have raised Alina with the help of her mother, Marissa, for the past four years. Marissa lived with me in a townhouse in Georgetown. Duke Braden and his sons Tyler and Joshua frequented the townhouse. I was shocked when I saw the picture of Marissa on the television saying she had been murdered. It had been two weeks since I had seen her and I knew she was being sent back to the Co-Op to be resold. Duke did not tell me why, only that Marissa had broken his trust and he would not have her in his house any longer. She screamed and begged to be able to take Alina with her. But, he forced her into the car and drove away."

"At first, I thought the man who bought her had murdered her. By this time, Duke was in the nursing home. I went to visit him but he was unresponsive. Soon after that, I was visited by Tyler. He instructed me to dispose of Alina. He told me to take her somewhere and leave her. He wanted me to drive north to Boston or somewhere. I couldn't just drop the child off alone somewhere cold. He came back and checked on me and found her still there. He became enraged and started throwing things. I was afraid of him and promised to take her in the morning and get rid of her. I packed our things and left the house. I have made contact with other women who were in the Co-Op and hid out with them. Then I saw on the news that not only Duke had died but Joshua's body was found in Texas. I suspected Tyler and I began to move from safe house to safe house trying to make sure he couldn't follow my trail to find me."

"Over the weekend, I was in the private apartment of Kristen LaMonte. She is the mistress of Judge Brigham LaMonte. The judge made a surprise visit to Kristen and found Alina and I there. The judge didn't say anything to me, but a few hours later Tyler Braden was at the door. Kristen refused to open the door and threatened to call the police if he didn't leave. He yelled in that I couldn't run and hide. He would find me and when he did he would kill both Alina and I. Then I heard on the television that his mother was also dead in a supposed murder suicide. I believe Tyler killed them. We moved around to two more houses, but I was afraid. I got a call on my cell phone last night and the person didn't say anything. I think it was Tyler Braden. I finally called the FBI because I believe Tyler Braden is a serial killer and both Alina and I are going to be his next victims if he is not stopped."

You can hear a pin drop in the room. Here is the eye witness we need to confirm our suspicions. We still can't convict him on the murders, but it gives us something to put an arrest warrant out that will stick. He has made death threats and we have a second witness to back the threats up. I ask Christina if she would consent to being put under witness protection. I leave to check the work being done on the safe house and request the DC office put Kristen LaMonte under protection.

As I walk out of the conference room I stop. Alina is awake and she is rubbing her eyes looking up. Samantha takes her hand and smoothes Alina's hair and kisses the top of her hair. "Hi, Alina. Christina is in the next room and you both are safe. I know it had to be pretty scary the last few days,-but you are safe now. My name is Samantha. Can I get you anything?"

Alina turns her head and looks at Samantha "My middle name is Samantha. My mommy named me after my grandma. Her name was Samantha too. Mommy told me she missed her mommy a lot. I miss my mommy too." Tears start to run down Alina's cheeks and Samantha picks her up and holds her against her breast.

Samantha is fighting tears and rocking Alina in her arms. "Don't cry, Alina. I know your mommy loved you. It's going to be all right. I will make sure no one does anything to you. "

I am about to step in and pick up Alina when she looks up at Samantha "You look like my mommy. She was pretty like you and had hair like yours. Did you know my mommy?"

Samantha shakes her head yes. She's crying now. "Yes I did. Have you ever heard the name Samantha Callahan?" Alina nods yes. "My name is

Samantha Callahan."

Alina turns her head sideways and looks into her eyes for a few seconds then wraps her arms around Samantha. "Mommy said one day my grandma would find me. Duke wouldn't let her contact you and let me meet you, but mommy said you would find a way. My mommy died and Duke died. All I have is Christina, but now you found me! My grandma found me! I knew you would if I wished really hard."

I walk over and put my hand on Samantha's shoulder. They are both crying now and holding on to each other. I know I am not going to be able to get Alina away from Samantha and I look at John and tell him to get a team assigned to my house. It may be safer anyway to have Christina and Alina separated. This will give Tyler Braden two targets. My house is fairly secure so that will help a team lockdown the location.

I order breakfast for everyone and Chip runs out to pick it up. After the incident with the head being found, our floor security has been tight. It is not unusual at this time for people to be barred from our office. Everyone in the building knows we feel violated and are keeping their distance unless called by us. We don't want anyone outside our team to know we have Christina and Alina with us. The DC Field office knows we have witness protection individuals. Outside our office no one has any idea we even have protected people with us.

I make the call to DC to confirm we can get two teams, one for our safe house and one for my house. I am not risking anything. I believe Tyler Braden has been in our office during the storm. I can't risk him getting word we have them and where we are hiding them. If he has any connection to anyone working in this building, or has planted anything in the building, I need to do everything I can to keep the location of Christina and Alina confidential.

After we eat breakfast, one of my team, Trina, leaves to get Christina and Alina a couple changes of clothing. Samantha has gotten Christina to lie down on the sofa. She's been up all night and is exhausted. Alina falls asleep in Samantha's lap again. We are in a holding period until everything is in place. We are all restless and trying to tiptoe around to not wake anyone.

Trina returns and we get them to both into new clothes. It has turned cold which makes it easier to disguise them in hats and coats. Christina will be easier to get out of the building. Alina will be more difficult because children are rarely here. We move Christina out at lunch time. She leaves through the front door and into a car as if they are going on an assignment. We decide to hold Alina until most people have left for the day and the night crew comes in.

When Alina wakes up, we ask her what she wants to eat. We all smile when she asks for pizza. I call the order in to a local place and notify the front desk to call me when it comes in. I order six pizzas so the team can have a pizza party. Alina is a typical kid and she is happy and excited to have pizza. Kids are great and they seem to be able to bounce back from so much. She helps Samantha put out paper plates and napkins. She sings and dances around the conference table.

John has offered to do the overnight. Two agents from the DC office are going to take the outside perimeter. After he eats lunch, I tell him to go home and get some sleep. I also tell John to bring Chris, his partner, over tonight and we will all do dinner. So far everything is going according to plan. By the time we finish eating, I get confirmation that Christina is at the safe house and they are on lockdown. Now we wait until things die down here for the afternoon so that we can sneak out ourselves.

About four, I confirm the outside perimeter of my house is secure and we have the all clear to move when ready. John will be at the house by six. Samantha starts to get Alina ready. They do the girl thing and visit the bathroom then we get her bundled up in a ski jacket, hat and gloves. I can tell she's scared and that might go against us. While I don't think anyone here is connected to Tyler Braden, I can't guarantee that.

Samantha and I are lucky we have an expert with us. One of the team puts Alina's booster seat in the back seat of my Jeep. Neither of us had a clue how the lap belt attached. I know I am facing a learning curve on a lot of things. I went from girlfriend to family in a very short time. I can't say that I am unhappy with the arrangement. It feels good to take her home. Alina jumps in the Jeep and fixes the seat belt and then sits in her booster seat. After that, she instructs Samantha on how to buckle her in. I have to smile. At least, we have a smart kid.

After we hit the road I tell Alina about Ebenezer and Chaucer. I warn her that they will be scared of her, but if she sits down they will come up to her and she can pet them. She just needs to be gentle. In the review mirror I can see her eyes light up. "I always wanted to get a kitty or a puppy but mommy said I wasn't allowed. Duke didn't want me having pets. I can't wait to meet them and I will be gentle. Mommy taught me to be gentle with the neighbor's kitty. I was allowed to go over and pet the kitty sometimes."

Traffic is a little heavy and we get into a back up leaving town. This makes me nervous and I get Samantha to help me watch the cars behind us. I want to make sure we are not being followed and we don't see Tyler Braden on the road.

The DC agents are already on site and stop us as I pull into the driveway. I roll down my window and show them my badge. While it feels strange to show my badge to get into my own home, it feels reassuring knowing if I have to leave that no one will get in without passing security. Alina has fallen asleep in the car and while Samantha gets the bag with her clothing, I pick her up and carry her up to the porch. As I fumble with my keys, Samantha leans in and unlocks the door, then turns off the alarm. Once again this is reassuring that she is taking control.

Alina stirs in my arms in time to see Ebenezer and Chaucer hopping out of the room to hide. She looks at me with a puzzled look "Kitties?" I tell her no and sit her down on the sofa. I get Chaucer and bring him over as an introduction. She squeals with delight and reaches out to pet him. I sit next to her with Chaucer in my lap. She reaches out and gingerly touches his fir and smiles. She is very gentle with him and he reaches out a paw to transfer to her lap. A friendship has been made between child and rabbit. He snuggles with her, his front paws and head on her lap, and his hind legs on the sofa. It is sweet to see her so happy.

I leave her with Chaucer and join Samantha in the kitchen. I trust Chaucer to jump down if he needs to get away. He is pretty good at taking care of himself, where Ebenezer would stay.

We get dinner started while she plays with Chaucer. I keep checking on them and notice Ebenezer has hopped up on the sofa and she's petting them both. It amazes me how easily she adapts. It speaks volumes to the environment she has been brought up in. She's very flexible for a child so young.

I hear the doorbell and head out to check and see who is there. John and Chris are standing waiting with one of the DC agents behind them. I open the door and wave the perimeter security off. We peek in on Alina and she is still being entertained by the rabbits. Ebenezer has decided to show off and is side hoping and flipping his ears on the floor. He stops and looks back at her to see if she's still watching and does a crazy hop again. Alina giggles and strokes Chaucer's ears.

The three of us walk into the kitchen and Samantha turns around. I see her eyes land on both John and Chris's guns. "I didn't know we were getting two agents inside as well. Seeing the three of you armed just drives this home." She then holds out her hand and walks up to Chris. "Hi, I'm Samantha."

John has a smirk on his face "Samantha, this is my partner Chris. In our relationship, I'm don't ask and, as a Virginia State Trooper, Chris is don't tell. We figured Adam could use the extra fire power. Chris is off the clock so he's volunteering his services for the night."

She smiles and shakes his hand. "It's a pleasure to meet you and thank you for coming. Here let me introduce you to Alina. She's the guest of honor and unfortunately the reason for all the security."

Chris holds up a finger and says "Wait, I have a bag at the door for the guest of honor. John and I did some shopping on the way over. Okay, I did some shopping as soon as John called me and told me what was going on, but don't tell him I told you he didn't have anything to do with this. It's a gift from both of us. In case you haven't noticed, he's a real he-man!" He goes to the door and gets a large shopping bag and walks into the living room. "Hi Alina, my name is Chris. I'm a friend of Adam and John and I have a present for you. I bet when you left your home you didn't have time to grab any toys. Am I right?" She looks up at him and nods her head yes. "I thought so. The first thing I did when I heard I was coming here was go to the toy store. Let's see what I have here. I bet you like to color. So, I got you a zoo animal coloring book and this big box of crayons." He hands them to her and she is grinning as she takes them and looks at them. "That's not all. I happen to know that Chaucer and Ebenezer like to play ball and I bet you would have fun playing with them so I got this jingle ball for you to roll to them. I bet you they will roll the ball back to you. Finally, you are in a new place and I don't want you to feel scared so I thought this big teddy bear will keep you safe and happy. He wants to be your friend."

He hands it to her and she begins to hug it. "Thank you, I love him. He's so soft and squishy." She runs up and hugs Chris. I stand there watching and realizing I have a lot to learn. I didn't think about a kid needing toys and I'm glad I have friends smart enough to think of these things.

Dinners ready and we go to sit down to spaghetti and meatballs with garlic cheese bread. I bring a glass of milk to the table for Alina and open a bottle of wine for the adults. We can't get drunk, but we can have a drink with dinner. I want everyone on their toes tonight. Before I sit down, I walk two plates outside to the guys on perimeter. While they are normally required to tend to their own needs, as fellow agents, I feel I should make sure they get a decent meal. Besides without a lot of luck, it would be nearly impossible for them to find food locally. For some reason it was decided to hide the stores and restaurants behind stands of trees and put either no sign or a very small sign along the road. If you don't know something is behind the trees, you drive on looking for some place to stop until you get to the approach to I-95 and then it is fast food haven for travelers who have stopped to get gas along the way.

I have to add a pillow on a dining room chair for Alina. I make another note to myself that we need to get a booster seat for her. I'm getting quite a list of things in my mind. It's funny a long time ago I saw Elizabeth and I in the roll of parents, but she was never ready. I thought that opportunity had died and now I love the thought of making a home for Alina. This kid in a few hours has changed my life. I know in the morning I have to get the paperwork started for Samantha to have permanent guardianship. Social

Services awarded emergency guardianship under witness protection to me. She is Samantha's granddaughter and she deserves to be able to make the decisions on Alina's life.

I can see Alina is getting tired and as soon as she finishes eating I pick her up and take her upstairs. Samantha goes up with me and we tuck her into the bed in the room next to mine. We reassure her that we are right next door and if she needs us she can just yell or come get us. Everything that has happened has been exhausting for her and in a few minutes she is sound asleep.

We go back downstairs. John has started a fire in the fireplace. They are going to take the first floor for the night. Samantha heads up for a shower and to check Alina while John and I run a check of the doors, windows and security system. John is in radio contact with the outside perimeter for the night.

As of ten o'clock, the house is in total lockdown. I let Samantha know if she needs to come down stairs she needs to announce herself. I have done an overnight security detail with John before and he tends to shoot anything big that moves. I remind him to not shoot the rabbits and head upstairs.

I find it hard to sleep. My body is exhausted from being awake for about thirty six hours but my mind is spinning. Next to me is the woman I have fallen in love with and in the next room is an orphan who needs someone to care of her. Things are happening quickly, and while I am happier then I have been since Elizabeth died, I feel my life is out of control. I hope I am able to live up to this new life.

DAY 25
DUTCH GAP, VIRGINIA

I smell bacon and look next to me realizing Samantha is gone. I check in on Alina to find she's also out of bed. Downstairs John, Chris and Alina are watching cartoons while Samantha cooks breakfast. I reach around her and grab a piece of bacon off the plate. She acts like she's going to smack my hand and I act like I am pouting. I'm a little shocked as she playfully spanks me on the butt. As she does it, I hear John laughing in the doorway. Everyone seems to have gotten some rest and there has been no attempt on the house. The night team comes in to brief us after briefing the incoming day team. We invite the night team to have breakfast before heading to their hotel. They are due back on duty in twelve hours.

John and Chris head upstairs to the guest room to get some sleep. Samantha and Alina settle into the living room with the crayons and coloring book and I pull out my laptop and start the paperwork for permanent custody. The house is quiet. Throughout the day, I check with the office to see how things are going both there and at the other safe house. Facial recognition software is being used on all traffic cameras in Richmond area and Tyler Braden's picture is airing on television with every news cast. The over head road signs on highways in Maryland, Virginia and Washington, DC are displaying the description and tag number of Joshua Braden's car. Police cars in all three areas are on the lookout for the vehicle with the potential of it now having stolen tags. There is a stop order for men driving similar red sports cars.

I hate waiting. I feel like a caged animal. I would love to take Samantha and Alina out to do some shopping and get her some toys and stuff for her bedroom. Unfortunately, it is too much of a security risk. Instead, I wait until John and Chris wake up and leave them in charge of the interior security and I go out to make a couple stops.

I go into Richmond and stop at a toy store. I am completely out of my league and find a sales person. I have no idea what a four year old girl would want to play with and what would make her happy. I want to find something that will give her hours of play since I don't know how long she will be stuck inside. The sales person takes me over to dolls. I'm sure she would like a doll, but I don't know how long she would play with it. I end up picking up a doll house with some additional furniture, a set of clay molds and modeling clay. As I am about to leave, I see a computer program for making paper dolls. The salesperson explains a four year old would not be able to make the clothing alone. She would need an adult to help her. I didn't see a problem with that. The program comes with heavy cardboard dolls and a disk to help design clothing that can be printed on either a color printer or on black and white and then hand colored. You can also print a stencil for new dolls if you want. I get a booster seat for the dining room and one for the Jeep since I will have to return the one provided by Social Services to bring her home.

My next step is the grocery store. I try to think like a kid and what they like to eat. I get some fruit, cheese, pretzels and graham crackers. I get a couple kinds of juice and some more milk. I decide to buy some chicken. Both Samantha and Alina seem to like Italian so I get the ingredients for lasagna. I figure maybe Alina can help lay the noodles in the pan and might enjoy that.

 Back at the house John helps me carry in the groceries and toys. I call Samantha and Alina into the living room. It's like Christmas morning for us. Alina is excited about her new toys. The dollhouse is a hit. Samantha sits on the floor with her helping her take the furniture out of the wrapping. They put the clay and molds on the coffee table. While Samantha loads the paper doll program on her laptop, Alina sits and arranges furniture in the house.

If anyone had told me two months ago I would be sitting at home with a girlfriend and her granddaughter moving into my house, I would have told them they were nuts. Instead, I am thinking about what I should do to Alina's bedroom to make it seem more like home. I know at some point I have to have a conversation with Samantha about things. Other then the melt down in the hotel about whether I was gay or not, we haven't defined our relationship other then we are here together. Fate put us in the situation and we both seem content to let it ride. Having them both here has struck a chord deep in my soul. I just worry that I have transferred my loss of Elizabeth by filling it with Samantha. I don't want to make a mistake and start a relationship involving a kid and then walk away from it.

We spend a quiet afternoon with Alina playing, Samantha doing some research on psychological profiles and me working on paperwork related to the case. John and Chris take turns relieving the guys outside so that they can go to the bathroom and warm up a bit.

The safe house is quiet and also had no attempts on it during the night. ~~also~~ Chip has come down from the office and is sitting inside with Christina. We get an update that she is talking. She is helping him understand some of the mindset of women who have been part of the Co-Op. Like all the others, she defends their practices and sticks by their historical background.

At five, I get up and go to the kitchen to get dinner started. Samantha comes in to help. We brown the meat, onions, pepper and mushrooms while the lasagna noodles cook. When the noodles are done, I drain them and let them sit while I work on the sauce. Then, I call Alina into the kitchen. Samantha gives me a strange look and I tell her to relax and let's see what happens. I want to give Alina the chance to help.

I get Alina to wash her hands and then let her sit on the kitchen prep table. I give her the bowl, ricotta, parmesan and mozzarella to mix and sit with her to help. She has never done this before and is tentative. She's careful and her brow creases as she concentrates on the job. Once that is mixed, I bring the baking dish over with the pan of sauce, the meat, the noodles and more cheese. Samantha sits down at the table with a cup of coffee and watches. I tell Alina what to put in the dish and she carefully spoons ingredients and makes layers with the noodles. When we are done, she is grinning from ear to ear. I tell her to sit there and I will be back as I put the lasagna in the oven. Next up I bring the loaf of Italian bread, a stick of butter that I left sitting out, some minced garlic, parmesan and mozzarella. After I slice the bread, she carefully follows my directions making the garlic bread. Finally, I bring her the bag of salad greens, carrots, celery and cherry tomatoes. I let her toss the salad in the bowl with two big wooden spoons.

Once done, we set the table and peak into the oven to see if the cheese is melting on top of the lasagna yet. Just before it's done, I put in the garlic bread. Then tell Alina to get John and Chris and tell them dinner is ready. I figure after they eat they can cover for the guys outside and let them get something for dinner.

Once she leaves, Samantha walks over and puts her arms around me "you have surprised me once again, Adam Clay. You are great with kids. You are also braver then me and just let a four year old make dinner. At first, I thought you were trying hard and had a sales person pick out some toys, but you are a natural born dad. You have a lot of patience with her. I am impressed." Then she leans in and kisses me. That of course happens just as Chris, John and Alina enter the room.

I hear a little giggle from Alina and I act like I am running across the room to her and pick her up. I give her a hug and announce that she made dinner and it's ready for us to all sit down and eat. John and Chris exchange looks then John looks at the food on the table "Alina made dinner? I'm impressed. It looks great."

After the outside team comes in for dinner and Alina tells them about their meal, Samantha takes her upstairs to get a bath and ready for bed. One of the guys on the security team compliments me on my wife and daughter. I don't bother correcting them. It's better they don't know their primary focus is the welfare of a four year old. Plus, I like the sound of wife and daughter.

The fire dies down and the day draws to a close. I throw a couple logs on the embers and bank the fire for the night. The day has been uneventful. Now if only we can catch Tyler Braden. I get into bed next to Samantha and put my arms around her. "I think we need to talk. That little girl next door needs a home. I know we don't have any type of formal relationship and it worries me a little. She needs stability and I'm afraid she will stay here and get attached. I don't want her hurt. I think we need to figure where we are going from here. Samantha, I'm rusty at the relationship thing. I haven't dated since Elizabeth died and you and I have been thrown together in this. We have never really even gone on a formal date and now I feel like I have a family. I want to do what's right for you and for Alina. You got out of jail and haven't been able to taste freedom or time on your own. Are we moving too fast and is that going to hurt her?"

Samantha runs her hand through her hair. I have watched her do this before when she is nervous or unsure of something. "Are you having second thoughts? I didn't mean to spring a child on you or start a relationship with a kid. I'm sorry! I know we are a burden and not what you bargained for. If you want when this is over, I will look for a place to live and we will move out."

I stop her, "no, Samantha. I don't want you to leave! I am happy. I spent my day thinking about getting Alina furniture for her room that is more kid friendly. I was thinking of changes I need to do to make the house feel more like your home. I am thinking about the future. The last thing from my mind is you two moving out. You and I need to build our relationship. From the first time I met you, everything has seemed so natural between us, but this has been so fast. Neither of us has had time to think. We have been caught up in this case and today I found myself pulling up the paperwork for you to apply for emergency custody of Alina. After this is over, I don't want her to be transferred from protective custody to foster care. I want to protect her and give her a home and a family. You have no idea how much fun I had making dinner with her."

I pull Samantha tight against me. "Elizabeth and I had talked about having kids. I wanted a family, she didn't. I didn't know before we got married that she didn't want kids. It wasn't something we talked about. We were crazy and in love. She had a career and the thought of taking time out to have a baby to her was too much to deal with. I thought eventually she would get established and come around. Then she died and I thought that was it. The love of my life was gone and I would have no other chances. Samantha, I want kids. I want to be a dad. I want to teach my kids how to ride a bike and teach them history. I want a son to carry on my name and a daughter I can give away at her wedding. Hell, I want grandkids eventually! Look, I don't need to know tonight. Things are still just too crazy, but I think I am here for the long run-- the kids, the family, okay we are going to have to talk about the dog because Ebenezer and Chaucer might be offended with the dog, but I need to know how you feel."

Samantha kisses me and I feel tears hitting my cheek. "Adam, I love you. Yeah it's crazy and we have not had time to live anything close to a normal life, but I can't think of anyone I would rather be with or anywhere else I would rather go. Do you realize I never thought a man would want to be with me for the rest of his life? Or someone would want to have a baby with me? I mean I'm getting older and if we are going to do this, we are going to have to make a decision in the near future, but yes! I want a family too. I'd love to have a baby with you. Alina is absolutely awestruck by you and you have been so great with her."

"Adam, can I lose Alina? I haven't even thought about that. Both her parents are dead and so are her other grandparents. I'm the only family she has. I just thought automatically she would be mine. Oh my God! You have to help me do what I need to keep custody of her. I thought when we brought her home she was mine."

I kiss her and tell her I'm here and we are going to make sure Alina stays with us. I don't know what tomorrow will bring, but tonight I go to sleep with my family under my roof. I'm not just about the job anymore, I feel whole. I didn't realize how empty I have felt since Elizabeth died, but now maybe I can go back to my life and live rather than exist.

DAY 26
DUTCH GAP, VIRGINIA

Saturday turns to Sunday and Sunday to Monday without any sign of Tyler Braden. I begin to wonder if his killing spree is over. The SAC has made the decision to scale back security on the safe house and my house. We will still have an internal and external guard. John and I feel safe going back to work and leaving Samantha at the house with Alina and Margaret Chu from our team. Outside is Eric Moss, an agent I worked with in the bank robbery and counterfeit division. Christina has two guards as well. I head into work feeling pretty secure in the decision.

Thanksgiving is a little over a week away and while at work I begin to think about the whole turkey and stuffing thing. I call John at his desk and ask what he and Chris are doing. Since Alina has begun to call them Uncle John and Uncle Chris, I figure we might as well do the family dinner if they aren't doing anything else. John of course offers to bring his turkey fryer to make some old fashion southern fried turkey. I have visions of the fire department putting out the side of my house and make a note to myself to check the fire extinguishers. I decide to buy a turkey breast also just in case the food of honor bursts into flames.

On my way home, I stop at the store to buy a cell phone for Samantha and put it on my plan. She had a throw away phone that she picked up while we were traveling, but it doesn't get strong reception at my house. I felt all day like I was out of touch with her and it drove me a little nuts. I checked in with her twice on Skype and of course checked with Margaret to make sure everything was ok. Alina loved the Skype calls. Half the team gathered around to say hi.

The other bit of good news is that the orphan's court confirmed receipt of the paperwork and awarded the emergency custody order. Permanent custody will take a couple weeks, but the clerk at the court house assured me that this was a pretty cut and dry case. At first she was concerned about Samantha's jail time until the New York DA's office faxed the release paperwork to them. That went a long way on green lighting the custody. The court is very sensitive in re-victimizing someone who has been falsely imprisoned.

Today has been a pretty good day and I walk in the door to the smell of tacos. Tonight, as promised, is Mexican food night with tacos, burritos and corn cake. I see the paper dolls have dressed for the occasion and are sitting on the dining room table in their festive best. Margaret has even gotten into the act and has taught Alina a few words of Spanish.

Before dinner, I sit down with Samantha and give her the new phone. I help her set it up and put my cell in as speed dial. Then she takes a picture of Alina and puts it as her wallpaper. We are about to sit down for dinner when the back door bangs open and the perimeter guard for the night, Tom, runs in. I grab my gun out of instinct only to find out it's snowing.

Outside we can see the Christmas lights on the bushes of the house up the street from us through the snow. It's snowing pretty heavy and the ground is getting white fast. Before we know it, Alina has darted into the yard in her bare feet and is dancing in the snow. I scoop her up and carry her back inside laughing. It's too late now to run out and get her boots and gloves so I may have to pick them up tomorrow before I go to work. If the snow sticks in the yard, it would be torture telling her she can't go out and play a little. As things like this come up, I realize just how much we have to do to make this Alina's home. She came here with nothing and as things like snowflakes happen we realize things we need. Seeing the Christmas lights, I realize in a little over a month we will have to do the Santa thing and I start thinking about Christmas trees and decorations. Somewhere in the attic are the decorations Elizabeth bought. Every year she would put up a tree before she hosted her office holiday party at the house. It was more decoration for the party then a Christmas tree. She didn't believe in exchanging gifts, only the obligatory holiday parties. I wanted the excitement of children seeing their gifts for the first time on Christmas morning and the laugher. Elizabeth was more the glass of wine Christmas

Eve and dressing up to go to family for dinner Christmas Day. She even waited to go to her brother's house to avoid the noise and clutter of her niece and nephew opening their gifts. She gave them savings bonds because she thought they played with toys for a few days and then moved on to something else. Buying them toys was a waste of money to her.

It seems every night I am going to bed thinking about things I want to do and what I think we need for the house. It has been a couple years since I bought anything other than food and toilet paper. My house is functional and a place to come home to between jobs. I think I also went on scene more then I needed to because I hated to come home to the empty house. I spent too many nights sleeping on the sofa in my office because I used the excuse of working late to justify a couple hour nap. Now I dream of canopy beds and putting together Alina's first bicycle. I already know Samantha will be a nervous wreck when I teach Alina how to ride a bike or take her out in the canoe.

DAY 27
DUTCH GAP, VIRGINIA

I wake up to four inches of snow on the ground. Tom has opened the garage door to use as a shelter and I can see his foot prints in the snow where he checked on things during the night. Over at the safe house, the perimeter guard spent some of the night inside and made rounds at random times.

My phone rings as I am heading out the door. Joshua Braden's car has finally been located. It has been sitting in long term parking at the airport for the last four days. There's no sign of him purchasing a ticket so he either used forged identification or has switched vehicles. Tyler seems to be able to move around the country without leaving a trail. That is very unnerving. I won't feel safe until he is behind bars. At least there is hope he has left the area and we can return to a somewhat normal life.

Work goes on in my office. We have over 400 leads to follow up on from this case. The DC Field Office is already dealing with two other girls who have been dropped off in public places as a Senator and a Congressman have resigned their office. Both left the country after abandoning the girls to escape extradition. Word has gotten out that we are tracking the men who are part of the Co-Op. Because most have a lot to lose, both as part of their position in life and bank accounts, they are taking their money and running.

This morning, we finally made the connection between the mechanical contractor who did the repairs on our building and how the head got into our building. One of their employees had been on medical leave and they didn't know he had been reported as a missing person. His family lives out of state and hadn't heard anything from him. This wasn't unusual since sometimes weeks went by without any contact from him. When he failed to call his mother on her birthday, the family started leaving him messages. They eventually had the police check the location and they found his badly decomposed body. Since the company was pulling employees from out of state, no one questioned the new guy. When we questioned the other two men from the repair, they picked out a picture of Tyler from a photo lineup. The men he was working with that day feel lucky to be alive. It also proves he kills for a reason. He didn't have a reason to kill them, so he worked with them all day and let them live.

Christina has told us about Tyler's temper and his erratic behavior. She thinks he may be on drugs or has a serious psychological problem. A couple times she saw him hit Marissa. I did not relay that information to Samantha. I don't think it would be good for her to know. Marissa was afraid of Tyler and so is Alina. She also told us about Tyler getting in trouble with Duke because he forced himself on her and raped her once. She told us Duke held a knife up to Tyler's throat and threatened to kill him if he touched her again. While that doesn't justify homicide, it was getting us a little closer to a motive.

John and I meet for lunch. I want to see if he and Chris are available one evening to add some fire power to an outing. Samantha and Alina have been cooped up in the house and they need to get out. Plus Samantha is doing laundry every three days for herself and Alina because they need winter clothes. I suggest an evening in Williamsburg. We can let the girls shop at the outlet mall and maybe grab dinner in one of the historic taverns. John calls Chris and we decide on tomorrow night.

John is just sitting there smiling for a minute, "You know, if I would have thought getting you laid would have changed you this much, I would have gone out and found a woman for you myself! Look at you! The whole office is talking about how you are smiling all the time, happy and pleasant. You, Mr. Serious-All-Work-Agent, have taken the time to talk to fellow agents and ask their opinions on canopy beds and little girl's toys. And what's this I hear rumored you asked about a good jewelry store? What is it you are buying Agent Clay?"

I smile at him and tell him it's a secret. He shrugs, "well let me just say if you are going, I have some places I would recommend. I might even be able to offer my personal opinion on selection. You do know Chris is dying to shop with her don't you?"

I have visions of Chris and Samantha shopping. She will be like his own living doll that he can dress and parade around. Chris is the decorator and planner of the couple. He keeps the house running and makes sure John has clean clothes and food. John is more the smell his shirt in the morning to make sure it is okay to wear another day kind of guy. I guess that comes with being a Marine and living through a tour of Afghanistan. He had to live in some rough conditions and he learned to just deal with what comes at him. He rolls with the punches and will sleep in his car if necessary. Christmas Eve, after Alina goes to bed, sitting back with a glass of wine in front of the fire is exactly when I am planning on giving Samantha her Christmas present. John and I have worked together for too long and he knows me too well. I know I can trust him with anything in my life. When I finally told him my inner thoughts on Elizabeth's death and how I blamed some of it on myself, I cried on his shoulder. Having him involved seems right. He and Chris should rightfully be around for the happy times in my life. They really are my best friends.

John calls Chris and I call Samantha to plan out tomorrow night. I also get a call from Orphans court while we are heading out. They want Samantha to appear tomorrow morning in front of a judge to determine the emergency custody and set the ball in motion for total custody. I spend the next thirty minutes explaining to one clerk after another why it is impossible for Samantha to appear in Richmond. The subject of the emergency custody is under FBI witness protection and it is too dangerous for either Alina or Samantha to appear in open court. No one seems to understand why a four year old would have a death threat leveled against her and why she has to be in hiding.

I finally end up with Judge Stanton, head of the Orphans Court, and explain to him that both of Alina's parents have been murdered. Her paternal grandfather has died under what is being investigated as suspicious causes and her paternal grandmother has also been murdered. The only surviving relative is Samantha and an uncle who is wanted for questioning in the series of murders. I get a promise of a return phone call from his office about the disposition of the appearance in the morning.

I don't even bother calling Samantha about this. She will insist on getting agents to cover Alina while she appears. I'm trying to get someone from the court to come to the house. I really don't care if the judge himself has to cart his elected ass over. Alina Braden is not going to appear in a court room and right now someone will have to get past me for Samantha Callahan to appear as well.

We head back to the office and I try to put the custody hearing behind me for the moment. I have five more potential members of the Co-Op in the Richmond area that have been turned in by friends, neighbors and family members. From what I am seeing, there may be a pedophile on every street corner. I'm sure not all of these will pan out and a few don't meet the monetary profile that has been established as the Co-Op. That's not saying they aren't run of the mill pedophiles. I keep thinking the jails are going to get pretty full of creeps who abuse children. Usually they don't fare well in general population. I wonder what happens when the percentage of child predators passes the non-predators. It could get ugly in there.

As I am heading out the door, I get the call that the court has appointed a lawyer who works under Judge Stanton to come to the house and hold a proxy hearing. He will be bringing a Child Advocate to do the home inspection and child interview as well as witness the proceedings. They need a second non-partisan witness and Margaret Chu has been approved as that witness.

Samantha is a nervous wreck when I get home. She's worried about whether the rabbits will be ok to run the house or whether the social worker will not approve then. People are use to cats and dogs, but most people don't understand house rabbits. I think about getting her drunk tonight so that she calms down. This is a side of her I haven't seen before. She's usually so secure in everything she does but she's worried about everything. I catch her in the kitchen cleaning under the vegetable crisper in the refrigerator. I pull her out telling her it's ok to have a house that is lived in and not a museum. If there's a piece of dried celery leaf under the crisper they will not take Alina. If she makes the house too perfect the social worker might be suspicious. To someone like me, a perfect house screams something is being hidden behind the front door.

We try to go to sleep, but we can't sleep. Now, I just can't wait until morning so we can get this over with. I finally doze off and wake to the sounds of her cleaning the bathroom.

DAY 28
DUTCH GAP, VIRGINIA

I brief Margaret in the morning and as I take a cup of coffee out to Chip I give him the information as well. I really don't want Chip to accidentally shoot some lawyer from orphans court for pulling into my drive way. If I don't green light this guy, Samantha might flip out on me. She is currently in the kitchen worried that after making breakfast the house smells like bacon and that for some reason might signal we don't have a healthy diet.

Promptly at nine, I see a black sedan pull into the driveway and Chip walk up to the driver's window. I let Samantha and Margaret know they have arrived. They both check Alina's outfit for any crumbs from her breakfast and check her hair. I just shake my head at them. It's okay for her to be a kid.

I get back into the living room as they start up the sidewalk. I expected them to be at the door by now but they take some time getting parked and out of their car. The lawyer looks old. He's wearing a long black wool trench coat, black fedora with a black, gray and white scarf around his neck. He walks bent over slightly and limps relying on his cane. I'm feeling a little guilty making this guy drive thirty minutes and come out in the cold. The Child Advocate is dressed in black slacks and an ankle length wool coat with heals. She walks behind him with her head down. I think she's watching for ice on the sidewalk. It's below freezing this morning and the potential for the sidewalks being slippery is possible.

I open the door as they step onto the porch and let them in. I offer to take their hats and coats but the lawyer gently declines, "No thank you son, we won't be here long." Suddenly, I hear Alina let out a shriek. She starts to scream, "No! No! Don't give me back! Please I won't go!" I have no idea what has scared her until I feel the cold metal of a gun muzzle against my neck.

I try to tell Samantha to run but it's too late. They have come into the room with Alina grabbing onto her leg trying to pull her back. He looks at Margaret and says, "Well you don't look like a nanny, so you must be the other agent. Give me your gun." Margaret looks at me and I nod my head slightly. "Good girl. Now you three go sit on the sofa!"

Samantha and Margaret sit on the ends of the sofa with Alina tucked between them. She is crying and Samantha is trying to hold her and comfort her while keeping her eyes on the gunman. Alina glares at him. In a scared little voice, she pleads with Samantha, "Please don't let Tyler take me back! Please!" I can see tears in her eyes. I try to stay calm. Tyler is shaking. I can't tell whether through fear or anger. I need to think and take control of the situation as fast as I can. Right now with a gun pushing into my jugular, it's hard to formulate my next move.

Tyler glares back at Alina, "shut up you little brat! I will kill you soon enough, but if you piss me off any more I will kill you now! Do you understand?" Alina nods her head and holds on to Samantha.

I take a deep breath. The woman has been quiet and she seems to be taking a few steps away from Tyler. She may be my weak link. I look at her, "what did you do to my agent outside?" Tyler jabs the gun into me harder and tells me to shut up. So, he knows she might be vulnerable too. "Did you kill him already like you are going to kill all of us?"

She shakes her head no and tells me Chip was hit on the head and is handcuffed in the trunk of the car. Tyler's head whips toward her "Shut up, bitch, or you die next!" I can see fear in her eyes. I can use her.

I decide to address Tyler. "So Tyler, you want to add killing three FBI Agents to your charges? Think carefully about that. When they catch you, don't expect any hero treatment. I hear it burns right before you die from a lethal injection. You lay there strapped down knowing it's about to happen in front of a gallery full of people who will watch you die. They take their

306

time and let you shake laying there waiting. Then your veins feel like someone has lit a fire in your body. That's right before you feel like you can't breathe. You start to suffocate..." He pushes me away from him and I fall against the fireplace hitting my shoulder. I look down and see a rip in my shirt and blood starting to stain it. Still, I have broken contact and begun to turn control back into my hands.

"Shut the fuck up and sit in the chair next to the sofa." His face is getting red and he's breathing faster. I need to calm him down a little so I become compliant.

Samantha gives me a terrified look and then addresses Tyler. "Why are you here? What do you want from us? What did you do to Judge Stanton or the lawyer he was sending here?" I try to get Samantha to look at me and get her to let me do the talking, but she's going into defense mode. She's like a lioness trying to protect her cub.

Tyler smiles, "I'm here because I'm going to kill you. I want to especially kill you, Miss Samantha Callahan. If you hadn't spread your pretty little legs that little bitch of a daughter wouldn't have even been born. It's all your fault! You started this by squeezing out that little cunt that ruined my life! As for Stanton, he's one of us. He called me last night before boarding a plane out of here. He's gone where United States laws can't catch him. He doesn't care what I do to you. He ran to protect himself."

I jump in. I hope to keep him talking. That gives me time. I slip my hand in my pocket and push the speed dial for John. I hope Tyler doesn't hear John answer. "Tyler, you need to explain this to me. If you are going to kill us, I think we at least deserve to know why." I hear the faint sound of John answering the phone and keep talking to cover it up. I hope John hears me. "You can't kill me before explaining why you killed all these people. I have been following you all over the country. I, at least, deserve to know why you did this before I die."

Samantha looks at me with her mouth open. I don't think she understands that I am stalling him, hoping John gets the message and gets back to us fast. Tyler looks jittery and bordering on erratic. "You killed them for a reason, didn't you Tyler. What did they do to you? Why did they deserve to die?" I am now banking on him feeling they had somehow wronged him. I just want to get him talking.

His eyes dart around the room. First to the woman he walked in with and then to each of us. When he looks directly at Alina, she tries to shrink back in the sofa. She is afraid of him and I wonder just what he has done to this child. He looks back at the woman "Bitch, you need to sit down in front of me. You are going to die, too. I just needed you to get in the door." He kicks the ottoman indicating where he wants her to sit. "Agent Clay, why don't you get up and move next to the great and wonderful Samantha Callahan and the little sluts spawn. Then, bitch, you sit in that chair." I get up and sit on the sofa as Margaret moves to the chair. We now have Alina sandwiched between us and can help block him from getting close to her.

As the woman sits down on the ottoman, he raises his gun and shoots her in the head. Her head slumps forward and pulls her body so that it tumbles to the floor. I hear Samantha scream as it happens. I look at her and tell her to stop. I need her calm. Her screaming could cause Tyler to turn to her and shoot wildly. He is that unbalanced. I need to bring him back into focus on his story. "Samantha is going to stop screaming and be quiet. She deserves to hear why you killed Marissa. Did Marissa start this? Was it something she did to you? Tyler, I have to know. Tell me. Let me understand this."

I have his attention again. He has stopped shaking and seems more in control. I try to evaluate if he is mentally ill or on drugs. I think it might be a combination of both. He killed his associate with no emotion whatsoever. After shooting her, he didn't even look as her body hit the floor. Meanwhile, Samantha's gaze is fixed on the blood spreading across the Oriental rug. Alina is sitting between us with her hands over her ears. I think she's trying to block Tyler out of her head. I'm sure the gun shot that close to her hurt her ears. I take a deep breath and try to connect to him. "So, did you think Alina was your daughter?"

He spun and looked at me. I see the gun waver slightly. "No! Dad thought she was his. He didn't know that fat fuck was doing his little fuck doll. When I found out Joshua was getting laid by the bitch, I thought I would get a piece of ass too, but she smacked me in the face and threatened to tell my father. Who the hell did she think she was? She was fucking my brother behind my father's back. Then Joshua told me to leave her alone." His voice gets sarcastic, "He said they were in love and he was going to ask dad if he could marry her. So, I got a DNA swab from the little bitch on the sofa and sent it to a lab to be tested. I got the fat fuck drunk and when he passed out got a swab from him too. Then, I went to dad."

"Dad was pissed when I showed him the paternity test. He smacked the fucking bitch around a bit. Showed her he was still her owner. Then he contacted the broker and put her up for sale. He told the slut Christina to dump the kid somewhere she would freeze to death, but she didn't listen to the man who paid her either! I checked and this little bitch was still there with Christina. I have to kill that bitch Christina when I'm done with you."

"Then we went to Virginia to meet the new owner. Dad and Joshua got into a fight. We had the buyer test fucking the bitch on the beach for the night and the broker stayed at the house. My fat fuck of a brother got down on his knees begging my father to let him marry Marissa." Again the sarcasm comes back in his voice. "He cried like a little girl and told dad he wanted to start a family with her. That they loved each other and he was proud Alina was his daughter and he told dad the slut was pregnant again. Dad punched him in the face. They started punching the shit out of each other and the broker came out and heard what was going on. The broker found out Marissa was pregnant again. He contacted the buyer on his cell phone and told him Marissa was pregnant and already had another child. The buyer cancelled the sale. Dad heard this, stood up and then collapsed on the floor. I started to do CPR and told Joshua he had to help me. That's when the broker went to the phone and started to call 911. I couldn't let him do that, so I got Dad's gun out of the drawer and shot him. Joshua freaked out on me, but I told him he had to help me carry dad to the car so we could drive him to the hospital. He was so scared he did what I told him to do. By the time we got back, it was time to pick up the buyer. I couldn't bring them back to the house, so I told Joshua to take the broker's car home and I will pick those two up and take them back to Baltimore. I told Marissa to get in the car while I talked to the buyer. She did what she was told. Then I went over the dune to get the old bastard. He had just spent the night fucking the bitch and he still had a fucking hard on from too much of the little blue pill. I couldn't kill him there because some guy was fishing along the waves. I drove to the wildlife loop and told Kali to go out into the woods I needed to talk to the buyer. I cut his dick off and shoved it down his throat. Then I held him down and watched him choke to death on his own dick. That was funny. I cut him a little. It feels good to feel the knife going in and out. It turned me on. It's like fucking a virgin and you feel it pop through the skin. Later, I watched for the guy fishing to leave and I took his old ass back to the beach. I dug a hole and buried him in the sand. I didn't think about a storm uncovering him."

"Now the little slut, killing her was fun after I killed the old guy, I stripped down and went out into the woods to find her. I was already turned on from the last killing. When I found her, I untied her bikini top on the way down the trail and took it off of her. Then bent her over the tree trunk and fucked her hard. I kept rubbing my knife across her stomach while I fucked her. She was scared and crying for Joshua. Then right before I came, I stabbed her and slit her open. Her body twitching and struggling got me off. That was the best fuck of my life. When I was done, I cut the bitch up some more. The tree was out over the water and I watched her blood dripping. It turned me on and I fucked her again before I threw her away. I went back to the house and the fat prick broker was still breathing, so I stabbed him over and over. It felt good, real good. I was on such a high. I drove to Baltimore and found my fat fuck of a brother sleeping. So I tied him up and put him in the trunk of my car. I was going to take him home to mommy dearest and tell her what her precious son did. I wanted her to know that he fucked daddy's whore too."

"We were almost home when the fucker tried to get away from me. So, I stabbed him. I have wanted to hurt him before, but he was always bigger than me, but tied up he couldn't do shit. I kept him high on drugs so he was quiet. His screaming ruined the music while I drove. He screamed when I cut both his hands off. So, I cut his head off to shut him up. I still had the sluts bikini bottom in my car so I butt fucked it up his ass. He was cooling off pretty fast though and I couldn't get off so I jacked off. Some of it hit his feet so I cut them off too."

I need to slow him down. I figure running lights the field office will need about thirty minutes. He's already most of the way through his story. "Why did you dump his body at the Traynor farm? Why there? It seemed so random."

He looked at me for a second. "I went to class with Traynor's daughter-in-law. She wouldn't even sit next to me in English 101. I asked her out and she laughed at me. The bitch treated my offer for dinner as a joke. Instead, she went out with John Traynor Jr. and they ended up married. Fuck her and fuck his family. I figured I would have some fun and let the cops invade their farm and think they were guilty."

I stop him again "I talked to your mother. She said she had been talking to Joshua on the phone and you via email because you had gone back to the Amazon. How did you fool your own mother?"

Now he is laughing "What kind of a mother doesn't even recognize her own children on the phone? Maybe you don't know this, but the great Helen Braden was a status loving cunt. My mother's world was about people thinking she was wonderful. She married my father and rode him to the top, but when she started to get old he went out and bought some nice fresh meat. That pissed her off, but she wasn't about to give up her money and status, so she left him fuck his little girls as she fucked society."

I think he's having fun now. He likes having an audience. "All I did was call mommy dearest from her precious Joshua's phone and she thought I was him. I emailed her from Joshua's apartment saying I was in the Amazon. That woman was so stupid."

He seems to be calming down some. I don't see him twitching and shaking as much. He appears to be more in control. "So, why did you go to Jekyll Island? Did you want to kill Jacob Montgomery?"

He snorts at me. "No. Montgomery was just the guy dad bought the whore from. Montgomery likes to fuck them young and break them in. Dad liked some tit on them. Montgomery wants them to have little boy's bodies. He's a queer who tries to be straight by doing little girls. He likes when they cry because to them he's so big. I just wanted to scare the old fucker and he ran like little girls he fucks."

Tyler is no longer sweating. His eyes are still darting from side to side and he's still breathing fast. I watch as he flexes the fingers on his left hand, opening and closing them. It's a nervous twitch. "Do you know you contributed to the death of everyone on his ship? They sunk during the storm. Only Montgomery and the kid lived. He went to Europe and is running. The kid told us all about you. She confirmed my theory that you were the killer. You messed up there. You left a lose thread. That wasn't like you. I have thought you were pretty smart, but that slipped by you. The kid heard your first name."

He looks thoughtful, "Montgomery must have said something to her. That's the problem with their kind. They think their little fuck toys are adults in children's bodies. Dad would consult with Marissa and let her make decisions, but he looked at me like I was a kid and too young. I was older then that bitch, but he valued her opinion more just because she laid on her back and spread her legs for him. Just like her mother, right, Samantha Callahan? Like mother like daughter. One whore fucks and breeds another." He walks over and grabs Samantha's breast. She moves to smack him and he slaps her hard across the face. "Oh baby, that's what I like, fight with me. Come on, look how hard you are making me!" He leans his crotch in toward her face and thrusts toward her a few times.

I have to keep controlling my breath. Right now, I want to jump up and grab him, but the gun is too near Alina. Samantha cries out as he grabs her hair and pulls her face toward his zipper. "Suck my dick slut!"

She looks up at him "Try it you son of a bitch and I will bite your dick off. Come on you cock sucker! Stick it in my mouth!"

Tyler lets go of her and pushes her head back against the sofa. "You are as much of a bitch as your daughter. The apple doesn't fall far from the tree. That little bitch threatened to do the same thing to me! I'm going to love killing you. Maybe I will do it the same way. Tie you up and rip your clothes off. Then I think I will fuck you. Yeah, you're getting old but I'd still do you."

"Oh and little Alina, mommies little girl. You didn't like it when I touched you. You cried and kicked me. What did you think you would do in life? Your grandmother is a whore, your mother is a whore, and you were born to be a whore! Only you aren't going to get the chance because you are going to bleed to death right here on this sofa." Out of the corner of my eye I see a movement and, like a cat, Alina springs from between Samantha and me. I see her land with her fingers poking near his eyes and her sneakers landing solidly at his crotch.

In the back of my mind, I hear my instructor at Quantico, "If you are in a live or die situation, there will be a moment in time that you have to make a decision. Do you sit back and let the person kill you or do you take the risk and go for them?" As her shoes collide with his testicles, I hear him groan. I grab his hand with the gun and twist it. I feel him losing his grip. With my other arm, I push Alina away from him. I see blood spurting from his face and into his eyes as her fingernails scrape across his face. I turn the gun toward him, fumble for the trigger and pull it. My body is still twisted and the recoil knocks me back onto the sofa. I see a look of shock on his face and look down to see blood spreading across his chest from a hole in the left side of his shirt. Then he sinks to the floor.

I hear crying and look on the floor next to the end of the sofa. Samantha is curled up cradling Alina in her arms. She is rocking back and forth. I lunge across Tyler's body to get to them. I don't know if the shot went through him and hit one of them. Instead, all I see is a fine mist of blood splattered on them from Tyler's chest.

I sink to the floor next to Samantha and wrap my arms around the two of them. It's over. Tyler Braden is dead. I reach into my pocket and grab my phone "John, are you there?"

There is silence for a moment then I hear, "Yeah man, are you guys ok? We are about three minutes out. I heard the whole thing."

I finally notice Margaret in the room. She's on her phone taking charge of the situation. "Boss, I got this. You are going to have to be debriefed anyway. You did a great job, but you need to get your family out of this mess."

She walks over and opens the door for my team as I coax Samantha to her feet. She looks pale and shaken but fine. I hold out my hands for Alina and she reluctantly hands her over. Like a little monkey, Alina transfers over to me and wraps her arms around my neck and her legs around my body. I lead Samantha around the bodies on the living room floor and start her up the stairs. Then look at John and promise to come back down after I get them settled upstairs. As I start up the stairs, Alina lends back and looks at me "Adam, can I call you daddy from now on?"

I have to smile. This kid has just witnessed two people killed in front of her, but she's young enough to not really understand. I'm sure this will be something we have to deal with in the future. For now, the importance of the moment is my role in her life. "Alina, let's make a deal. You can call me daddy if you start calling grandma mommy. If not, it's going to look really weird to people that your daddy is married to your grandma."

Samantha stopped on the stairs and looks back at me, "please tell me you didn't just propose! We already have the world's strangest relationship on record, but I will not take a proposal over two dead bodies on the living room floor!"

EPILOGUE

It has been a few whirlwind weeks since I closed the case file on Kali's murder. Of course all that we uncovered in the investigation will keep agents around the country busy for quite a few years. Throughout the holidays, one after another of the rich and powerful has been falling when their dirty little secrets of kidnapping and child sexual assault are aired in public. In the next year, country club prisons will be filling up with America's most famous pedophiles. Tonight is just uncomfortable for me. The last place I ever expected to be was dressed in a tuxedo sitting in the balcony of the Capital building. I had to get dressed this afternoon in a monkey suit and wait for over an hour to pass through security and now what has seemed like an endless night of pomp and circumstance. Finally, the Speaker of the House stands and announces the President of the United States of America. I watch as he makes his way down the aisle shaking hands and giving out hugs to his friends. Finally, he makes it to the podium and everyone quiets down and sits.

"Mr. Speaker, Mr. Vice President, members of Congress, distinguished guests, and fellow Americans, I stand before you tonight a humble man. Over the last year, we as a country have come together to pick up our economy and get Americans back to work. We have strengthened our schools and strengthened our borders. More then everything else, we as a country have come together to strengthen ourselves. As I look out across this audience tonight, I am saddened to see a few empty chairs. I know tonight there are some districts in this great land that would like answers and will have to elect new representation. Yet, they hold their children close as they face the horror that has unfolded since just before Thanksgiving. This holiday season, more than any holiday before, we have delivered gifts to families who thought all was lost, when we began to return the lost children back to their homes. Tonight, I want to start my address to this nation by honoring the FBI team that brought many of America's missing children home. Ladies and Gentlemen, fellow American's watching from home and to those military servicemen watching from abroad, please join me in honoring FBI Special Agent Adam Clay, FBI Special Agent John Duncan and Dr. Samantha Callahan Clay. In four short weeks, this dedicated team of professionals brought down the biggest pedophile ring this country has ever known. Tonight America's children sleep safer knowing these criminals are on their way to jail. Agent Clay, your beautiful new wife, Dr. Samantha Callahan Clay and Agent Duncan, America thanks you tonight for your fine service. I would like to announce, as of this date, one hundred and eighty-seven children have been located and are in the process or are already back home with their families. So far three hundred and twenty-eight people have been indicted in this child trafficking ring. We owe it all to you. And to Dr. Clay, I offer to you my sympathy because if it was not for the tragic murder of your daughter, Kali Callahan, this group would still be running their business kidnapping, trading and selling children as part of their child sex ring. There is a bill that was introduced to Congress last week in honor of your daughter. The Kali Callahan Child Protection Act will go a long way in providing tools to law enforcement, educators and medical staff so that we can bring the faces of all the missing children onto the computer screens of people who work with children around the country. We have come a long way from faces on a milk carton, to faces scrolling on the computer screens around the country. Let's bring them all home and make kidnapping a child too hard for a criminal to get away with it anymore!"

Everybody under the dome is standing and facing us. The sound is magnified to a deafening roar as every hand claps and people cheer. Beside me, Samantha stands with tears streaming down her cheeks and falling into the curly blond hair of Alina resting on Samantha's shoulder. I still marvel how a four year old can sleep through just about anything. Even the sound of the joint house of Congress clapping and cheering doesn't wake her. As for me, I guess it's about time for me to take my new family home to meet my parents. I can feel my cell phone vibrating in my pocket and my sixth sense tells me it's my mother. I'm due a few days of vacation and now that the President of the United States has announced my marriage and my new daughter to the country, I should introduce them to my mom and dad.

ABOUT THE AUTHOR

Sharon Dobson was born in York, Pennsylvania and spent her childhood between a farm in Monkton, Maryland and a summer house in Chincoteague Island, Virginia. She now lives in Reisterstown, Maryland with her family and pet house rabbit, Gizmo. She is an avid hiker and history buff, getting her writing ideas from the places she visits and what she sees along the way.

Made in the USA
Lexington, KY
12 July 2013